Jus' Restin'

Captain Gary Wilder

Enjoy!
Capt. Gary Wilder

First published by Dog Ear Publishing
4010 W. 86th Street, Ste H
Indianapolis, IN 46268
www.dogearpublishing.net

dog ear
PUBLISHING

ISBN: 978-160844-447-2

This book is printed on acid-free paper.
This book is a work of fiction. Places, events, and situations in this book are purely fictional and any resemblance to actual persons, living or dead, is coincidental.

Printed in the United States of America

Dedication

$\mathfrak{F}$or my favorite little buddies and long-awaited grandsons, Jack Wilder Theron and Sam Alexander Theron. Well, for that matter, any other little folks who come along and want to call me Grandpa G!

May we read this book together over the years to come in the true spirit of Jimmy Buffett's "The Captain and the Kid," and enjoy each other's company through these words as long as our lives will allow.

My story is based upon a great many truths, with a little imagination tossed in where needed. As you get older, your wisdom will sort out the fact from the fiction – and that's where the fun is to be found.

Aargh, me Mateys, I can't wait for our first readin' together!

In Memory

Kasey, The Sea Dog

1992–2006

Chapters

Captain Dude 1

5 + 5 = 5 14

The Bar 44

The Green Monster 54

Indian Maidens 76

Bottom Time 95

Shame on the Moon 106

The 180' Line 125

Crab Ledge 151

Lobzilla 175

Hump 109 185

End of the Line 206

Maritime Surprise 230

The Coast is Clear 249

Rock & Roll 270

The author would like to acknowledge the following people for their contributions to the creation of *Jus' Restin'*:

Front Cover Photo – Pam Trudel

Back Cover Photo – Captain Gary Wilder

Editing – Emily Bunker

Writing Coach – Nicolla Burnell

Chapter Sketches – Tim Joyce

Technical Support – Eric Wilder U.S.C.G.
Air Station Cape Cod

Rodney Crowell – Lyrics from "Shame on the Moon" – permission by Granite Music Corporation

Author's Note: The characters and places in this novel are based upon people and places I have known and enjoyed for years. Most of the characters are composites of the many people I have met while fishing and diving the waters of New England and have avidly supported the writing of this story. Others are purely fictitious.

As the author, I would like to thank the many people who have endured and supported my efforts to bringing this dream of writing to fruition. First, to my wife and daughters, for being the sounding board for ideas as the book began to take shape and get underway. Next, to Nickey, my writing coach, who gave me the inspiration and guidance to take the chance and put my ideas to paper. Also, to my editor Emily, who took my best efforts and turned them into the story I always envisioned it could be. And lastly, to all my friends and relatives who have had to listen to an aspiring author, who always thought he was just about finished, never realizing how long a journey this would be. To all of you, my sincere thanks.

Chapter One

Captain Dude

Captain Rod could faintly hear the clicking sound of tiny seabirds' feet moving along the bow rails, but that was all that was needed to wake him this morning. He threw aside his blanket and gave Kasey, still sound asleep, an affectionate look. A little pat on the head and she rose to her feet with a long stretch and vigorous headshake. Her collar tags rang in the start to a new day.

A glance out the moisture-soaked cuddy windows revealed fog that was "thick, like pea soup," as old New Englanders would say. At least it wasn't raining. Stepping outside the pilot-house, the captain figured that the low lying fog would soon burn off, as the fading moon could be seen shining high overhead in the early morning salt air. The marine radio was switched on to get the latest forecast for the day. It was just shy of 06:00.

Captain Rod used to dive more a few years back, but between juggling a full-time job at the nuclear plant and running a charter boat on weekends, chasing giant bluefin tuna was quickly taking priority for his free time. All indications told him that's where the real money was to be made fishing these days; the sushi market for giant bluefin tuna was lucrative, if all his plans could just come together. On the other hand, this captain still enjoyed the camaraderie that went with a day of scuba diving under the waters of Cape Ann, and the logbook indicated that was the focus of today's charter.

Cape Ann, in Gloucester, Massachusetts, is popular among New England divers. Its beautiful rockbound coast has over 25 miles of coves and beaches, with numerous islands just offshore. Depending on wind and sea conditions, a diver can usually find a calm entry point from shore.

The destination this morning was Foley Cove: a picturesque hideaway tucked into Cape Ann's northwest corner. A deep lee towards the south, Foley Cove is sheltered from the prevailing summertime westerly winds. Its calm waters make it a prime site for small boat fishing, daytime picnics, nighttime boat anchorage, and, above all, boat and shore diving. A blow from the north, however, could produce some nasty water in this normally-tranquil cove.

Captain Rod had successfully dived the cove several times over the years, first from shore and later from boats. He was quite familiar with the bottom terrain from the innermost shoreline out to the 70-foot depth at the open water entrance.

The crew had requested this dive site because the shoreline starts as typical beach sand, then gradually turns to a mix of sand, silt, and mud as the depths move past fifteen feet heading out to open water. On the western shoreline, rugged granite rises from the ocean floor creating a solid stone wall at a steep angle to the surface. This underwater wall has deep cracks and crevices, which are home to the primary quarry of recreational divers: *Homarus americanus,* the New England lobster. Flounder and fluke are also common to the silty bottom and rocky terrain. These species are very popular quarries.

The fish can be speared but the "bugs," the nickname for lobsters, have to be taken by hand. Occasionally a keen-eyed diver can even find sea scallops, a seafood treat. Each makes great table fare for a good underwater hunter.

A few select and very fine homes with beautiful views of Ipswich Bay stand 75 feet atop this granite wall. The eastern shoreline of the cove is low and rocky, with many small homes of Cape Ann's fishermen dotting the shoreline.

Foley Cove is a fine spot for a number of activities, and with a weather forecast of a five to ten knot wind out of the southwest, it would be a smooth ride to the dive site with calm water. The flat sea conditions would make diving from the boat, exiting from the water, and boarding much easier for the divers.

Rod planned to anchor the boat on the west side of the cove, in approximately 45 feet of water and about 200 feet from the rock wall shore area. This should be accomplished by 09:00, with the dive crew ready to descend after about twenty minutes of dress-out time. The crew that morning was from a dive shop where the captain had maintained both a personal and professional relationship for many years, and where he had trained with their instructors to become qualified as a PADI (Professional Association of Dive Instructors) Divemaster. This enabled him to hire out his boat to divers.

Waiting patiently for the day's crew to arrive at the Harborside Marina, Rod ran through his mental checklist to ensure that the boat was ready to leave the dock. Once completed, he would then attend to other duties and concentrate on welcoming the divers aboard.

The engine space and bilges were checked for signs of oil or coolant leaks; all fluid levels were normal. He switched the battery selector to position #2, always keeping one of the two batteries as a fully-charged spare, in reserve for emergency starting. While the engine warmed to operating temperature, the captain checked the safety gear. Lifejackets – the number one safety item – were on board for all. He then tested the 406 EPIRB (Emergency Position Indicating Radio Beacon), and verified that the emergency O_2 (oxygen) was up to pressure and that the first aid kit was in place.

Moving to the helm, a quick scan of the instruments and gauges revealed running oil pressure at 55 psi, volts at 14, temperature steady at 170 degrees, a fuel tank at ¾ full, and an engine running with a smooth idle. Everything was normal. The gauges provide the vital signs of the boat, so this checklist is performed countless times in a day. He then gave the engine the final test: taking it up to 2,000 RPMs in order to listen for anything abnormal. The engine had been repowered in the spring with a new Volvo-Penta 350. She sounded really smooth, so the cover was closed and the engine shut down. The captain loved instruments – no room for idiot lights. If there was a problem, he wanted to see it developing, not when it was too late.

It was time to set the music on the stereo for the day, with no commercials. Tunes play a key role in setting the tone for the day's activities, and the captain made sure there was something in the music library for everyone.

The time was now 06:30 and with the crew not due to arrive for another hour and nowhere in sight, Rod took the first mate across the street for her morning constitutional. Kasey had a bladder that could last forever, and knew the morning routine well. A purebred German Shepherd, she had the quintessential markings of the breed: light brown flanks blending to a jet black back, a black snout, and ears that shot upward when something or someone had her attention. She was a wonderful dog, loved people, and always accompanied her master on his charters. She had little use for other dogs, however, and would let them know it upon sight.

One of the regular folks on the dock, another early riser nicknamed Archie, saw them returning down the ramp in the early morning fog. Archie was a gregarious boater, and was always the life of the party on the docks, day or night. "Hey Cappy, did 'Drop-a-Log' do her thing?" he asked, pointing to Kasey. He was working his typical humorous accent, a big fan of the old TV show *All in the Family.*

They laughed and the captain replied, "A lunker, I'll be sure to note it in her 'logbook.' "

"Where are you headed today? Fishing or diving?" Archie wanted to know so he could plan his evening meal. The boat often returned with fresh scallops or fish to be shared on the docks in the evening. The marina was a fun place to be with friends on a summer night.

"Divers today, heading over to Foley Cove for a little training exercise. Who knows what we might bring back later." Archie gave a mock salute and returned to his business.

Back on board, breakfast was set down for Kasey, followed by housekeeping activities on the boat. Then, after half the day's quota of push-ups and a quick shower at the bathhouse, all was ready. The fog was thinning overhead and a light breeze, as predicted, was picking up. Fair weather clouds and a temperature of about 75 degrees pointed to a fine day on the water.

Just then, the captain heard several honks of a horn in the distance, from a vehicle crossing the old wooden timber bridge leading to the marina. The dive crew was arriving right on time. He quickly untied the lines and moved *Jus' Restin'* over to the service dock, adjacent to the gas dock, which would ease the task of moving the scuba gear to the boat. With the lines secured, Kasey and her master went up the ramp to welcome the crew. They would closely oversee the gear going down to the dock and on board the *Jus' Restin'*.

"Ahoy, Captain!" exclaimed P.J. Durkin, the dive instructor and organizer of the class. P.J. was tall and lean and thinning a bit on the top, having just turned the corner on fifty. Always upbeat and professional, he was just over six feet tall and in terrific physical condition, with boundless energy and panache. What really grabbed one's attention right off was his mustache. A classic handle bar: reddish-orange, with two finely coiffured loops curling up and in on either side. It was a beauty. Waxed and waterproofed. He sure did keep it looking fine. He claimed that when he pinched his nose to clear his ears, his mustache straightened out and then curled back to the original shape!

"Aargh, good *marnin'*," replied the captain in his best Jolly Roger accent, soliciting grins from the rest of the divers. "It's great to see you, P.J.! We've been looking forward to having you on board again." They exchanged a hearty handshake and P.J. gave Kasey several long strokes on her head and neck. P.J. then introduced his crew to their hosts for the day.

"I'd like to introduce you all to Captain Rod Gray, the skipper of the *Jus' Restin'* and Plum Island Charters. This fine canine is his first mate, Kasey. Captain Rod certified as a rescue diver with me a few years ago, on his way to completing his Divemaster rating. He won't be diving with us today, but he'll remain on board to assist us with our training and final qualification as rescue divers."

Although P.J. Durkin was responsible for the divers when they were in the water, Rod had overall responsibility for the dive logistics and everyone's safety. His decisions would therefore be final regarding any safety issues or problems encountered during the trip.

"That's right," smiled Captain Rod, "no bubbles from me today."

"OK then, I think it would be easiest if you all introduced yourselves to Captain Rod and presented your certification cards."

By letting each of the divers introduce themselves, Rod was able to ask about their dive experience, whether they had dived from boats before, and any medical issues he should be aware of. As Divemaster, Rod would assist P.J. with final equipment checks before each diver was given the OK to roll overboard, and would help them when they returned to the boat.

P.J.'s students were volunteer EMTs from their hometown fire department. Located on the Merrimac River, their department also musters a volunteer dive rescue team. This would be their last training dive before the final exam the next day, which P.J. had prepared for them. Today's dive would focus on the last phase of the training, conducting search patterns, followed by lunch and a second recreational dive for Cape Ann bugs.

"Hello Captain, my name is Sarah Barnes. We've all been looking forward to diving on your boat. P.J. tells us you guys have had a lot of fun training together and that maybe, just maybe, you might share some of those stories?"

Captain Rod reached out and shook her hand. A quick look at her certification card verified that she was rated Advanced Open Water, meaning she had successfully completed training to a maximum depth of 90 feet. Sarah was a cute petite girl, about 5'3", with short, curly, strawberry blonde hair. She seemed very upbeat and energetic, excited to be diving that day.

"Good morning Sarah and welcome! Please, take your gear down the ramp to the boat, but don't load the boat until we're all there. I'll stow the gear." Captain Rod glanced at P.J. and continued, "We'll have to see about those stories a little later. Who knows, maybe we'll make a few of our own today. Again, welcome!" he said with a warm smile.

Sarah was happy to see the *Jus' Restin'* waiting and tied to the service dock. She went purposefully about her way to get all her gear down to the landing.

Next in line was Bob, a mountain of a man with curly light brown hair and a full beard. He had to be 6'4", over 275 pounds, and solid everywhere. What wasn't covered by hair was speckled with freckles. He had a handshake that told the captain he was all business. "Hi, I'm Bob Weeks," he said as he handed Rod his card. "Same routine as Sarah?"

Captain Rod nodded and Bob was off, focused on the task at hand: carrying some of his equipment and the rest of Sarah's. Rod noted to P.J. that the dates and qualifications of Bob's and Sarah's cards were the same. P.J. looked at Kasey and then to Rod and quipped, "They're a team, been engaged over six months."

"Then how come she's not carrying his gear?" came a third new voice, with an air of sarcasm. Rod and P.J. both looked over to a short, roly-poly guy in his early twenties with a buzz-cut hairdo. He had coffee in one hand and a doughnut and cigarette in the other. "Just kiddin' Dude. Roberto Martinez here."

Rod looked him up and down: 5'2", 225 plus pounds, he figured. "That would be Captain Dude, to you, young man. Still, welcome aboard! Let's get that gear down on the dock. We leave in ten minutes."

"Aye-aye," spouted Roberto with a salute. This wiseacre almost spilled his coffee as he fumbled for his gear and made his way to the boat.

P.J. and Rod exchanged another firm handshake, each being truly glad to see the other again. "So what do you think P.J.," Rod whispered, "if he were an inch taller, would he be round?" They both had a good laugh and Rod helped P.J. with his gear.

Kasey led the way down the nearly-horizontal ramp to the boat. The divers were waiting on the dock as Captain Rod stepped over the gunnel and onto the deck of the *Jus' Restin'*. Sarah gave him a long look. He wasn't nearly as tall as her Bob; she figured 6'1". She noted he was tan all over, had a salt and mostly pepper mustache and goatee, and had hair that was almost snow-white except for a black patch in the back. Rod joked with friends that Jay Leno had copied his hair, but had his black spot in the front. Rod used to work out three times a week when he was younger, but there didn't seem to be much time or interest for that these days. Fifty pushups morning and night and a three-mile walk with Kasey was about all he mustered for a routine now. It helped to slow the inevitable. He was getting a little heavier in all the wrong places, but liked to joke that he was "a piece of prime rib with a little extra trim on it." Sarah guessed his age to be late forties. She was close.

A six-tank rack on the deck just forward of the engine was filled with brightly colored yellow and green dive tanks. These aluminum tanks are commonly known as "80s," which means they can carry 80 cubic feet of air compressed to 3,000 pounds per square inch (psi). P.J. explained to his students that the compressed air in the dive tanks could essentially fill a rectangular prism that was four feet wide, five feet long, and five feet high. How long a tank lasts depends on the depth of the dive: deeper dives and rapid breathing consume air at a faster rate.

Rod knew that P.J. was legendary for his ability to stretch a tank of air for all it was worth. The safety rule of thumb when diving is to surface with a minimum 500 psi remaining on the gauge. P.J., on the other hand, who preached the gospel of reserve air, would take it to near zero if he was on the trail of some quarry and thought nobody would find out.

Rod motioned for P.J. to come on board. As the two of them stowed the gear, they instructed the students on how to load a dive boat properly. Stability was a key factor that was always considered on a boat this size. Gear that had to stay dry was moved forward into the port side of the cuddy cabin, while the captain's gear was segregated on the starboard side. Kasey's spot was also in the cuddy, so the center had to be kept clear for her favorite pillow!

P.J. explained that port was left and starboard was right. "It's easy to remember: 'left' has four letters and so does 'port.' Now you'll never forget, right? Oh, I mean...OK?" He laughed, knowing he probably just confused them.

All the other dive gear was stored on the deck: six tanks in the rack, two inside the pilothouse on the port side, and the rest of the equipment to the sides in an orderly fashion. This was a gear-intensive sport, so everyone was responsible for keeping things organized. P.J. was a stickler for order and that pleased Rod, since it took the burden of policing the decks off him.

With all the gear stowed under P.J.'s direction, Captain Rod now gave a quick brief of the day's itinerary. Also before shoving off, he reviewed the safety features on board the *Jus' Restin'*. He pointed out where the lifejackets were, in their yellow bags in the cuddy, followed by the locations of the three fire extinguishers, the 406 EPIRB radio, and the life raft on the topside. Rod then asked P.J. who he thought was the best swimmer of the group. Roberto was quick to interject that he was, by far, the most qualified. Rod replied that this was good news because the life raft could only hold four people, so if it had to be deployed, Roberto could pull Rod, P.J., Sarah, Big Bob, and Kasey. The ice was broken and everyone had a chuckle.

Rod described the electronics package next. "I have Foley Cove as our destination this morning – the waypoints to get there are already plugged into the GPS, which is short for Global Positioning System. The radar will be on, but the fog is lifting as we speak so we shouldn't have to refer to it for our ride across the bay. Once we clear Plum Island Sound, we'll have relatively deep water for the duration of the trip. The FM/VHF radio is scanning channel 16, the emergency channel, and weather channel 1."

"What channel do you listen to for the fishing info and local chatter?" asked an inquisitive Bob.

"That would be channel 9, the gossip station. A lot of it is in fishermen's code, so it takes awhile to figure out. If we have a weather alert, the radio will switch automatically to the weather channel."

"And how do we use that?" asked Sarah, pointing to the marine toilet.

"The head, as it is more commonly referred to, is very easy to operate. A lever and a pump handle. I'll show you when the need arises."

"And for the guys without aim, there's always the 'mother-in-law's cup,' " chimed in P.J., as he picked up the big mug from inside a five-gallon bucket.

The mother-in-law's cup, a giant blue and white plastic mug, is an object for many uses. Rod had picked it up on a boondoggle from work at some attraction in Atlanta. He liked to joke that he bought it special for when his mother-in-law came on board. Its primary function was to aid the men, rather than have them try to relieve themselves over the gunnel. It was a proven statistic, at least Rod believed this to be true, that the number one cause of men drowning was from falling overboard while doing what they do best.

"Well, what the mother-in-law doesn't know will never hurt her!" laughed Captain Rod, as Sarah watched P.J. put the cup back in its place. "Just kidding, Sarah." He gave her a reassuring wink, which seemed to do the trick. "Do you folks have any questions before we cast off?"

"Captain, how long will it take us to get to Foley Cove?" she asked, refocused, eager to get under way to the dive site.

"It shouldn't take any longer than forty-five minutes. It's just about twelve miles." She was satisfied with that and he continued. "Anyone else?" Rod scanned their faces for questions, but all were eager to go. "OK, let's shove off!" He went back into the pilothouse and fired the engine, then motioned to P.J. to cast off the lines. All was ready for a day of fun and games on and under the waters of Cape Ann.

Rod eased the boat away from the slip and out into the channel. He pushed the stereo into service, with the rocking blues of Delbert McClinton throbbing out of the speakers located under the gunnels and in the pilothouse. He looked back over his shoulder to see an approving Roberto, dancing with two thumbs up.

"Captain Dude!" he exclaimed, as he rocked to the beat of some great Texas blues. Rod turned back to the wheel with a smile and peered out over the bow, down the Parker River, and towards the Sound, thinking, *Captain Dude...I think I like that...*

Once under way, P.J. joined the captain in the pilothouse, Sarah sat on the engine cover, and the others stayed seated on their gear. All were enjoying the scenic cruise out of the marina, down the river towards Plum Island Sound. There were many boats for the first quarter-mile, either on their moorings or on docks belonging to houses by the water's edge. Brightly-colored kayaks speckled the water paddling towards the sea, taking advantage of the outgoing tide.

Captain Rod gave a short blast on the horn and waved to an old man walking across his lawn, heading for his dock. Ambling towards the waiting skiff, he carried his clam rake and catch baskets in one hand and tucked his other hand into the small of his back.

"That's Willy the Clammer. He digs steamers out here year round, even in the winter. Well, that is if the Parker River doesn't freeze. He's quite the character. Wears that old green lifejacket – refuses to wear orange. I guess that's the attitude you take when you're 85 years old and 100 percent Irish. Likes his green."

Willy heard the horn and recognized his friend's boat. He gave one big wave with his free hand, from far left to right.

"Willy won't be able to start digging clams for at least four hours, so I bet he'll get in a little striper fishing first. He knows these waters and flats better than anyone around here." Rod and P.J. both waved back as the bow of *Jus' Restin'* passed the first navigation buoy.

The orange and white buoy cautioned headway speed only: 5 mph maximum. It was just past slack high tide and the current was now ebbing back out to sea and gaining speed. This was an advantage to the boat, since it could add a couple of miles per hour to its speed over the ground (SOG), saving fuel at the same time. A win-win situation, Rod thought as he approached the #36 buoy, the beginning of the marked channel to open water. There are 36 buoys, in descending numbers, to navigate to open sea. Once they reached the mouth of the Ipswich River at Crane Beach, it was a straight shot across the bay to Foley Cove. On a clear day this was easy, but nearly impossible in the fog without GPS or the old faithful compass. Rod marveled at how sailors used to navigate by the stars, but he was an electronics navigator and liked it that way.

The red #36 buoy means the end of the no-wake zone, so it was time to throttle up. The #36 is the end of the line in the trail of buoys that marks the channel from the entrance at the mouth of the river. These aids to navigation, as they are called, are a series of red and green floating markers adorned with reflective strips. They identify the safest passage for travel. The red ones are always on the right when returning from the sea, and are cone-shaped on the top and even-numbered. Those on the opposite side of the channel are green, can-shaped, and odd-numbered. The buoys are big enough to be easily identified with the naked eye or with radar at nighttime or in reduced weather conditions.

Rod motioned to P.J. to let the crew know they were picking up the pace. Easing the throttle steadily forward, the Volvo was quick to respond, rising to the optimum cruising speed of 3,400 RPMs. P.J. reached for the overhead grab rail, quickly regaining his balance. Now they were under way and making way, at close to 21 knots or 24 mph: a respectable cruising speed for the boat, considering the personnel and heavy dive equipment on board.

P.J. asked Rod why he was pushing the toggle button on the throttle.

"Adjusting the outdrive. It's a maneuver known as trimming. This will cause the bow to either lift or lower, maximizing the speed over the water without changing the throttle position. I have to adjust the port side trim tab to compensate for Big Bob's weight and bring the boat level, side to side. The trim tabs are flat plates at each of the stern corners, which can be adjusted down into the water, lifting that side of the boat and making it ride evenly over the surface. Just like flying a plane, I think!" laughed Rod, who hoped to learn to fly some day.

The divers were busy talking and taking pictures. By the looks on their faces, they were enjoying the wind rushing through their hair, caused by the boat's newly-acquired speed. The hissing of the smooth water spraying to the sides of the boat filled the air, and the whine of the engine and outdrive only added to the experience. Everyone admired the shoreline and seascape of Plum Island Sound and the Parker River Reserve. It has remained virtually unchanged over time.

The water was placid, with the wake from the boat breaking up against the riverbanks and the marsh grass standing tall against the morning sun. Because of a strong moon tide that day, a higher-than-normal plus tide, the tide and the top of the banks were almost even.

P.J. and Kasey were getting reacquainted – Kasey enjoyed the attention of someone who knew the right spots to scratch. Captain Rod just sat back in his helm seat, sipping the coffee that Sarah had brought for him. This was always the most relaxing part of the ride, heading out through the channel in the early morning.

The sun was shining brightly now, and the fog was falling away behind them over the shoreline. With plenty of water below, and little or no chance of running aground in the tricky waters of the sound, *Jus' Restin'* could go outside of the marked channel and make a straight shot by Middle Ground, past Grape Island, and on to the western tip of Crane Beach.

Captain Rod's mind was running ahead, down the river; he was always trying to anticipate problems before they arose. But he had no idea what the now-tranquil Plum Island Sound held in store for him on the return trip later that day.

Chapter Two

5 + 5 = 5

The captain cut *Jus' Restin'* to the inside of the red #10 nun buoy just past Bass Rocks, and set a course that would take the boat along Crane Beach, the pride of the town of Ipswich. The beach was already filling up at 08:15. With the temperature predicted to be at least 90 degrees that day, the beach was sure to be hosting a large crowd; open spaces would soon become scarce. A faint smell of suntan lotion wafted on the offshore breeze when the captain rounded the #4 buoy and adjusted the course for Foley Cove. It was a beautiful summertime day, with blue skies and light breezes, as *Jus' Restin'* headed onto Ipswich Bay.

Rod pointed out to P.J. that there was a pretty good sea swell, the remnant of a tropical storm that had passed about 300 miles offshore over the previous couple of days. "Not to worry P.J.," Rod explained as his eyes scanned the horizon. "The weather report says three to five feet, mostly in sea swell. It will be like riding a big piece of Christmas ribbon candy: smooth with lots of highs and lows. Forecasters are also saying a chance of severe thunderstorms."

"Yeah, but if it were six months from now, they'd be saying a chance of flurries! That's how the weathermen cover the bases!" P.J. laughed at his own joke.

"Seriously P.J., with the temps predicted for today, we really need to keep aware of changing conditions. It can kick up quick."

P.J. agreed and returned to the crew to recap the conversation with Rod, then sat down to enjoy the remainder of the ride to Foley Cove.

Bright waters shimmered ahead of the bow as *Jus' Restin'* pushed her way across Ipswich Bay towards Halibut Point, where Foley Cove would appear shortly on the starboard side. With a clear view ahead, and only five miles to go, it would take less than fifteen minutes to get there.

The Annisquam River, the only route to Gloucester Harbor without going completely around Cape Ann, was 45 degrees relative off to starboard. Depending on where people are fishing, it's a way to get fresh fish to the buyers on the docks of "Dogtown," as the whaling widows call the seaport. It's also the scenic route to the waterfront restaurants and bars, as well as a shortcut to Boston's north and south shores.

Rod was just finishing his coffee when Roberto entered the pilothouse. "I didn't have my C-cards on me when you asked, Captain Dude, but I have them now. Here you go."

Rod took the cards from Roberto, all six of them. "Let's see what we have here: Open Water, Advanced Open Water, Underwater Photographer, Underwater Hunter, Wreck Diver, and Ice Diver." He looked back out over the helm and joked, "You've been a busy dude. Where's the card for Underwater Lover?"

"I'm working on that!" he snapped right back, motioning his head towards Sarah. Rod smiled and just shook his head. The boy sure is ambitious, he thought, and certainly didn't lack for a great imagination. "So tell me about the boat Captain Dude. What makes her tick?"

"Well, she's my baby," replied Rod, giving the helm wheel an affectionate pat. "A Parker 2520, Sport Cabin. I bought her at the New England Boat Show. Met Linwood Parker there, the owner of the company. After a long chat with the man at the top, the deal was sealed."

"How big is she?" Roberto eyeballed her overall length.

"Well, she's just over 25 feet, has a 9'6" beam, and a 250 hp Volvo-Penta under the engine cover. Not too much power – just enough. Her drive system is the duo-prop, a counter-rotating, two-propeller drive."

"Nice. How fast will she go?" asked Roberto, eyeing the GPS to see their current speed.

"Top speed under calm conditions is about 30 knots, which equals 34.5 mph. Not the fastest boat on the water, but stable and reliable in a moderate sea."

"How far can she go before you need gas?" Roberto wanted to know all the basics and Rod was happy to accommodate; he could talk forever about *Jus' Restin'*.

"The fuel capacity is 173 gallons. We can conduct many charter operations before refueling. She truly has a great range of operations for a small boat."

"I really like this cabin. It's quiet inside and you don't get wet when the weather kicks up like those open boats. Tunes inside, too!"

"They call it a pilothouse, the signature of the manufacturer. It provides many comforts: protection from the weather, heat from the engine for warmth in cold operations, a marine toilet, and a v-twin berth cuddy cabin for overnights. Kasey and I often sleep on the boat."

"You do diving and fishing charters. That must take a pile of gear."

Rod went on to explain that much thought had gone into outfitting his boat. For dive charters, a removable/stowable ladder made returning to the boat easy. A rescue backboard was fitted under the starboard gunnel for training and actual emergencies, and the pilothouse had an emergency oxygen tank. If a rescue situation arose, or a diver had to be airlifted from the deck, the *Jus' Restin'* could be located easily and the stricken diver or fisherman airlifted to an onshore emergency facility.

For fishing charters, there were six rod holders on the overhead of the pilothouse for storage and for trolling striped bass. The gunnels and transom corners had rod holders for all types of fishing, each capable of handling the heavy duty Penn International #130 class rods and reels, which are used specifically for giant bluefin tuna. There was also a pair of sixteen-foot telescoping outriggers on the overhead for trolling the large squid rigs and assorted big game lures that the tuna are known to favor.

On top of all this, there was real-time survival gear on board: a Mustang suit for Rod and two "one size fits all" Gumby suits for the mates, equipped with hood, gloves, and booties. Each can be donned in less than a minute with just a couple of practice runs. These are bright orange insulated suits, designed to withstand the cold New England waters. Similar to a diver's wet suit, if they do fill with water they retain their warming capabilities. Each suit comes equipped with a whistle, a light, and patches of reflective tape that can be seen by searchlights. The suits are literally total body lifejackets.

The 406 EPIRB radio, if activated manually or by immersion in the sea, sends out an emergency frequency signal to a group of satellites, then relays the signal to a central emergency facility. This in turn relays the data to initiate a SAR (search and rescue) mission to be conducted by the United States Coast Guard.

A Coast Guard Falcon jet, helicopter, or surface craft can track the 406 EPIRB's signal. The EPIRB is versatile: it has a 25-foot cord and can be attached to a person's wrist, tied to a life raft, or can float freely on its own. It is bright yellow and emits a small, intense strobe signal that is easy to see. All pertinent information regarding the *Jus' Restin'*, such as type of boat, captain's name, and home port, was on file with the emergency facility.

Rod knew he had a superb boat, and he maintained her in pristine condition. The equipment was 100 percent functional at all times, or at least thought to be so. Having overall responsibility for the personnel on board, he liked to leave little to chance; it was best to be prepared.

Foley Point lay just ahead as Rod returned Roberto's C-cards and thanked him for his interest in *Jus' Restin'*. P.J. entered the pilothouse, recognized their location, and motioned "five minutes" to the others while Roberto returned to his gear. Bob finished his water and Sarah enjoyed the last of her iced coffee. The two of them were enjoying their time together.

Captain Rod stood up, pushed his helm seat back, and began to throttle down and come about into the cove. He brought the boat to a slow headway speed since there could be divers anywhere in the cove, and on a weekend there usually were. Regulations require boats to fly dive flags when divers are in the water, and also require divers to tow an appropriate number of flags. One flag could cover several divers, as long as they all stay together. The same flag rules apply to shore divers.

P.J. and Rod knew that just as rookie divers tend to get disoriented, occasionally so do those who are more experienced. As a precaution, P.J. positioned himself on the bow as a lookout to survey the waters ahead. Flags, bubbles, and heads bobbing on the surface all indicated that someone could be on the surface or just under close by. Hitting a diver is unforgivable, and moreover, avoidable. Good luck was shining on them because there was only one other boater in the cove, and he was fishing.

"Perfect! I think the three-to-five-foot seas must have scared some people away. This is great: as the UFC's Big John McCarthy always says, 'Let's git it on!' " Rod was obviously gleeful that the cove was wide open, and that the water and weather were perfect.

The three trainees began the task of assembling their gear while Rod and P.J. anchored the boat. Rod maneuvered the boat to the spot where he wanted to drop the anchor. He motioned to P.J. and the anchor was freed from the pulpit, its chain rattling and reverberating through the hull as it spiraled to the bottom. The Danforth #13 anchor has fifteen feet of 3/8-inch chain, along with 300 feet of half-inch nylon line. Nothing too big – just right for this boat in shallow and calm waters. Since the tide was going out, and there was a very light wind, Rod told P.J. to pay out about 100 feet of scope. The rest remained in the anchor locker. P.J. secured the line to the bow cleat and awaited Rod's signal.

Rod slipped *Jus' Restin'* into reverse for just a moment and then into neutral. He looked out the forward window as the bow began to swing and the anchor line tightened: the hook was set. The engine was shut down and P.J. got a thumbs-up from the captain. He was about to change hats and become Divemaster, but first it was time to set the mood with some Jimmy Buffet music. The tunes began with "A Pirate Looks at Forty," a great song about a sailor lamenting how he had been born at the wrong time in history: two hundred years too late.

"OK, first diver down needs to check the anchor." Rod's voice was setting the tone that the diving was about to begin. P.J. volunteered for the duty.

"What's our depth?" asked Sarah, cupping her eyes and peering over the side.

"The depth sounder is indicating 51 feet, and the tide is dropping," Rod replied. Sarah was still relatively new to diving, and 50 feet was her comfort zone.

"This is just what I like." She appeared very happy with the report.

Rod supervised the divers as they grabbed their respective tanks. Holding the tanks steady between their knees, they slid the BC's on and secured them with Velcro straps. Next came the first stage regulator clusters, which consist of the main regulator and four black pressure hoses attached to the main valve on the tank. The hoses supply the second stage regulator, which divers breathe through; the spare regulator for emergency breathing; the instrument console, which says how much air is remaining in the tank; and a compass for navigation. The last air hose is connected to the BC for buoyancy control. There are many components, and each is essential to a diver's ability to function safely in the deep underwater environment.

Rod noted that the newbies had fine-looking new equipment. Bright yellows, greens, and pinks for Sarah, while P.J.'s buoyancy compensator (BC), on the other hand, looked like a bulletproof vest that had fought with him in Vietnam and lived to swim another day. P.J. had fallen behind the latest scuba technology, still relying on his proven older gear. But his equipment was tried and true, meticulously maintained, and always performed well.

One of the reasons scuba diving has become so popular is due to the advances in equipment and the buoyancy compensator is a key component. The experience is about buoyancy: too little (negative) and the diver sinks like a rock. Too much (positive) and he floats like a cork or rises too quickly to the surface. Either way, a diver can get into trouble quickly if he isn't able to control his buoyancy.

The buoyancy compensator (BC) is an inflatable vest that is combined with a high-pressure air cylinder (usually an aluminum 80) attached to the backside with a strap. Getting one's buoyancy right is pretty simple: put on all the necessary dive equipment, get into the water, and then keep adding lead weight until you start to sink. This amount of weight is added to a diver's weight belt and stays the same for each consecutive dive. If a diver wants to stop descending, he just adds a little air from his tank into the inflatable BC by pushing a button; if he starts to rise, he simply lets some air out of the BC with the pull of a string.

The amount of weight to add or subtract varies depending on whether the diver is in fresh or salt water. New England divers generally learn how to dive in fresh, and then graduate to the ocean. They seldom return to fresh water. Comparing freshwater diving to the ocean environment is like comparing black and white TV to IMAX.

As Divemaster, Rod understood that new divers try to achieve perfect buoyancy and therefore tend to expend air at much higher rates. Experienced divers, on the other hand, can generally control their buoyancy with their lungs alone, after initial and subsequent adjustments. If an experienced diver wants to rise while swimming across an uneven ocean floor, he simply inhales a large breath of air, which allows him to rise automatically. He can then swim over the obstruction, exhale, and sink back down again. Once a diver's buoyancy becomes "neutral," it's like floating in space. The weight of all the equipment is negligible, and the feeling of weightlessness is experienced underwater. Astronauts train underwater in order to experience weightlessness and practice maneuvers prior to going into space.

With the BCs ready to go, next comes the task of suiting up. All the divers would be in wetsuits, which meant that they would all experience the thrill of cold New England water filling the air gaps in their suits as they descended. Dressing is always performed in the same sequence: pants (bibs), boots, hood, and jacket. Next is the weight belt, followed by the BC and tank, fins, mask, and lastly, gloves. At this point a diver is ready for a final equipment check by the Divemaster. With so many pieces of equipment essential to success and safety, the Divemaster's final check is crucial.

"When everyone has their bibs and boots on, we'll have our pre-dive brief," said P.J., reviewing his checklist to himself. He knew that divers waiting in the hot sun with black rubber suits could easily overheat, thereby raising anxiety levels, so he made it as quick as possible.

"This will be our last training dive today – your final exam is tomorrow back at my camp on Pawtuckaway Lake," P.J. explained. "We will perform two circular search patterns at a 60 and 120-foot radius from the anchor, with each of us spaced fifteen feet apart. The rope has a knot every five feet for reference; we will leapfrog each other to our initial positions along the rope, complete one revolution around the anchor, and then stop. We'll leapfrog again to each of our final positions, then complete one more revolution." P.J. scanned their faces to ensure they all understood, as this had already been taught in the classroom.

"Here's today's quarry," interjected Rod, holding a small, bright green, underwater flashlight.

"Whoever finds Captain Rod's flashlight will give the appropriate signal, then each of us will follow the line back to the anchor," P.J. continued. "I will then coil the line, and we'll ascend the anchor line and return to the boat. If anyone gets down to 500 psi air pressure, and nobody has found the flashlight yet, signal the person next to you and then surface via the anchor line – slowly. Take a safety stop at fifteen feet. Captain Rod will be here to assist you back into the boat. Any questions?"

They understood the dive plan, and with the hot sun beating down they were anxious to get into the water. Big Bob was sweating heavily and wanted in right away. Rod checked the sounder and reported that the water temperature was 64 degrees at the surface. They all knew that wouldn't last long: with the thermocline just a few feet below, the temperature of the water could drop another ten to fifteen degrees in an instant.

The thermocline is a separation of water by temperature. As a diver descends, he can actually see the phenomenon with the naked eye. It has a wavy appearance, something like heat rising off a hot road. Even if the diver doesn't see it, he would certainly feel the temperature drop against his face. The area around a diver's mouth is the only part of the body exposed to the water; the rest of the body is covered by the neoprene suit.

Rod launched *Jus' Restin*'s life ring overboard, with 125 feet of yellow polypropylene line attached to a cleat on the inside gunnel next to the pilothouse. This would stretch out behind the boat, allowing the divers to hang on until all were assembled in the water and ready to descend. Another benefit of the 125 feet of line was that if anyone overshot their return to the boat, they could swim to catch it. On many dives, strong currents were encountered, and this safety ring had saved the day more than once.

"Everybody, listen up," barked P.J. "One last item... compass headings. The wall is 270 degrees to the west, the beach is 180 degrees to the south, and the far shore is 90 degrees to the east. Open water is 0 degrees to the north. Always know your heading and check it often." P.J. reinforced that it was essential that everyone understand their position relative to a compass heading. "It'll be interesting to see if the sea swell will have an effect on our visibility."

Bob and Sarah helped each other finish suiting up, while Roberto and P.J. tended to themselves. When everyone was nearly ready, Rod gave P.J. a quick check and P.J. rolled gently over the side into the cool green water. Rod handed P.J. his BC and tank over the side. P.J. was the only diver Rod knew who liked to put on his BC that way. He made it look easy – P.J. made everything look easy! He was so at home in the water. In a moment he was ready and waiting patiently for the others to follow.

Rod gave each of them a final check. He adjusted some straps and verified that their weight belts were on. He checked that all tank valves were open and that the air in their tanks was approximately 3,000 psi, followed by a couple of quick shots of air to each BC. He wanted to make sure that every diver floated immediately after entry.

He clenched his fist and tapped it on the top of his head – the universal OK signal. This meant each diver could now roll over the side and into the cool waters of Foley Cove. Rolling into cold water is always a thrill, yet can be unnerving to a novice. A diver goes in upside down, so the bubbles everywhere can really be disorienting. After bobbing to the surface, the view through the mask mimics tunnel vision: half above water with the blue sky, and half below where the green depths await.

Breathing on the regulator, a swimmer hears a combination of sounds: hissing air when inhaling and gurgling bubbles when exhaling. This eventually becomes background noise, negligible after a few minutes underwater. The diver then checks to see where his buoyancy is and adjusts the BC accordingly.

Cold water begins to trickle into the air gaps and replaces the air in the suit, making a diver more negative. The sensation is felt down the middle of the back and up the legs until it hits the crotch...YEOW! But soon the water warms to body temperature and feels quite comfortable. After a brief rest to calm oneself and gain composure, with the heart rate slowing down and breathing becoming normal, the diver is ready to descend.

A diver's senses are affected in different ways once submerged. Objects appear 25 percent larger and closer than they really are, hearing becomes more acute, and because the diver cannot breathe through the nose, the senses of smell and taste are gone. The sense of touch is minimized by the thick gloves.

Rod once did some diving in the Keys and the Bahamas, but he soon became bored. Although he enjoyed the bright colors of the fish and corals and almost unlimited visibility, it lacked the one thing that held Rod's interest most about diving: bounty. If he found something of interest in the waters of New England, it was his. Whereas in the warmer tropical waters, strict regulations keep divers from removing or even touching objects on the ocean floor. He understood that with the sheer number of divers in tropical waters, this was probably a good thing. Without restrictions, people might harm the delicate underwater environment. He was glad that less pressure on the environment from cold water divers meant that these limitations generally didn't apply here in New England.

Rod threw the 120-foot search line and then the dive flag to P.J. He had already let out 60 feet from the coil of line attached to the dive flag, just enough to keep the red and white striped flag and the yellow buoy at the surface with some slack. The divers would be towing it from the bottom. P.J. signaled for the rest of the divers to enter the water.

Sarah was the first over the side and surfaced right away; P.J. acknowledged her fist-to-the-top-of-the-head signal. She drifted back to the yellow neoprene lifeline, grabbed on, and waited for the others. She could see her Bob getting ready to go.

Bob was as strong as he was big, an impressive sight as he prepared to roll out. Rod joked that he hoped the water was deep enough for him as he went over the side with a huge splash, severely rocking the boat from side to side. Rod grabbed Roberto, who weebled and wobbled and almost fell out the other side of the boat. It isn't easy to keep one's balance wearing all that gear and long fins, even on a stable deck! Bob gave the OK signal.

P.J. also gave the OK and then pointed at Roberto. Rod nodded as Roberto backed up and rested on the gunnel, ready to go. "Dunkin' Dude, are you ready?" joked Rod, winking to P.J. Roberto leaned back and was over the side. No OK sign from the Dude, but it was obvious he was all right as he made his way to the safety line.

P.J. motioned for everyone to use their snorkels to conserve air until he was sure they were relaxed, calm, and ready to descend. P.J. handed the keeper from the line of the dive flag to Bob, who was elected to pull the flag. A keeper is a bright yellow plastic holder, with a line wound around it and an open loop in the center. It barely fit over Bob's forearm, secure at his elbow. He could still swim free while marking the location of the training class below the surface.

Rod climbed up on the gunnel and ran the three-foot by five-foot bright red and white striped dive flag up the port side outrigger of *Jus' Restin'*, where it flapped gently in the breeze 25 feet above the water. P.J. saw the flag and knew all was ready. It was time to start diving.

After everyone returned P.J.'s OK signal, he gave the thumbs-down and swam forward to the bow and anchor line. The others followed on the surface. Once at the anchor line, P.J.'s head went under, his fins came up, and he slipped below the surface. Bursting bubbles marked his presence under the water.

He was pleased to see the visibility looking good, but he wouldn't know for sure until he could see bottom. P.J. liked to descend head first, as he had no trouble clearing his ears under the ever-increasing pressure. It's important for divers to clear their ears every ten feet or so, depending upon the individual. Just the simple act of swallowing, or pinching the nose through the mask and blowing, usually does the trick. The dive has to be terminated if the diver can't clear his ears, because the pain is excruciating.

Arriving on the bottom, P.J. checked the anchor, firmly setting the flukes into the muddy bottom. He determined the visibility to be about ten to fifteen feet; not bad, but he hoped the divers would kick up the bottom and cloud the waters, because this would enhance the training. He clipped one end of the search line to the anchor shackle and prepared to pay out the line. He was already on the lookout for game. After the dive was completed, followed by a lunch on board, he would show these newbies how to fill a game bag with some good eating. But first things first: find the flashlight.

Bob and Sarah descended together, feet first, with one hand each gripping and sliding down the anchor line. They stopped at 25 feet according to Sarah's depth gauge, signaled their ears were OK, and continued to the bottom where P.J. was waiting.

Roberto was next and he crashed to the bottom like an anchor. His buoyancy was obviously very negative and he would need to adjust his BC. His landing kicked up a lot of silt, which, combined with the negligible current, would now take awhile to clear. This in turn meant that tugging on the line would be the primary means of communication between the divers, further testing their skills. This was just fine with P.J.

P.J. gestured for Sarah to be first, meaning she would swim along the rope for three knots and stop. Roberto would be second at the 30-foot interval, Bob third at the 45-foot knot, and P.J. with the remaining coils of line at the 60-foot knot. Remembering their classroom training, each knew that this technique was similar to a marching band making a clockwise turn. The diver closest to the turning point moving the slowest, and the diver farthest out swimming the fastest, controlling the speed of the sweep.

With everyone ready to go, P.J. swam away from the anchor, paying out the line and counting the knots. Twelve knots would get him to his position. The rest followed behind with Sarah stopping at her allotted spot, Roberto at his, and Bob counting out his nine knots. Soon all were in position, and P.J. stretched the line tight. He carried the remaining 60 feet in a coil with him. When the line was ready, each diver made an identifying mark in the sand, so they would know when the 360-degree pass was completed. P.J. gave the appropriate signal – two tugs on the line – and the search pattern began. The divers held the line in front and swam forward.

In the meantime, Captain Rod turned his underwater dive light on, tossed it over the stern, and watched it sink out of sight. They wouldn't find it on the first pass because he had tossed it beyond their range. Hopefully they would find it on the second, ensuring a successful training session. Rod then climbed to the top of the pilothouse and sat on the life raft to monitor the trail of bubbles, and to watch Bob's flag bobbing on the surface.

It was a gorgeous morning, complete with seagulls screeching on the shore and fighting over a morsel one had stolen from another. Divers were walking their gear down the rocky shoreline to the beach from a small parking lot above the rocks, their voices faint in the distance. Rod returned to the pilothouse and kept an eye on the flag, since it would be coming near the boat soon and he didn't want it to tangle in the boat's outdrive. He knew that this was basic but good training. If a rescue team ever got to this point in a real-time situation, however, it would be a body recovery not a rescue. But if the divers were trying to locate a specific item in a known area, this was one of the best ways to do it as quickly as possible.

Underwater, everything was going as planned. P.J. had already scooped up three scallops as he swam the outside leg, and put them in a small catch bag while keeping the line taut. Sarah's job was the least eventful because she had the shortest distance to swim, but she was enjoying immensely getting her buoyancy just right. Bob was an avid sportsman, and this was one activity she and Bob could enjoy together.

Roberto surprised a small monkfish nicely camouflaged underneath him. As the startled fish swam off into the blurry distance, Roberto noted that it was shaped like a stingray, but behaved differently in that it lay flat and camouflaged against the bottom. This is a unique species, with a kind of fishing lure attached to its head. The fish wiggles the "lure," and small baitfish check it out and try to bite it. With lightning speed the monkfish then snaps open its huge mouth, creating a powerful suction, pulls in the curious fish, and slams its mouth shut. Poof! Baitfish gone and monkfish happy, all in the blink of an eye.

Bob was getting the most action, because he had come across two "ghost pots." A ghost pot is a lobster pot that has broken away from its buoy, lost to the ocean floor forever. Sometimes divers find them as singles – Rod once found what he figured to be at least ten ghost pots snagged together and jammed into some rocks. They provide the one thing that most sea creatures like: cover from predators. Bob turned over the pots as he passed by and saw two lobsters swim quickly away. He figured one of the bugs, a respectable size, could have been a three-pounder.

Lobster pots and divers are a topic for heated discussions among lobstermen and divers all along the New England coast. You don't mess with a lobsterman's gear. That's it, case closed. Maine and New Hampshire don't even allow divers to harvest lobsters, but it's legal in Massachusetts. With the advancement of diving equipment, lobstermen and divers have been at odds for years, but the Environmental Police and the Gloucester Police monitor the popular dive sites and help keep everything on the up and up.

Down below, the first circle was completed and the divers stopped at their respective starting points, then turned and followed the line to P.J.'s 60-foot position. P.J. held up his pressure gauge for all to see and indicated for everyone to check their own air supply. P.J. gave the OK sign and each returned his signal.

P.J. was off again, this time to the full extent of the line. Sarah, Bob, and Roberto followed and took up their positions as before. P.J. gave the correct number of tugs on the line, the signal to start, and they were all under way for the final pass. Eyes scanned side to side, everyone wanting to "rescue" the flashlight and earn some bragging rights back on board.

Just a little more than halfway through the second pass, Bob spotted the green flashlight, almost out of sight and settled into the mud. He grabbed it and jerked the line three times in each direction, the signal that he found the light. Everyone stopped right where they were. P.J. followed the line back to Bob, acknowledged the find, and continued to swim past Roberto and Sarah. They all fell in behind P.J. as he returned to the anchor and coiled the line as neatly as if he was standing on the deck. Then he motioned with an open hand to Sarah, as if to say "ladies first," and they all ascended the anchor line behind her.

Sarah popped up first to see a smiling Rod awaiting them on the bow. He had put the ladder in its place at the stern, and dropped in two lines with brass snap clips for the divers to attach their weight belts to before exiting the water. The clips are suspended four feet underwater, making it easy to attach and release the weight belts. When the divers surfaced, they would pop the snaps on the chest straps and release their BCs. Rod, in turn, would lift the BCs with tank and regulator into the boat. The divers would then float leisurely to the stern of the boat, take off their fins, and climb the ladder aboard.

It's easy if you follow the sequence. Sarah, however, made a serious mistake...she released her BC and tank before releasing her weight belt. This made her extremely negative and she quickly sank below the surface with no air supply. Only one thing to do: drop the weights! Now! Sarah struggled with her belt as she continued to sink. Why wouldn't the belt release? She began to panic, frantically grasping at the buckle. She was a good six feet under the surface and heading down fast. Watching the hull of the boat drift further away, she continued her fight. Suddenly, she felt a hand from behind release the buckle. Her wet suit, a natural lifejacket, immediately propelled her upwards.

She exploded to the surface, gasping for air, but eventually regained her composure after resting on the ladder. P.J. swam to the line and clipped in her weights as she slowly climbed the ladder back into the boat. Once on board, Sarah looked back at P.J. floating like an otter beside the boat. He winked at her and said nothing.

Bob and Roberto were unaware of all the drama and exited the water after Sarah without incident. All were back on board, ready for a bite to eat and to kick back for an hour or so between dives. Captain Rod lowered the dive flag from the outrigger and welcomed everyone back. Kasey returned to the cuddy cabin to get out of the way of the divers and gear. She liked to sleep there with the portal windows opened – it was cool and out of the direct sunlight, with gentle breezes moving the cuddy air. After all, she was a seadog, knew her place, and played the role well.

The tanks were changed and the gear properly stowed, ready for the next dive. Lunch was next on the agenda. While everyone located their food, Rod cleared the engine cover so it could be used as a lunch table. The cover was about three feet square and painted as a red and white dive flag. Rod figured this was a good thing because if he ever had to evacuate someone, a searching helicopter would have an easier time finding *Jus' Restin'*. But first Rod had to retrieve his lunch...from under the engine cover.

"What are you having today?" asked P.J. with a snicker, slowly shaking his head side to side.

"Leo's Calzone Volvo," returned Rod with a laugh and the accent of an Italian waiter.

Everyone looked to see what was so funny; Rod, in the meantime, picked up a half-moon-shaped piece of aluminum foil from the front of the engine. He closed the cover and slowly opened the mystery package to reveal a hot veal cutlet calzone from Leo's Sub Shop, complete with gooey mozzarella cheese running out the sides.

"Fresh from the oven!" exclaimed Rod, feeling a nudge on his leg. Kasey was right there, sniffing the tasty treat permeating the air. "I got us a large one, so there is some for everyone." Rod got out his fillet knife and sliced the calzone into seven long strips. "Get it while it's hot!"

"Oooh-oooh, nature's perfect food!" sighed Bob, who did a great imitation of Homer Simpson, one of his favorite TV characters. He dove in for his share of the meal.

P.J. asked the captain if he could feed Kasey her piece. Permission was granted, so P.J. cut Kasey's slice into three morsels and proceeded to feed her...but first she would have to earn them. He began with the first silent signal: raising his open palm to the vertical position. Kasey sat and her big canines snapped shut, making the first sliver history. Second signal: palm down and horizontal to the deck. Kasey lay down and the second treat was gone. Lastly, with an open palm, P.J. swept his right hand down to Kasey's nose, then stepped away. Kasey didn't move. He waited 30 seconds, then gave her the last delicious piece of calzone.

"Good dog, Kasey! You have taught her well," said P.J., smiling with approval. He glanced at Rod and then back at Kasey.

With the little dog-and-pony show over, everyone enjoyed the food they'd brought. The calzone soon disappeared except for one lonely piece. After putting everything away, the divers kicked back, knowing they needed to wait another half hour or so before going in the water again. This would insure that any residual nitrogen that they might have in their bloodstreams would be expelled before the next dive.

"Hey, who ate the last piece of calzone?" Rod asked. A silence fell over the boat. Rod waited, but still nothing. "I'll get to the bottom of this. Kasey, come!"

Kasey came out of the pilothouse, where she had tried to retire, and stood before her master. He pointed to P.J. and asked Kasey if he had taken it. No response. Next, he pointed to Sarah and asked the same question. Again, no response. Finally, Kasey was asked if the culprit was Bob or Roberto. Still she was calm – it wasn't any of them. P.J. interrupted and asked Kasey if Captain Rod had eaten the last piece. Kasey began to bark violently and viciously towards the captain. Without anyone noticing, Rod had slowly raised his right hand to his ear lobe and was pulling at it with short, quick jerks: Kasey's signal to put on a barking display that could make one's blood run cold.

"You caught me! Stop!" laughed Rod as Kasey ceased her barking. He dropped his hand and patted Kasey on the head, acknowledging that she'd obeyed his command. "Good girl! We still make a good team don't we, P.J.?" Rod and P.J. laughed at their own antics.

This was a trick the threesome had played on people before. Kasey, a key part of the act, was five years old and 80 pounds of muscle: a magnificent looking animal. One wouldn't want to be on the receiving end if she meant business. She could be very intimidating, but Rod knew she was good-natured and would never threaten people unless she was told to or had good reason.

It was time for the second dive, but being in no hurry to get started, Rod took a moment to hear everyone's opinion of the first one. Roberto volunteered his sighting of the monkfish and that he wished he'd had a spear with him. "I heard the best meat is in the long tail, and I'd sure like to try some of that," he said, licking his lips.

"Well, I rolled a couple of ghost pots and let a nice keepah get away," chimed in Bob.

Sarah added, "I didn't see that much on the bottom, a small flounder and a couple of crabs, but I did notice several big schools of tinker mackerel that were passing by the anchor line on the first circle."

She looked around as the others nodded in agreement that they too had seen the mackerel. Rod commented that this was a good sign, knowing that striped bass loved them. Maybe some fishing action on the return trip might produce a striper or two for the grill at the marina that evening.

While everyone was busy preparing for the second dive, Rod scanned the waters around *Jus' Restin'*. A tan-colored lobster boat was approaching the stern, on a direct course towards their location. It was a typical "down-easter" craft, with the large flared bow sweeping back towards the low water stern, and a hydraulic stainless steel capstan for hauling pots on the starboard davit. A squint to the eyes revealed that it was the *Amy Anne*, a boat that Rod had seen working these waters many times, though he didn't know the captain personally.

"What's this jamoke want?" cracked Roberto.

Rod shot him a stare that made him understand his comment was not appreciated.

"Good morning, Captain!" shouted Rod, the *Amy Anne* pulling alongside a short distance away. "What can I do for you?"

"Hey there, I'm Josh Duffy, and I've got a little problem I think you can help me solve. I believe I have a buoy and some warp line wrapped around the prop shaft. It's thumping pretty hard. Maybe one of your divers could check it out and cut it free for me?"

"No problem, I'll gladly do it myself. Come around to the stern and I'll throw you a line." Rod went behind the helm seat and returned with a twenty-foot spring line that he normally used on the dock. He tied the line to the port side stern cleat and was ready to throw it as the *Amy Anne* approached. Captain Duffy's mate was on the bow and grabbed the line that Rod let fly. They were tied together in a moment, with the *Jus' Restin's* anchor holding their positions.

P.J. volunteered to go overboard and do the job, but Rod replied that by going over himself, he would get credit for a dive and could update his dive logbook. P.J. rolled his eyes, for they both knew this would not qualify as a dive. Rod went into the pilothouse, where his dive gear was stored to the right of his helm seat. Rod put on his dive trunks, mask, snorkel, and fins. No need for the larger scuba fins without all the usual scuba equipment. He did grab his Kevlar gloves, dive knife, and pony bottle. The pony bottle is a miniature dive tank, with a capacity for thirteen cubic feet of air at 3,000 psi. It has its own regulator and is designed primarily as a spare air supply in case of emergency, to be a part of one's backup dive gear.

Rod came out onto the deck, carrying everything he would need to help Captain Duffy get back under way. This was an opportunity for some goodwill, and he would do it right. He took the dive knife and strapped it to his inner left calf, then attached the Velcro straps of the pony bottle to his left forearm, with the regulator at the elbow. Next, he donned his fins, mask, and gloves, and rolled over the side. Popping to the surface, he gave the customary fist-to-head signal as the current carried him to the *Amy Anne*. When he approached the starboard quarter, Captain Duffy leaned over to shake hands. Rod reached up to accept his gesture.

"Captain Rod Gray at your service. This surgery shouldn't take too long." He glanced at his dive watch: it was 11:55.

Rod let go of Josh's hand and put his regulator in his mouth. He grabbed the chine of the hull, and pushed himself below the surface and under the stern of the lobster boat. The sun was shining brightly through the water from the far side of the *Amy Anne*, lighting up the boat's hull and prop shaft with an amber glow. Rod approached the prop shaft and it was immediately evident that Captain Duffy was right: a green, yellow, and white painted buoy, with about ten feet of warp line (a lobsterman's terminology for the lines connecting his lobster gear), was wrapped tightly about the shaft. He grabbed the prop shaft with his left hand to hold his position, and with his right he got the knife strapped to his leg.

The knife had two cutting edges opposite each other. One was a ragged, diamond-tipped blade for cutting stainless steel line – popular with striper fishermen – and the other, a razor-sharp, all-purpose serrated blade. The latter would make short work of this problem. Within moments, the line was freed and Rod, holding the buoy and excess warp line in his left hand, surfaced where he had begun. The mate was waiting there with a wide smile, knowing that now he wouldn't have to dive and clear the prop. He took the buoy and line with a thumbs-up. Rod returned the signal and proceeded to swim on his back to the *Jus' Restin'*.

Passing his fins and mask to P.J., he climbed back aboard. He moved his gear to the pilothouse and placed it on top of his dive bag, to be stowed while the others were taking their second dive. Next, a quick wipe with his favorite towel, a large green and white Dartmouth College towel he'd bought at one of his kids' swim meets. The special souvenir had been with him for years. Now dry, he slipped on a tee-shirt and came back onto the deck.

"Captain, thank you!" yelled Captain Duffy from the bow of his boat. "I've got something for you to show my appreciation. Do you have a bucket?"

Rod found his five-gallon white utility bucket, removed the mother-in-law's cup, and gave it a quick rinse. He tossed the bucket to Captain Duffy, who disappeared behind the large cabin of the *Amy Anne*. He promptly returned, untied the line from the *Jus' Restin'* that was attached to his bow, and slipped the line through the bucket handle. He held his arm up high and watched the bucket slide down the line to Rod's waiting hands. Rod grabbed the bucket as Josh let go of the line, and issued a salutary wave while they drifted away with the current from their temporary mooring.

"Thanks!" yelled Rod, placing the bucket in the pilothouse, out of the sun. He returned to the divers, who by now were anxious to get under way.

With P.J.'s role as instructor now over, Rod seized the opportunity to perform the pre-dive brief and have a little fun at the same time. "You've all said that your goal is diving for bugs. Very well. Each of you will carry your own dive flags with your permit numbers visible. Remember, no spears for lobster: they're to be taken by hand only! Ghost traps are fair game. You must gauge all your lobsters underwater and return them to where you found them if they are 'shorts' or 'eggers.' The females will either have eggs under their tales or a 'V' notch in one of the tail fins."

Rod knew from experience that it's a challenge to catch a lobster. It takes nerve as well as skill. "If you want to wait a few minutes, I'll tell you the secrets to catching lobsters." All agreed, so Rod began. "Lobsters have a few defensive tricks, so it's not easy. They swim backwards, with the ability to see and navigate in reverse. If they are approached with no cover to protect them, their strong tails can propel them with short bursts of speed, covering a good 50-to-60-foot distance. All lobsters have a lair somewhere close by, where they return to eat their catch and hide from other predators. As they grow, they move on to larger holes, leaving their homes to smaller lobsters."

Rod yielded the deck to P.J., who was chomping at the bit to share what he knew about bugs. "You can sneak up from behind and try to grab the carapace, the main part of a lobster's body. From there, inch your hand forward to fold the two large claws together, pick the lobster up, and then gauge it for legal size. If it's legal, you can put it into the dive bag. Catching them in the open is the easiest way, but they're primarily nocturnal feeders, and prefer to hide during the daylight hours. Diving for lobsters at night is strictly illegal. They are usually in their holes during the day, which means that you have to stick your hand into the hole, sometimes up to your shoulder, to reach the prize."

He looked at their faces and knew they were hooked. "This is where the nerve part comes into play. Lobsters have two claws, and a good-sized lobster can crush your finger if they grab hold – and they won't let go! Plus, they always push them-selves upwards to the roof of the hole, where the spiny spikes that cover their head and claws can engage the overhead and keep them from being pulled out."

Rod took over the tag-team training. "If you come across a place where you think a lobster may be hiding, try to do something that might tease him out. Inch your finger to the edge of the hole and wiggle it, but don't let him see you. If that doesn't work, it's cobra time."

"What do you mean?" asked Bob, intent on learning the secrets for catching a big one.

"Well," P.J. said, as he lifted his hand, "you hold your hand up, just like a cobra ready to strike. Move stealthily towards the opening to the hole. Then, when you feel the distance is right, strike!!! Remember, you'll encounter the lobster's claws first: they're open and waiting for that hand to come after them. You have to go right on by the claws, and then push the lobster down. Turn your hand to the left or right and keep him pinned down, just like in the open. But you'll have to turn him around in the hole, so that he comes out tail first and can't hook those spikes into the roof of his hole. Sounds simple doesn't it?" He looked around to see some anxious faces. "But wait until you shine your light into one of those promising openings and see a six-pounder, with those big white molars on that crusher claw waiting just for you. Then you'll find out if you have the nads to go after him! That's why it's called hunting."

"Piece of cake!" exclaimed Roberto. "Let's get going, I think I'm going to have a banner day!"

"Wait just a minute, now. Before you all go under, I'd like to make an observation," said Rod, looking sheepish. "Let me point out that the captain, *mwah*, has also dived today. It lasted less than five minutes, descent was less than five feet, and I have," he smiled as he got the five-gallon bucket from the pilothouse, "five nice lobsters!"

Rod passed the bucket around for all to see. P.J. broke into joyous laughter and proclaimed, "The standard has been set. A challenge! I accept the challenge!"

The others knew their work was cut out for them, but it certainly wasn't impossible. This was the lobsters' turf and there were lots of them waiting down below – all sizes – and although improbable in Foley Cove, a ten-pounder might be found.

"P.J., I suggest a surface swim on snorkel to conserve air. Head towards the west, and then hunt the wall down to the bottom where the sandy ocean floor meets the rocks. That's always a good area since lobsters like to dig holes under rocks. They can be anywhere, so keep a sharp eye open. And don't forget, everyone has to take a dive flag and make sure that the numbers are displayed. I'll keep your permits with me in case the local police board us. Are there any questions?" Rod asked.

"I don't have a flag, Captain Dude," said Roberto.

Rod stroked his goatee and thought to himself for a moment. "Well, you can take mine, which isn't exactly legal, but I need to know where you are. Hopefully, there'll be no issues, but you *will* have your own flag the next time you dive for lobsters. Understand?" Rod wasn't asking; he was letting the rookie know to get his act together.

He took out his dive flag from his personal equipment. Permit number 0840: bold black numbers on the white stripe of the red flag. He gave it to Roberto, then proceeded to check the divers as they entered the water. They all surface swam away from *Jus' Restin'* over to the granite wall on the western side of the cove, their dive flags bobbing along behind them.

The captain could now relax a bit, get out the binoculars, and check out other boats and the sights on the shore. This certainly was a target-rich environment for sightseeing the local color.

It wasn't long until the entire team was underwater, searching for the elusive lobster. P.J. was the first to score: a nice two-pounder hiding under some seaweed at the bottom of a deep crevice. Sarah looked on and signaled her approval to P.J. She decided she would follow him to learn his tricks before attempting to catch one herself.

Bob and Roberto were together at first, but Roberto opted to dive alone and headed north along the wall. He was soon a good distance from the others. Rod could see all the flags, and with a glance through the binoculars, saw 0840 bobbing in an area with many lobster buoys. *What's he doing over there, away from everyone else?* was the question that crossed Rod's mind. Other dive boats had been slipping into the area, so there were flags and divers in all directions now.

Rod settled into his helm chair. Looking down and to his left, he could see Kasey sleeping in the cuddy. What a life, he thought – a seadog's life. His mind drifted to P.J. Theirs was a strong friendship with many common interests, one being German Shepherds. In his other life, P.J. was a state police officer, stationed for the past twenty years in his hometown of Topsfield. The last ten years of his career had been as a K-9 officer. His dog, KaKo, was a huge male whom P.J. had accepted as a one-year-old. Many years of companionship followed, with decorations for exemplary service going to them both. P.J. would take KaKo everywhere; they were a popular sight around their small town, a favorite with young and old, and a deterrent to crime in their community.

But nothing lasts forever. KaKo passed away in his sleep this past winter, which broke P.J.'s heart. He pondered resigning his position, as KaKo could never be replaced, and thought he would try to reinvent himself. Rod wondered how the metamorphosis to Vice Squad was going and decided to look for a time to talk with P.J. on the return trip. He looked down at Kasey, knowing that her day and his would come some day, too.

Suddenly, the VHF radio came to life. "Securite, securite, securite, hello all stations, this is the United States Coast Guard, Boston Group. The National Weather Service has issued a severe thunderstorm watch for coastal Massachusetts, to include the Merrimac River south to Cape Cod until six pm. These storms could bring torrential rains, possibly including large hail. All craft should be on the watch for changing weather conditions and seek appropriate shelter. This is the United States Coast Guard, Boston Group, out." Securite, ("see-cure-a-tay") is the Coast Guard's word that an important message is to follow.

Well, isn't that interesting, Rod thought. *Clear skies overhead, but I can't see to the west with that granite wall blocking my view. Radar is blocked as well. Better just keep the radio on and stand by.* He checked the radio to ensure it was still scanning after the message, which it was. He would have to wait and see.

Suddenly, a pounding on the hull got Rod's attention. He looked over the port side – nobody – then over the starboard, and there was Sarah with eyes as big as he'd ever seen. They seemed to fill up her entire mask. She ripped the regulator out of her mouth and sputtered, "P.J. was going for a big lobster and has gotten his arm stuck in a crevice. Bob and I have tried again and again to pull him free, but no luck. What are we going to do? We need help!" She was panicking, and Rod knew he must calm her down if they were going to have any chance of freeing P.J.'s arm.

"Where is he located?" Rod pressed.

"About ten feet from the bottom, on the rock wall; he has the dive flag on the arm that's stuck. You should be able to see him."

"Yes, I see his flag. Bob's is right there too," Rod pointed as he looked towards the wall. "Quick, take my spare air and knife and give them to P.J. He'll know what to do. In the meantime, I'll set up my steel 120-cubic-foot tank with a regulator, which can give him a couple of hours of air so we can buy some time. I'll also notify Gloucester Dive Rescue while you're gone." Sarah nodded her head, took the pony bottle and knife, and went urgently back to P.J. "Swim on the snorkel and save your air! P.J. may need it," Rod barked.

Rod sat back on the engine cover and called to Kasey. She came to his side and he patted her slowly, staring into her attentive eyes. Suddenly, he started to laugh, just a little at first, then a real belly roll.

"Kasey, P.J. just threw them the old 'Arm Stuck in the Crevice' trick!" This could get interesting. He could only imagine P.J.'s theatrics: his arm being forever trapped in a tight crevice. He would drag it out as long as possible and hopelessly flail away for Sarah and Bob, who had probably 'dropped their own logs' by now. This scenario was especially funny for Rod, as P.J. had played this trick on him before. Rod had pulled and jerked on P.J.'s arm for the longest time, but to no avail. P.J. had been down to less than 200 pounds of air when Rod showed him his options: 200 pounds on his gauge and going fast, or the knife. Just give me the sign, buddy. Rod made a sawing motion to his pal after pulling his knife from its sheath. P.J. then pulled out his regulator with his free hand, blew Rod a kiss underwater, and miraculously pulled his other arm free and clear.

Rod knew he'd been had! He reached across and locked an arm around P.J.'s newly-freed arm, gave him his octopus (spare emergency regulator for situations like this), and the two divers headed for the surface. Rod continually punched P.J. in the ribs to ensure he was breathing properly! P.J. was breathing just fine, laughing bubbles all the way to the surface.

Training aside, Rod was getting a little concerned, as he now had two unknowns in front of him. What was the weather like beyond the granite wall with the beautiful homes? And second, how long would P.J. play out his charade in the crevice? At least Roberto was heading back; Rod could see that his flag was coming closer to the boat. About five minutes later, Roberto was at the stern holding up his dive bag.

"You da man!" exclaimed Rod as he hoisted the bag aboard. It was loaded with dark green creatures. "There have to be twenty lobsters in that bag!"

"He's the man all right!" came a loud voice from over the port side of the boat, amid ship. "I caught him robbing lobster pots and filling his bag. I tried to stop him, but he flipped me off! He's a damn poacher!" shouted a diver fifteen feet from the boat, bobbing on the surface. "I followed him right back here to your boat!"

"I'm the captain," said Rod, extending his open palm to the diver, as if to tell him to stop. "Let me take care of this."

"Well I've got his numbers, 0840, and I'm reporting his poaching ass to the Environmental Police." He submerged and was gone, his bubbles heading in the direction of the charter boat 100 yards to the port quarter.

Rod went over and grabbed Roberto's loose gear and threw it to the deck. He then reached over and "assisted" Roberto back into the boat, flopping his 200 plus pounds on the deck like a big codfish. "You have pissed me off, Dude!" he yelled at

Roberto. "Get your gear off, stow it, and shut up!" Rod grabbed the bag of lobsters, turned it upside down, and began releasing the contents over the side from whence they came.

At that moment, the VHF radio came to life. "*Jus' Restin'*, *Jus' Restin'*, *Jus' Restin'*, this is *Checkers*, 0-9." Rod stopped and threw the catch bag into the corner of the pilothouse as he grabbed the radio and replied, "This is *Jus' Restin'*, go ahead Chet."

"Hey Rod, just got a phone call from my sister in Lowell. Said they were experiencing the worse thunderstorm she'd ever seen. She checked the TV weather and the radar shows that it's heading right down the Merrimac River Valley towards us. Where are you located?"

"Foley Cove. Got several divers in the water. Can you see anything yet?"

"Nothing yet but it's surely coming. Could blow out before it gets here. Lowell's 40 miles away, but you'd better play it safe."

"Roger that, Chet, and thanks for the heads-up. *Jus' Restin'* standing by 0-9."

"*Checkers* returning 0-7."

Rod knew that Chet was truly concerned or he wouldn't have called. Chet Fisher was a good friend of Rod's and a long-time diver and mariner of the Cape Ann area. He operated the towboat *Checkers* out of Harborside Marina. If Chet was concerned, that was good enough for Rod. "Time to make things happen…" he muttered.

"How much air is left in your tank?" he barked at Roberto, who was sulking and staring at the deck.

"Still got 800 pounds," he replied scornfully.

"You get your butt overboard and get a message to P.J." Roberto quickly put his gear back on. He hadn't made much progress removing it since Rod's blasting. Rod got the slate board from his dive bag and wrote "P.J., all return to boat NOW!"

Roberto was underwater in a flash, swimming with Rod's urgent message towards the three flags grouped near the rocks.

It was decision time, and Rod had been trained to take the conservative approach. He picked up his mike and switched the radio to intercom, which energized the loud speaker on the roof. "Attention on the beach," boomed his voice over the loud speaker, carrying well into the cove. "There is a severe thunderstorm heading towards the Cape Ann area. Govern yourselves accordingly."

Rod knew that the folks on the beach had heard his warning because they waved back at him. Now he had to warn the divers underwater. Rod found his toolbox and grabbed the heavy duty, twelve-inch adjustable wrench and one of his steel dive tanks. He lowered the tank halfway into the water, and banged it five times. Ten seconds later, five more times. He repeated this for a full minute. For the life of him, Rod couldn't remember the warning signal for diving, but knew that it was five short blasts for boaters. He assumed that everyone would hear his warning and head for shore, as noise travels a great distance underwater.

Bob was just about to attempt his first amputation on P.J. when Roberto burst onto the scene. He passed the message board in front of P.J., and as Gomer Pyle would say, "Shazam": his arm popped free. P.J. signaled to the disbelieving Sarah and Bob that he was OK and to follow him. Roberto fell in behind the others. Within ten minutes, they were all back to the boat and hanging onto the line.

Bob and Sarah were obviously upset with P.J. for putting them through that episode, Roberto was bummed out because he was busted, and Rod was on edge because of Roberto and the uncertain weather.

P.J. asked jokingly, "What's the matter? We were just about to play doctor."

"Not now P.J., we've got issues. Get everyone on board, right away."

P.J. helped everyone onto the ladder and fed the fins and gear into the boat and to Rod. As soon as P.J. was on board, Rod fired the engine, and went up onto the bow and began to pull the anchor. P.J. wanted to know what was going on and what he could do. Rod recalled his conversation with Chet and said they were going to get under way as soon as possible and return to the marina. Then he stood up, stopped pulling the anchor, and looked right into P.J.'s eyes.

"Another diver caught Roberto poaching lobsters out of traps while pulling my flag. The guy who caught him is going to report the numbers to the Gloucester fish cops – just what I need!"

P.J.'s shoulders slumped as he realized one of his people had just broken the law and that Rod's integrity was now on the line. A bad reputation could ruin his charters, and news traveled fast through Gloucester. Rod cautioned P.J. not to discuss the lobster issue until he had decided how to resolve it, and to make sure everyone was bagging up their equipment and getting ready for the return trip. P.J. retrieved and stored the boarding ladder. Rod finished hauling the anchor and secured it properly with the safety latch.

"Bob: up on the bow. Keep a lookout until I tell you to come back."

Bob moved forward right away, alongside the pilothouse, and hung onto the grab rails on the roof as he moved forward. He stopped next to Rod at the helm. Looking towards the shore, Bob could see that people appeared to be packing up and leaving the beach; they were heeding Captain Rod's warning. P.J. supervised the efforts on the deck and relayed the captain's concern regarding the weather.

Rod switched on the radar and GPS. The radar would take 70 seconds to become operational, as it required a startup period. The other electronics were now functional. He eased *Jus' Restin'* into a slow 180-degree turn to starboard, passing the dive boat with the citizen cop on board, then headed out towards open sea. Idling alongside the granite wall, he was still unable to get a view to the west.

"Just another 100 yards and we can see the west," Rod murmured to himself. The rocky cliff slowly lowered and the sky opened up to a full view of the horizon. The incoming storm couldn't have looked more ominous, and it was heading directly into their path through Plum Island Sound.

Chapter Three

The Bar

Rod motioned for P.J. to come into the pilothouse, while the others and Kasey sat on the deck, or the "cockpit," as it is called by nautical types. P.J. closed the door behind him and waited for Rod to initiate the conversation.

With the captain and their dive instructor now out of earshot, the three divers opened up on each other, yelling over the noise of the engine. "What were you thinking, Roberto?" demanded Bob. "You've jeopardized the captain's license and reputation. You swam off leaving me alone, which our training has taught us not to do. And stealing lobsters! What's with that?"

"I don't know. I just wanted to beat Captain Rod with the most lobsters. I tried going into their holes. You saw me...no luck. I figured nobody could see me if I was alone; who'd know the difference? That's why I went off on my own. Well, I was wrong. Really wrong." Roberto looked down at his feet, shielding his eyes from Bob and Sarah. "I don't know how I can make this up to all of you. I really don't know what to do. I feel awful."

"I'll tell you one thing, you're in deep trouble. Right now the captain and a state trooper are inside deciding your fate as we speak. From what I've seen, they can be upbeat and easygoing, but both are professionals and they're going to deal with you in their own way." Bob shook his head in disgust. "I wouldn't want to be in your boots."

"And what about P.J.?" blurted Sarah to Bob while pointing at P.J. in the pilothouse. "Pulling a stunt like that 40 feet underwater? He scared me half to death! And you, Bob, were you *really* going to cut off his arm?" Sarah demanded.

"If he had given me the go-ahead, I think I could've done it. We've had to rescue people trapped in crashed cars with the Jaws of Life – it's our job to be cool under fire. But if we had stayed together, there would've been more air to share and maybe we would have been able to put our heads together and come up with a viable solution," snarled Bob, trying to remain calm while shooting a glare at Roberto. "The captain has two steel 120s on board, and P.J. could have breathed for a couple of hours on them while we figured it out and got more help. I wonder how P.J. thought we handled his 'emergency.' "

Rod studied the sky: it was like night and day. Bright sun and clear skies overhead, and what appeared to be a large dark blanket approaching on the western horizon. The leading edge was about 45 degrees to their position. He switched the selector on the radar to its 24-mile range, which now reached out to show the immensity of the storm heading their way. Two large black areas appeared in the upper corners of the display, and he knew right away that this was the weather Chet had warned him about. If the dark areas came together on the screen, this could be *really* big. The storm was eighteen miles away and coming towards them. Rod would be watching the screen closely from now on.

The *Jus' Restin'* eased by the last of the boats in the cove and came around the tip of Foley Point. Rod pointed the bow towards the entrance of the Ipswich River and the #2 buoy, which would mark the beginning of their journey back through Plum Island Sound. He pushed the throttle ahead and took the engine to 3,800 RPMs, bringing the boat to an aggressive 25-knot run to the buoy.

Fingering the buttons on the GPS, Rod called up the way-point for the #2 buoy. The GPS had over 100 waypoints in its memory, each a specific location that the boat frequented, with coordinates that could also be located on a roll out chart. A quick check of the GPS data showed that with the boat's present speed, it was a calculated 12:35-minute run to the #2. Rod would use this time to review the issues at hand: impending storm, Roberto's disrespect for the law, and his lobster number being reported to the police. What else could happen?

Rod glanced anxiously at his watch and saw that it was 13:45. With low tide at 14:12, he determined that the tide would be nearly slack at the mouth of the river. It would then turn and flood back in, filling Plum Island Sound as it had for eons. Due to the exceptionally low water resulting from the strong moon tide, the return to Harborside Marina would require him to follow the 36 buoys closely. This serpentine course would take twice as long as the high water this morning. Time was increasingly becoming a factor in determining Captain Rod's decisions.

The weather was changing fast as the *Jus' Restin'* made its way to the entrance of the Ipswich River and Plum Island Sound. It wouldn't be long before the sun disappeared behind the ceiling of clouds and Mother Nature unleashed her summertime fury. August was always primetime for the thunderstorms that marched eastward across New England.

"Many of the longtime boaters at Harborside Marina believe the Merrimac River has a strange influence on thunderstorms. They think it acts almost like a meteorological magnet, with the storms tracking the river valley to the ocean," Rod rambled to P.J., while scanning the skies.

"I'm sure you're aware of the three major tidal rivers between Portsmouth, New Hampshire, and Cape Ann," Rod went on to say. "First, there's the Piscataqua River coming out of Portsmouth, then the Merrimac River in Salisbury, and finally the Ipswich River here at the mouth of Plum Island Sound. All three river mouths create dangerous passages because of the vast quantities of water held in each river basin as the tides ebb and flood. It will be interesting to see, in a few short minutes, what the mouth of the Ipswich holds in store with the low tide, shallow waters, and large sea swell breaking on the bar. It's going to be some kind of fun. Believe me!"

Kasey started to fidget. Storms weren't her favorite activity, and conditions were worsening quickly. She began to whine softly for the pilothouse, but nobody was paying attention, nor could anyone hear her with all the noise.

"Well, P.J., are we having fun yet?" Rod laughed sarcastically. "We have some obstacles in our way, the first being the bar at the mouth of the river. We have one thing in our favor: the tide is changing, so it will soon be flooding the sound."

"Why is that a good thing?" P.J. was looking for some good news and was all ears.

"When the tide is still ebbing, the sea swell stands up against the falling tide, making for a bigger break over the bar. But because it's nearly slack and about to turn, I'm confident it won't be too bad even though we still have to deal with the sea swell. The waves should roll across the channel and break on the shoals to the west. The bigger issue, however, is the storm. It's coming fast, and the radar indicates it's less than fifteen miles away."

"*Jus' Restin'*, *Checkers*, 0-9." The VHF radio broke the silence.

"*Jus' Restin'* switching to 0-7. Go ahead Chet."

"Rod, where are you located? This storm is getting closer, real quick. We can hear distant thunder now and it's heavy. I'm back here in my slip at Harborside."

"Right now we're approaching the #2 buoy; another eight minutes to the bar. Then at least another twenty back through the channel to the dock."

"Are you really going to shoot for the dock?" asked Chet, challenging Rod.

"I have a contingency plan if this storm hits before we can make the dock. I'll call you for an update from Harborside once we clear the bar. *Jus' Restin'* standing by on 0-7."

"*Checkers* standing by on 0-7." Chet moved to the stern and looked at the approaching storm over the transom of *Checkers*. He was concerned for all those aboard the *Jus' Restin'*, as well as for the boats in the marina. A powerful storm could wreak havoc with boats in slips and on their moorings in the river.

"A contingency plan? What do you have in mind, Rod?" P.J. asked.

"Well, we'll have to get across the bar first, so I have a few chores for you. First, get the lifejackets out of the cuddy and everyone into them, and check that they're on properly. Second, secure the gear low in the cockpit. Third, I want the crew seated with their backs against the pilothouse, looking towards the stern. Their elbows should be locked together with Sarah in the middle. And lastly, bring Kasey forward with us."

P.J. repeated the orders back to Rod, who acknowledged that they were correct, and then went to work.

Rod reached to the back of his helm chair, lifted off his life-jacket, and slowly put it on, adjusting each of the individual straps until comfortably snug. With just five minutes to the buoys, Rod's thoughts were consumed with the tasks at hand.

The outside environment was becoming noticeably darker when P.J. opened the door and entered the pilothouse with Kasey. "Into the black we go...sun is behind the clouds now, and it's really dark overhead. How far to the first buoy?" asked P.J.

"A couple of minutes – it's just under a mile." Rod pointed to the #2 as the two of them peered ahead, looking to see what the channel held in store. A glance to the sky showed it taking on a rather spooky appearance.

"The swells have been moving at a speed of about twenty knots," Rod continued. "We've been going over them, in the same direction, all the way from Foley Point. The difference now is that the waves will be building in size and gaining speed as the water shallows up under them. Our problem is that when we turn 90 degrees into the channel, the waves will be approaching from our port side at a perpendicular angle. They'll lift us up and try to push us sideways towards the shallow bar on our starboard side." Rod raised his eyebrows and shook his head, indicating danger. "No. No. No. We don't want to get into a situation where a wave is propelling us ahead and down the forward slope – it could roll us over."

"Well, what do you think? Is it safe to go? Can we do it?" questioned P.J., concerned that maybe they should lay to the outside of the river and ride it out.

Rod looked to the southwest and saw that the waves were breaking in the shallows off the starboard side of the channel. Each wave held its large hump until it cleared the channel, then built to a curl with spray coming off the top of its eight-to-ten-foot crest. Finally it would break, crashing on the bar with a thunderous roar.

"I think we'll be OK here," said Rod, scanning side to side. "The channel is a mile from the #2 to #4 buoy, and then we'll be clear of the bar. It's a little over a quarter-mile wide. My plan is simply this: we'll cut the inside of the #2, then hug the port side of the channel – which is marked by the green #3 buoy – halfway through." Rod pointed out the green can buoy to P.J. "If any waves start to pull us to starboard, we'll just steer left, down the backside of the swell, and get back on track to the port side of the channel and keep heading for the red #4. We're going to kick her in the ass and just go for it!" Rod exclaimed, assured his plan would work. "Piece of cake. Should be through in less than two minutes. Tell everyone to get ready and stay seated."

P.J. was confident in Rod's explanation of traversing the bar. He cracked opened the door and gave the palm-down signal, as if he was telling his dog KaKo to sit. Everyone understood and prepared for the ride through the channel.

Rod took one last look at the breaking waves over the bar and then turned *Jus' Restin'* 90 degrees to port, just missing the #2. He pushed the throttle all the way forward and trimmed the outdrive up a touch. This would achieve maximum speed through the channel and over the bar. *Jus' Restin'* responded with 4,400 RPMs and just over 30 knots.

The ocean surface was noticeably smooth, except for the sea swell. *The calm before the storm,* Rod thought. With the boat heading almost due south through the channel, Sarah, Bob, and Roberto could see what lay ahead and to the left. For the past fifteen minutes, they'd been looking backwards over the stern at clear skies. It was a sight to behold! Waves crashing to their left, the ugliest sky any of them had ever seen, and the *Jus' Restin'* going at a fever pitch for all she was worth.

The first swell was hardly noticeable as they rode a gentle side-to-side course over the rounded wave, pushing down the port side of the channel. Rod could see that waves were breaking on the shallows at the far end of the channel. He pointed this out to P.J. and said he wasn't concerned since they'd be turning a hard 90 degrees to starboard at the #4 buoy, thereby avoiding these waves.

What Rod hadn't planned on was a 34-foot Uniflite, a big old fiberglass sport fishing boat that was usually moored in Essex Harbor. From a distance it looked like it was on anchor, but as they got closer they could see the vessel was now rounding the #4 and coming out through the channel. At top speed, this boat was lucky to do fifteen knots, but it could still create a horrendous wake. That, coupled with the sea swell and the fact that Rod had to steer towards the center of the channel to give the Uniflite the right of way, made life more interesting. Dangerous, too.

More and more boats were showing up behind Rod from all over Ipswich Bay. A few big Gradys and a Donzi flew on by without trouble and headed west up the Ipswich River alongside Crane Beach. Those who couldn't carry that speed elected to follow the *Jus' Restin'*, and soon a small armada was navigating through the channel. They all went up and over another swell, a bigger one this time, then approached the #3 buoy at the midpoint of the channel.

The Sport Fisherman apparently wanted his half to be in the center of the channel: it was decision time for Rod. He knew it was always best to pass port-to-port, but that would put him dangerously close to the building waves, breakers, and sand-bars. He therefore elected to make a sharp turn to port and then straighten right back, a clear signal that they would pass star-board-to-starboard. Rod also knew that the waters to port were deeper and safer, so he could take a little extra edge to port if necessary.

They went over the next swell, and this time the outriggers whipped side to side, accentuated by the pitch and roll of the boat. Rod held the wheel firmly and joked to P.J., "Is it raining in here?"

"Jus' sweatin'," replied P.J. with a weak smile, his head bobbing nervously. Beads of sweat rolled down his cheeks.

Rod looked back over the helm and yelled, "hang on, here we go!" just as the wake from the Uniflite was upon them. Rod throttled back hard so as not to crash into it, and planned to ride up and over the three waves he was anticipating. P.J. grabbed Kasey to keep her from flying around the cabin. In the meantime, the dive gear was sliding forward in the cockpit; Bob stuck his feet out to stop its progress.

The *Jus' Restin'* eased over the first wave and then slammed into the trough, with the leading edge of the second wave looming ahead. The bow nearly went under because the boat was now riding lower from the momentum and extra weight, but she recovered and managed to rise over the second wave. She dropped hard into the trough again as the third and final wave approached.

Rod looked to the port and there it was: another sea swell building offshore. The #4 buoy was nearby, but the new swell and the last wave from the Uniflite's wake were about to con-verge. Rod slammed full throttle, and the duo-prop dug in hard.

"Up Jumbo!" Rod yelled with a laugh. They went up the third wake of the Sport Fisherman, with the sea swell right behind them and closing.

Over the third wave they sailed. They were nearly airborne as they crashed down into the bubbles and churning water from the props of the old Uniflite. The bow went under, and a wall of green hit the windshield; the Volvo growled under the strain, but the RPMs regained slowly and steadily. She started to accelerate again and the race was on!

"Everyone still with us?" asked Rod.

P.J. looked out the rear window and saw that the crew was still hunkered down, hanging on for dear life. As he raised his eyes over the stern, he could see an enormous sea swell curling and advancing fast.

"Everyone's still here, including that huge wave coming after us!" yelled P.J.

Jus' Restin' was like a surfer exiting from a curl, racing sideways against the building wave. The other half of the Uniflite's wake was crashing on the sandbars to the right. The sea swell began to pick them up and thrust them forward.

Bob, Sarah, and Roberto were hanging on and truly scared. The stern of the boat was high on a crest one moment and deep in a trough the next, with subsequent waves trying to crash over the stern and into the cockpit. The combination of the breaking waves, a screaming engine, and being airborne off the deck as they blasted over the wake was an exciting yet frightening experience, with a significant danger factor thrown in.

Rod swung the wheel to starboard and made a beeline for the #4, knowing that if he cut this buoy to the inside, he would surely "polish the props" on the edge of the bar. He had cut the buoy way inside on a previous trip and scuffed the propellers hard.

There was no way they could make the #4 staying inside the channel without hitting the buoy and getting sucked into the curl. So they went outside the channel to starboard, just missing the large red #4 nun to port.

Meanwhile, Sarah, Bob, and Roberto had each other's elbows in a death lock. They stared at the thunderous wave that kept reaching forward, trying to engulf them and the *Jus' Restin'*.

The boat suddenly lurched forward, causing the propellers to scuff the bottom on the edge of the channel. Luckily the hull never hit. The engine recovered and the RPMs surged, bringing a wide smile to Captain Rod's face. *Jus' Restin'* swung back into the channel again, right on course, as the sea swell thundered onto the sandbar to starboard.

"Just cleaning the wheels!" Rod whooped. He and P.J. exchanged high fives as *Jus' Restin'* steadied her speed and continued down the channel. But the feeling of relief that settled over the crew as they raced along the shoreline was to be short-lived. The real challenge lay to the west, and by the looks of the sky, the crew of the *Jus' Restin'* would be engaged soon enough.

Chapter Four

The Green Monster

Captain Rod took a deep breath and a long exhale. Even at dead low, there would be plenty of depth for the return trip as long as he didn't drift outside the channel again. He throttled back to 3,800 RPMs and checked his gauges: the temperature was running high at 185 degrees, fifteen degrees above normal. He attributed the temperature rise to running hard and long over the bar and sure enough, with the reduced RPMs, the temperature slowly drifted back to normal.

Rod got P.J's attention and pointed to the screen. "Take a look at the radar: rain's happening at eight miles. The whole upper third of the screen is black. I'm going to call Chet to see what's going on at the marina." He grabbed the mike from the helm. "*Checkers, Jus' Restin'* 0-7…"

"Go ahead *Jus' Restin'*," responded Chet immediately. "Rod, where are you located?"

"Just passing the #6, coming up the channel by Crane's. What's the weather at the dock? Anything started yet?"

As Chet and Rod were talking, Bob, Sarah, and Roberto sat upright on the deck, looking over the stern at the small fleet coming in behind them. Several boats, maybe seven or eight, were following in their wake as they traveled along the shore. The beach was a flurry of activity: those who hadn't left yet were doing so as quickly as they could, heading for the stairs that would lead them to the shelter of their vehicles in the parking lot.

Chet was getting nervous as he relayed the state of affairs back at the marina. "It's as black a sky as I've ever seen, just boiling grey and black, and yet so calm on the water. There isn't a ripple here at my slip. I saw several lightning strikes in the distance, followed quickly by heavy, heavy thunder. It's going to blow at any moment. My radar shows rain closing at four miles now."

Rod studied the radar, a unique piece of equipment. Not only can it pick out objects near and far away, all the while calculating the distances, but it can also display oncoming rain. Accurately. And it is fully functional day or night, in all weather. Based upon what he saw, Rod made his decision.

"Chet, we're not coming back to the dock. There's no time and there's no advantage to being there." Rod again looked over his shoulder to the crew on deck and then back out over the bow. "I think I know a place to hide and ride this out. We're going for the Green Monster between the #16 and #18 buoys."

"I think I know *just* what you have in mind. Good idea and good luck! *Checkers* standing by on 0-7."

"What are you talking about, the 'Green Monster'?" P.J. questioned. He had no idea what Rod had in mind.

"You're a Red Sox fan. Just wait: you'll see in a couple of minutes. But when we get there, I'm going to want everyone inside the cuddy and pilothouse. Go below and get the cuddy ready." Rod felt a furry body shivering up against his leg. "Hey, look at Kasey – she's stepping on my foot! She always does this when she's scared."

Rod laughed and patted Kasey's head, but that did little to calm her down. Kasey had been caught on her run back home, all alone, when a storm struck the past summer. A tree fell and pinned her under its branches. As she lay helpless waiting for someone to free her, as she was pelted by hail and heavy rain. When Rod arrived home and released her, she trembled for hours, never recovering from her fear of storms.

Rod steered hard to starboard, rounding the #10 buoy at Bass Rocks as two boats passed on his port side and headed up the headwaters of the Ipswich River. Meanwhile, he continued towards the Ipswich Yacht Club and farther into Plum Island Sound and the Parker River. The sound is a tidal basin fed by several small rivers and estuaries, including the Ipswich, Eagle, Rowley, Parker, and Plum Rivers. Each river feeds into the main marked channel in which they were traveling.

"I don't know what they have in mind, but they're capable of speed that we are not. Good luck to them."

Rod looked ahead as boats were moving about in the channel, trying to get onto their moorings and ride out the storm. He decided to ignore the posted speed limit and so did the boats behind him.

The door suddenly opened, with Sarah standing in the doorway. "Can we come inside? It's freezing out here!"

"Sure Sarah, come on in!" Rod shouted as the cold air rushed into the pilothouse. The windows had been closed, making the pilothouse nearly airtight, and he didn't realize the temperature had dropped so rapidly outside.

"Go right down into the cuddy, grab the green and white towel, and get comfortable. P.J., the other two should stay outside – I don't want all that weight forward yet."

P.J. motioned to Bob and Roberto to stay put, while Sarah went below to warm up. Looking out the side windows, Rod pointed to the exposed sandbars on either side of them as they raced up the channel past the #12 buoy, around the point, with the #14 just ahead.

"Rod, rain is three miles away now, straight ahead. I can't wait anymore. Where are we going and what is the 'Green Monster'?" P.J. was as nervous as a little kid. He just had to know – now!

"The Green Monster is one of my favorite fishing spots inside the sound. It's a 25-foot-deep channel at low water, tight to the western banks of the channel." Rod paused as a small boat flew past their starboard. "Here's the deal: remember how the surface water was even with the grass on the way out of the channel this morning?"

"Yeah, it was right up to the grass, just about even – above it in some places."

"That's right! Well, with a normal eight-to-nine-foot tide drop, plus this being a moon tide, we've gotta have ten feet of wall between the top of the banking and the surface of the channel." Rod shifted his weight as the boat rolled on an oncoming wave. "My plan is to approach the banking at 90 degrees to the wall, and then push the bow of the boat, with the anchor out front like a hook, *right into the mud wall*. We'll keep the boat in this position with the engine running slowly, holding us tight, while the winds blow. A perfect bulwark." Rod grinned. "What do you think?"

"I like it, I like it a lot! The wind will just blow right over the top of us! Sounds like the safest place to be...to me, anyhow."

"Great. Just in case it all goes to hell, I'll put you on record as approving this plan!" They laughed as *Jus' Restin'* flew past the #14 buoy with the Green Monster a quarter-mile away and in plain sight. As he approached the #16, Rod began to throttle back, as did several of the boats behind him...even though they didn't know what he was planning to do.

"P.J., take the helm, approach the banking slowly, and go for the middle. I want to help direct the other boats that have been following us, looking for cover. But don't make contact yet!"

"You got it." P.J. took the helm and steered the boat for the center of the banking, throttling back to ensure a slow approach. He breathed a sigh of relief because he knew they were going to make it, though in the knick of time.

Rod came out of the pilothouse into the cold calm air, and noticed something very strange: the sixteen-foot outriggers were hissing with static electricity. They were becoming electrified by the approaching storm!

"You two: inside right away, into the cuddy. Put Sarah between you. Hurry!" The two big guys headed forward, causing the bow to lower noticeably.

A couple of boats flew by up the channel, but three boats stopped next to the *Jus' Restin'*. They didn't know what they should do next. Rod yelled that he was taking cover behind the banking and strongly suggested they do the same. He knew that there would be zero visibility on the water once the wind and rain started, so these boats would almost certainly run aground and be at the mercy of the storm. They were center console boats, with no real protection from the weather: recreational fishing boats with a crew that probably had very little experience in rough weather. *And this was going to get rough.*

Rod returned to the pilothouse, and P.J. stepped aside to give him the helm. "Sure you don't want to steer, hang onto this stainless steel wheel with all the static?" Rod laughed, since P.J. was sweatin' heavy again. Just then, a tremendous crack of lightning lit the darkened sky, followed immediately by booming thunder. The hull reverberated. "Oh baby! Here we go again. Sit tight everyone!" Rod said as he peered down into the cuddy.

He eased the pulpit up to the banking, and sure enough, the grass was a good two to three feet above the roof of the *Jus' Restin'*. The distance quickly closed between the anchor and the Green Monster. He made contact and pushed ahead into the thick mud, then throttled up. The anchor went about a foot into the mud. He eased off the throttle, keeping the boat in gear and the hull perpendicular to the land mass.

He shut down the electronics, because all hell was about to break loose. A lightning strike would probably toast everything electrical – and themselves too for that matter – but no sense in trying to attract one. Rod and P.J. looked up through the front windows at a turbulent sky that would have made Steven Spielberg's special effects look tame.

Then it started. The grass began to move, slowly in this direction and then in that, as if it couldn't make up its mind. This is what they were waiting for: the forward edge of the storm was upon them. Bob and Roberto were looking out the portal windows on either side of the cuddy. They saw that the boaters who had been following them were trying frantically to get on their rain gear and lifejackets. Although these mariners didn't seem to understand which one was more important, they were soon ready to engage Mother Nature.

POW...POW...POW-POW-POW-POW-POW.

"Hail!" P.J. shouted.

The wind gusts brought half-inch hail that pounded the fiberglass roof and decks, creating a deafening roar inside the pilothouse. The water was calm where they were, but 100 feet beyond the stern, waves were being whipped up by the ever-increasing wind. Rod saw two bright yellow kayaks approaching from the right, desperately paddling to find shelter. The water was jumping all around them, and the hail was coming down at a tremendous rate. It was falling so hard that slush was building up on the surface of the water.

"P.J., take the helm and hold her steady. I'm going to help these people aboard!" Rod directed P.J. to the helm. "Bob, come with me!"

Rod pulled his hat down tight, opened the door, and went into the cockpit. Pelted by hail, he now felt the full blast of the weather. Bob was close behind as they went to help the kayakers on the starboard side of the boat. It was difficult to walk on the deck because it was so slippery with ice and slush.

"Grab my arm, pal, I'll pull you in!" Rod yelled. He made a forearm-to-forearm grip and pulled. In an instant a thin, dark, middle-aged guy was over the gunnel. "Go inside with the others! Bob, pull in the kayak and lay it on the deck."

Bob followed orders, and P.J. opened the pilothouse door for the first of the kayakers. Rod went back into position for the second kayaker to come aboard. He leaned over the side, and it was like a dream: as in his first motorcycle accident, time seemed to slow to a crawl. He made eye contact with a petrified young woman who was reaching frantically for Rod's outstretched hand, her bright green eyes looking like beacons. Their arms locked together and Rod lifted her into his arms and then to the safety of the *Jus' Restin'*.

"Inside, quick!" Rod shouted, as Bob brought her kayak aboard. Directing Bob to go back inside, Rod elected to spend a moment huddled outside under the overhang of the roof, evaluating the weather and assessing the situation. This was positively the place to be. Any other location in the sound was sure to feel the full might of the storm. He feared for the boaters in open water who were at the mercy of the storm; a small boat offshore would have little chance of survival if caught off-guard in this weather.

The three boats that had followed them to the Green Monster were to port and having difficulty maintaining position against the wind. Rod stepped outside again and motioned them to raft up together and to the *Jus' Restin'*. He took a line from the first boat and tied it to his mid-ship cleat, then yelled for them to do the same to each other. He directed the first boat to keep the engine running in forward, and to hold steady. The skipper acknowledged.

Rod looked over the stern and determined that visibility was limited to a mere 50 feet. Suddenly a tremendous gust of wind blew off his hat – in a flash it was riding the waves down the channel. He reentered the pilothouse, which was now full of frightened mariners, and saw that his new passengers were shivering from the cold and wet. He turned on the heat, and adjusted the throttle to just under 1,000 RPMs so that the combined weight of the boats rafted to him wouldn't affect his position on the wall.

"Welcome aboard folks. Are you two OK?" Captain Rod asked, trying to calm their fears. He had to yell to be heard over the howling wind.

"Were we glad to see you! That hail really hurt!" remarked the woman with a French accent. "This is our first time out here and we weren't sure where to go when we saw the storm approaching."

"Well not to fear. I'm Captain Rod. This is P.J., and Sarah, Bob, and Roberto are down below."

"Bonjour, my name is Suzanne Brouilette, and this is Ahmed Jafari. Again, thank you ever so much for bringing us aboard!" She gave Rod a big hug, and Ahmed offered an embrace and a handshake.

"Well, this is just starting, so get comfortable," said P.J., who was looking intently at the blowing grass above the front windows.

The banking had a slight overhang and thus limited their view, but through the side windows they could see the sky light up with huge bolts of lightning that vibrated the fiberglass hull. The wind kept increasing, like the shifting into higher gears on a semi truck. It would rise with a gust and hold that velocity, then another gust, then another, and so on.

"I figure we're in close to 50 knots of blow by now – I pity the small boats in open water," said Rod. "These waves will be building in quick succession. Not a pretty picture for those off-shore."

Rod retreated into his thoughts as the others discussed the storm. He knew that the boats tied to their docks at the marina would be thrashing against the dock lines, like bulls before they're released at a rodeo. The storm would test every piece of line and hardware, looking for the weak link that would allow a boat to be torn free from its berth. There were also at least 100 boats in the channel leading up to and beyond the marina, tethered to either a mushroom anchor or a concrete block buried in the mud. Those boats, which relied on suction to hold them steady, were probably twisting and turning in the wind and surf. Because of the storm's direction, the marina could not escape: it would feel the full power of this summer blast.

The hail had transitioning to heavy rain without letup. The temperature inside the cabin was now comfortable, and Rod noticed something quite pleasant. Suzanne's perfume had begun to float on the air with the new warmth, making for a nice atmosphere. *Much better than the usual suntan lotion*, he thought. He caught P.J.'s attention and made a sniffing motion with his nose like a rabbit, along with a Groucho double eyebrow raise. P.J. smiled and pointed to the window, as if to tell Rod to pay attention to the job at hand. Rod smiled.

He peered into the cuddy to see how Bob, Sarah, and Roberto were faring. It was tight quarters down there, and after a quick assessment, Rod determined that Roberto didn't seem quite right. He asked if he was OK. Roberto said yes, but Rod knew better. He'd been very quiet, which usually means something's wrong...especially for a talker like Roberto. The cabin was airtight and with seven people inside, all of whom were probably hyperventilating, the oxygen level had to be dropping.

"Open the portal windows a touch and let some air in there. We'll do the same up here."

Rod felt the air shift inside, and he was confident this would be beneficial to all on board. He then moved to the control panel and turned on the lights in the cuddy, the red light in the pilothouse, and the anchor light on the topside. The rain and wind continued to pound the boat with a deafening rhythm, and water leaked in from the overhead. But all in all, Captain Rod was satisfied that everything was secure for those aboard his boat. This, unfortunately, was not the case a mile up the channel to the north.

*

Willy the Clammer was in trouble. He had enjoyed a wonderful morning: he'd caught a nice, fat 38-inch striped bass that he attached to a line and let hang over the side of his boat. As the tide dropped, exposing the sandbars, Willy surveyed his choices and picked a clam flat with a deep drop-off on the backside. He anchored his skiff where his fish could hang in a few feet of water, out of the heat of the noonday sun. Seems he had forgotten to bring his cooler and ice that day, and leaving his catch on the deck would have ruined it.

Willy had clammed for a couple of hours, had hit 'em pretty good he thought, and it was timeout for some lunch. As always, he had his foldout chair the grandkids had given him, and with the incoming tide a couple of hours away, there was plenty of time for his usual nap. All was right with the world as he nodded off to sleep.

After a peaceful rest, he raised his head and opened his eyes; it took a moment to register, but soon he knew he was in serious trouble. Stiff from the two-hour nap, he slowly pushed himself out of his chair and turned to look into the face of the oncoming storm. A short distance away the first lightning bolt struck, and the wind began to gust so much that he could hardly keep his balance.

Looking back at his skiff, he analyzed the situation at hand. Should he leave? He knew that with a small motor and very little speed against the rising wind, his boat wouldn't make much progress. And where would he go, anyhow? Home was a twenty-minute ride on a good day. He looked at the ground and saw that he was standing on the highest point of the clam flat, and it was probably a couple of feet above the water line. He had a plan, a simple one, but a plan that could work. He was going to stay right where he was.

Willy shuffled to his boat carrying his folding chair, clam bucket, and lunch box, and placed everything in the bow. He got out his lifejacket, along with his crusty old Gloucester fisherman-style rain hat and jacket, and put them on. Then he walked back to the one item he'd left on the sand: his clam rake. He would literally draw his line in the sand and make a stand against Mother Nature. He got down on his old tired knees, picked up the rake, and gave it a long stare. It was a tool he knew all too well, but now it was to be used for something he'd only dreamed about.

The rake was short, its handle just under eighteen inches, but it was unique: this rake had five long tines, each over ten inches long, and was made of heavy steel spread across a steel header. Willy raised it high over his head and drove it into the sand. It didn't go all the way in, but he didn't want it to yet. Next, he reached over the front of the rake with his right hand and slid his fingers into the gaps between the tines. Finally, with his right palm against the rake and his left hand on top, he pushed it as far as it would go into the sand, right up to his fingers.

His hand was now locked like a cowboy's to his rope on a bull, ready for the ride of his life. He lay down on his rounded belly and grabbed the handle with his left hand, then stretched himself out as streamlined as possible against the strengthening wind. He put his head down, resting his forehead between his biceps, and prepared for the worst. Willy was a tough old bird and he knew his chances; the old boy was ready to make his final stand.

The hail was the first to hit. It started out as a few pellets, then quickly increased with ferocity. His jacket and hat protected him pretty well, but from the waist down he was fair game and it hurt! Willy thought back to the times when he used to play here and have BB gun fights with his teenage pals in the marsh grass. He chuckled, thinking how his buddies had pinned him down on this sandbar, with no cover, and showed him no mercy for all the times he had stung them in just the right spot.

Mercifully, the rain soon took over, and he knew he could bear the pounding. But the thunder and lightning were frightening! The storm seemed to be centered directly over him. Lying face down, he could see the mud light up from the lightning overhead, and the thunder almost lifted him off the flat as it reverberated into the sand. The waves in the channel were building and washing onto his little island, inching their way up the sand. With the incoming tide, they would be upon him in no time.

*

Rod pointed out the lightning to the north, which seemed to be moving east at a good clip. "The beauty of these storms is that they don't usually last more than an hour, so we must be close to the midpoint – maybe even a little past."

Jus' Restin' was now camouflaged in marsh grass and leaves. Anything that wasn't tied down was blowing in the wild, swirling wind. The tide had changed now and was flooding in...starting to pick up speed...filling the sound. No other boats had come through the channel since they'd arrived at the Green Monster, but that was about to change.

Fish Tales was following her electronic chart plotter up the channel, coming around the #16 buoy, and approaching *Jus' Restin'* on her port. She was a 38-foot Sport Fisherman with a seasoned captain aboard. The captain throttled back just a bit to keep his wake down once he made out the lights from the boats huddled against the banking, then resumed his speed after passing by. *Jus' Restin'* and the others rocked and rolled on the wake, but the little band of boats held their position. *Fish Tales* disappeared into the wind and rain, traveling up the channel with the guidance of modern technology, given that visibility was near zero.

*

Willy lifted his head just enough to see that the wind-whipped waves were a few feet away. The combination of the incoming tide and wind had brought the waves to him sooner than he'd anticipated. He got up to his knees and elbows in order to keep his head above the approaching water, while still securing his position.

Just as another lightning blast hit, he saw the ghostly figure of *Fish Tales* approaching from the left. Her red and green navigation lights were becoming bigger and brighter, but soon all Willy could see was the green light as she passed by, about 150 feet away. He tried waving but realized nobody would see him because the crewmen were inside, attention fixed on their instruments.

And then it hit him: the wake from the *Fish Tales* was coming! He tried to lie back down as fast as his old bones would move, but he wasn't fast enough. The full force of the first wave – a four-footer – broke right on top of him and crashed on the sandbar.

Just like in the rodeo, Willy was out of the gate! His left hand was ripped from the rake's handle and shot high into the air, but he was still able to hold on with his right hand. The force of the wave almost lifted the rake out of the sand. After the wave passed, he fell down and tried for a different grip – but not in time. The second wave managed to buck Willy off the rake and yank it free, sending him tumbling past his anchored skiff. The third wave just pushed him into the deep water.

He was now adrift, the wind and the waves shoving him simultaneously east towards the shore and north with the tide.

He turned his back to the wind, and waves broke over his hat. He'd been very cold on the sand bar because of the hail, rain, and cold air. But now the 75-degree water, normal for the sound this time of year, was keeping him warm. He knew he could survive with the conditions at hand; he just needed to wash up to a place where he could climb ashore.

*

The lightning was well off to the east as the wind began to diminish. Even the rain was losing some of its punch. "I think the worst is over, what do you think?" asked P.J., with the others looking on hopefully.

"I think you're exactly right, P.J. Let's turn on the radio and see if we can contact Chet at the marina." Rod switched on the radio to channel 7 and hailed Chet.

"This is *Checkers*, go ahead Rod," came Chet's familiar voice over the radio.

"Hey Chet, all's fine here. What's going on at the marina?"

"The storm is almost done. Light rain and wind: it'll be over in a minute or two." Chet scanned the view out his window. "There appears to be a lot of damage on the roadway up above, with trees and power lines down. No power at the docks and some boats have broken free. I'm about to walk the docks and assess the situation."

"Very well Chet, we'll be here awhile yet, then see you at the dock. *Jus' Restin'* returning to channels 1-6 and 0-9."

Rod placed the mike in its holder and began whistling the theme from *Gilligan's Island.*

Everyone except Suzanne and Ahmed started to laugh as they now knew the worst was over. Rod opened the door of the pilothouse and the wind rushed through, bringing in an abundance of cool fresh air. The rain and wind continued, but the storm was losing intensity fast. Rod stepped into the cockpit and pumped his fist to the other boats. Their captains and crews cheered, knowing that they had survived what Mother Nature had dished out that day. He signaled to stay put a little longer, they signaled their agreement, and he returned to his crew.

"Ahmed and Suzanne, where did you folks put in today?"

Ahmed said, "I believe it was a public area. Right next to an old bridge, back up the channel a couple of kilometers. I'm really not sure how far away."

With the noise abating, Rod noticed Ahmed's foreign accent. He figured he might be from the Middle East.

"You must be talking about the town dock," P.J. surmised. "We'll be going right by there on the way back. You might as well stay with us so we can drop you off."

"Excellent idea P.J., but before we leave here – a toast!" said Rod, as he pulled a little purple bag out of the tool locker. "Bob, there are some plastic cups in the box by my gear; please grab them and bring them outside. Thanks."

Rod pulled the throttle back to an idle, then motioned for everyone to follow him into the cockpit. With everyone outside among all the gear and kayaks, there wasn't much room to stand. But everyone, even Kasey – who had finally stopped shivering – found a spot. Bob passed around the cups, while Rod gave each of them a "spot of grog" to enjoy. Rod hoisted his cup and said, "To old friends, new friends, and Mother Nature!"

"Here, here!" cried Suzanne, "and to our captain!"

Rod laughed and everyone cheered. He was glad they'd gotten through it all safely. "*Aargh*, it's good to be alive!"

With that, they all tossed back the Crown, thankful they'd weathered the storm. Rod motioned to the other boats that it was safe to head out, so they untied from each other, pulled back from the Green Monster, and headed up the channel – each with an exciting survival tale to tell.

"Bob, take the bucket and see if you can rinse the debris off the windshield, and P.J., make sense out of the gear and kayaks in the back. I'll get us ready to be under way."

Back at the helm, Rod switched on the electronics and the navigation lights, since it was still raining. Bob heaved a couple of buckets of water forward, clearing the bow of mud and grass. Rod eased the boat into reverse. The anchor was secure in the mud, but pulled away from the banking without a problem when a huge hunk of mud fell away and splashed into the river.

Rod spun the wheel to starboard, pushed the throttle forward, and rode the incoming tide back up the channel. The sun was now starting to break through the clouds and small patches of blue could be seen all around. He made a hard right turn at the #20. It would be straight ahead now for a half mile to the #23, then a long left hand turn by the #25 and #27. No sense in hurrying, he thought, so he set the throttle at 2,600 RPMs: a leisurely ride back to the town launch would allow time for some small talk with his new guests.

Sarah and Roberto were in the cockpit area helping P.J. and Bob get the equipment squared away. Ahmed and Suzanne had taken over P.J.'s spot in the pilothouse, and Kasey was back in the cuddy on her favorite blanket.

"We dodged a bullet today," commented the captain to his guests.

They smiled in agreement, as Rod continued to scan the waters ahead. Something caught the corner of his eye: a small boat on anchor, off to starboard. He slowed a bit and eased *Jus' Restin'* over to the far side of the channel to get a closer look. This was not a normal place for a boat under the circumstances, and a closer look revealed a familiar sight...Willy the Clammer's skiff, but no Willy.

The tide was covering the clam flat where Willy's boat was anchored, but it was evident by the ripples on the water that it was extremely shallow. Captain Rod eased *Jus' Restin'* onto the bar, and heard the sand rubbing against the hull as he came to a stop and shut down the engine. He climbed onto the bow and looked all around – no sign of Willy.

"Here we go again, things happen in threes they say! P.J., get Willy's boat and tie it to the stern. Bob, put the kayaks over, one on each side of the boat. Suzanne and Ahmed, I want you to look at this." Rod got out the chart for Plum Island Sound and opened it on the engine cover. "Who knows what happened to Willy, but with the wind from the west and the tide flooding generally north, he's gotta be somewhere along the eastern shoreline. Suzanne, I want you to paddle along the shoreline, which is the marsh banking. I will take my boat up the channel, and Ahmed, you split the difference between us. When we find him, and we will, signal the others."

Suzanne and Ahmed leapt into their boats and paddled off in search of Willy.

"Sarah, take my binoculars, go topside and keep a lookout on the life raft. He could be anywhere. P.J., is there a lifejacket in the skiff?"

P.J. hustled to the stern and looked in the boat. "Negative."

"Good, he's got his jacket on," Rod replied, "we'll find him quick." Backing the boat off the sandbar, he picked up the radio mike and called Chet. "*Checkers*, 0-7." Chet answered right away. "Chet, we have a problem. Just found Willy's boat, but no Willy. We're starting a search from buoy #23 north along the channel over to the eastern shore. Call the Coast Guard and the Harbor Master and advise them of the situation."

With Chet handling the communications for him, he could concentrate on the search. They moved along the channel to the #30 buoy, Rod listening in as Chet talked with the authorities on the radio. At the #30, an unmarked splinter channel opened up to the east and Rod steered to starboard, bringing him on a course to rendezvous with the kayaks.

Each time Suzanne paddled around an outcropping, exposing the next bit of shoreline, she hoped to find Willy. Maybe he'd been picked up already or was walking on the shore somewhere. She couldn't see inland with the high banking and grass to her right, so she continued on. Ahmed, 100 yards to her left, wasn't having any luck either.

Suddenly Sarah yelled that she could see the top of a paddle waving. Rod asked where, and Sarah replied "at two o'clock." Rod looked to starboard, about halfway between the bow and mid-ship, and sure enough there was a kayak oar waving above the grass line on the far shore. He corrected his course and headed for the signal.

Suzanne came about on a small outcropping, the entrance to one of the estuaries that winds back into the marsh grass and feeds into the sound. There, sitting on a little spit of sand, was Willy the Clammer! He was shivering, and his hat was drooping down over his eyes: a pitiful sight. He heard Suzanne calling his name.

"Willy," she cried, "is that you?"

"You betcha! It's me alright!" He tried to get up, but he was so cold and exhausted from his ordeal that he could barely move. Suzanne ran her kayak onto the sand, got out and knelt at Willy's side, and gave him a big hug. Willy looked at this beauty and asked, "Am I in heaven?" They both laughed and she told him he'd be fine – Captain Rod was nearby and would find them soon. She stood up and waved her paddle high over-head so everyone could see her location.

In a moment Ahmed was on the sand and at Willy's side, giving him the once over and checking his medical condition. He gave Willy the OK sign and a soft pat on the back. Willy pointed his shaking finger excitedly at the outriggers of the *Jus' Restin'*, which were coming around the banking and into the estuary.

"There they are!" yelled Sarah, "just ahead!"

As he maneuvered into the estuary, Rod looked out the starboard window and a big grin spread across his face. His eyes welled up when they met Willy's – Rod feared he might have lost his old friend. He gave a couple of short blasts on the horn and there was a round of applause.

Rod picked up the mike and called the Coast Guard on channel #16. He informed them that Willy had been found and was in good condition. The "Coasties" thanked him, and he returned his radio to scan. A moment later the Coast Guard bulletin announced the termination of the search for the lost mariner.

With everyone back on board, and the skiff and the kayaks in tow, *Jus' Restin'* proudly made her way back to the Parker River. Her crew enjoyed the magnificent rainbow that had developed to the east, with the dark clouds of the passing storm as its backdrop. The sky was nearly clear to the west, and the warm sun was beating down on them as they headed towards Willy's dock. Willy's wife had heard all the chatter on her VHF radio in her kitchen, and was waiting nervously with her friends on their dock when *Jus' Restin'* eased up to meet the reception committee.

Once they tied up the boat, Bob and P.J. helped Willy onto the dock and into the waiting arms of his wife of 60 years. It was a grand reunion. Willy had many neighbors who thought a lot of him and he was moved by their presence. As everyone said their goodbyes, Rod gave Willy a wink and a salute out the window. He returned the gesture with his traditional Richard Nixon wave.

The channel revealed the extent of the damage. Large oaks and maples and other debris had toppled onto the lawns of the waterfront homes and into the water, now a muddy brown from the heavy rain runoff. Two small boats were partially sunk and resting on the shore, having broken from their moorings, and one old sailboat had a splintered mast. But overall, the fleet in the harbor appeared to have weathered the storm pretty well. The town dock was bustling with activity. People were checking their boats, and the Harbor Master was performing a surveillance of the area from his boat. The rescue teams that had assembled to search for Willy were now packing up, having never deployed. After a short wait, a spot opened at the dock and Captain Rod tied the boat up right away.

"Well, here we are, the next stop on the tour. Is this the launch you left from this morning?" Rod asked. He thought it was and sure enough, Ahmed spotted their car in the parking lot. P.J. and Bob pulled in the kayaks and set them on the dock, along with the paddles and lifejackets.

"Captain Rod, thank you ever so much for rescuing us from the storm. We will be forever grateful." Ahmed extended his hand and Rod gave him a hearty handshake.

"My pleasure Ahmed. Please come back and visit, the boat is slipped on the other side of this bridge."

Ahmed said goodbye to the others, climbed over the gunnel, and waited for Suzanne.

"Captain, am I extended the same invitation?" Suzanne asked, in a soft French accent that made the captain's knees wobble.

"*Aargh*!" was all Captain Rod could muster, laughing and smiling broadly.

"Then I shall see you again, my captain," she whispered, as she gave him a tight hug and a kiss on the cheek. She stepped out of the boat and onto the dock, waved to the rest of the crew, and said goodbye again to Rod. She and Ahmed picked up their kayaks and headed down the dock. Suzanne stopped one last time to give the crew another wave.

"You know P.J., I think my philosophy of 'catch & release' needs to be reexamined." They laughed and watched Suzanne and Ahmed head for the parking lot, then went back into the pilothouse. Rod started the engine and headed for the slip, a short distance away.

The service dock at the marina was jammed with boats dealing with storm-related problems, so Rod elected to go into his own slip. The divers would have to carry their gear up the ramp of the floating dock, which was steep now because of the low tide. There was nothing Rod could do about that.

Once backed into the slip and tied fast, Kasey bolted over the gunnel, her bladder about to explode. Rod grabbed her leash and told P.J. to do whatever was needed, and that he would be back as soon as shore duty was completed. Down the finger dock they went, heading for the upper yard and the bushes Kasey so desired.

Steam rose from the hot top as the cool air and warm wet ground made for a humid atmosphere. The marina was in a state of calm with no electrical power, no water at the bathhouse, and people hanging around discussing the storm and the damage it caused. Rod passed *Checkers* and caught Chet's attention. Chet was talking on his radio and getting ready to shove off and tow in some stranded boats. He and Rod waved to each other. They would get together later to run over the day's events, and to enjoy a little "navigation fluid." This was part of their daily routine.

Kasey was right where she wanted to be, in the thickly-wooded lot nearby. With no one in sight, Rod decided to join her. As the day faded behind him, there was still one issue left to address: Roberto. Captain Rod decided it was time to let him twist in the wind.

Rod and Kasey wandered about the entrance to the docks, exchanging stories with the other boaters and trying to determine if anyone from the marina was unaccounted for. Nope, the report was everyone was fine. As P.J. and his crew assembled their gear at the head of the ramp, Bob brought the SUV to the ramp to be loaded. Sarah, Roberto, and Bob made quick work of packing the rig, while Rod and P.J. wrapped up the business side of the trip. Before long, they were all milling about the SUV and discussing the storm and the next day's final exam.

"Captain Rod, we'll be starting at 08:00; can we expect to see you there?" asked Sarah, eagerly looking forward to the next adventure.

"You can count on me. Should be fun!" Rod shook her hand and then Bob's, who was standing next to her. Roberto extended his hand, but Rod ignored the gesture. "Stand by a moment," said Rod, as he walked alone to P.J.'s truck.

P.J. and the crew looked puzzled, not knowing what Rod had on his mind. He found what he was looking for under the front seat: P.J.'s 9mm Glock and his handcuffs. He took the cuffs and put them in the waistband on the back side of his shorts without anybody seeing. Time to turn up the heat.

"P.J., as a state police officer, I want you to do your duty. Place Roberto under arrest for poaching undersized lobsters and illegally tampering with a lobsterman's gear. I took these from under your front seat – I believe one size fits all," he remarked as he handed the cuffs to P.J. and stared at Roberto. It was hard to tell whose jaw dropped farther, Roberto's or P.J.'s. Sarah and Bob wanted nothing to do with this situation and slid away to the bathhouse.

Rod began to berate Roberto. "I made the laws and expectations of diving for lobsters perfectly clear to you, and I even cut you some slack regarding the use of my dive flag. It came back to bite me, but now it's my time to bite back. P.J., *you* take care of this. *You* arrest him, *you* call the Environmental Police, *you* call the Gloucester Police, or do whatever *you* have to do, but *my* name will be cleared. Do *we* all understand?"

"You don't have any evidence! It's my word against yours!" blurted Roberto, remembering Rod shaking out his dive bag overboard. He thought he had trumped the captain: no evidence, no crime. He'd played his only ace. A moment ago Roberto thought he was leaving this problem behind him at the dock. Now reality was hitting him between the eyes, and he was scrambling.

"Stand by," Captain Rod demanded, as he headed off with Kasey to the *Jus' Restin'*. Once inside the pilothouse, he began searching. "It must be here, this is where I threw it." And sure enough, behind his dive gear was Roberto's dive bag. He grabbed it and held it up to the sunlight. In the tangle of the nylon mesh were two undersized, juvenile lobsters. "Bingo!" Rod handed the bag to Kasey, who carried it in her mouth like a Frisbee while trotting back to the group. He opened the bag to Roberto's groan and P.J.'s forlorn expression, and motioned to P.J. to follow him for a sidebar conversation.

"P.J., here's the deal. I don't really care what happens to Roberto, he's all yours now. Maybe you can work some magic with the EP officers, I don't know. But he needs to feel the long arm of the law here." Rod looked back at Roberto standing all alone. "The big issue for me is having my name cleared. If word gets around that Plum Island Charters condones poaching, my business will go out with the tide. I can't afford that and I won't allow it to happen. My family has been lobstering for over 100 years; mine is a respected name and," pointing at Roberto, "*he will not cause it to be tarnished.*"

"I understand Rod. I'll tell you what I'll do. I'll cuff him and put him in the back of my truck while I make some phone calls. I don't believe he's a felon at heart, but I'll do a quick check and also call the Gloucester Police and Environmental Police to try to diffuse this issue. One way or another, I'll clear you of any responsibility. OK?"

"Deal. I'll see you tomorrow at 08:00." They shook hands and P.J. returned to the truck and the waiting Roberto. Rod left in his old Ramcharger with Kasey in the back. He caught a glimpse of P.J. placing the cuffs on Roberto, with Bob and Sarah looking on from the porch of the bathhouse in disbelief.

Pulling away from Harborside, Rod looked into the rear view mirror to see Kasey sitting with her real Frisbee in her mouth. "All right baby, it's your turn. Let's go play," and off they went down the road.

P.J. watched Rod crossing over the old bridge, kicking back for the rest of the day, while his day had just become a lot more difficult. He was very uncomfortable with the situation. For one thing, he wasn't in the habit of looking for some "consideration," or "magic" as Rod called it, from other police. Secondly, he wasn't that familiar with the marine laws governing lobster fishing or which laws had been broken. Lastly, was Rod playing a variation of the Arm in the Crevice game? He thought not, so until a solution had been worked out, Roberto must sit and ponder his own fate.

Chapter Five

Indian Maidens

𝕬fter Kasey's daily Frisbee workout, an acrobatic display
with 25 to 30 throws at the local town common, the time
came for her customary three-mile walk. Rod planned to take
her along the backwaters and marshlands of the Parker River, a
quiet and picturesque area with few homes and little traffic.

He was thankful the greenhead fly season was over,
because a walk here during their one-month reign of terror
might have required a blood transfusion. The dreaded fly is
about a half-inch long, has iridescent green eyes, and seldom
bites within easy reach of retaliation. Instead, they prefer hard-
to-reach locations such as the middle of the back, behind the
knee, or on the ankle. Their bite feels like someone took an alli-
gator clip and attached it to your skin.

Rod never understood why – infrared maybe – but whenever he started the boat engine during that notorious one-month span, it was like ringing the dinner bell. Let the carnage begin! The bug is so infamous that many town folk wear tee-shirts proclaiming Town Bird status: to kill one is illegal because they're protected.

The greenhead does not fly solo in the battle against mankind. There is also the hated midgie, a bug almost too small to see...but oh so irritating. Folklore says the native Indians called them "no-see-ums," and that under a microscope they are nothing but a set of chattering teeth. Walking through a swarm of midgies feels like walking into a biting cobweb. The only relief is a stiff breeze because when the wind picks up, they vanish as quickly as they arrived.

And what marshland would be complete without the common mosquito? These are twice-a-day insects: early in the morning and just in time to ruin a beautiful sunset. But in spite of doing battle with all three of them, Rod had yet to come up a reliable method of eradication – only ways to cope and endure.

One hot summer night, Rod almost succumbed to some particularly bloodthirsty mosquitoes. After a successful offshore fishing trip, which was enhanced by a generous tip, he decided to splurge a little with a nice dinner on Plum Island. After cleaning the boat, showering at the boathouse, and making the social rounds on the docks, he was ready to head out. Having another charter first thing in the morning, he made his bunk in advance so he could come straight back and hit the sack.

After a fine dinner and a sampling of his favorite local microbrews, it was time for bed. Crossing the gunnel and onto the boat, he noticed the pilothouse door was open. No big deal: rarely is anything tampered with at Harborside. He must have simply forgotten to close it. He entered the pilothouse, closed the door, and lay down on his bunk where his head sunk blissfully into the cool pillow. It took a moment to register, but soon the whine of the "moes" built to a high pitch. Then, the biting. Rod turned on the light and saw mosquitoes by the hundreds!

He flew out of the cuddy, sputtering and swatting the miserable buggers that were attacking his arms and legs.

How to get rid of them? A blast of bug spray would do it, but then he'd have to sleep in that atmosphere. *Not a good idea. What would MacGyver do? I have to use my resources wisely.* Then it hit him: the Black & Decker handheld vacuum cleaner! Feeling like Davy Crockett going back into the cave after the bear, he charged into the pilothouse, got the vacuum, and plugged it in. It roared to life.

"Take that you little bloodsuckers!"

Ten minutes later they'd all disappeared into the nose of the machine, which now buzzed like a beehive. Rod stepped out of the boat and onto the dock, and walked a good 100 feet away; after checking the wind direction, he let the mosquitoes fly. Back in his waiting bunk, stillness never sounded so peaceful. Moments later, Captain Rod was in la-la land.

*

When Rod was five his parents divorced, and he went to live with his aunt and uncle for a few years. Their son was four years older than Rod and their daughter was one year older. They were wonderful people, and he was happy to share their home until he was old enough to move back with his father.

His aunt had recently passed away, and his cousins had their own families, so Uncle George lived alone now. He had a small cottage in scenic Essex, landscaped to perfection, with a two-bay garage. Essex, a quaint town of horse farms and ship-building, is twenty minutes from the marina. Uncle George and Rod had a special relationship: there was always room at the inn for Rod and Kasey. George especially loved having Kasey around, since it reminded him of his favorite dog, Jack, another German Shepherd.

"Well, this is a pleasant surprise for a Saturday night!" exclaimed Uncle George. "Did you get caught in the storm? Wasn't that something?" He was eager to hear Rod's stories about the day.

George was an impressive man: 6' 3", lean, with a contagious zest for life. He had short curly white hair, a golden tan from daily walks on the beach, and maintained a good weight for his age of 79. Being around him was like going down memory lane. He and Rod's father started off as brothers-in-law, but over the years they became the best of friends; Uncle George reminded Rod of his father and it felt good to be in his home.

"Today was a close one for sure – we found cover just in time."

Uncle George sat on the edge of his chair, not wanting to miss a single detail. "Sounds like you had quite a time. Are you going out early to fish tomorrow?" he asked. He was hoping Rod would make his favorite apple cinnamon pancakes for breakfast, if he wasn't leaving too early.

"I'm supposed to be at a lake in southern New Hampshire for a class with rescue divers by eight o'clock. I was thinking we might go out for dinner tonight. How about some seafood – you interested?"

"Sure, but only if I'm buying!"

Uncle George enjoyed going out to eat, and seafood was king in Essex. He fed Kasey while Rod got in the shower; soon they were heading to Uncle George's favorite restaurant on the shore road, The Blue Marlin.

It was a beautiful late summer evening, with the cool air from the Canadian high-pressure system a welcome change from the heat. The restaurant was crowded but that was the norm here because the food was good and worth the wait. Uncle George had fried clams and scallops, his weakness, and Rod had the surf-and-turf: steak tips and fried haddock plate, with coleslaw and home-cooked baked beans. A couple of Sam Adams Summer Ales in frosted mugs made their meals complete. Both of them saved a little for Kasey, who was snoozing in the backseat of the truck.

Uncle George watched Rod enjoying his meal, especially the beans. "You remember what your father used to say about beans and Saturday night?" he asked, testing Rod's memory.

Rod finished his mouthful and looked up with a smile. He took a sip of the ale, then turned on his Maine accent and replied, "Sad-dee night, beans and lovin', gawwwd, how I hate it!" They had a big laugh, and Uncle George told Rod he sounded just like his father. He'd be proud of him, working that Down East lingo.

After dinner, they went back to the house for a chitchat about the old days, then it was off to bed and lights out. Morning came with Kasey whining for Rod to take her outside. Out they went to a clear sky and cool breeze – a refreshing start to the day. When they returned, Rod noticed pancake mix on the counter next to the apples and cinnamon. *Oh, the power of suggestion,* he chuckled to himself.

"OK if I leave Kasey with you? I'd like to take the bike to New Hampshire today," Rod said as he mixed the batter. "But only if you don't mind." He knew this was only a formality, as Uncle George thoroughly enjoyed Kasey's company.

"Of course I'll take her! You can leave her with me forever!" Uncle George and Rod laughed, each knowing Rod would never part with Kasey. With breakfast behind them, the threesome headed out to the garage.

"How are you going to carry all that dive gear on your bike?" Uncle George asked as he swung open the old wooden doors.

"I don't need to take everything. My buddy P.J. has extra tanks and weight belts, so I'll just bring my gear that's on board the boat." Rod removed the cover from his bike and there was his Goldwing: jet black and ready to go. During the summer months at the marina Rod liked to keep his bike accessible, and Uncle George didn't mind. "First gotta check the fuel gauge to make sure you didn't run the gas out of her while I was gone." Rod was only half kidding, since Uncle George had been a Harley rider for years and, 79 or not, he might get the urge and go for a ride.

"She's just the way you left her. Fire her up and let's hear her purr."

Rod fired the engine, but before the bike could warm up he was dressed for the road and waving goodbye, heading for the Harborside Marina.

Life was getting back to normal at the marina. Power had been restored, and the marina crew was cleaning up the debris from the storm. Rod went aboard *Jus' Restin'* and collected his gear. He carried the equipment to his bike, and was in the process of loading it when Chet approached him with a wide smile. "You missed the excitement yesterday. The Environmental Police were here about an hour after you left. I figured you had a problem with one of your divers."

"You could say that. No respect for the working man," replied Rod with a look of disgust. "What happened to him?"

"The guy got belligerent with the cops. They would've taken him to the Iron Bar Motel if it wasn't for your friend P.J. He managed to calm him down, so the fish cops only issued a citation. The law states that if anyone is apprehended with 'short' lobsters, the fine is anywhere from $100 to $500 per lobster. The kid wasn't too happy – started arguing with them. If P.J. hadn't intervened he was going to the hooscow!"

"He's lucky I dumped most of his bag – what he originally had would've cost him dearly!" Rod shook his head as he finished securing his dive gear. "But I gotta go now so we'll catch up later, Chet. Heading up to P.J.'s place and I don't want to be late."

Rod started the bike and was off, winging north on I-95 into New Hampshire with a 25-mile ride ahead of him. His destination was Pawtuckaway Lake, a warm water lake with private homes on the south side and a state park to the north. P.J. had a cottage there and Rod was familiar with its waters. But now it was time to enjoy the morning ride as he laid on the throttle.

After passing the sign "Maine and Points North," Rod found himself drifting back in time to Uncle George and one of his cousins. Her birth name was Beatrice, which cried out for a nickname – something short and catchy – so she became Bertie at an early age. She had an infectious laugh and thought everything Rod did was funny. He always did his best to entertain her because she was a cousin, sister, and best friend rolled into one.

One of Rod's favorite memories was going "Down Home" with his father, Uncle George, and cousin Bertie. For some reason Rod's father, whose name was actually Hubert, and Uncle George, whose real name was Jerry, had abandoned their birth names. Instead, they called each other "George"; everyone played along and the names stuck.

Down Home is a little seacoast community called Brooksville, a part of Cape Rosier that juts into western Penobscot Bay. It's a part of "Down East," the rockbound coast of Maine from Penobscot Bay to the Canadian border. Rod's father's family were all "Mainah's," with the majority hailing from Brooksville. Rod idolized his father; whenever he told tall tales from Down Home, Rod was a captive audience, hanging on every word. He would try desperately to mimic the unique Maine accent for which his father had such command.

One summer, rumors of a vacation in Brooksville started to swirl. When Rod found out Uncle George and Bertie were going too – oh happy day! The time finally came to head Down Home. The two Georges rode in the front seat (with Rod's dad as captain and Uncle George as navigator), Bertie was in the backseat with her Nancy Drew books, and Rod was on the deck of the back window. Their '53 Plymouth was a spacious playground for an eight-year-old since seat belts were still a long way off in the future.

Soon they were on US Route 1, on their way to their overnight stop: Rockland, Maine, "The Lobster Capital of the World." Rod's father had cousins there, so it was a convenient place to rest and visit relatives. A few rites of passage had to be completed first, however. The first was the Piscataqua River's "hummin' " bridge, the gateway to Maine.

As they passed the sign welcoming them to Portsmouth, New Hampshire, Captain George came over the intercom to announce that this was the town where Rod was born, and where the "other side" of his family had its roots. As the blue Plymouth cruised downtown, Navigator George instructed everyone to roll down the windows and be ready for the first sign that Maine was near. They drove down State Street, through the Strawberry Bank section of town, and there they were: the tall, green, twin towers of the Memorial Bridge, the border crossing between New Hampshire and Maine. The towers looked huge to Rod and Bertie, who were both standing up in back looking over the front seat. They didn't want to miss a trick.

"Prepare to enter Maine!" Captain George commanded as he let off the gas pedal to allow the traffic in front to pull ahead. His timing was perfect: when his tires hit the steel latticework of the bridge's road surface, there weren't any cars in front of them. He gunned the old flathead Plymouth and she accelerated as only that six-cylinder could. The hum of the tire's pitch began to rise as the Plymouth gained speed. Higher and higher it rose.

Navigator George issued the next command: "Breathe only through your nose!"

Rod and Bertie closed their mouths tight. The car went faster and faster, and the pitch of the tires got higher and louder. Then it hit them...it was euphoric...the smell of salt air from the Piscataqua River below as they rocketed into the great state of Maine! The kids shrieked with joy as their fathers laughed and enjoyed the thrill – they were making memories that would never fade. These two guys were a tag team, and Uncle George set the stage for the next act: how to speak like an Indian.

"Well, now that we're in Maine, you kids really should learn to speak the native tongue. Do you want to learn some Indian words?" asked George, who had just hung up his navigator's hat and put on his Indian guide hat.

"Oh yes, let's start now!" screeched Bertie, eager to get the lesson under way.

"Well, first we'll learn how to properly say the name of the river we just went over. People in Portsmouth today call it the Pis-CAT-a-qua River. The early settlers called it the Pis-ca-TA-qua River. The word has been pronounced many different ways, but for the native pronunciation we'll have to ask the chief." Indian Guide George looked over at the George behind the wheel and signaled that it was his turn to dazzle.

In his best Indian accent, Captain-turned-Chief George began the lesson. "Name easy to learn. Speak slowly to start. Then say faster as get better. Listen close to the way of the native words: Pizz-ah – qua-tah – wah-tah." The chief slowly repeated himself: "Pizz-ah – qua-tah – wah-tah. You try, little squaw."

Bertie tried and had it down after a couple of attempts. Rod kept up with Bertie, as they were both good at Indian languages. The two of them sat back and practiced while the Georges in the front seat barely contained themselves.

"How long before little pale faces figure out scam?" Chief George asked with a smirk.

"I know one thing: when they do, they'll never forget it!"

Each had a good laugh as the Plymouth continued past the Portsmouth Navy Yard. They traveled on up through Portland, Brunswick, and Bowdoin College with its huge pine trees, then over the bridge next to the Bath Iron Works where Navy warships were built. An hour later they entered Rockland and sure enough, there was the banner stretching between two buildings on Main Street that claimed, "Rockland, Maine: The Lobster Capital of the World."

They found their way to cousin Dottie's house. It was a joyous time, since Rod's father hadn't seen his cousins in ages; there was much to catch up on and a few beers to help them along the way. After a tour of the waterfront and a signature lobster cookout in Dottie's backyard, the kids were off to bed. The adults joked and laughed far into the night.

Everyone was up early the next morning. They said their goodbye's right after breakfast, since the kids were eager for the final leg of their journey to Brooksville.

"One more time, what was the name of that river?" asked Dottie, winking at Uncle George. The kids obliged, and the adults had another one of those great, subdued laughs that only a parent can enjoy.

They were Down East now, and on their way Down Home to the enchanted town of Brooksville. Back onto US 1, they stopped in the seaport towns of Camden and Rockport, and then traveled north along the western shore of Penobscot Bay. After a visit to Perry's Nut House, a local tourist attraction, George the navigator pointed out that the Bucksport Bridge would be coming up on the right, and for the kids to keep an eye out. Bertie spotted it first. George the captain pulled into a rest area just before the bridge and let the kids get out to take a picture.

"Wow, that's a high bridge! Do we have to go over it, Dad?" Rod asked, afraid of being so high in the air.

"Not to worry Rod: you and Bertie can stay on the floor, and we'll let you know when we're safely on the other side. OK?" The captain looked at the navigator and winked.

Relieved, the kids looked at each other and sighed. They didn't want to look way down to the water below. That *had* to be scary! The Plymouth pulled out of the rest area and made a tight turn to the right onto the span over the river.

"OK kids, down on the floor!"

Rod and Bertie huddled on the floor behind their fathers, looking at each other with terror. The front seat riders were enjoying the view of the picturesque Penobscot River, with Bucksport in sight to the left.

"Are we over the bridge yet?" yelled Rod from the safety of the floor.

"Almost!" replied his father, biting his lip as he smiled at the other George. They went another few seconds, then Captain George said, "OK, we're on the other side!"

The kids jumped up to look out the window and saw that they were dead center in the middle of the bridge, 135 feet above the water! "You tricked us!" yelled Rod, who hit the floor and refused to get up for five more miles. Eventually even Rod laughed at the joke, but he wasn't going to be had again – no way.

Up ahead was what they'd been waiting for: the road sign for Brooksville. They were almost Down Home. Almost.

"We don't want to show up hungry, so we'll stop at a little place by the water that you kids are going to love. It's called the Bagaduce Lunch. Hot dogs, hamburgers, and the onion rings are the best. They've got haddock and scallops too, if you want to try them." Rod's father knew that his son really liked onion rings. This place was special for him as well: it was here that he'd learned to enjoy "rings" as a kid. Heavy on the batter!

They stopped to fill the cooler with some Knickerbockers for the dads and bottles of tonic for the kids. The band of travelers rode a little farther when the navigator announced that their destination was just ahead. Nestled on the banks of the

Bagaduce River, overlooking the big pine trees along the water, was a little red and white diner. The Bagaduce was a tidal river, and it was ebbing out to sea at a good clip when they arrived.

The Plymouth rumbled onto the gravel parking lot, and navigated over to and under the shade of the tall pines. After ordering their food, Bertie and Rod ran off to the pine grove by the water to choose a picnic table, and the Georges carried the cooler down to the lunch site. It was a perfect place for the kids to play and explore nature while the fathers could "have a Knick" before arriving at Uncle Gorham's house. They had asked the counter person to hold the order back for a while, to give the kids a chance to play a little after the ride. But this was only a ploy to allow the men time to lighten up the cooler a bit. Two beers later, their number was called and the food arrived right on schedule.

Rod's Dad yelled out a "Let's eat," and that brought the kids running. They'd been playing at the water's edge and were excited to see the food on the table. In a flash they were working their way through their soon-to-be favorite choices. Bertie was in seafood heaven, sampling everyone's lunch. Rod was finished first, having devoured his hot dog and rings, and asked if he could go back to the water. Bertie soon followed. The fathers relaxed and watched their kids having the time of their lives; they were finally Down Home. Not only was life good, but just as the sign at the state line said, "It's the way life is supposed to be."

"My dad used to take me here when I was a kid," Rod's dad mused in his Maine accent. "It's like déjà vu. Cay ah faw ah notha bee-ah George?"

"Shoo-ah George, pass her over!"

This went on for another hour or so. If they'd stayed any longer, Bertie, who could see over the dash, might have had to learn how to drive – in a hurry. When the kids ran back to the table, Chief George looked at his faithful guide and decided it was time to turn on his broken Indian accent and have some fun at the expense of the Bagaduce River.

"Penobscot Indians call this river, 'Bag-a-Douche.' Long time ago, Indian maidens come down from village to fill their douche bags in running ocean waters. Waters good medicine.

All squaws wash with waters. Chief and tribe all very happy after nice bath!"

The chief managed to maintain his composure throughout the lesson, but his faithful guide was dumbfounded. "How do you know all these things, Chief?" asked his guide, looking away from the kids' line of vision.

"Me know many things, teach just little bits at a time."

With that said, the kids ran back to the water's edge for one last look around, while the near-empty cooler was carried back to the Plymouth. The chief gave a whistle that could be heard in Castine, and the kids raced back up the hill to the car. Once inside, they started reciting the story of the Indian maidens to each other.

The chief looked in the rear view mirror and saw that the kids were playing with something. "What you capture from river?" he asked.

Bertie held up a tonic bottle that was full of water. "Bag-a-Douche water. You said it was like medicine. Can we keep it?"

"Shoo-ah, good idea!" Ahhhh, he smiled.

"You're going to pay one of these days!" his trusty guide whispered in a low voice.

The chief winked and they were off to Uncle Gorham's house. But there was time for one more adventure. "Listen, does anyone want to fly car like airplane?"

"Sure, but how can we fly?" Rod asked. He was not a fan of heights and after all, this *was* a car.

"Magic Hill ahead, but everyone must want to fly!"

There was a resounding yes, so the chief changed back to his captain hat and instructed the navigator to "extend the wings." The navigator was puzzled, so the captain reached over and slid the heater and defroster controls all the way to the right. The kids had no idea what the levers did, so they looked outside expecting to see wings coming from the sides of the car.

"Wings extended" said the navigator.

Up ahead was a steep hill with no view over the top, since its elevation dropped rapidly on the opposite side. With low bush blueberry fields to the right and left, and no "other" planes in his pattern beyond the hill, the captain was confident of a safe takeoff. "Going to full power!" he shouted as he down-shifted and gunned the engine. He figured close to 65 mph would be required to launch.

"Prepare for takeoff!" yelled the navigator when they hit the top of the rise.

The kids held hands as the Plymouth broke the surly bonds of earth and went airborne. Off the seat, weightless and scream-ing, they felt their stomachs trying to jump through their mouths. That old Plymouth *Spitfire* flew magnificently through the air, seemingly forever. What a thrill ride! The tires even chirped a little, signifying a safe landing.

"People are going to start calling us the Wright Brothers, Captain!" exclaimed his navigator, having just earned his wings.

"We do it for de' fun!" whooped the captain.

Everyone laughed as the navigator lowered the flaps to slow this fine craft, not wanting to overshoot Uncle Gorham's "taxiway," a narrow gravel driveway consisting of two ruts with grass growing high between them.

The 150-foot incline led them to the back door of Uncle Gorham's cottage. Rod peered out his window and thought what a neat place this was: its shingles were worn and its paint had long ago faded, and reddish-green ivy grew over old rose trellises. He would soon discover its unique characteristics to include the squeaky well pump and the thrill of a ride in the "two-holer-backhouse."

Everyone got out to stretch and laugh about the ride. Bertie was holding her bottle of magical water, bragging that she hadn't spilt a drop! Rod's dad walked over to the screen door that led into a hallway filled with rubber boots, rain gear, and a wooden box with an assortment of empty bottles. Rod wrig-gled in beside his father to get a look through the lower screen, as his dad hollered through the mesh screen and second door leading into the kitchen.

"Gorham, you home in they-ah?"

"That you Hubie?" Gorham didn't play the George game; he liked their original names best. Rod was about to meet Gorham, and he would *never* forget this first encounter.

The little house on the hill faced due south, sitting about 100 feet above the waterline of Penobscot Bay. The screened porch on the front of Gorham's home overlooked some of the finest real estate in the state of Maine. The sun was shining so brightly off the water that, even with his hands cupped around his eyes, Rod could hardly see inside the house. A tall thin man appeared quietly in the doorway, blocking the sunlight and creating an indelible silhouette that burned into Rod's memory.

"By *Gawd*, that must be Little *Rawd* with *Berrrrtie* right behind him...come on in!" said the friendly voice with the thick Maine accent. Gorham, a tall handsome man of 70 with a full white beard, stood before them.

The door opened and everyone went inside to a warm welcome of handshakes and laughter. Soon the kids were begging to go down to the dock and see Uncle Gorham's lobstah boat. They were given the OK, while the older boys sat on the porch and caught up on old times. They had a clear view of the kids as they played by the dock and shoreline.

It was Sunday afternoon and the beginning of what would be the most wonderful week of memories in Rod's childhood. There were many things to do, but his number one mission was to get into that boat, pull the traps, and catch some lobstah! This was going to happen early the next morning and he could hardly wait.

The kids did the breakfast dishes while Uncle Gorham put on his high rubber boots and jacket. With everyone set to go, the band of fishermen walked in order of height down to the shoreline: Rod in the lead, followed by Bertie, then Hubie, Gorham, and Jerry closing up the line. There was still a thick Maine fog hanging on the water, but Uncle Gorham assured everyone that it would clear soon enough – no need to worry. They all climbed aboard, then Gorham explained the day's activities and assigned chores.

"Seeing as how *I'm* the captain, *I'll* steer the boat. You big fella's will pull in and set out them they-ah pots." Gorham looked down at Rod, who was anxiously awaiting his assignment. "And you chummy, you are in charge of fillin' the bait bags. Bertie, you need to come up he-ah and help me spot the booh-ee's. All my booh-ee's look like this." Gorham picked up one of his buoys from the deck, a beat-up old wooden burgundy float with three faded white stripes around the center. "Everyone ready?"

"Ayuh, we're ready!" said Bertie, who was as excited as everyone else.

Gorham prepared to start the engine. She was an old boat that had seen a lot of work over the years and, like her captain, was in the twilight of her career. *Finest Kind* was powered by a small diesel, which had replaced the old original "one-lunger." Her instruments consisted of a compass, an ammeter, and a temperature gauge. That was all Gorham needed.

As they chugged along the rocky shoreline, Uncle Gorham explained to Bertie that the boat was like a clock, and that the bow was *always* at the twelve o'clock position. Everything else was relative to the bow: the stern was at six o'clock, and so on. She nodded and called out the first buoy right away. "Buoy at two o'clock!"

Sure enough, there it was as Gorham maneuvered the *Finest Kind* into position for the Georges to make their retrieval. The Georges made a fine tag team as they hooked the buoy with the gaffe, pulled in the warp line, and set the pot on the work platform. The lobsters needed to be removed through the large open cover, and gauged and pegged. A new bait bag was then tied into the pot.

The kids were excited to see what waited inside the wooden slats of the pot. Gorham pulled the boat into neutral and came back to supervise the operation, handing Rod's dad the gauge for measuring the lobsters.

"Go ahead Hubie, show 'em how it's done," Gorham encouraged.

It had been many years since Hubie first learned the skills of a Down East fisherman, but he took to the task as if it was only yesterday. There were three red crabs, a starfish, and two lobsters inside the trap; he pulled out the crabs and starfish and tossed them over the side. Next, he pulled out the lobsters one at a time, their tails flapping madly. Taking the gauge and placing it between the eye socket and the beginning of the first tail segment, Hubie recognized these as keepah's. Gorham smiled and pointed to the box of wooden pegs. Each claw was closed with a peg, so that the bug wouldn't damage itself or the others that would soon be joining this bug in the catch box.

"Now chummy, it's your turn. Take that bait bag and shake it out over the gunnel." Gorham pointed to the side of the boat. Rod understood and followed directions. "Next, take the cover off that barrel and get a fish head to put in the bag."

Rod first looked at great Uncle Gorham with bewilderment, then to his father for reassurance. His father just nodded toward the barrel. Carrying the empty bait bag to the barrel, he lifted the cover and took a look inside: it was full of fish parts and other sea creatures, all in some state of decomposition. But what really grabbed Rod and Bertie was the smell! "Whew! That stinks!" said Rod.

"That's what makes her good! Reach right in they-ah and fill that bag. I'll show you how to tie her in the pot."

Rod reached in and grabbed the head of a bluefish that was bobbing on the top of the brine, while Bertie wretched at the smell. The men were all laughing, but Rod did it and everyone cheered him on. He brought his hands up to his nose, which was a big mistake...he ran to the gunnel where his breakfast went over the side.

Gorham handed Rod a rag and told him to wipe his hands and not to be sniffin' bait anymore. Everyone had a good laugh. The young fisherman recovered enough to suggest that everyone take turns baiting the bags – Gorham chuckled and agreed that was a good idea. He showed the group how to put the bait bag back into the pot, and then instructed the crew on setting out the pot.

"Always throw the buoy first, next the line, then the pot. That way, the line won't get tangled and the pot can't drag the buoy to the bottom, causing you to lose your gear."

With the routine down, the rest of the morning was spent doing what Down East Maine-ah's do: fish for lobsters. They had a productive day, hauling over 70 pots, with 56 keepah's in the catch box. Gorham had over 200 pots, which he checked twice a week.

The fog had cleared and the sun shone brightly as they went to their last stop, the lobster car: a large float that replicates a lobster pool like the ones at fish markets. Gorham would store a week's catch of lobsters here, then sell them on Sunday to fish dealers. It was empty now, but with luck they'd have a fine harvest to sell by the end of the week.

The remaining days went by too fast, as good times always do, with lobstering in the morning, followed by mackerel fishing for the bait barrel. The afternoons were spent picking low bush blueberries, visiting relatives, and walking to Buck's Harbor for the best black raspberry ice cream ever. Life here was wonderful, and Rod wished their vacation would never end.

Saturday morning arrived all too soon. Armed with a paper bag full of fresh blueberry muffins from cousin Katherine, they said their goodbyes and got into the car. As they pulled onto the road, Rod looked up to see Uncle Gorham on the porch waving goodbye; as hard as he tried, he couldn't hold back and burst into tears. This was the greatest place to be and he didn't want to leave, ever. But all good things come to end, and so the foursome headed back from whence they came, enjoying new stops along the way. After all, a vacation isn't really over until you're home.

A week later it was back to school for third grade. Thoughts of summer, although emblazoned in Rod's memory, were fading like bubbles breaking in a boat's wake...until the teacher gave the class their first assignment: an oral report on what they did last summer.

Which story would he tell? Uncle Gorham? Lobsters? The stinky bait barrel? Maybe the blueberry fields? And then it hit him and his eyes lit up with joy. He would teach the class how to talk like an Indian and understand Indian customs. This was going to be the best report of all, he was sure of it!

That night, with Bertie's help, he proceeded to put to pen the story of the Pizz-ah – qua-tah – wah-tah River and the Penobscot Indian maidens. He would honor the Indians and make the chief proud!

The next day his classmates excitedly told their stories. Rod thought they were all very interesting, but he was sure his story would take the prize. A definite gold star! Mrs. Reardon finally called his name and he marched to the front of the class, his story in one hand and a paper bag in the other. He was confident and ready to go. Bertie had coached him because, after all, she *was* in the fourth grade. He took his time and read clearly because he wanted everyone to understand what he had to say.

He started with the Piscataqua River, first what it's called today and then reciting its original name. He had figured out the little scam, but played dumb; he was developing his sense of humor. He had the class repeat it in unison until everyone got it right. "Piss-a-quart-of-water" never sounded so good! The teacher, Mrs. Reardon, just stood in the back of the classroom tapping her lips. With the first half of his story behind him, he launched into the tale the Indian maidens, which he considered to be the greatest story ever told. In the end he proudly produced the tonic bottle filled with the medicinal Bag-a-Douche River water!

The class applauded wildly, but Mrs. Reardon was in shock! She managed to praise young Rod for his story, however, and the details he included. After the other students completed their reports, she gave them a five-minute in-class recess and went across the hallway to the teachers' lounge. She asked the other teachers to come to her classroom, without giving them a clue as to what was in store.

Once everyone took their places, Mrs. Reardon explained how the children had just described their summer adventures. Then she asked Rod if he would please retell his story so that the teachers could enjoy it as well.

"You betcha!" replied Rod. He dashed to the front of the class and put the teachers through the same routine, audience participation and all. They were speechless. Mr. Bowen, the only male teacher, excused himself and could be heard laughing uncontrollably all the way down the hallway. All in all, Rod thought he did a good job, even if he couldn't understand what Mr. Bowen thought was so funny about the water. Sure enough, though, he got his gold star!

Ah, but that wasn't the end of it. A few weeks later, when the two Georges were attending parent's night at the elementary school, Mrs. Reardon pointed out Rod's paper. "It's the one with the gold star," she remarked with a sly smile.

Together they read Rod's story with tears in their eyes. "I told you! I told you that you would pay someday!" whispered Uncle George, elbowing his brother-in-law in the ribs.

"Paid with a gold star! Unbelievable! Ugh. Chief always say, 'Never let truth get in way of good story'!"

The Georges looked back at Mrs. Reardon, who smiled and shook her head. She knew some kids would never grow up, and that was a good thing. A very good thing.

Chapter Six

Bottom Time

After Rod's nostalgic cruise down Memory Lane, the exit for Pawtuckaway Lake State Park appeared ahead, next right. Some time had passed since Rod had been to P.J.'s summer place, but he remembered the way and was soon pulling into the dirt driveway and through the soft sand, towards the shed by the water. The time was 07:58, and after a quick recon of the area, he determined that he was the last to arrive. All the players from the day before were milling about the dock, attending to their gear and getting ready for P.J.'s final exam.

Warm lake water against the cool morning air caused a fog so thick that there was at most 100 feet of visibility, and not a whisper of wind. The weather had been bright and sunny all the way to the lake so Rod knew the fog was temporary. A few of the swamp maples along the water's edge had begun to turn on

their autumn color: a sign that the end of summer was near. He parked his bike and was beginning to unload his dive gear when P.J. walked up, smiling as usual.

"How was the ride up? Nice I'll bet. Cool and clear after that hot weather, a welcome change."

P.J. was pleasant – no hint of any issues – so Rod decided to cut to the chase before meeting with the rest of the folks. "OK P.J., give me the dirt. What's up?"

"All right. I figured by your demeanor that you weren't bluffing, so I called the Massachusetts Environmental Police. They sent out one of their officers from Gloucester, and he arrived about an hour after you left. I explained all the gory details, then he interviewed Roberto. With no past record, the officer decided to just issue a citation for having the two lobsters. But because you had dumped several others, he told Roberto that he was going to recommend the maximum fine, which could cost him up to a grand."

"I understand Roberto didn't handle that very well?"

"No, Rod, he didn't. He thought that since this was his first offense, he should get a verbal warning only. The officer told him that if he'd seen all of the stolen lobsters, he'd be in jail now. He said he should consider himself lucky!" said P.J., shaking his head. "The thought of a $1,000 fine tipped Roberto over and he started cursing the officer. I had to tell him to shut his mouth – NOW – or this guy might ratchet up the charges. Roberto finally calmed down and accepted the citation."

"What about the issue of my numbers, you know, my dive flag?"

"He said yes, they had in fact received a call about your numbers and poaching. He wasn't happy that you let Roberto use your flag, because, well, *you know the rules*. But now that the citation is issued, he has no problem with you and will touch base with the Harbor Master to make sure all is understood." P.J. paused for a moment, reviewing the events in his mind. "I think that does it...did I cover everything?"

"I guess so. How's the mood with our group this morning?" asked Rod, glancing down towards the dock.

"I've told them to put it behind them. They have their final exam shortly, so they need to be able to focus on the task at hand."

"Sounds like good advice; I hope they take it. Anything else?"

"Yes, we do have a small problem. Because *we* left the marina so late yesterday, we couldn't get back to the dive shop before it closed, so the tanks didn't get refilled. We left them at the shop; they'll fill them tomorrow when they open." P.J. shrugged his shoulders and added, "I do have three full spares in the shed, however, one for each of the students. The problem is I have no air for you – I hate to see you come all this way and not dive. But if you could be a safety swimmer, that would be greatly appreciated."

"Not to worry P.J., I can use the relaxation and take a back seat. Safety swimmer works for me just fine!"

"Thanks. This shouldn't take very long."

"My pleasure. What do you say, are we nearly ready to go?" Rod stood by, his gear in hand.

"Suit up and we'll begin. I'll see you at the dock."

P.J. gave Rod a thumbs-up and headed down the lawn to the divers, who were already in their wet suits minus the hoods and gloves. Sarah was floating about in front of the little beach next to the dock. Roberto and Bob were going over some written material.

Rod took his wet suit, mask, snorkel, and fins and went down to the shed, a simple shack outfitted with a changing area inside. In short work, Rod was dressed out and listening to P.J.'s diving plan. After a hello from Bob and Sarah, and the silent treatment from Roberto, Rod figured it was time to start the day's activities. He gave a signal and P.J. began.

"Today is the culmination of the last four weeks of training for your Rescue Diver Certification. Six dives supported the techniques we discussed in class. Now I have a number of exercises, some individual, some as a team, with which you can display your proficiency..."

"Hello Mr. P.J.!" shouted an excited little boy running full speed across the lawn, cutting him off mid-sentence.

P.J. recognized him right away: he was the five-year-old son of Pete and Laura Miller, who lived two cottages down. His big brown eyes were wide open, and the hood of his red, white, and blue Popeye jacket was tied on tight.

"Hey little buddy! How's my Scotty today?"

"We're going for a canoe ride! Have you ever been in a canoe?"

"Oh sure, they're great fun!"

"Good morning P.J., looks like more training today. Sorry to interrupt, but I need to borrow a lifejacket for my boy. Can you help me out?" asked Scotty's dad, whose deep voice rumbled through the dense fog.

"I wish I could, but the neighbors down the other way borrowed all the kids' jackets last weekend for a swim party and haven't returned them yet – sorry. Take a stroll over and get what you need."

"Oh well, we have cushions for the canoe; he can sit on one of those. He'll be OK."

"I don't think so, Sir. He needs a jacket," said Sarah from the dock.

"He's been swimming at the Y for two years and swims like a fish. He'll be OK. We're only going out a little ways. Besides, with a canoe you're only required to have cushions."

"You're not hearing me, Sir. Kids under twelve must wear a jacket! It's the law," Sarah insisted.

"I appreciate your concern, miss, but I think we'll be just fine." Pete looked at P.J. and said, "There's a law for everything these days. Isn't that right P.J.? You should know! Well, thanks anyway, sorry to disturb your class." With that, they were off, disappearing into the fog as they headed back from whence they came.

P.J. raised his eyebrows, nodded to Sarah that she was right, and picked up where he'd left off. "I'll keep a score of the exercises. Remember, 80 percent is the required passing grade. So here's the deal: I've placed a cinder block on the lake bottom, 100 yards 120 degrees from the end of the dock. Once you find the block, I want you to set up a search pattern to find..." P.J. stopped mid-sentence. He grimaced and twitched a little, then said, "Sorry, Mother Nature, gotta go. Stand by until I get back." P.J. headed up the hill towards his cottage, doing his version of a John Cleese silly walk and trying not to lose control along the way.

Everyone chuckled as P.J. made his way towards certain relief. An uncomfortable quiet settled over the foursome, and each of them fidgeted nervously. Rod walked into the water alongside the dock, inspected his fins, and looked over P.J.'s handiwork in the new dock that he'd installed that spring.

Scotty's voice could be heard in the distance, along with the paddles banging against the sides of the canoe as they floated away in the distant water. The visibility was so limited that it was hard to tell exactly where they were, but the fog carried their voices clearly.

"Daddy, I want my juice box," said Scotty, loud and clear.

"Not now Scotty, I can't reach it. Wait until we get to Robin's Island."

"I can get it, Daddy."

"No! Don't you stand up. Stay where you are...I said don't stand up!"

The sound of the oars hitting the gunnels, and the canoe turning upside down with a splash, ripped through the fog.

"Scotty, where are you? Scotty! Scotty!" Then, a blood-chilling yell for help. "Help! Help! My boy's fallen in. I can't find him! Help me!"

For a split second all eyes on land came together: it was decision time again.

"We're coming, keep calling! I'll get P.J. and tell his wife to call 911!" blurted Bob, who was off like a shot for the house.

Rod put on his fins and prepared for a surface swim. He checked his watch: 08:46. Roberto was in a state of shock, not knowing what to do. Bob, having alerted P.J. and his wife, ran along the shoreline to see if he could pinpoint Pete and Scotty's location.

"Roberto, get your gear on!" yelled Rod. "I'm going to swim out and try to find them. I'll call to you and Sarah. Get moving!"

Rod got in the water and rolled onto his back. His legs were strong, and with his long fins, he could propel himself quickly over the surface. He stopped once, turned over to get his bearings, and yelled that help was on the way.

Big Bob could hear Pete Miller calling frantically for his boy. No way could he see them, but judging from the direction the voices were coming from, he calculated an angle where they might intersect with a line from the dock. Armed with that information, he ran back to the dock to see Sarah hastily putting on her gear. They looked out and saw Roberto swimming into the fog.

"Bob, I'm heading out," Sarah said. She waved her hand at the old shack and added, "Get the backboard out of the building for me, quick!"

Bob ran to the shack and got the emergency backboard. Sarah placed it in front of her and kicked in the direction of what she figured was their approximate location. Looking back, she yelled for Bob to stay where he was and work with the EMTs when they arrived, and to get P.J. up to speed. Meanwhile, P.J. reappeared and ran down the lawn towards Bob, while his wife stood in the doorway of the cottage shouting into her cell phone.

Rod stopped swimming and listened to the calls for help. He figured he was no more than 100 feet away and sure enough, with the fog just a foot or two off the surface, he could see the canoe. He yelled and Pete waved back. Rod swam as hard as he could towards the canoe, just in time to see the outstretched hand of the man he was trying to save go under the surface. Rod tried to dive under to grab him, but his wetsuit would have nothing to do with it: his buoyancy was too positive.

Rod looked around and saw an upside-down canoe, an Igloo Playmate cooler, and two square yellow cushions floating on the surface of the water. He checked his watch – it was 08:48 – then yelled towards what he believed was the dock. He told everyone to hurry and try to follow his voice because both the boy and his father were now underwater.

Roberto was first on the scene and Rod instructed him to dive straight down and start looking, but to keep his fins above him so as not to disturb the silty bottom. Roberto acknowledged. Rod checked his watch again, 08:49, then turned to Sarah and signaled for her to stop in the water.

'Take a compass heading to me!" Rod yelled. He could see Sarah look through her console and gave her a thumbs-up. "Dive to the bottom and swim towards me. Roberto's already down there."

Sarah pushed the backboard in Rod's direction; it skirted across the water right to him. Then her fins went up and she disappeared under the surface.

With no wind or current to deal with, combined with the quick response of the divers, Rod was confident they would find the boy and his father in time to save their lives. All he could do now was wait.

With pressure building, Roberto cleared his ears as he went headfirst, straight down. Fog was overhead, so visibility was diminished, but there was good clarity to the water. He put a shot of air into his BC when he reached the bottom, which made him lift slightly; this was good, he thought, because it would keep his feet from stirring up the silt. He began to look for signs of the little boy or his father. Nothing. He decided to swim a box search pattern: fifteen kicks straight ahead, a 90-degree turn to the right using his compass, and repeat until he was back to his original position.

Sarah had reached the grassy bottom by this time and could see nothing out of the ordinary. She continued to swim until she saw Roberto, who was completing the third leg of his search pattern. They swam towards each other with their hands and arms stretched wide open, signaling nothing, hoping the other had had some luck.

As they knelt on the bottom, Roberto noticed what appeared in the distance to be bubbles mixed with debris adrift in the water column. They swam about ten feet apart and headed towards the disturbance. Sarah was the first to see a large figure lying in the silt. She came upon what turned out to be Scotty's father, then looked around to see if Scotty was nearby. She pointed Roberto towards a patch of colors about ten feet away.

Roberto swam off and found a little body face down, wearing a red, white, and blue Popeye jacket. Roberto's heart pounded as he picked up the child, afraid to look at its face, and shot for the surface. His thighs burned as he broke the surface with all his might. He emerged five feet from the canoe and the waiting Rod.

"Quick, give me the boy. Now go back and help Sarah!"

"Sarah's found his father," panted Roberto. "I'll go back and help bring him up. Give the boy CPR: he's not breathing!"

Rod put the little guy, who was covered in weeds, facedown on the backboard and looked at his watch: 08:52, six minutes bottom time! What happened next was only matched by what was going on under the water.

Rod took off Scotty's hood and brushed away the weeds from his face...lying there in front of him was a rubber mannequin of a little boy! It had been stuffed with fifteen pounds of lead sinkers. At first Rod was furious, but his anger turned to relief as he now felt P.J.'s presence and realized this meant that father and son were OK.

Sarah and Roberto had found Scotty's dad. He was dressed as they had seen him on the beach, except that he now had two thirteen-cubic-foot spare airs hidden under his jacket, a weight belt, and a small pair of goggles. He was planning to stay on the bottom until the air ran out or he was "rescued." With air bubbles popping on the surface all about the canoe, the two divers and the drowning "victim" surfaced.

"Adult male on the surface, 08:54. Get them on the backboard! CPR for both of them!" yelled Rod.

When Roberto and Sarah saw the Scotty mannequin, they understood that the whole scenario was a scam, the defining moment of P.J.'s training...their final exam.

"Can't do CPR on the board. Assisted breathing only!" barked Sarah.

"Good job Sarah – breathing it is!" replied Roberto.

The "victims" were now on the backboard, with each diver performing simulated breathing for the one they'd "rescued."

Next, Rod propelled the backboard towards the dock and the shore help.

Roberto couldn't help but admire Sarah's calm composure and femininity as she performed her duties. His thoughts drifted to the last time he tried to make a move on something that wasn't his...so he went back to the task at hand.

"Compass heading?" inquired Rod.

"185 degrees reciprocal to the dock. Steer to the right," responded Roberto.

Rod kicked as hard as he could in order to get back quickly and to burn up the adrenalin from the "rescue." P.J. could have clued him in, but on second thought, how would that have helped? Rod could use the refresher, too. P.J. would use any trick, especially if he thought someone had his or her guard down. He finally had to crack a smile as the barge carrying the so-called victims reached Bob and P.J. on the dock. Rod checked his watch one last time: 08:56.

"Bob, continue CPR on the boy!" shouted Sarah.

Bob got ready, got a quick look at the victims, then howled, "What the hell is going on?"

He looked up at the crew, who were stone-faced and recovering from the fastest, most exciting ten minutes of their lives.

P.J. reached behind his back and got out a small note pad that he'd tucked into his belt. He waited a couple of moments while everyone decompressed. "OK, let's talk about it while it's still fresh in your mind. I have a few questions." He scanned their faces. "How do you think you all did with the test? How long from start to finish? What were you thinking about? And lastly, would you have saved them?"

The lively conversation was in full swing when a familiar voice was heard in the distance. "Mr. P.J., Mr. P.J., did I do a good job?" asked Scotty as he ran towards the group with his mother in tow.

"Yes, you did, we're very proud of you!"

"How did you pull this one off, P.J.?" demanded Sarah, having fallen for P.J.'s second life-and-death scenario.

"Under the cover of fog, Mrs. Miller and Scotty went quietly out in a rowboat beside Mr. Miller, who was in the canoe.

Once Scotty voiced his part of the drama, they slipped away, leaving Pete, one of my fellow instructors, and you guys to do the rest."

P.J. smiled and thanked Scotty for his help, then thanked his mother. Tears were streaming down Roberto's face as he looked at little Scotty standing on the shore. He broke down and whispered, "I thought he was dead. I thought we were too late when I found him. I just knew he was gone."

Everyone felt bad for Roberto because, after all, he'd been through a rough 24 hours.

"All right then, let's get ready to start the test!" yelled P.J., clapping his hands together.

The words were barely out of his mouth when everyone starting throwing their gloves and hoods at him. "Test nothing. Let's spark up the grill and have a bite to eat. It's time to relax!" ordered P.J.'s wife, who had prepared a barbeque with P.J. for the occasion.

P.J. gave everyone a double thumbs-up, meaning the test was in fact over, and that they had performed up to his expectations. He danced up the hill with his thumbs still up, confident in the skills of his new rescue divers.

After a couple hours of ribs, potato salad, sodas, and dive talk, they loaded their gear for the ride home.

"So how'd we really do?" Rod pushed P.J.

"I was very pleased with all of you. A great job!"

"Well, you got me again. I don't know how you keep coming up with these panic drills."

"A little of nature's smoke and mirrors always helps! It's what I like to do. Hey, maybe someday I'll save your life or you'll save mine. If you want to be a good diver, you've just got to train, practice, keep diving, and be ready for anything."

"All right, good enough. But I'm going to put diving on the back burner for a while. With vacation time and some comp time from work, it'll be fishing for the next month. I have several charters lined up and whenever that's not happening, the boat will be chasing giant bluefin."

"Any luck with the tuna fishing?"

"Nah, just a lot of 'tuna wishing' so far, but some guys have picked up a couple giants off Maine, big ones – 700 pounds plus – and they're moving south. Hopefully, we'll be waiting in their migratory path and finally hook up with some of those bad boys!"

"Well, sounds great and good luck! Call me if you need anything. Really, call me if you need a mate on the boat. I can't fish very well, but I can surely cut bait!"

"That goes for me too! I can fish, but don't have any experience with tuna. I'd love to learn!" said Bob, who'd been eavesdropping.

"I'll keep you guys in mind."

Rod fired up the bike, thanked P.J. for the chow, and waved to Sarah and Roberto.

Roberto signaled for Rod to stop. "I just wanted to apologize for yesterday. I hope I didn't jeopardize your reputation in any way." Roberto did his best to look into Rod's eyes.

"Well, Roberto, I hope you've learned a lesson. You knew what you were doing was wrong when you did it. Doing the right thing when others aren't looking, that's integrity. Actions have consequences. I'll survive this episode, and maybe you'll be a better man for it. Let this have a positive effect on the rest of your life. Good luck." Rod held out his hand, and Roberto accepted it.

Rod would now make a trip home, then head back to Uncle George, Kasey, and the *Jus' Restin'*.

Chapter Seven

Shame on the Moon

od took the bike on the backcountry road towards his home in the small town of Greenland, New Hampshire, twenty miles to the east. Arriving just after noon, he came in quietly; it was naptime for his wife Lilly, who worked the evening shift on Memorial Hospital's medical-surgical floor. Neither of his daughters were home. Both were college students enjoying their summers off.

Amy, the youngest, was working on a ranch in Jackson Hole, Wyoming. This was her first experience in the mountains and wide open spaces of the West. Her older sister, Cari, traditionally a traveler during the summer months, had elected to stay closer to home to work at a restaurant owned by a friend of Rod's in the downtown area of Newburyport. The girls had grown up fast, too fast, and he missed having them with him on the boat. They would be returning to their New England colleges in the fall.

No matter how quiet Rod could be, Lilly was a light sleeper and was soon awake and getting the complete report on the activities of the past couple of days. She had lost interest in the business side of the boat scene, but still enjoyed the friendships at the marina and would occasionally accompany him on a charter trip. She preferred to show up at the end of the day for the dockside activities on her weekends off.

They met during her college days and married in their early twenties. She was half Irish and half French, slight of build, with long dark hair. She enjoyed a good time along with the joys and responsibilities of raising two girls. It was a challenge for them to find time for each other with all the activities of their family and professional lives.

"So, what's your schedule looking like down the road?" asked Lilly as she busily moved about the kitchen.

"Looks like the next few weeks are charters and tuna, with some fun and games mixed in. It's going to be really busy, but hey, that's what the boat is all about right now."

"Have you found some guys to fish the tuna with you?" Lilly was concerned about Rod going out alone.

"Yeah. I think I have at least three or four who I can count on. Lots of people would like to go, but it can be dangerous and I need reliable people. P.J. Durkin would like to go, plus a new guy, Bob, and there's always Mumbles and Koo Koo, two of the best striper guys I know."

"Have those two ever been offshore? I thought they were just inshore striper fishermen." Lilly started to laugh a little because people didn't just *have* nicknames, they earned them. She knew these two characters could make quite a tag team.

"We'll see. Tuna have been reported coming down the coast, and I intend to be waiting for them. Plus, I've got several cod and haddock trips on the books, so we'll play it smart and keep the tuna gear on board...just in case we find the whales and birds working offshore."

"Well, it sounds like you have it all figured out. I sure hope you get into these tuna. College bills are really starting to mount, and catching some tuna could sure take some of that pressure off." Lilly poured herself a cup of coffee. "I'm working a lot up until my vacation starts just before Labor Day. Be careful and call when you can. Amy will be coming home for the holiday weekend, so we should plan a day out on Sandy Point with the girls before they go off to school again. Speaking of girls, how's my Kasey girl doing?"

"She's fine, spending the day with Uncle George."

Rod checked the "honey-do" list on the refrigerator: nothing pressing there. He glanced back and saw Lilly sitting down to the computer, which was becoming her favorite pastime. She loved to gamble, just like her grandmother Mini, who used to take her as a kid to Rockingham Park to bet the trotters. Online poker with play money was addictive. Rod and Lilly used to go to the Connecticut casinos, but Rod got tired of what he called "feeding the Indians," so Lilly relegated herself to make-believe gambling. And she was getting good.

"How much are you up now?" joked Rod, checking to see the latest tally.

"My account says over $225,000. Thank you very much!" she replied proudly. "Who knows, someday, I may become a professional gambler like those guys on TV."

Someday. Rod smiled. The patented answer they always gave the kids was *anything is possible; aim for the stars.* "Well, I'm going to grab some fishing gear from the shed and be off again. Come down to the marina and we'll have some fun on the docks. A lot of people are hanging out – you know how that works. Give me a call when you can."

A hug and a kiss goodbye and Rod was off to the shed and his supply of fishing gear, while Lilly went to lie down. She closed her eyes for a few more winks before heading off to work.

Rod grabbed several seventeen-ounce diamond jigs for the cod trips and three Green Machine rigs for tuna. With the diving gear already on the bike, there was little room for anything else. He figured if he really needed something special, he could always go to Surfland Bait and Tackle and get the latest scoop on fishing from Kay and her girls who ran it. The shop had it all, was close by the marina, and was always worth the trip.

Knowing that the Sunday traffic would be stacking up at the Hampton tollbooth, Rod elected to take the scenic route through Portsmouth and along the ocean via Route 1A. New Hampshire had a short coastline, but it was a scenic mix of rocky shore and hard sandy beaches. There was a cool sea breeze coming onshore and the traffic was tolerable. It took about an hour to get to Salisbury Beach, then over the Merrimac River into Newburyport, and finally back onto Route 1A, the coastal road to Essex.

Uncle George and Kasey were kicking back under a big Crimson King maple in the side yard as Rod pulled into the driveway and made his way to the shed. Kasey ran to his side, whining and howling and shaking with joy at Rod's return.

"Hey there, how's my girl?" Rod patted Kasey and gave Uncle George a big hello.

"How did the diving go? Did you pass your test?"

"Oh sure, P.J. was up to his old tricks," Rod laughed as he backed the bike into the shed. "He does a great job with realism, but he can scare you half to death doing so!"

Rod filled his uncle in on the details as he unloaded the motorcycle. "I'm going to leave all my dive gear in the shed. The tuna gear takes up a lot of room on board, and if I need to dive, I'll just come and get it."

"No problem, you can leave Kasey too!"

"No way! My seadog is coming with me, but I'll bring her back in a few days for a couple of day trips. You two make a good pair, don't you Kasey!" Rod clapped his hands and Kasey was right at his feet, a worn Frisbee in her mouth.

"Better give her a few throws or she'll never leave you alone!" laughed Uncle George.

Rod grabbed the disc and let it fly. Kasey was addicted to the thrill of chasing Frisbees. As a pup, she had no interest in sticks or balls, but took right to the Frisbee. It was nothing for her to chase the disc 25 consecutive times as far as Rod could throw. The signal that she was tired and had had enough was when her ears lay down on her head when she returned.

Rod and Kasey headed back to Harborside to prepare for the fishing trip the next day and to kick back. They would enjoy the marina activities for the duration of this lazy Sunday afternoon and bask in some glorious weather.

The marina was back in full swing, with the gas grills smoking and the stereos playing everything from Jimmy Buffett to Frank Sinatra. Frank was a tradition on Sunday evenings with one of the local radio stations. *Checkers* had been busy: she was just being tied up to the service dock with an eighteen-foot bow rider in tow. Kasey led the way as they approached "Bourbon Street," the liveliest section of the marina. Archie, the usual master of ceremonies, was standing on the swim platform of his boat leading the frivolity.

"A beer for the captain," he said as he saw Kasey rounding the corner first. A Corona was soon in Rod's hand.

"Thanks, Archie. Looks like you have everything under control here." A lot of people were enjoying the day on the docks.

"You bet. The food is cooking, the beer is cold, and the 'Golden Cleaters' are on standby." Archie pointed his finger to the two old salts sitting in their deck chairs, light beers in their arm holders, keeping a watchful eye for mariners returning to their slips.

The "Golden Cleaters" were the consecutive winners of Harborside's prestigious "Golden Cleat Award," given by the marina staff to boaters who rarely, if ever, untie their boats and leave the dock. Their self-appointed mission was to assist people into their slips after a day on the water. With over 100 boats at Harborside, a running tide that can hit four knots under the docks, and any combination of libations consumed onboard, this is the setting for calamity (and entertainment!) that can happen on a moment's notice. The fact that the Cleaters had slowed down a little over the years in their response time added a special unknown to the equation.

Rod enjoyed the party on Bourbon Street for about an hour, trading fishing news and gossip with his friends, then headed down the docks to *Jus' Restin.'* He opened the boat, set out Kasey's pillow, then iced down some stray beers that were in the dock box. He put the two dive tanks that were on board in a rack on the dock.

There was a little window of time for a quick snooze, but that didn't last long. The Golden Cleaters were soon climbing aboard, trying to fend off an arriving boat that was normally slipped next to him. The customary fee for this dockside assistance is one beer, or something of equal value. The Cleaters were paid off and were soon back in their chairs, keeping an ever-vigilant eye over the marina activities.

Rod left Kasey on board, with her leash attached since other dogs frequented the docks, and headed for his stash of bait for the next day's charter. He maintained a small freezer that he'd bought from Chet in one of the yard buildings; Chet used to run charters before he transitioned to towing. They were planning to fish for stripers, so he grabbed three blocks of frozen herring, a favorite of Plum Island's stripers, plus a small bag of shrimp for Kasey and him to enjoy later.

Back on board, he turned on the stereo, popped a Moosehead from the cooler, and began to read the latest issue of The Fisherman Magazine. This little magazine would give him an overview of what had been happening the past week up and down the coast. For the most part, it was pretty accurate. But Rod knew conditions changed daily, and he was curious how yesterday's storm might affect the bite the next day.

He nearly dropped off to sleep in his deck chair, his hat pulled down over his eyes and the sun shining brightly in his face. Kasey was the first to detect a change; she lifted her head and sniffed into the wind. She got to her feet and strained on her leash, her nails scratching the hard deck, as someone approached the boat and stood alongside the gunnel.

"Bonjour, is this vessel for hire, Captain?" said a soft voice. The accent and the smell of perfume gave away the voice's identity.

"Suzanne, good afternoon! What a pleasant surprise – come aboard!" He leapt out of the chair and held her hand as she stepped into the cockpit.

"Your website, which I got from the business card I took from your dash, said you do evening sunset cruises. I thought, what a great idea! So here I am...what time do we leave?"

"Well, you're in luck. Kasey and I are at your service." He bowed. "Here, let me take your bag. Do you have a jacket? It can cool down quickly when the sun sets."

"Yes, it's in my bag, along with some bottles of wine for the ride if that's OK..."

"Actually, it's encouraged if not outright mandatory on this type of cruise! We like to refer to it as 'navigation fluid.' You make yourself comfortable, and I'll prepare to cast off."

"Before we leave, a check for your fee. I'll put it with the business cards."

"Thanks, you've obviously thought of everything!"

Rod went into the pilothouse, fired the engine, and checked his watch: just after 17:00. He looked out the window at the Golden Cleaters, who were now joined by Archie and Chet.

Evidently, Suzanne had made quite a stir with her entrance on the docks, having to walk the gauntlet by Bourbon Street to get to the boat. Curiosity now held the gawkers in its grasp a conspicuous distance away. *Who is this goddess and what does she want?*

Rod smiled and gave them a salute. "Gotta go to work!" he yelled while casting off the lines. "I think a cruise inland up the Parker River will work nicely, Suzanne," he said as he eased out of the slip and turned to port.

The channel was clear as Rod rode the incoming tide up the river into the late afternoon sun. Then, the familiar popping of a cork. He looked back to see Suzanne getting a couple of wine glasses from her bag. Rod surveyed the beauty who had reentered his life by surprise this fine afternoon. She had shoulder-length brown hair with streaks of auburn, and looked to be about 5'6". No more than 40 years old. Her clothes were obviously upscale and fit just right. She was like the ocean's surface: smooth and mysterious up top, with serious structure under the surface.

"After we pass under the train bridge, we'll shut down the engine. This river goes for a couple of miles inland and we'll just drift the tide and enjoy the scenery. Sound agreeable to you?"

"You are the captain – sounds wonderful to me." She heartily agreed as she stood in the afternoon sun, holding two large glasses of red wine.

"Lord, give me strength," Rod muttered to himself as he negotiated through the narrow, low-ceiling train bridge to a wide open section of the river. They drifted quietly through the marshlands of the Parker River. Rod put on a special mix of tunes that would play many of his favorites for hours without interruption.

"As they say, you ain't from around here, are you girl?" Rod quipped.

"You are right. I was raised outside the city of Arcachon, in southern France. My family has always worked in the winery business. Here, try one of our creations." She handed him a glass.

He gave it his best swirl and sniff, inhaling its wonderful aroma. They raised their glasses, and Suzanne toasted their new friendship and the scenic vista surrounding them. Rod examined the bottle: a Chateau Cos D'Estournel. He didn't know a lot about wines, but he knew this didn't come in a box!

"So, tell me, are you visiting, or do you live here in the States now?" asked Rod, trying to get a clearer picture of the mystery woman in his presence.

"Actually, I'm working here, off the coast. Ahmed and I both work aboard the research vessel *Atlantic Zephyr*, which has been surveying the waters off Cape Ann for the past couple of months."

"OK. I've seen your vessel several times. What kind of research, if you don't mind my asking?"

"We are looking for a boat that we believe may have sunk here over 50 years ago. Unlike trying to find the Titanic, whose sinking was well documented, we have only sketchy information. We are not really sure if the vessel even made it here."

"Sounds difficult. What kind of information do you have to work with?"

"At this point, it's all conjecture. But we do believe our information to be relatively sound, based upon discoveries that have surfaced over the last year. Essentially, a copy of a ship's manifest from the end of World War II was discovered in some archived materials in France. It lists many items of antique value, such as Old Ivory dishes and items of that nature, but we believe there was also gold and jewels – contraband that was stolen by occupying German forces, and then spirited away during the closing days of the War." Suzanne sipped her wine. "If we find it, we figure there's a substantial fortune to be had. But there is no verifiable evidence that the ship ever arrived at her destination. One of the crewmembers of the boat actually lived in Rockport under an alias until he died last year. We think the ship either sunk offshore or was scuttled when it arrived here." She leaned forward and whispered, "Sounds very cloak and dagger, doesn't it?" She was obviously excited about her expedition and her role in it.

"Another glass of wine and I'm a believer!" said Rod.

"There is actually more to the story, but maybe we'll save that for another time." Suzanne poured another glass of wine.

"Well, I can only imagine what you're trying to accomplish; finding a downed boat in these waters must be tough. What was the name of the boat?"

"The *Ebony*, a 48-foot black-hulled, two-masted sailing vessel, originally berthed in Bordeaux."

"Interesting. Sounds like a great job. With today's technology, you've got a good shot at it. Good luck!" Rod raised his glass to Suzanne's.

They continued their drift up the river, enjoying the setting sun, as Suzanne opened a second bottle of wine. She cleaned the glasses and poured a white wine this time. Rod noticed it was a Chateau Carbonnieux, another fine-looking label. He remembered the shrimp he'd brought: something to add to the menu, along with the salsa and chips he had on board. It was a nice treat and even Kasey managed a shrimp or two.

The tide was high as they approached the bridge at US 1, a roadway they wouldn't be able to get under at high water. The sun was beginning to set, while an August full moon was due to rise in the east.

"Let's motor back a ways, then drift the outgoing tide for a moonrise cruise to the marina."

"Very well, Captain," she said smiling, her French accent sounding better with every syllable and sip of wine.

They cruised through the twisty backwaters until they were on the widest part of the river. About a mile from the marina, but still in slow-moving and tranquil waters. The white wine from the second bottle was going down smoothly as they drifted along the grassy backwater shoreline. The stripers that had come in on the rising tide were now starting to feed in the golden light. They could be heard popping on the surface: the schoolies up top and the bigger fish cruising underneath.

"Would you like to try your hand at catching a striper? I believe you signed on for the deluxe cruise." Rod laughed as he motioned to the fishing rods that had been placed in the overhead holders in preparation for the following morning.

"Sounds like fun. What will we use for bait?"

"We still have a few shrimp left: let's give them a try first. If we can get under the little ones, we might pick up a keepah for you to take back to the ship with you."

Rod baited the hook and made the first cast, in order to show Suzanne the technique and where to try to place the bait. He retrieved the line and passed her the rod. She pointed to a swirl near the surface about 75 feet away, then set the shrimp just upstream of it by about ten feet. She looked back and smiled as Rod's jaw dropped.

"First time fishing, huh?" He laughed and shook his head; she obviously knew her way around a fishing rod. She hooked a small schoolie, and the gentlemen that he was, Rod released it for her.

"Do you have any surface lures?"

"I hope so because Kasey just ate the last of the shrimp! It's time to 'walk the dog'!"

Rod went into the tackle box and got out a floating Spook fishing lure. This would surely do the trick. He changed up the tackle and handed the rod back to Suzanne.

"Just cast where you want it to land, let it sit a bit, then twitch the end of the rod a couple of times. That will make the lure dart left and right. Let it sit there, reel up the slack slowly, and do it again. Slow action is the key. It's a technique called 'walking the dog.' It works well – you'll see."

She nodded in agreement and let go with a spectacular cast, right to the edge of the channel and next to an overhang of mud and grass. Her technique was flawless on the retrieve. Wham! A big striper was on and peeling line, heading back up the river. She adjusted the drag, held the rod high, and played the fish like she knew exactly what she was doing. After a ten-minute fight, she maneuvered it next to the boat. Rod reached over the gunnel and lipped the fish by hand to bring it on board.

"Beauty!" Rod exclaimed as he placed the fish against the tape measure on the gunnel. "It's 38 inches; gotta weigh 20 to 22 plus pounds." They examined the fish, fresh from the ocean, with little sea lice on its tail. "OK, it's decision time – do I put it in the box or shall we release her?"

Suzanne looked at the fish and thought for a long moment. "No, I think we'll let this fish enjoy the rest of its life. What do you think, Kasey?" Rod held the fish under Kasey's nose.

"You're the boss, sounds like an excellent idea to me. Would you like to do the honors?"

Suzanne reached over and took the twisting striper from Rod's hands and lowered it gently over the side. With a splash of its broad tail, the fish was gone.

It was nearly dark now as Rod scanned the area around the boat to get his bearings. The lights from the marina could be seen in the distance, no more than half a mile away. He switched on the navigation lights and the two cockpit lights under the gunnels. The moon had just risen over Plum Island and was now emerging as a huge orange ball on the eastern horizon.

"Isn't that incredible," remarked Suzanne, pointing to the moon as she poured the last of the wine into their glasses. "Are we almost back already? It seems like we just left."

"I'm afraid so, but there's no hurry. What do you say we put the boat in its slip? With this fine wine, I'd be susceptible to any number of maneuvering blunders if we continued down-river."

Actually, Rod knew that backing into the slip on the out-going tide was the easiest way into the slip, and it was completed without incident. He tied the dock lines and *Jus' Restin'* was shut down until morning. Then he heard a familiar sound.

Pop! Suzanne was opening another bottle of wine. Rod found himself praying ever so softly. Out on deck, he rearranged the chairs to maintain a friendly distance and decided to take the conversation back offshore. The latest bottle of wine was delicious, and there was no sense hurrying. This was the best charter he'd had in a very, very long time!

"I know something on the topic of locating a ship underwater, although not a lot." Rod settled back into his chair. "In 1939 a submarine, the USS *Squalus*, went down just northeast of here on Jeffrey's Ledge, in 250 feet of water. A true hero of the times, Charles 'Swede' Momsen rescued many of the the sailors on board. This had never been done before. He saved them with a little help from my grandfather."

Rod lifted his glass again and continued. "As a civilian, Gramps was in charge of all the materials and supplies at the Portsmouth Naval Yard, and supported Swede's efforts from shore. Whatever he needed, Gramps made sure he got. My mother was proud of her father and she recounted the story many times to me. My own father worked on submarines at the base, and I used to have a great collection of ID tags for the submarines that were built and maintained at the Navy yard. Since I was a little kid I've always been fascinated with submarines, especially the nukes. My father was devastated when we lost the *Thresher* over the continental shelf. He never got over that."

"That's interesting. We have discovered many ships on the ocean floor, even a few submarines. But they were all relics from previous wars. Sunken ships are very special: they all have a tale to tell."

"Suzanne, I'm curious, what's your function on the ship?" Rod queried as he sipped his wine.

"I am responsible for all sonar tracking and data interpretation. My ship employs a SMX80 side scan sonar display. It's the latest technology."

"I'm impressed! There must be a lot of responsibility with that job."

"Oh, it has its days, just like your job. I'll bet you get a few surprises every once in a while." She smiled as she took another sip of wine.

The wine was taking effect, and Rod was doing his best to interpret the signals he was receiving. He noticed that Suzanne was starting to slur her words, but it only enhanced her accent. This could get complicated.

"How did you come up with the name for your boat?" Suzanne asked. "It is a fine boat by the way – it saved my life!" She hoisted her wine glass again, and they toasted *Jus' Restin'*.

"For several years a farmer lived behind our home. He was the nicest old man, never married and had no children. When I met him my father had just passed away, so I guess you could say I was the son he never had and he took over my father's role. We became the best of friends. For years, Kasey and I would go to his house when I came home from work; after playing Frisbee, we would peer through his porch screen and knock on the door. I'd always yell, 'Arthur, what are you doin'?' and his reply was always, 'Jus' restin' ' in that old Vermonter's accent. Anyway, when he passed away he left us the farm. Some of the proceeds from the estate bought the boat and the rest is, as they say, history."

"What a nice man! I'll bet you have a lot of fond memories of him." Suzanne began to fidget, then whispered, "Excuse me, but is it alright if I use the head?" She started to stand and nearly fell over. Rod caught her against the gunnel.

"Suzanne, are you OK?" he asked, holding her steady.

"Oh, I'm fine. I haven't felt this good in a long time. This has been wonderful – thank you so much!" She was obviously succumbing to the effects of the wine.

"Let me turn on the lights in the cuddy, and you can have some privacy while I take Kasey for a quick stroll. We'll be right back."

She agreed and Rod took Kasey on her leash and headed down the docks, which were now lit by soft yellow lights. Bourbon Street was quiet: the Sunday revelers had headed home, another weekend behind them. As he started up the ramp to the top of the service area, he glanced back at *Checkers* and saw the orange glow of Chet's cigarette. Chet stepped out of his pilothouse and gave him the Robert De Niro: two fingers pointing to the eyes and then at Rod. Chet held up his night vision binoculars and laughed.

"Yeah, I'm watching you, too!" Rod said, keeping Kasey on course for her mission in the woods. In just a few minutes, Rod and Kasey were back onboard with Suzanne. "Mission accomplished. Kasey, on your spot!" Kasey went into the cuddy and jumped onto her pillow.

As Rod sat down he heard several loud voices from a boat returning to its slip. These guys, clearly intoxicated, were attempting a landing three slips away. They were docked on the outside of the slips where there was no danger to other boats, so Rod decided to let them fend for themselves.

"Suzanne, come on inside the pilothouse, please."

She went inside as Rod flipped the switches that controlled the stereo and the cockpit and cuddy lights. The boat was now in darkness, except for the yellow lights of the docks. They stood in the shadows, sipping their wine, watching the antics down the dock.

"This could get interesting: these fella's are tanked."

Kasey started to stir and Rod gave her the signal to stay. She obeyed.

After a rough landing, the four men got out of the boat doing what drunken sailors do: joking, burping, and cussing as they unloaded their gear before making the trek along the docks to the parking lot. They would have to pass right by Rod and Suzanne. The loudest of the bunch was wobbling his way towards the *Jus' Restin'*. He stopped at the dock box and stood there, in a stupor, looking at the fishing rods in their holders. Then he spotted the dive tanks. He put down the gear he was carrying and picked one of the dive tanks out of the rack and began to examine it.

"Kasey!" Rod whispered, and Kasey was at his side in the doorway of the dark pilothouse. Holding her collar with his right hand, he reached back with his left and counted up four switches from the bottom of the console. He held his finger on the switch.

"Hey, guys, look at this – a scuba tank! I always wanted one of these! I might not have caught any fish but this is a keepah. Who the hell would leave this stuff on the dock?" bellowed the drunk, holding the tank high above his head like he had just won the Stanley Cup.

"That would be the captain, and I suggest you buy your own!" barked a voice out of the darkness. Rod flipped the switch and the halogen floodlights lit up the entire area as if it were a Fenway Park night game. Next, he released Kasey...she went directly to the port quarter and, having picked up on Rod's ear tug signal, proceeded to scare the life out of the would-be thief.

"Put that back, you jerk! What's wrong with you?" said the captain of the recent arrivals, a new boater at the marina whom Rod was about to meet.

Rod motioned to Suzanne to stay where she was, and went out on the dock with his fish bat in hand.

"I wasn't going to take it, I was only kidding! Really, I mean it, really!"

"You're right, you aren't going to take it – I'm not kidding, and I mean it, really!"

Rod stood blocking the exit as the new captain got between him and the drunk. Rod signaled Kasey to be quiet, and again she obeyed. The new captain grabbed the tank and put it back in the rack, then apologized for his crewmember. Rod was wondering what was going to happen next when he heard a voice from behind.

"There a problem here?" said Chet, now standing beside Rod.

"No, no, my buddy here made a mistake and we were just leaving."

At the sight of Chet, Kasey happily bounded out of the boat. But seeing Kasey close up only hastened the escape of the new arrivals. All the way to the parking lot their voices could be heard...yelling at and teasing the poor fool, mixed with hearty laughter. This was a tale they would enjoy telling for years to come.

Rod thanked Chet for his support, and Chet gave him the De Niro again. After an inquisitive glance over to the boat, he said goodnight and sauntered back to the *Checkers*.

Rod knew that anytime you mixed alcohol and water, things could happen. He looked at his watch: 21:15. With the excitement on the docks now behind them, Suzanne exited the pilothouse into the bright moonlight. "Shall I turn on the lights and music while we finish the wine?" she asked in that French accent that was getting more and more pronounced.

"Are you going to be able to drive? You sound wonderful to me, but I don't think you could pass a sobriety test. I'd give you a ride back, but I wouldn't want to chance it either."

"It's still early, and I don't have to be back to the ship until 07:30. I can always sleep in my auto. Not to worry. Here, let me fill your glass." She reached for the bottle but it was empty. "Like I said, not to worry!" She reached into her bag and pulled out a little bottle of sweet dessert wine. "This will make a wonderful finale to our evening. You'll see."

"Whoa, you have a small wine cellar in that bag! What do you have there – may I see it?" Rod held the bottle next to the deck light and read in his best French accent, "Chateau Suduiraut...I'm already impressed!"

They sat and relaxed as they discussed their activities for the forthcoming week. Rod shared how he would be running fishing charters but was really looking forward to starting the tuna season. Suzanne explained that her ship would be mapping an area a few miles east of the Dry Salvages.

"Earlier you said there was more to your vessel's research. Could you explain any of that? I'm always interested in what goes on out there."

Suzanne was silent for a long moment, deciding if she wanted to answer Rod's question. Then she recounted a story that she claimed she overheard among the crew.

"Just like the rest of my mission – based upon rumors," she said, laughing at her own words. "It seems that an Austrian-born physicist, Frieda Werfel, a student and collaborator of Lise Meitner, was instrumental in the mathematical research that led to the development of nuclear fission. She was marked by the Nazis as a Jew and would certainly have been sent to a concentration camp. She escaped in 1939, along with her secrets, to Sweden. This is just a rumor, but it is believed that her work continued in secrecy. She died in 1946. If her writings are found, they could shed new light on atomic theories that could have dire consequences. Quite possibly, her work may be part of the contraband on board the *Ebony*."

She looked up at the stars and pointed out the Big Dipper. "But the longer I work on this project, the less I believe any of it to be true. Sometimes I doubt if there really is such a ship on the bottom. But if the *Ebony* is out there, I'll find her one way or another." She raised her glass again, "To the *Ebony*, wherever she may be."

Rod took a sip of the sweet wine and pondered Suzanne's remarks. "If that's the case, maybe she *should* stay on the bottom forever."

A silence fell over the boat, except for the music, which continued playing into the night. They both drifted into their own thoughts, basking in the moonlight. The cumulative effect of the wine had now taken its toll, and Suzanne was curled up in her deck chair, ready to nod off. Rod analyzed the situation at hand: Suzanne couldn't drive her car and couldn't stay in his boat – no man alive could be trusted to resist that much temptation – so he had to come up with a plan. And then it hit him.

He looked over the stern at the *Happy Times*, a 28-foot cabin cruiser berthed in the slip diagonally across from him. It was owned by a couple who were real party people. They had offered it to Rod to stay in any time he liked, as his quarters on board *Jus' Restin'* were quite spartan. Best of all, it was never locked. This could work.

"Suzanne," Rod whispered, "I have a place where you can sleep, and nobody will bother you."

"Not even you?" she smiled, as she tried to rise out of the low deck chair.

"I'll do my best to behave myself. Here, let me help you up." He helped Suzanne get to her feet. With the sudden rise, she got dizzy and wrapped her arms around Rod.

"I like your plan, but only under one condition: you dance one song with me."

"OK, understand – requesting dance with the captain. You've got a deal."

If Rod was going to dance, it would have to be something appropriate. He cued up one of his favorite artists, Rodney Crowell, and what he thought was his best song ever, "Shame on the Moon."

The music began and Suzanne sunk into his arms, swaying to the soft music. Rod thought back to his first dance party, when he was twelve years old...that was magic he would never forget. He was twelve again and it felt good, even better than before. Rod wished he had picked "In-A-Gadda-Da-Vida" by Iron Butterfly because that song would have lasted seventeen minutes, but he was already on thin ice. No sense in tempting fate. The song was over way too soon, but a deal was a deal so it was time to move.

"That was nice, thank you Rod," purred Suzanne. "Now, where do I rest my head this evening?"

"Just follow me, Kasey and I will show you the way."

Rod got Kasey's leash and the threesome slipped inside the cabin of *Happy Times*. Rod quickly made up a bunk for Suzanne for the night. She lay down, the light from the moon shining through the curtains onto her face, her eyes slowly closing. As he went to pull away, she placed her hand on his cheek.

"You are such a gentleman. Thank you for a wonderful time and for helping me. I know I had too much to drink, but I was having such a good time. I'll never forget this evening. It was wonderful. Merci."

That must have been the last thought through her mind, because she then closed her eyes and fell asleep. Rod covered her with the blanket, and he and Kasey stepped onto the deck of *Happy Times* into the cool night air, the bright moon making it seem like daytime. He looked in the distance and saw Chet, his cigarette aglow in the doorway. Rod gave Chet his best De Niro and laughed.

There was a large bench cushion in the stern, so Rod got his pillow and blanket, tied Kasey's leash to a cleat, and lay back. He looked up at the moon and stars while "Shame on the Moon" played in his mind...

Once inside a woman's heart
A man must keep his head
Heaven opens up a door
Where angels fear to tread
Some men go crazy
Some men go slow
Some men go just where they want
Some men never go
Ooh, blame it on midnight
Uuh, shame on the moon

He sang the lyrics over and over to himself, hoping he'd made the right decision. For now, he would employ the code of the submariners: run silent, run deep.

Chapter Eight

The 180' Line

Rod awoke to the sound of slamming doors and loud conversation coming from the upper parking lot. The *Happy Times'* big soft cushion, combined with the wine from the previous evening, had made for a great night's sleep. He checked his watch – it was 05:45, so the voices had to be coming from his charter arriving a bit early. To be early was to be on time.

He looked out over the stern of *Happy Times* and surveyed the group milling about the lot. It was easy to tell a charter group: each person wore some variation of sweatshirt or jacket and carried a cooler and bags of food. Somebody would have a special rod, maybe a gift or loan from a friend or a favorite uncle, and someone else would be passing around seasickness medication. Rod thought this group appeared to be under control; the cup might not be challenged today.

He opened the door of the *Happy Times* to see Suzanne still curled up and sound asleep. He gave her a little nudge to get her under way, since she needed at least 30 minutes to drive to Gloucester, plus time to get herself together. "Hey, it's time to rock and roll," he whispered softly. "It's quarter to six and my crew has arrived." Rod looked around the cabin...he didn't want to forget anything. Evidence. "You can use the bathhouse and shower or whatever you like. How's your head feeling this morning?" he asked, biting his lower lip.

She slowly sat up and determined that there was no permanent damage. She was ready for a new day and managed a smile to prove it. "That was such a relaxing evening. I hope I didn't put you in an awkward situation." Suzanne stretched as she looked about the inside of her accommodations. "I have all my things in the auto, so I should be able to change and meet my ship right on time," she said, smiling and looking at her watch. "This was just perfect! We are usually on the boat for two weeks at a time, so this was a nice break." She stood up and completed her morning stretch, then added, "Do you think I could come by again sometime? This is such a wonderful place and I've enjoyed your company so much."

"Absolutely! I would suggest that you call first – it might be best."

"Wonderful. I'll grab my bag and be off. Goodbye Kasey, keep an eye on your captain." She bent down to pat Kasey, then turned and planted a short and sweet kiss on Rod, catching him totally by surprise. "That's for being the best host a person could want! We shall meet again...you'll see!"

Another quick look about her surroundings, and she was off, over the stern of the *Happy Times*. She waved goodbye and made her way quickly along the docks.

Kasey and Rod were close behind, each needing a trip to the woods before shoving off. They intercepted the charter at the top of the ramp; after the introductions, Rod pointed the foursome in the direction of the slip. He told them he would return shortly and asked that they wait on the dock.

With Kasey's morning glory behind her, they went back through the parking lot. There was only one car Rod couldn't account for, so he figured Suzanne for the red Toyota. He passed the bathhouse and continued down the ramp under Chet's watchful eye. Chet knew everything that went on in the marina, or at least he thought he did. He bobbed his head and smiled as Rod made the turn for his boat.

"Are we ready to catch some fish?" piped Captain Rod, attempting to generate some excitement in his crew.

"Yeah, you bet we are. How's the fishing been lately?" one of them asked.

"It's been a little bit slow. Let's hope the weather has had a positive effect on the bite."

Rod learned not to tell people "you should have been here yesterday" because there were always slow days. He found it better to start the trip low key, then do his best to find the action and make their day a fun experience. He had a way of putting fishing in terms that everyone could understand. He explained to the crew that a charter trip was like a game of baseball: the Stripers vs. the Bluefish. Every hour was like an inning. Sometimes you score big at the beginning, sometimes it's a grand slam at the end. Some days it's a pitcher's duel, and other days a homerun derby. The anticipation and excitement of each fish, every turn at the plate, was what made it fun.

After the safety briefing, the engine was started, the lines cast off, and the boat was out of the slip and heading down the channel into Plum Island Sound. There were a few spots Rod liked to fish early, and striper fishing was typically best early or late in the day. Soon they were coming upon a favorite spot: the Green Monster. One small boat, a center console, was drifting along its face with the incoming tide.

"You should have been here the day *before* yesterday!" said Rod, laughing at his own private joke.

They eased in about a hundred yards behind the other boat, cut the engine, and began drifting herring chunks in the 25-foot-deep trough. Rod pointed out that the fisherman in the other boat had landed a nice fish. The man brought the fish alongside, removed the hook, and then released it. Two in Rod's group were hooked up right away; Rod just smiled and took a deep breath. Fish on in the first inning always takes the pressure off the captain, and he was grateful.

As they were about to complete the first pass in front of the Green Monster, the center console came about and passed by. Her captain was waving, heading back for another drift. One of the crew came into the pilothouse and asked who the man in that boat was – he looked very familiar.

"We don't call this spot the Green Monster for nothing...does that help?" said Rod.

The crewmember bolted back outside to take a second look, and sure enough, it was the greatest left fielder the Red Sox ever had! #8 had been fishing the Plum Island area for years and was a familiar face on the water.

"Take me out to the ballgame!" one of them yelled. The guys were really excited when they realized who was fishing with them that morning. It was going to be a great day.

After a couple of passes, it was time to try a new spot; if you didn't hit them right away you probably weren't going to. Stealth was everything. They continued their quest down the channel towards the open ocean. Two drifts by the rocks in front of Crane Beach produced two nice keepers for the box, then they went out past the #2 entrance buoy for some double duty.

Rod wanted to troll up the 180' line towards the mouth of the Merrimac River, then make a loop back to the marina through the Plum River on high tide. A good plan for a half-day charter, assuming the tide cooperated. The 180' line – where the ocean depth drops to 180 feet – is on all the charts. It's part of an area called Bigelow Bight, and it skirts along Ipswich Bay approximately three miles offshore, making a large curve that goes on for miles.

Stripers are a federally protected species brought back from near collapse. It's against the law to keep those that are caught outside the three-mile limit; catching and releasing them is also frowned upon. But bluefish are plentiful, and they are true fighters. These fish would make for some great action until they reached the Merrimac, where the legal stripers were waiting. Rod passed out trolling lures and everyone was soon back in the water – a good spread, with two lures on top and two running ten to fifteen feet under the surface. Birds were working ahead, so it wouldn't be long before they'd be onto some fish.

But Rod had an ulterior motive for fishing here. This is nature's superhighway for the giant bluefin tuna, their fall migratory path for the millennium; for reasons only speculated there's something about this route that attracts the fish. Rod saw several boats ahead on the ball, working their chum slicks, trying to entice any tuna in the area to their hooks. According to the radar, these boats were following the 180' line like a fence. A respectable quarter-mile separated them. Rod planned to stay to the inside, between the boats and the shore, and troll a portion of the five miles as they headed for the mouth of the Merrimac River.

He was checking the depth sounder when a cry of "fish on" came from the cockpit. Rod smiled broadly and throttled back, while taking another look at the sounder. Here was what he'd been waiting for: the telltale big, red, inverted checkmark-shaped echo. Right under him at 110 feet! Tuna! Rod could hardly contain himself. He hit the MARK button on the GPS and put in the date as a code, marking the spot for when he could return and try his hand at these giants.

Bluefish were dancing on the surface, fighting for their lives, trying to shake the hook. Rod figured the tuna must have been feeding on the blues, who were probably feeding on mackerel, because the screen was incredibly active with yellow, green, and red echoes up and down the water column. This became evident when one crewmember caught a bluefish that had been chopped in half. Rod's adrenalin was pumping.

"Tuna did that!" he said. "If he'd been a little more accurate, he would have gotten the whole thing! Then you would have had a 'tuna on' for about three nanoseconds!"

The guys couldn't believe that the ten-pound fish they'd been fighting was just reduced to less than half its size in one bite. Most folks didn't care for the strong flavor of bluefish; others loved it. They also made great bait for Rod's lobster pots, so four and a half bluefish went into the fish box with the stripers.

"Reel 'em up! Set up for drifting the herring again. We'll be at the mouth of the Merrimac River in ten minutes."

Once the lines were all in, *Jus' Restin'* was throttled up for the run to the entrance of the river. On a Monday morning, with few boats about and a strong incoming tide running, it was likely to be a very productive day.

The Merrimac can be an unpredictable and dangerous place to fish one day and relatively calm and peaceful the next. It depends mostly on the time of the tide and the prevailing winds. Today didn't seem too bad: a quick current at the mouth, four to five knots maybe, then slowing down after the jetty. Once past the rollers at the mouth, there were several shoals that held fish at different times in different places, depending upon the tide. Rod figured they would get at least five maybe six good drifts before the time constraints of a half-day charter dictated returning to the slip. He planned to stay a little longer to ensure deep enough water for the trip back through the Plum River. He'd come up with a "nice guy's" reason to fish longer – which usually translated into a bigger tip!

The fishing was fast. Rod cautioned the crew to be selective with the fish they kept, since they were only allowed two each. There might be bigger ones, but by the same token the bite could turn off like a switch so it was up to them to decide which ones to keep and which to release. Soon everyone had their limit, but some time remained before the water was sufficient to ensure a safe return via Plum River.

"I have a secret spot and I need a couple of fish myself. Let's move."

So everyone reeled in, and within a few minutes they were on Joppa Flats. It didn't take long until Rod, using a spook and walking the dog like the evening before, was onto a big fat striper. Another of the fishermen had hooked one the same size, prompting Rod to comment that they were "cookie cutters": stripers tend to school with fish their own size and age. With both fish landed, Rod now had his two fish in the box. It was time for the run to the dock.

This was a favorite ride of Rod's. The channel is very tight through the marshlands of the Parker River National Wildlife

Refuge, with many twisties. First, a no-wake ride under the drawbridge leading to Plum Island, and then throttle up and let her rip! It reminded him of the TV shows he'd watched as a kid with airboats flying through the Everglades. Quick successive turns left and right, with a good speed on, and *Jus' Restin'* leaning hard through the turns. The crew was really enjoying the finale! The ride ended right at the spot where Rod had found Willy the Clammer two days before. Next, a no-wake cruise to the service dock and cash-out time.

"Captain, what a great morning! We limited out! And the ride back, now that was cool!" said the approving leader of the group. The crew was all smiles and extremely satisfied with their trip. Rod was particularly happy since he knew that they didn't always end like this. He reflected on the worst charter he ever had...

Three brothers had hired the boat to take their father out on Father's Day. They had hats made to commemorate the "First Annual Father's Day Expedition," and none of them, not one, caught a fish. He even offered them a free trip, but they didn't come back. That's the thing about fishing: there are no guarantees.

Rod tied the boat to the service dock and offered to fillet the stripers, but they all wanted to take home their fish whole, both for pictures and for the chance to do the filleting themselves. Rod filleted his two, demonstrating his technique so that they could try it on their own catch later. The leader of the crew followed Rod into the pilothouse to settle up. The fee was $325 for the charter, and the crewmembers chipped in $10 each for the tip. All in all, Rod figured he had a pretty good start on the day, and it was only 11:30. Everyone shook hands and off they went, carrying home some fine Plum Island stripers.

One of the summer-help kids from Harborside was right there on the gas pump, and *Jus' Restin'* was quickly taking on 50 gallons. Meanwhile, Rod made his plans for the rest of the day. First, he would ice the striper fillets he'd kept and get them ready to travel. Next, he would put the bluefish for his lobster pots in the freezer and wash down the boat. After that, he would drop by the bank to deposit money into the boat account, then head to Newburyport to deliver the stripers to his friend's restaurant and visit with his daughter Cari, who worked there. And finally, he would find two fishermen to go tuna fishing in the morning! Priority number one!

With the boat duties behind him, he went to the bathhouse to get the shower he'd missed that morning. He was ready to leave when he remembered Suzanne's check. She said it was with the business cards, so back to the boat he went, only to be intercepted by Chet. He was really a man of few words.

"Give it up!" he demanded, trying to keep a straight face. Whatever mystery surrounded the nighttime guest, Chet wanted it cleared away.

"Sorry Chet, strictly business. I couldn't possibly discuss client information." Rod held out his palm, "Can't do it, confidential." They both laughed as Rod continued on his way back to the *Jus' Restin'*.

Once inside, he opened the cover of the Tupperware container that was secured to the dash. There it was, right on top, folded in half. He opened the check to see that it was for $250: $75 over the base fee. Nice. The way Rod figured tips, they were his, a perquisite. All other fees went directly into the account. Not bad – he now had $115 extra cash to play with as he liked.

But there was much more important information to be gleaned from the check he held in his hand. He looked at the header and saw that it was a corporate check, drawn against a company he'd never heard of with a European address. The signature belonged to a man, a company officer. He noticed a number written on the edge of the check in thin pencil, just like the mechanical pencil that was kept in the Tupperware box. It was a phone number.

He stood there pondering the number. What did this mean? "Run silent, run deep" crept into his mind. OK, let's be smart here. He always liked to know who was calling him when the phone rang, so he decided to put the number into his cell phone and give it a contact name. Suzanne wouldn't work – that's like running on the surface exposed to gunfire. But he needed a French name. He started to laugh: he would use "Pierre" or, as his father used to say, "Pee-Air, the Dehydrated Frenchman." Must have been an early translation from Penobscot Indians!

Rod believed that life was like an AC sine wave, a continuous series of ups and downs. He was now riding an uphill curve...things were going his way and life was good. But he also knew one thing about riding the wave: something had to happen to signal that it was time to head back down the curve. The trick to life was knowing when that point in time happened and to adjust accordingly.

The Newburyport downtown district was sunny with a fair amount of activity, having just enjoyed a busy weekend of vacationers. Rod and Kasey found a parking space on State Street, close to the front door of Captain Jack's Grille. The lunchtime crowd should have thinned out by now, but the place was still hopping. A good sign because this was Jack's first year with his restaurant, and you never know how the public will take to a new spot. Rod buzzed the windows down halfway and left Kasey in the backseat. There was a nice breeze and he could keep an eye on her from the entrance.

"Captain Rod! Good to see you – have a brew!" said the bartender, reaching into the cooler for a frozen mug and pulling on the tap for some local Fisherman's Brew. It was a new micro taste, an amber lager, and it was doing very well (with some assistance from Rod). The slight hangover from the night before was a distant memory, so he gave the bartender the sign of approval.

Rod had grown up with adults who liked to party. That, coupled with an apprentice program in the construction department of a power company whose motto was "Too much is just enough," had set him up for a life of daily happy hours. Although drinking on charters was strictly forbidden by regulation, Rod occasionally bent the rules.

The bartender was an interesting guy from South Africa named Gerald. He had an accent that Rod tried desperately to imitate, but Cari thought her father only sounded like a drunken Englishman. Gerald aspired to become a wine sommelier, and Rod was keeping an eye on him because he had *his* eye on his little girl.

"Thanks G. To the first one of the day; let's hope it's not the last!"

Rod liked the new microbrews. He had to be careful, though, because some of them could deliver the worst headaches imaginable due to their exotic recipes. But this was a friendly brew – no problems here.

"Captain, my captain!" Two arms wrapped around him from behind.

"Hi baby, how's my Little Chicken today?"

"Just fine Dad, we're really busy. Jack's a happy guy today. We had a great weekend, great crowd, and I got lots of tips! We'll talk in a bit; gotta go for now."

Rod's eyes followed his daughter as she headed to a table by the window, a young couple enjoying their meal and watching the downtown scene. His mind drifted to Cari's new relationship. They were both athletes enjoying a healthy lifestyle. Cari was tall and thin, with short brown hair and a slight case of swimmer's freckles. G was a few inches taller, thin, with short curly brown hair. Rod admired their dedication to fitness; it was getting harder and harder for him to find the time and ambition to exercise. They seemed to enjoy each other's company very much, and he was glad for them both.

Rod took a long, last swig of beer and headed for the kitchen with his cooler of striper fillets. Jack was working the grill with Sasha, the new chef he'd hired: a Ukrainian girl whose cooking talents added a whole new flair to the menu.

"Ahoy there, what have you got for me today?" said Jack, who was standing at the flaming grill. He was glad to see his pal, knowing that there was something in the cooler for him.

"This morning's catch. Stripers. Four big fat fillets," replied Rod, snatching a steak tip from the grill. "I gotta get me a few of those, and don't forget the rings, please."

Sasha peeked into the cooler and smiled with anticipation. Fish was her specialty so this was going to be an entree on tonight's menu.

"Fishing is looking up, Jack. Maybe some tuna in your future – I'm going out early tomorrow."

"Yeah, baby, that would be nice." Jack licked his lips. "Ah, sushi and tuna steaks! We could be a hit with that combo. Hook 'em up, Captain!" Jack was excited about the prospect of fresh tuna. He was just starting to get a name for himself on State Street and this could only help. Jack and Rod had been friends forever and had a business relationship that was easy to maintain. Jack never paid for his fish and lobsters and Rod never paid a tab. No fish, no food or beer, so Rod made sure he always had Jack's best interests in mind.

Back out to the bar, Rod contemplated the last item on his checklist: assemble a crew for tomorrow's tuna trip. His steak and onion rings arrived, along with a loving smile from his favorite little waitress. He thought he would call Bob Weeks, his big guy diver from the weekend. He dialed his number.

"Bob Dude, this is Captain Dude. How are you?" he asked, having a chuckle over Roberto's assigned names.

"Just fine, what's up?"

"Going for tuna tomorrow, spotted them in Ipswich Bay this morning. You interested?"

"Sure, you bet – I'll be there! What time and what kind of sandwiches do you want?"

"Be at the marina by 04:00 and bring enough chow for three. I'm going to get one more person onboard. He'll take care of the drinks. OK with you?"

"Sure enough, see you in the morning. Thanks for the invite – should be a blast!" Big Bob was excited. He was an avid sportsman but had never gone for the big game. This could be the experience of a lifetime.

"Hey mate, did I hear you say you were looking for another fisher for your boat? I've got the day off, so I could help you out."

Rod looked up and saw that the bartender was serious. "What kind of fishing experience do you have? I've watched you trolling for my daughter, but that doesn't count." He raised his eyebrows and waited for a response.

"Evidently I haven't used the right bait yet with Cari, but she's looking. I'm patient. However, I've caught many yellowfin tuna back home in South Africa. I know my way around a Penn reel." He sounded very sure of himself.

"Perfect. Be at the boat at 04:00. You bring the drinks and I'll take care of everything else. We're slipped down at Harborside Marina."

Rod watched the weather forecast on TV over the bar – it all looked good. He finished his meal and one more Fisherman's Brew.

"Well, Gerald says he's going fishing with you in the morning. He says he knows how to fish so I think he'll be an asset," Cari declared. She was pleased he was going, because she was becoming interested in Gerald and it would give him and her dad a chance to get to know each other.

"All righty then, I'm off to get the bait and prepare the craft. See you in the morning G. Bye, Cari!"

Kasey sniffed Rod as he climbed back inside the truck. The smell of onion rings and steak permeated his clothes. "I know what you want," he laughed, as he pulled the steak tip in the napkin from his shirt pocket. "Here you go, baby!" There was no chewing, just a heavenly moment of flavor.

After a quick stop to get the 100-quart cooler that was kept next to the bait freezer, Rod arrived at the shady pine road that led to the bait-processing plant hidden in the backwoods of Rowley. This refrigerated building supplied fresh bait primarily to lobstermen, as well as frozen bait to the numerous bait and tackle shops along the coast.

These guys had the freshest bait and today it was herring, one of the tuna's favorites. And the price was right. Rod could get a full cooler, which was equal to a "tote box," for $17: a real deal. A tote box was a hefty black plastic container with handles at the ends; Rod had several next to his freezer for handling the fish during the cod and haddock trips. He could run a chum slick for hours with this supply of bait.

The cooler was really heavy now, so Rod commandeered a two-wheel cart with Chet's help to get the bait out of the truck and down onto the boat. He separated a portion of the bait into another large cooler and iced them both. It would be twelve hours before the fishing started and the melting ice, mixed with the blood of the herring, would make a superb gravy for enhancing the slick.

Now it was time to prepare the rest of the gear, which not only served to flush out any problems, but was also like a pre-game show: a comprehensive review of the factors that could, and ultimately would, play a part in catching a giant bluefin. Rod always liked using analogies and metaphors to put things in perspective, so he compared the process of fishing for the giant bluefin to a complex series electrical circuit. For the circuit to operate, all the components in the circuit had to function correctly, one after the other. If any one component failed, the circuit wouldn't work, the light bulb wouldn't light, and the tuna would live to swim another day.

In his mind he replaced the components of his imaginary circuit with bait, hooks, crimps, lines, lures, leaders, rods, reels, harpoons, tail ropes, gaffes, block and tackle. There was a lot to remember. Electronics, charts, locations, water depth, ocean current speed, time of the tide, birds, whales, dolphins, 406 EPIRB, survival gear, boat reliability, weather, skill, and above all: *attention to detail*. If he could minimize the variables and eliminate the mistakes, with a little bit of luck, *Jus' Restin'* would indeed land The Big One.

The price of tuna had gone up over the years, and many fishermen had joined the fray, reaching for the big bucks. The final price paid was again similar to the electrical circuit...factors included fat content, weight, was it bled correctly, was it iced sufficiently, what is its overall appearance, and, the biggest factor of all, what is the Japanese market paying? That's where the giants go. But it still wasn't over. Lastly, the captain would have to decide if he wanted to accept the fish dealer's offer or put the fish on consignment and hope for a good price when it arrived at market in Japan. From "fish on!" to cashing the check was a tortuous path, but it could be a huge payday. If a 750-pound giant – with all the right stuff – came to the fish buyer, it could fetch $20 or more a pound. $15,000! Not a bad day's pay.

But just like poker, you had to put it down to pick it up, and the gear reflected the investment. A new rod and reel combination ran $1,800, and there had to be at least two. The raft, survival suits, and EPIRB radio all added a substantial amount. After the boat, this is an additional investment of at least $10,000 – just to get a couple of lines in the water. The mother-in-laws had fronted Rod the money for the tuna gear, so there was even more pressure to succeed.

Tuna fishing is a dangerous game and it can take its toll on mariners. The federal government dictates that when fishing more than twelve miles from shore, boats must be outfitted with survival gear. Fishermen in small boats have been swamped over the stern in rough water, leading to loss of life, when big powerful fish towed them backwards. The prospect of a $15,000 payday can cloud the judgment of many a skipper, causing him to take chances he normally wouldn't take.

But the biggest variable of all, the main component, is the tuna itself. They are a migratory species, and the younger fish tend to stay in their own age groups. The smaller ones are called "footballs" because of their shape and relatively small size: 25 to 100 pounds. There are several classifications as they increase in size, until the final category of "giant bluefin." These are the only ones that can be sold at market. They have to be a minimum of 73 inches in length, just over six feet, and roughly 250-300 pounds. Unlike the schooling football tuna, the giants can tend to be solitary. The world record was an astounding 1,496-pounder caught in Nova Scotia, Canada.

The giants can, and do, travel long distances each day in search of food. But if food is plentiful, they'll stay in one general area for extended periods of time. These fish have personalities: all are tough competitors, but some are just like junkyard dogs. They're tough. And fast, very fast! A giant is capable of bursts of speed in excess of 50 mph, peeling line at an incredible rate. That's why there are over 400 yards of line on a reel, nearly a quarter-mile – and sometimes that isn't enough. Many fishermen have been "spooled" by some monster that wouldn't stop. These tuna rod and reel combinations are the elephant guns of the oceans; they're made of the finest materials and are certainly up to the task.

Rod went to the dock box and brought back the rods and reels that he kept under lock and key. These were bent butt rods: the huge gold Penn 130 two-speed reel is attached to a short bent handle that rests in a special swivel rod holder in the gunnel. The fiberglass rod is inserted into the handle and screwed down tight with a special locking ring. The rods have rollers to handle the line, since eyelets cause friction. One end of a six-foot-long quarter-inch stainless steel cable with brass snap swivels is attached to the bent butt handle, and the other end is attached to a cleat under the gunnel. This keeps the rods from going overboard if they're ripped from the rod holders...more likely from the hands of the fisherman as the rods get moved around the cockpit during a fight.

Taking the special leader material out of its case, Rod made up the line that would hold the bait. Great care was taken to keep the tuna from seeing any of the terminal tackle, especially if it might reflect light.

Every component was of top grade materials. The main line consisted of 400 yards of Dacron, and was similar in design to the Chinese finger toys Rod played with as a kid. One end of the leader, 100 yards of 300-pound test plastic monofilament, was inserted about six feet into the end of the Dacron line. The line was tied tight with nylon at the six-foot point and at the other entry point. It was a chore to make up the line in this fashion, but it was nearly foolproof. There was no way this line could part: the harder a fish pulled, the tighter it grasped.

Next, at the end of the mono, he slid a small plastic slide with a loop on it. This is where he would attach the balloon. Lastly, a stainless steel swivel. Because of the sheer size of the line, knots would have been weak and inefficient; aluminum crimps were therefore used instead. After they were attached, black electrical tape was applied to hide their shiny appearance.

The final piece of line, a twenty-foot shot of fluorocarbon – virtually invisible under water – was crimped with the opposite end left bare until it was time to start fishing. At that point, a razor sharp circle hook would be attached. The circle hook was the best choice because it can bury itself deeply into the fish's jaw with no help from the fisherman.

With the rods ready, the harpoon was brought on board, along with the tail ropes, safety cables, and anchor setup. Rod would go over these items and their responsibilities in the morning. Right now it was time for Rod and Kasey to take their afternoon walk and to play Frisbee. After dinner and a good night's sleep, the games would begin at 04:00.

The alarm went off at 03:30, just enough time for a shower and a stroll with Kasey. The G-man and Big Bob had arrived and were admiring the moon that was heading into the western night sky. Rod looked at the moon and reminisced about the night before. He felt young again...alive.

"Ahoy, Captain! G-Man here!" Gerald was all smiles and ready to go.

Big Bob was getting the food out of his truck when he spotted Rod coming towards him from the bathhouse. "Captain Dude! I got the onion rolls! And the coffee! And Kasey, here's something for you, pooch." He reached into a small bag and got out a hamburger patty from last night's meal. Kasey gave it a sniff and in a couple of bites, it was gone. Big Bob now had a friend for life.

"Good morning guys, it's going to be a big day – I can feel it!" said Rod. He actually hated to get up early. The early morning darkness had a profoundly depressing effect on him, but the company of these two made the darkness seem brighter.

They all went down to the boat and settled their personal gear into the cuddy cabin. Bob wiped down the windows, which were heavy with dew. Rod fired the engine and turned on the night vision red cabin lights, along with the navigation and cockpit lights. Then came the radar, GPS, and VHF radio. Everything was functioning normally.

"We're ready. Let's cast off the lines, Dude" commanded Rod.

Bob let out a bellow of laughter. "Aye-aye, Captain Dude. Lines are away."

The G-man poured the coffee, and they headed under the bridge and down the channel. The moon, the electronics, and the shore lights were illuminating the way.

"We marked a spot yesterday where we saw several arches. It'll take about 45 minutes, so keep an eye forward as we head out the channel."

The guys took positions on either side of the pilothouse and hung onto the roof grab-rails. Slowly down the channel in the early morning darkness they went, ready for an adventure. After making their way through Plum Island Sound and approaching the #2 buoy, the waypoint was called up on the GPS. With a slight course correction, they were bearing down on the site where Rod had spotted the tuna the day before. The radar showed several boats already on station, spaced apart equally. The tuna men with the big sport fishermen rigs had fished all night. The waypoint showed up on the radar, with a good-sized gap between two boats that were already on anchor. The boats' anchor lights became visible as they approached.

"This is perfect," said Rod. "We'll steam ahead just a little, drop the anchor, and drift back right on target." Looking all about, he adjusted his position in the mix of boats. "It's a good thing to have plenty of room, away from other boats. If we hook up, we don't want the fish to run into their anchor lines."

Jus' Restin' had a specially-designed anchor setup specifically for tuna, all contained in a tote box. One of Johnny's famous "Tuna Specials." It consisted of an anchor and chain much larger and heavier than the one on the pulpit, with over 500 feet of 5/8-inch nylon line. It was fitted with two floating magenta-colored Gloucester balls, one of which had *Jus' Restin'* stenciled on it. This anchor would hold in any conditions. If a fish hooked up, the anchor line could be easily let go, so that the boat could drift away and prevent the tuna from getting entangled. The boat could come back later and either retrieve the anchor or set back up on the buoy.

With the anchor now set, it was time for the captain to discuss his expectations and hand out assignments. "Right up front, I want it known that there has never been a tuna on board this boat. This is the first season we've gone 'tuna wishing.' " Rod looked at their faces for some kind of reaction, but there was no deterring his crew. "You probably saw the squid bars in the cuddy. Well I'll tell you, those have been trolled all over

Pigeon Hill, the Cove, New Scantum, Halfway Hump, and Jeffrey's Ledge. I think a tuna tried to crash one of them once, but it missed and never tried again. Bluefish will tear them up. So far, for me, pretty much ineffectual."

Pointing to the big coolers on the deck, he began again. "So it's time to try a new tactic called 'chunking.' These coolers, as you've seen, are full of fresh herring that we're going to use to make a chum slick – an oceangoing smorgasbord. We'll place our two chunks, with these 8/0 hooks buried inside..." He held the hooks up. "...right under their noses. They won't be able to resist!" He set the hooks down, then spit in his left hand and slapped it hard, just like Big Papi. "What do you think? Sound like a plan?"

"This will work. I know it will, Rod – I've seen it work," offered the confident G-man.

"What do you want us to do?" asked Bob, chomping at the bit to get going.

"This type of fishing is like the control room of a nuclear power plant or an airline cockpit: hours of boredom, punctuated by brief moments of sheer terror. So, to minimize confusion, I've decided which tasks each of us will be responsible for when we hook up...and we will hook up, right?" All three of them gave a high five, and the tone for the day was set.

"Bob, I've watched you work with the lines so I want you to release the anchor, but only after I signal that the engine is running. Next, I want you to clear the deck of anything not related to the landing of this fish. Put everything away forward in the cuddy. Understand?"

"Got it, release the anchor on your signal, clear the decks. Got it!"

"G-man, I want you to immediately start reeling in the other line. When you get it on board, cut off the hook bait and throw it in the chum cooler. I don't want anyone getting caught by a flying hook. Then take that fishing stick and put it overhead in the center rod holder."

"Understand. Other line out and then cut the hook. Rod overhead. I'm there."

"You may be wondering what I'm going to do after starting the engine. Well, I'm going to the corner with the rod bent over like it's about to break, with line peeling out, and simply watch and enjoy the moment!" Rod smiled, walking to the big gold reel at the stern of the boat. "This Penn International 130 knows its job. My mission is to keep that line headed out over the stern, on a 45-degree angle away from the corner." He raised his arm, making a hatchet-like motion to show Big Bob and G where he expected the line to go.

"We need to let the fish pull the boat backwards," Rod continued. "Try to wear him down with the resistance of the flat wide stern. We'll all take turns reeling, trying to get him close enough to stick 'em with the harpoon. Once he's harpooned, if we don't kill him he'll run again." Rod picked up the dart, which was attached to a buoy with 75 yards of quarter-inch nylon line. "So be careful where your feet are because you don't want to get tangled. A fish can pull you right over the side and under. And we have to be very, very careful of the stern drive; if the line hits any sharp edges, like the props or trim tabs, it will be cut like a knife because of the tension that's going to be on that line. And the fish will be gone."

Rod looked down at the deck and then back to his crew. "And lastly, because I'm relatively new at this, I may bark orders at you and change them a moment later. Please, don't take it personally – just the heat of the moment." Rod looked about the cockpit to see if he'd forgotten anything, but nothing stood out. "OK then, any questions before we start?"

"Wow, there's a lot to this," Bob added, with the G-Man in agreement. "Just let us know what to do, Cap!"

The sunrise was still a half hour away, and the "golden light," as it was called, was just turning on. The lights on the shoreline were barely visible, and the moon was still bright and low in the sky. It was time to get the chum slick started and the lines in the water.

Rod brought out a five-gallon bucket, a cutting knife, and the "chuminator." This was a gift from G.W., *Jus' Restin*'s primary physician and the best mechanic on the North Shore, according to Rod. He was also a good friend. The chuminator was an old mop handle with a soft plastic grip, with the bottom four inches of a one-quart plastic container screwed onto one end. It was engineered to be dipped into the bucket of chum, retrieve three or four pieces of herring, and plop its contents over the side at a rate of once every minute. The tool was perfect for the job.

Gerald got his knife out and cut the bait, a whole herring, into three pieces.

"G, cut them into four or five pieces – we don't want to feed them, only to entice them. Besides, they'll last longer. Rule number one: don't ever, ever, ever stop chumming! That would be like a bloodhound on the scent of a trail coming to the edge of a river – a break in the trail. The tuna could swim off to one side or the other and never find the slick again. So keep chumming!"

With the chumming chores under way, it was time to focus on the lines. "Bob, come on over here and help me get these lines ready. We need to put on the stingers, the hooks with bait. Grab a couple of the best-looking herring, and cut off their heads."

Rod took the end of one line, which had the diameter of a ballpoint pen refill, and pushed it into the fish near the tail. He worked the line along the spine and exited the large bloody opening where the head used to be. He wiped off the line, slid on the crimp, and slid the line through the eye of the hook and back into the crimp. Bob handed him the large crimping tool, and Rod squeezed the handles, making a smooth compression of the metal crimp. Then he made a second crimp and pulled the fish line back, causing the hook to disappear into the body of the bait.

"Now you see it, now you don't!" The hook was buried deep inside – no telltale signs of danger for a wary fish. "OK, now we'll add a sinker about ten feet from the hook. Bob, grab that box of sinkers with the rubber bands attached."

The sinkers were already stealthy: they were wrapped with black electrical tape and a black rubber band. A 32-ounce sinker was selected from the box. Rod counted out ten feet from the hook, looped the rubber band onto the fluorocarbon leader, and pulled it tight.

"Now it's party time. Time to display our colors." Rod produced a small bag of large, bright, heavy-duty tuna balloons, with all the traditional color selections. He thought back to the weekend after 9/11...he was headed offshore for a cod fishing charter and he passed the tuna boats fishing the 180 line. Every fisherman down to the last man was using red, white, and blue balloons. He never forgot that amazing display of patriotism.

"You boys pick the colors – pick some lucky ones."

Bob reached in and got a bright yellow balloon.

"How about that one?" said Gerald, pointing his fishgut-dripping finger at the pink balloon.

"Pink? Pink? Oh boy! Now hear this, I'm changing your name from G-Man to Girly-Man!" yelled Bob, having a good laugh at Gerald's expense. Humor at someone else's expense was always the best kind. Gerald looked to Rod for support.

"Hey, don't look at me for help – you picked it!" laughed Rod, as he started to blow up the yellow balloon. "We spotted the tuna yesterday between 90 and 120 feet. We'll set the yellow for 90 feet and the pink for 120. We can always adjust them if we mark fish at a different depth."

With the lines ready, Bob lowered the first bait over the side. When he got to the sinker, he measured twenty arm-lengths in order to get the bait down to a depth of 120 feet. He secured the pink balloon where he stopped counting. This line would go out first, since it would be the farthest from the boat and deeper into the chum slick. The same process was completed for the second rod, with the yellow balloon set for a 90-foot depth, about 75 feet closer. The balloons rode gently on the smooth calm surface a fair distance behind the boat; they would be the first indicators if a fish took the bait.

With both lines now in the water, the chuminator began sending herring over the side at the prescribed rate. The chum slick looked like a giant plume from a smoke stack: concentrated at the source, and then spreading out over a large area as the bait drifted down on the current. Trying to place the bait at just the right position in the slick – so that the chum would sink at the right rate and right by their hook baits – was a guessing game. The speed of the current dictated everything. The technique worked very well in theory; the tuna, and any other fish in the area, would pick up the scent of the bait and home in on the source. The fish would then unsuspectingly swim into the slick and suck up the pieces of chum. Chomp, chomp, chomp...until they reached the hidden hook. Then all hell would break lose. Fish on!

There was still time to enjoy nature at its finest. The sky was turning a pinkish-orange as the sun neared the horizon. The air was calm, and not a ripple could be detected on the water. The crew could see other fishermen in their boats with balloons trailing behind, lying in wait, ready to ambush these truly magnificent creatures who can eat 1/3 of their weight in a day. The giants were on the prowl, and the crew of the *Jus' Restin'* was ready and waiting.

And waiting...and waiting. The morning was dragging, so much so that Rod decided to catch a little snooze. He opened the portal windows, arranged some pillows, and settled in next to Kasey for a nap. He lay there in the cool and refreshing shade of the cuddy, stroking Kasey's head and drifting off to sleep. He was sound asleep when the alarm went off.

"Fish on!" yelled Bob.

Rod leapt out of the cuddy and banged his head against the overhead on his way out of the pilothouse. Once on deck, nearly dizzy from his collision, he saw Big Bob with one of the small rods from the overhead with a striper on the line. "Dude, what are you doing?" he asked in frustration.

"Well, we saw stripers coming up in the slick, right at the stern of the boat, and thought we would take a couple."

"OK, here's the deal," Rod began, rubbing his pounding head. "We're just inside the three-mile line here – although not by much according to the chart plotter. The commercial striper season is still open, so you guys can fish for stripers, too. Put them in the blue fish box, and remember, they must be a minimum 34 inches. We'll sell them later. But *don't* yell 'fish on' again! Unless it's a tuna. OK?"

They agreed. Rod turned and headed to his bunk, only to yell back, "And keep chumming!"

Rod went back inside and lay down. His sentimental favorite Jimmy Buffett song, "The Captain and the Kid," was coming out of the speakers. Thoughts of his father and this song could bring him to tears. He missed his father so much and wished he were here to share this time with him. He lay back with the tunes playing in his head and drifted off to a deep sleep. This time he managed a half hour, but it seemed like only seconds.

"Yellow! Yellow! Yellow! Fish on! Rod, get out here!" Bob was frantic. Rod ran out into the bright sunlight and saw the pink balloon only.

"Where's the yellow?"

"It's gone! Under!" yelled G. "Look at this rod: it's bent over and taking line!"

It was happening, just like they dreamed it would, right before their eyes. Rod peered down into the water from the starboard corner, imagining this fish feeling the hook driving into its jaw. The rod bent over like it was going to snap, the tip throbbing under the pressure as the line played out.

"Battle stations!" Rod yelled. "Woo hoo, we're on, mark the time: 09:10!"

G headed for the other reel, while Rod fired up the engine. On Rod's signal, Big Bob released the anchor line. Rod looked out over the bow and saw the Gloucester ball with his boat's name on it staying on position, while they drifted away with the current. He went back to the corner and watched the rod and reel, following the angle of the line into the water below.

"Look, over there! The yellow balloon just surfaced. It's free of the line!" yelled G, just as the balloon popped about six feet into the air. Everyone's adrenalin was pumping as the line went out in bursts alternating with quiet. The rod tip was making ever so subtle movements.

"He's headed east, so let's bump the boat forward and turn it east-north-east to get us away from the boats here on the 180' line," said Rod.

He went to the helm and carried out his plan, trying to maneuver the fish where he wanted it to go. He didn't want to take any chances on it getting tangled in the anchor lines of other vessels. The moves of the *Jus' Restin'* didn't go unnoticed; other fishermen watched and cheered them on.

"I'm going to try and get some line back. Let's see what he's got," G said. He started cranking the massive gold handle of the big Penn reel, putting even more pressure on the hook. This maneuver aggravated the fish; he put on another burst of speed and took 50 more yards of line. Then, without warning, the line went slack.

"Reel, reel, reel," barked Rod. "He's changed directions!"

G must have put 50 cranks on the reel when the line snapped tight and headed directly down.

"He's going under the boat!" yelled Bob.

"Give me some direction. Where does the boat want to go?" asked a frantic Rod.

"Reverse to starboard!" replied G.

Rod bumped the shifter into reverse, along with a little throttle. The boat snapped about, bringing the line back to the angle they wanted.

"Neutral!" yelled G. Everything was as it should be again, with the fish taking more line and the threesome fighting to get it back. They would replay this scenario over and over again for the next hour and a half. Gain some line, lose some line, the fish turning and heading off in another direction. The chart plotter looked like a little kid playing with an Etch A Sketch for the first time. This fish was literally dragging them all over Ipswich Bay.

Now a new problem was presenting itself: spectators. A number of boats were watching the battle for the bluefin and so far they were keeping their distance, but this just added another variable to worry about.

The fish started making a wide circle under the boat: a "death spiral," which Rod had heard about. This signaled that he was nearly spent, but it created a whole new dilemma as far as handling the boat. The line kept getting under the boat, making it difficult to keep the proper alignment. The fish then made a sudden movement and the line went under, rubbing against the drive.

"No!" yelled Rod. "Not the drive!" He ran to the stern, scrambling over the engine cover while putting on his leather gloves. "Hold my feet!" he yelled as he lay over the transom, trying desperately to hold the line away from any sharp edges. Then, for no apparent reason, the line went slack. Rod lay there, looking over the stern into the water below, when he noticed the line moving away from the stern and begin to tighten up again. "Fish *still* on!" he gasped, shaking his head. "God, we've gotta keep that line away from the drive."

Bob and G looked on, feeling dejected, as though it was their fault.

"Hey, focus! Nobody's fault, that tuna just keeps changing directions. Patience." Rod smiled and returned to the helm.

Now the fish was coming to the surface, another move they hadn't seen yet. The line kept changing its angle as it came up and up and up. Then, it happened. The tip of the tuna's half-moon tail, followed by his dorsal fin, broke the surface. He was swimming on the surface and he was huge! Rod grabbed his binoculars to get a closer look at this majestic but exhausted fish, its tail swishing slowly from side to side. The iridescent blues and greens were spectacular, as was the row of bright yellow triangle-tipped fins along the upper length of its body between the dorsal and the tail.

"I think it's time, boys! He's cooked!" Rod checked the harpoon by feeling the sharply-filed edges of the big brass dart at the tip of the ten-foot aluminum pole. The stick was ready, the line clear. "OK, let's reel him to the boat – slowly. When he's close enough, I'll stick him. Keep a slight pressure on the hook; don't let the line go slack!"

Rod went back into the pilothouse, turned the wheel just a little towards the fish, and put the boat in neutral. G kept reeling at a slow pace, keeping the line taut. This reeling action was now pulling the fish in, causing it to roll and expose his right side to the harpoon.

"Keep coming to papa, keep coming," Rod was whispering to himself as he picked up the harpoon. Taking a position next to G on the reel, he waited as the fish came closer and closer. The sinker was now out of the water, bouncing gently on its rubber band, dripping water, and approaching the end of the rod. Holding the harpoon high above his head and to the right, Rod waited anxiously for the exact moment. The sinker was now at the first roller, the fish ten feet away. "Keep reeling, slowly."

"I can't! The sinker is jammed at the roller!" muttered G, staring at the rod tip.

Rod was almost in range – just a couple more feet! "Keep reeling. The rubber band will break. Keep going!" He could see the eye of the tuna. They seemed to be staring each other down. It was time to pull the trigger and let that harpoon fly! As Rod took aim, G pulled on the handle as instructed and the rubber band broke. The sinker splashed right in front of the fish; he responded with a surge of his huge tail flapping violently, as Rod simultaneously let the harpoon go. He watched the dart pass just above and behind the fish's head and disappear into the water.

The next sound would surely live on in Rod's mind forever: that of fluorocarbon running against the edge of the starboard trim tab, a rumbling that vibrated throughout the boat. Then, the unbelievable...BANG! The rod snapped violently upwards, then returned to a relaxed position as the broken fluorocarbon drifted in the wind, curling around the rod tip. The fish was gone! That's all there was to it. He was gone. Gone. The time was 10:35.

Chapter Nine

Crab Ledge

The next couple of days were spent conducting charters and telling the story of "the one that got away." The more Rod told the story, the more excited about tuna fishing he became, which only served to aggravate him over his last performance. He had that bluefin sold and tuition checks in the mail a half hour before he even saw the fish on the surface. As they say, "It's not over until the fat lady sings"; with tuna the expression is, "It's not yours until the tail rope is on."

The tail rope is a ten-foot long, 5/8-inch nylon line, with a loop spliced into one end. This attaches to a cleat on the boat. On the other end is a sleeve of clear plastic tubing over a quarter-inch stainless steel cable connected to a large stainless steel snap swivel. The idea is that after the tuna has been gaffed and subdued, the tail rope is attached, causing the swivel to slide along the plastic cover and cinch tight like a lasso. Then – and only then – is the tuna actually caught. Rod had never gotten to that point and wondered if he'd ever get another chance.

To be a successful tuna fisherman, you had to know where to look. Being new at the game, he was not a member of any "good old boy" network. All information, although always welcome, was therefore usually secondhand and impossible to verify. Tuna fishermen didn't give up their secret spots to just anyone, and cards were played very, very close to the chest.

There was one excellent source of information, however – a reliable source. So Rod decided it was time to take a ride to the Fisherman's Outfitter, the shop where he'd bought his tuna gear. Johnny, the owner, was an accomplished tuna fisherman and was always willing to divulge secrets. One of his steadfast rules was that tuna always move: an area could be hot one day and dead the next. Keep looking for the birds and whales. That's where you'll find the tuna. He also gave up the names of a few tuna boats to keep a lookout for on the water.

"If you see these boats, you're in the right area, so start fishing!" said Johnny.

Talking with Johnny was an uplifting experience because he was so animated and positive. Rod was sure he would be onto another fish the next time out. They talked about the fish that was lost, and Johnny just laughed – welcome to the game! Johnny heard that there was an active bite happening down on Crab Ledge. He pulled out a chart and pointed to an area about ten miles east of Chatham, off Cape Cod.

"That's gotta be 100 miles from Harborside!"

"Hey, you can steam there in your boat, with good water, in five hours. You've got the right boat for this." Johnny's face got seriously excited. "Fish all day, zip into Stage Harbor at night for some fun and games in Chatham, then back out in the morning. Fish some more and return to home port at the end of day three! A couple of tuna over 800 pounds landed from there two days ago and the price is up!" Johnny rolled up the chart they'd been scanning. "They use live bluefish as bait down there this time of year." Folding his arms, he continued, "Hey, this is what tuna is all about: chasing them. The Cape is one of the hottest spots in the world. The premier spot, just waiting for you to go get 'em!"

"Helluva plan. I'll talk to my crew and see if they're up for it. Personally, I like the idea. Thanks John, you're the best!"

More customers entered the shop and Johnny was right there to greet them. Rod wandered around the store for a while, scanning the different gear. He picked a few items from the shelves that he really didn't need as yet, but he knew this information was valuable and Johnny had to make a living, too.

Back at the slip, Rod pulled out his charts and pondered Crab Ledge. He was excited and his mind was clicking, running over the logistics. The plan could work; it certainly had the potential to be a big winner. It was a long steam, but *Jus' Restin'* had the range to make the complete trip on less than a tank of fuel. Plus, Rod had a cousin, Norm, who lived in Brewster, about ten miles from Chatham. He'd enjoyed some success with fishing, and had plenty of room at his home for a couple of overnights. Rod was sure he'd like to join the action. He called Norm, who said he was welcome to stay at the house and that he'd fish with him the middle day, Saturday.

Rod tuned the marine radio to the weather channel to get the latest long range report. High-pressure building over the New England area, continuing fair weather for at least the next four days. Winds five to ten knots, becoming light and variable. With no charters booked for the next few days, all that was needed was a crew.

Big Bob and G were both unavailable due to their work schedules, so he called up the reserves. First, Koo Koo. Just dialing the phone, Rod began to chuckle to himself. On his first day working in the power company's construction department, he was assigned to Koo Koo to learn the ropes. Koo Koo had earned his nickname due to his total lack of fear of heights and generally outlandishly crazy personality. He could pass as a stunt double for Danny DeVito and was just as funny. His real name was Paul, but Rod loved calling him Koo Koo.

Koo Koo was an avid fisherman; the two of them had fished for stripers in the discharge canals of the New England Power plants where they used to work shutdowns. Their career paths eventually took them in different directions, but they still maintained their 30-year friendship and fished together whenever they could.

"Koo Koo, it's time! Time to get us a big one!" Rod had to almost yell because Koo Koo was never a fan of ear protection and was now nearly deaf.

"What? Big what?" he asked. He'd developed a habit of saying "what" as a first response to anything, a defense mechanism to gain time to try to decipher what had just been said. Plus, he liked to play games with what people said and he was quick.

"Tuna. You ready to try for some tuna? Giants, off Chatham. Planning for three days. Do a couple of overnights in Brewster. Should be a lot of fun!"

"What? A giant tumor? Only three days left? Oh, that should be a lot of fun!" he replied, laughing on the other end.

"Hey, knock it off, Koo Koo. You heard me! I know you did. Are you in?" Rod sat back, amused, waiting for the next response.

"What? Tuna? Chatham? Three days? Sure, when we going?" was his enthusiastic reply.

"I want to leave tomorrow morning, trying to get one more guy. Can you be here at Harborside at 04:00?"

"What? 04:00? Harborside? OK, I'll be there."

Koo Koo was ten years older than Rod and had retired early. Getting time off was no issue to him, and Rod knew he was already packing.

The next call went out to Ray, AKA Mumbles. He got *his* nickname because he mumbled everything. Mumbles was an old friend from the camping days, when the girls were little. He was a good all-around fisherman, and he and Rod had spent a lot of time salmon and trout fishing together. He reminded Rod of Uncle Grady on the old *Sanford and Son* TV sitcom – the only difference being that Mumbles was white. He was so good-natured that nothing ever got to him; he would be an asset to the crew. He said he was on board to go and volunteered to bring the sandwiches.

The plan was set. Kasey would have to do shore duty with Uncle George because after all, with three guys and their personal stuff, plus the tuna gear, they would need the space. Uncle George and Kasey would be just fine together, walking the beach and playing Frisbee.

Rod began to organize the boat. The anchor setup would remain on the dock; no need for that, because no chunking this trip. He would take the squid rigs and the green machines for trolling, as well as a couple of boat rods to catch bluefish for bait. All the other tuna gear was still on board. Next, it was over to the gas dock to top off the fuel tank, and to make sure the head tank was emptied. The motor and all the fluid levels were checked. Three twenty-pound bags of ice went into the big blue fish box. She was ready to sail.

The next morning arrived quickly. Mumbles and Koo Koo had met briefly at a summer cookout years before, but had never fished together. They were soon mumbling and questioning each other like old friends. Rod just looked on and laughed, watching them interact. One guy who didn't speak clearly, talking with a guy who didn't hear well. This was going to be fun!

Spreading out a couple of charts on the engine cover under the brilliance of the halogen flood lights, Rod gave his crew a briefing of the plan that would get them to Crab Ledge, off Cape Cod, and back. First, they would steam over to the entrance of the Annisquam River, then go inland on the river, exiting via the Blyman Drawbridge and into Gloucester Harbor. As they headed out through Gloucester Harbor at Eastern Point, a waypoint for the BE Buoy would be called up in the GPS. The GPS would plot a course across Massachusetts Bay right along the length of Stellwagen Bank, a federal marine sanctuary where the fishing is great.

Stellwagen Bank is a known tuna hotspot, right down to the BE Buoy ten miles off the tip of Provincetown. Rod thought they might want to troll this area if they marked fish, especially if the whales were present and feeding. From the BE Buoy, the *Jus' Restin'* would make the final dogleg of the journey along the northeast tip of Cape Cod National Seashore, the outside arm of the Cape, for about the last 30 miles. Then it would take a heading east and start looking for the whales on Crab Ledge.

Everything was ready. Time to shove off for three days on the high seas. The sun was just making its way above the horizon as they cleared the jetty at Gloucester's Eastern Point. It was a spectacular sunrise. This was going to be an outstanding day, with calm waters, an occasional ripple on the surface from an invisible zephyr, zero clouds, and unlimited visibility.

Jus' Restin' ran a steady 21 knots across the calm green surface, her crew enjoying the smooth ride – not always the case for these New England waters. Looking to starboard, Koo Koo pointed out the 540-foot smoke stack of the Salem Harbor fossil power plant. Paul and Rod had climbed that stack twenty years before, to perform strobe light maintenance. They recalled being able to see Provincetown and the entire outline of Cape Cod Bay clearly from the top.

Farther to the southwest, the Beantown skyline was visible. A pinkish-orange brilliance, the reflection from thousands of windows of the city's buildings, welcomed the rising sun. Overhead, a steady stream of jetliners were making their final approach over the water to Boston's Logan International.

"It's 26 nautical miles to the BE," said Rod. "We'll be there in an hour and twenty minutes, plus or minus the current. And keep your eyes open for steam!"

"What do you mean, steam?" asked a puzzled Mumbles. "Is there something wrong with the engine?"

"Whales!" replied Rod. "When they surface, they blow the air out of their lungs and the air mixes with the water that's in their blowholes. Looks like a blast of steam coming out of the water. You'll see."

Ray and Paul kept a sharp lookout as *Jus' Restin'* made her way SSE over a tranquil Massachusetts Bay. Several commercial boats could be seen trawling for cod, along with recreational boats that were fishing for cod and haddock. It was an uneventful ride for the first hour, and the radar showed only scattered boats. Rod switched the radar down to the three-mile range when they got within five miles of the BE buoy.

"Anybody want to venture a guess why it's called the BE buoy?" asked Rod, breaking the silence. Neither of the guys knew, but they were about to get a lesson in aids to navigation whether they wanted it or not.

"Here's the scoop," Rod began, as he scanned the boats ahead. "You've probably heard of the Boston Shipping Lanes? Well, they're the routes designated by the federal government to control the shipping traffic from New York, around Cape Cod, and into the Boston Harbor. We're talking big ships: LNG tankers, cruise-liners, commercial container ships, and big tugs with tows behind. Coming up the coast from the south, a ship would encounter the BA buoy first, southeast of Nantucket Shoals, then the BB, BC, BD, and lastly, the BE buoy. All spaced several miles apart, all the way around Cape Cod."

Rod positioned his arm, mimicking the shape of the Cape, and pointed out the position of each of the buoys. "In recent years, right whales have been taking a beating, getting hit by these vessels. So they may make a bigger angle around the tip of the Cape by moving the BD buoy farther offshore. This will help protect the whales."

"What about us? What are our chances of hitting a whale? Do they even know we're here?" asked Mumbles, who was intent on getting a closer look at a whale.

"I would think so, but who knows?" Rod shrugged his shoulders as he checked the radar and continued to scan the waters ahead. "The law says to stay a minimum of 300 feet away from any observed whale and no more than seven knots of speed. If there's a surprise surfacing, we need to stop the propellers and wait until it's clear to move again. Up till now, I've only observed them on whale watches. Fishing around humpbacks could be interesting – we'll have to watch and learn when we get into the mix with other boats."

"Hey Cap, check the screen." Koo Koo pointed to the radar, which showed a cluster of boats two miles dead ahead, scattered about the north side of the BE buoy. There were birds working in the distance, but no whales could be seen.

"Let's rig the squid bars and troll through. We'll see what happens. I don't want to linger here, but I do want to give this spot a chance." Rod throttled back to an idle and asked Paul to take the helm. "Koo Koo, will you be able to see over the bow?" asked Rod, while giving Mumbles an elbow.

"What? Very funny! I'll just stand on the seat. I'll be OK, but thanks for asking!" Paul laughed and continued to chew his unlit cigarette. He was trying to quit. He'd quit hundreds of times but this was his best shot so far.

Rod went about the task of setting up the squid bars, with Ray's assistance. Both tuna rods were now ready, in the midship holders, as Rod let out the first of the two squid bars. A squid bar consists of a 3/16-inch stainless steel bar that's about four feet wide and painted black. The snap swivel from the line is attached to a three-foot leader that connects at the center of the bar. It pulls a spread of twelve brightly-colored plastic squid bodies that are about a foot long each; in the center is a string of four of them, spaced two feet apart. Trailing at the end is an imitation squid of a different color, and is the only one to have a hook. It's huge. The Stinger, as it's called, is hidden within the skirt of the lure, out of sight of an unsuspecting tuna.

The idea is to make the squid bar surge over the surface, imitating a school of squid trying to escape from a predator. Tuna are known to attack from the rear and pick off the weakest in the school, hopefully the odd-colored one that looks like it's trying to keep up with the pack...wham-o, fish on!

To get the desired action, the lures, one on each side of the boat, were set to run in the first couple of waves generated by the wake. The waves would suck the lures under, causing them to surge forward and skitter across the surface. This would create a spraying action. To accomplish this, the outriggers were lowered out to the sides with the tuna lines running to their tips, which made the squid bars follow perfectly in *Jus' Restin'*'s wake. The guys all agreed it sure looked like a good way to fish, but up to this point the technique had been unsuccessful.

They still hadn't seen any whales, but the tuna fishermen were thick in the small area around the BE. Some were anchored and chunking, some trolling squid rigs and green machines, others drifting live bait. For Rod, there were simply too many boats – so after a 30-minute troll through the pack, they reeled up and were back on course for Crab Ledge.

None of them had ever seen the Cape Cod National Seashore from a boat, and it was worth the trip. The high sand dunes, well over 100 feet in some places, came right to the shoreline. The sand cascaded downward in certain areas, reminding Rod of the landscapes he'd seen while riding motorcycles in Utah and Colorado. They ran the next hour and a half about 100 yards offshore, the waves breaking on the shoreline, and enjoyed the calm waters and scenery.

"OK boys, we need to keep our eyes open for birds," said Rod. "Gotta pick up some bluefish for live lining. Johnny says that's the trick out here this time of year."

They were right off Nauset Inlet when they finally spotted seabirds diving on baitfish, which were being pushed up to the surface by the bluefish below. Within twenty minutes of trolling broken-back lures, they had all the bait they'd need. A total of five bluefish in the livewell would be sufficient.

"Time to get a little bit of Intel," Rod said as he picked up his cell phone and scrolled through his contacts.

"What? Who you calling now?" asked Koo Koo.

"My nephew – I want to hear what he knows about any tuna action out here on the Ledge. He's my ace in the hole!"

Rod's nephew Eric was an Aviation Maintenance Technician, First Class. This meant he was the mechanic and winch operator on a United States Coast Guard HH-60J Jayhawk rescue helicopter, presently stationed at Air Station Cape Cod. He had transferred up from Savannah, Georgia, the previous year and was now enjoying being back home in his native New England.

"Uncle Rod! How you doin'? Are you out fishing?" said the familiar voice on the other end, imitating some character from the Sopranos.

"As a matter of fact, we're just a mile offshore heading for Crab Ledge, east of Chatham. Didn't know if you might have any super secret Homeland Security information about tuna sightings in this area. That's a service you provide relatives and taxpayers, isn't it?"

"Well, I'm home right now – don't have a clue. But when I go on duty at 18:00 I'll check with the crew coming off and let you know this evening. How does that work for you?"

"Sure, that'll work fine. We'll be back onshore by then – staying at Norm's place the next two nights – then heading back to the North Shore after a little more fishing on Sunday morning. Yeah, OK then, we'll chat later. Thanks pal. *Jus' Restin'* standing by."

Rod had a good feeling as he closed up the phone and hung it on the dash. He was proud of Eric being in the service of his country. He only wished his father, Eric's grandfather, could see him; he'd be very proud of his grandson.

The coordinates for Crab Ledge, 41° 41'.000 N latitude by 69° 47'.000 W longitude, were punched into the GPS and a new course came up on the screen. "Five miles to go! Start looking for whales, birds, and boats," commanded the captain.

It wasn't long until Ray's eagle eye was locked on. "Steam! Starboard bow!" he yelled out, pointing to a plume rising into the air from the calm surface a half-mile ahead. "Humpbacks! Look at their tails when they dive! Wow!"

This was the first time Ray and Paul were in the presence of the majestic humpback. The closer they got, the clearer it became that they were approaching a large group of feeding whales. Maybe twenty or more, spread out over a vast area. Geysers of steam and upright tails could be seen all about to the east.

The radar showed several boats fishing within a mile of their location, mixed in with the whales. Yet another group of boats was about three miles to the east. It was time to start watching the sounder and look for the telltale arches of tuna. So far the screen was relatively clear, except for small groupings of bait up and down the water column. Rod slowed the boat and let the engine cool a bit, then shut it down and came out on deck to meet his smiling crew. They were all eager to start fishing. They would try drift-fishing these lively bluefish along the outskirts of the whales.

"Let's get a couple of these sucka's in the water," urged Koo Koo, ready to go.

"There's a special way to rig 'em. Watch this and pay attention," Rod replied. He took a six-inch needle from the rigging kit and put about three feet of nylon string, which resembled dental floss, through the eyelet.

"Let's get our first candidate out here," said Paul, pointing to the livewell. After some grabbing and thrashing, he had a twisting, eighteen-inch, five-pound bluefish ready for surgery.

"We're going to make a bridal type of loop through the top of his head," Rod explained as he pushed the needle just under the surface of the flesh on the top of the fish's head. The point of the needle exited two inches from where it entered, then Rod pulled the thread through until only six inches remained on the other side. He went back to the insertion point and repeated the process two more times. Cutting the nylon from the needle, he tied the loose ends together, then manipulated the threads until they were all equal. Finally, he made a little bridal sling that consisted of six equal loops of the nylon, which is where he attached the 11/0 circle hook with more nylon thread. "We don't want to actually put the hook into the bluefish itself; we want the total hook exposed. Now pass over the black magic marker."

Rod colored the white thread to hide its appearance. The hook was already black, so the bait was ready to go over the side and do its thing. The rig looked like the tail hook from a fighter jet that was snagging the cable on an aircraft carrier. It was a good setup.

"We'll set this one for 50 feet and let the next bluefish free swim," Rod went on to say. He took his scissors and trimmed the powerful tailfins just a touch, so that the bluefish couldn't swim with the power it normally possessed. He then lowered the bait into the water. "Trick of the trade. Shhh." They set up the first line with a sinker and a red balloon and let it out about 200 feet behind the boat.

The second fish was rigged the same way, minus the balloon. The blue, with a smaller sinker attached fifteen feet up, was free to swim on its own. Its natural instinct took over and it headed straight for the bottom, steadily taking line on free spool. After what Rod figured was 125 feet, Ray was given the signal and the drag on the reel was inched ahead just slightly, so that the bluefish couldn't pull any more line by its own power. If a big fish started to take the bait, it would be able to run with it without feeling any resistance until one of the guys slid the drag handle to the "strike" position. This would allow the circle hook to set itself.

"OK, lines are in the water – let's eat!" said Koo Koo. "How about those sandwiches, Mumbles, I'm starved!"

Rod and Paul got out the sodas and paper plates, and Ray got out a bag from the cuddy. "Ahhhh, we've got a small problem with the samiches," mumbled Ray, with a sheepish grin spreading across his face.

"What?" asked Koo Koo. "What do you mean a problem? Let me see that bag." He took the bag from Mumbles and pulled out two huge packages of sugar wafer sandwich cookies: one vanilla, one chocolate.

Mumbles spoke in a voice so slow and low, even for him, that it was hard to understand. "I didn't have time to make sandwiches, and the deli was closed so early in the morning. So that's what I got instead."

Koo Koo looked at Rod and then back at Mumbles. He shook his head and without skipping a beat, held up the chocolate package and hollered, "Who wants roast beef?" Then the vanilla, "or we've got turkey! The three basic food groups: sugar, lard and dough!"

Everyone laughed. What else could they do? Luckily, there was a small stash of cheese crackers and peanuts in the cuddy – all the makings of a well-balanced meal. As they enjoyed their noontime rations, Rod shared some of the secrets that he had gleaned from publications about the fine art of fishing tuna.

"Those bluefish are down there screaming! Sending out distress vibrations that predators are going to pick up on. They make for great bait. Plus, unlike fishing for stripers, slack water is primetime for tuna. That's just an hour away. So keep an eye on the lines, the whales, and watch to see if the other boats are having any luck. If a fish hits, you know your jobs. Let's get 'em!"

The current was slowing, evidenced by the chart plotter, which showed how little they'd moved in the last half hour.

"Hey, hey, hey, listen!" Mumbles was pointing at the reel with the bluefish down deep. "I just heard that reel click a couple of times."

They all moved closer to the reel and sure enough, the line started to tighten and play out with a few more clicks of the reel. Suddenly the line was flying.

"Let him go, let him suck it all in!" cheered Koo Koo, his eyes fixated on the reel. "Let's give him another minute and then set the hook. What do you think?"

Everyone nodded in agreement, sounded good to all. The reel continued to spool out slowly – click, click, click – and then another short burst.

"OK, Koo Koo, hit 'em!" yelled Rod as Koo Koo pushed the drag lever to strike position and reeled for all he was worth to set the hook. The rod doubled over and line began to fly off the reel, the tip of the rod bouncing under the pressure from the surging fish below.

"Fish on!" was the battle cry. Everyone cheered. The fish took line and Koo Koo gained it back. After a few minutes, Mumbles took over and tried his hand at subduing the monster. This went on for about twenty minutes until the line started to angle up to the surface and they were able to gain back most of what they'd lost. The fish was just under the shimmering surface, about 75 feet away.

Then came the first clear sign of what they had hooked. They could see the swept-back pointed tip of a tail breaking the surface, along with a pointed dorsal fin. Wait, this wasn't curved like a tuna's. What was on the other end of the line? A blue shark, and a big one at that.

"Blue dog!" shouted Rod. "First one of these I've caught, or even seen up close for that matter. Let's be careful here. We're not going to try to take him since he has no cash value. And there are lots of teeth so we need to be smart."

Rod wanted to be cautious because he knew little of how to release these fish. As the shark came alongside the boat, they saw the exposed hook that was caught in one of the gill plates on the left side of his head. It had to be a good ten feet in length, and its body was beautiful shades of blue: dark on the top, lighter on the sides. He reached over the side with his pliers, naively thinking he was going to get his hook back. With a violent thrash of its long body and tail, the shark swam away from the boat, taking line again and leaving Rod with plenty of water dripping from his face.

"What's Plan B?" asked Mumbles, as the guys laughed at Rod looking like a little kid caught with his hand in the cookie jar.

"Ahhh, let's just get him close this time and cut the line. He can keep the hook!" muttered Rod, standing on the deck.

In a couple of minutes the shark was alongside again, and this time Rod cut the line about three feet from his head. The creature slowly slipped away, back to the deep waters. The crew repaired the line and set out another bluefish, then sat back and waited for more action.

Koo Koo pointed out that they weren't on the edge of the whales anymore, but rather in the thick of them. There weren't many birds about either, so the whales had to be diving deeper for baitfish, then periodically surfacing for air. This was unlike the feeding habits Rod had witnessed many times in the past. Commonly referred to as "bubble-netting," this technique was perfected through evolution.

Typically, two or three whales hunt together for a large school of fish. Sand eels, a four-to-six-inch fish, is their main staple on Crab Ledge. The whales dive under the school, then swim around in a circle, letting air out through their blowholes. The air bubbles rise, creating a cylinder of expanding and breaking air bubbles; this frightens the baitfish into a ball – nature's safety in numbers – inside the rising wall of bubbles. When the bubbles and fish have almost reached the surface, the whales swim up rapidly from underneath with their mouths wide open. They rise as much as ten feet out of the water, their mouths now full of food. Then they close their lower jaw to squeeze the water out through the screen-like baleen of the upper jaw, and swallow their dinner.

The whales' imminent arrival is announced by hundreds of birds flying directly to and landing on the breaking bubbles. They wait for the whales to surface and then pick the fish right from their jaws!

This whole process is what attracts tuna. Once the bait is balled up, they're easy pickings for the sleek, fast tuna. The giants burst through the wall of bubbles with their mouths wide open, scooping large quantities of bait from the ball. There's enough for everyone, as Mother Nature provides for all.

"Balloon! Fish on! Fish on!" yelled Koo Koo, jumping out of his chair and tripping over a sputtering Mumbles. Both of them headed for the same rod.

"Ray, get the other line out of the water!" screamed Rod as he fired the engine. He came back out on deck to see Ray reeling as fast as he could, the bluefish bait skimming across the surface towards the stern.

Koo Koo was clearing the remaining "roast beef" and "turkey" sandwiches when they all stopped for a moment to look at the reel and the red balloon. The balloon was flying across the surface, and the line was going out at an unbelievable pace. Suddenly the balloon changed direction: it was now coming left to right across the stern.

"Hurry, Ray, reel!" barked Koo Koo.

Before Rod could get back to the helm, the line had changed position so much that it was now running across Mumble's shoulder, burning his skin and knocking him down to the deck. Koo Koo quickly climbed across the engine cover, unclipped the other reel from its cable, and pulled the rod and reel onto the deck – bringing the flopping bluefish with it.

As Mumbles cut the bait free, Rod spun the boat hard to starboard, bringing the line back out over the stern to the six o'clock position. The boat was left in neutral as the threesome stood at the stern and watched the balloon head for England. Little did they know they were on a Nantucket sleigh ride in reverse. Next came the most awe-inspiring sight any of them had ever seen.

"Mammal on!" whooped Mumbles, as a humpback whale breached and let out a high-pitched screech. Nearly its full body twisted in the air, then fell back into the water with a tremendous splash. Koo Koo pointed to the hook that was impaled on the gleaming white pectoral fin of this huge creature.

"Full drag, snap the line!" was the command, and Koo Koo pushed the drag fully forward. The reel went lock solid, and the line tightened then snapped with a bang. It had released at the weakest link. Koo Koo reeled the line back – the only items missing were the hook and the bait.

"Maybe we acted prematurely! What's the market price for blubber? Sure looked like a keepah to me!" laughed Mumbles, his arm bleeding from the line burn. "That whale had to be at least 30 tons and 40 feet long!"

"I wish that never happened," said Rod. "I don't think it's a good idea fishing this way. No more fishing deep with these creatures around. Let the other bluefish go." Rod was upset; these were docile creatures and he was disappointed that one of them had been hooked. "That whale must have swum into the line and gotten hooked as the bait went over its fin."

Rod just shook his head. He'd invaded the whale's domain and violated his existence. "Hey, let's forget it for today." Rod glanced at his watch and looked to the west. "It's almost three o'clock now. Let's head for Stage Harbor and get our slip for the night. Then we can meet up with my cousin."

The boys started to square everything away as *Jus' Restin'* came to life, her bow pointing west and heading for the entrance to the Southway. This channel, which was between Nauset South Beach and Monomoy Island, was similar to Plum Island Sound. A half hour later, they passed the alpha buoy marking the entrance to the channel.

When they entered the channel, the charts became useless because the channel changes constantly with the shifting sands. They came upon a clammer getting into his boat, ready to bring the famous Chatham clams to fish buyers. (Rod was sure Willy would take exception to the word "famous" in comparison to his Ipswich clams.) He hailed the clammer and asked for directions to Stage Harbor; the man motioned for them to follow and off they went, weaving a zigzag course for twenty minutes around at least 40 buoys. The attendant on duty at the dock, a smiling Jamaican named Shrimpy, informed them that there were no slips available but that they were welcome to tie up at the gas dock for their two nights in town.

"Norm, we're here at the marina. Whazz up?" asked Rod, using his cell phone while Koo Koo and Mumbles secured the boat and surveyed the new scenery.

"I'm just getting out of work. Going to stop by Goose Hummock's and get the latest scoop and a couple extra lures. Grab your overnight bags and take a cab to the Squire in downtown. I'll meet you there in one hour. See ya then."

One of the patrons at the marina offered to give the boys a ride downtown. They accepted and piled into an old pickup truck. None of them had been to Chatham before, and they were quite impressed with the quaint little village. There were many shops and restaurants, but only one major watering hole.

They went through its front door and took the big round corner table at the entrance by the window, allowing them a clear view onto Main Street. Anyone going in or out the front door had to pass by them – the perfect seat for fun and games. The weekend crowd was starting to arrive and the joint was cranking up; the aroma of seafood, steaks, and ale permeated the festive atmosphere.

Norm came in and joined the table just as everyone decided to stay put, have dinner, and enjoy the local color. The food was top shelf and you couldn't beat the frozen mugs of beer. Koo Koo was busy bantering with the locals. Rod's phone began to buzz, so he escaped to a bench on the sidewalk in front of the Squire. It was his nephew Eric.

"Hey! What's the latest? Any Intel from the last crew?" asked Rod.

"Sure. Seems they spotted numerous schools of footballs busting the waves about fifteen miles out. They said it was right along a rip line. Nothing really big, but a lot of action. Not too many boats either." He gave Rod the coordinates and they chatted a few more minutes.

"I've got a question for you: if I ever need your services when I'm back on the North Shore, how long would it take for you get to me?"

"Well, it depends on a couple of things. First, are we on the ground or airborne at the time we receive the distress call? And secondly, how far offshore are you when you make the call?" Eric did some quick calculations in his head. "Time is everything. Typically, if we are on the hard deck, we're going to need 30 to 45 minutes to be on the scene for the Cape Ann area. Why do you ask?"

"No particular reason – just a comfort thing, that's all."

"What you need to remember is this: if you think you're going to need us, don't wait to call. Hey, it's what I live for!" Eric was serious. "If we're out there tomorrow, I'll look for your boat. Do you still have the dive flag on the engine cover?"

"Still there." The boys were banging on the window for Rod to come back inside. "All righty then, we'll try your numbers and report back tomorrow. Thanks, pal. Keep up the good work – we're proud of you! We'll be looking for you overhead."

Back inside, the party was in full swing. Mumbles was beginning to show symptoms of an acute case of mumble-osis, and Koo Koo and Norm were trying to outdo each other telling jokes to the women at the next table. When Rod came back in and sat down, Norm pointed towards the two guys at the far end of the bar.

"Hey Rod, you want to have some fun? You're an old Elvis fan. Start singing something from the King and watch what happens. Those dudes just love Elvis."

Sure, he'd love too. His beer-balls were in full swing! But what would he sing? Then it hit him. This would do it. He stood up, cleared his throat, dropped down a couple of octaves, and gave his best Elvis impersonation of *It's Now or Never*...which wasn't all *that* bad.

It was as though somebody had just pushed their start buttons. One of them grabbed a beer bottle like it was microphone and continued the song, never skipping a beat; the other singing back-up harmony.

The Elvis Brothers continued and the whole bar section joined in, belting out their best impersonations of The King. Everyone was having a great time. This was the place to be on a Friday night in Chatham. The party went on until near midnight when Norm finally managed to herd the boys into his truck and back to his place.

The next morning came way too fast. After a hearty breakfast of donuts and aspirin, the foursome pulled away from the gas dock and headed out for a new adventure chasing tuna. It was nearly the crack-of-noon. Once they cleared the Southway and were heading to the open ocean, Rod plugged in the numbers Eric had given him the evening before.

"Looks like about six miles past yesterday's position. Let's check it out." said Rod. He adjusted the throttle and trim, checked the radar, and signaled to Norm. "Norm, take the helm while we rig the green machines."

Norm followed the course on the GPS, while the others rigged the rods. The green machines were new lures, and everyone was excited to see if they would be the key to getting some tuna on board. The lures consist of two parts. The first is the "bird": a yellow wooden football-shaped device with two four-inch wings. About eight feet behind the bird is a long green plastic lure, similar to the plastic squid, but longer and narrower and with red beads leading to the stinger. It looked like it would work, but the proof would be when it hit the water. The bird acts just like a bird in a backyard birdbath, splashing and making all kinds of action. The plastic lure runs just under the surface, silently pursuing the bird.

After a half-hour ride, they were on location. The tide was running full and the rip was easy to identify. The Cape is famous for "fishing the rips," and this promised to be a good spot. They let the lines out about 100 yards behind the boat and the birds went to work. It wasn't fifteen minutes before the first tuna hit, crashing the lure and fighting for its freedom. It was a football, easily subdued after ten minutes. These rods were really meant for the giants, but you never could tell what was going to hit so you had to be ready to the max.

The tuna weighed 55 pounds and just over 48 inches: a keeper, but nowhere near big enough to sell. It was put on the tail rope, and a knife cut to one of the main lateral arteries ensured that the fish was properly bled. A second tuna was caught within the hour, a fine 90-pounder. Even on the big reel these fish were formidable when they got near the boat. The day continued like this, but the rest of the fish were released since there's a two-fish limit per day.

The biggest laugh of the day came at lunchtime, when Norm came out with his sandwiches. Mumbles was looking on and had to ask what kind he had brought.

"Ham – does everybody like ham?"

"Oooh, strawberry!" snickered Koo Koo, thinking a pink bag of cookies was on the menu. They all had another laugh at Mumbles' expense.

They were back on the dock just in time to put in 50 gallons of fuel before the marina closed. Even though he didn't need the gas, Rod liked having plenty this far from home. They went to Norm's house to fillet and ice their catch. Cold beer and fresh bluefin on the grill – it didn't get any better. It took a couple of hours to complete the process, but when they were done there had to be over 60 pounds of bluefin in the cooler, all iced and ready for the trip home.

The next morning Norm gave the guys a ride to the marina, and they were off for the final leg of their weekend excursion. The plan was to try the BC buoy, a spot about ten miles farther. Then around noontime they would turn NNW, set the GPS for Gloucester, and head for home. This morning the whales were everywhere, more than the first day, along with huge flocks of seabirds working the bait balls. Nature at its finest. There was one other unexpected addition here: boats. Lots of them.

They decided to set out the green machines and fish the outskirts of the action. This went on for a couple of hours, adding a nice 65-pounder to the fish box. Nobody else was catching anything as far as they could tell, except the whales, which were putting on a tremendous show for the spectators.

Rod asked Koo Koo to take the helm as he grabbed his camera to take pictures of the feeding whales. He climbed alongside the pilothouse next to the starboard window and snapped several quick shots of a whale surfacing about 75 feet away. Koo Koo was getting nervous and looked to Rod for guidance on where to steer the boat.

"Just go where you like. But if you see birds flying towards a particular spot, acting like a whale is coming up, steer away."

Koo Koo nodded and they continued the troll doing six knots. The captain finally had a chance to relax, a rare occurrence because he was usually at the helm overseeing the activities of the boat.

Suddenly, and without warning, the boat slammed to a stop. All forward motion ceased. It happened so fast that Koo Koo fell out of the helm chair and onto the deck of the pilot-house. He hung onto the helm wheel. "What did we hit?" he yelled. "I don't want to drive anymore!"

Rod had been holding the roof grab-rail, looking back towards Mumbles in the stern and watching the lures do their work, when he went flying forward. His right hand released the rail and his right knee buckled when it was hit by...*something*. He swung wildly to starboard as the boat yawed to port. He looked to his right and saw a huge black mass moving past his right leg, crushing down the starboard bow rails against the forward deck. Rod's momentum started to swing him over the side. His right arm flailed wildly towards the water while his left hand held onto the roof rail as tightly as possible. His eyes finally caught up to the location of his right hand: it was a mere six inches away from the wide-open eye of a humpback whale.

The whale had surfaced while feeding, and its wide-open mouth collided with the *Jus' Restin'*. The entire starboard bow was in its mouth! The whale's tail pumped with forward momentum and pushed the boat sideways to port, making it heel over to starboard.

"We're gonna take water!" yelled Mumbles (who was not mumbling anymore!), "it's gonna come in!"

The boat was heeling a good 25 degrees to starboard. The whale held the boat in that position, pushing it sideways for what seemed an eternity. Then suddenly it opened its mouth and slid backwards into the water, releasing *Jus' Restin'* from its jaws. The boat snapped wildly back to port, nearly ejecting Rod over the bow.

"Neutral!" yelled Rod, as he watched the whale sink under the surface. He went down to the cockpit and found Mumbles back to full mumble mode, talking to himself and scared half to death. Koo Koo was back on his feet and had the boat in neutral as ordered. A calm of disbelief fell over the crew.

"Aargh, Queequeg, prepare Captain Ahab a coffin!" Rod laughingly yelled at Mumbles as Koo Koo joined the two at the engine cover.

"Nobody is ever going to believe this!" offered Koo Koo, shaking his head.

"Oh yeah? Well, look at the rails!" added Mumbles, pointing to the bow.

About six feet of the starboard rail was twisted like a pretzel, pushed flat to the fiberglass deck. It was covered with baleen, a hair-like material from the whale's mouth, and a few streaks of bright red blood. They all stood there trying to fathom what had just happened.

"Reel 'em up! We're gonna fix those rails. We're outta here while we're still afloat!" ordered Rod, half joking, half serious. "They say things happen in threes, and that's number two!"

He didn't have to tell the crew twice: the lines came in FAST. Rod inspected the bow rails. Mumbles was an exceptionally strong guy, and with some direction and a little help from Koo Koo, they got them back into reasonable shape. It took about twenty minutes of pushing, pulling, and prodding, but when it was all over they didn't look bad at all.

"OK boys, I think it's time to head for home." Rod went back into the pilothouse, pushed the throttle forward, and *Jus' Restin'* came about and left Crab Ledge behind in her wake. There was a southwesterly breeze to meet them when they left the protection of the National Seashore, but it only made for a following sea off their port quarter. No problem. After a couple of hours, the "Eyes of Ann," the twin lighthouses of Thacher Island off Gloucester, could be seen in the distance.

Rod switched the radar to the six-mile range and sure enough, there was the target he hoped he would see. When he got within two miles, his suspicions were confirmed: the *Atlantic Zephyr* lay dead ahead. He picked up his cell phone and scanned his list of contacts...time to call Pierre. He waited for an answer, not sure it would come.

"Bonjour, this is Suzanne," replied the soft voice.

"This is Captain Rod, and how are you today?"

"I am just fine. What a surprise! To what do I owe the honor of your call?"

"I'm trying to return a favor. Are you on board your ship today?"

"Yes, we are here, east of Thacher Island. Are you on the water as well?"

"Yes, about two miles off your stern. If you can come to the rail and drop a line, I have a special treat for you. Can you get away for a moment?"

"Certainly, I'll be on the platform at the bottom of the stairway, starboard mid-ship."

"OK, I'll see you shortly." He hung up and called Mumbles to the helm. "Steer towards that ship – I have a couple things to do."

Mumbles took over the helm as Rod got the five-gallon bucket, covered the bottom with ice, and put two big bags of bluefin fillets on top. Next, he went into the cuddy and rooted around the storage container until he found what he was looking for: a nice sweet wine, a half-bottle of Chateau d' Yquem, that the G-man had brought as a gift. He placed the bottle into the bucket and covered the fillets and wine with more ice, leaving the upper half of the wine bottle exposed. *Perfect,* he thought.

Rod took over the helm while the boys wondered what this big ship was all about. As they approached the *Atlantic Zephyr,* Rod could see Ahmed standing on the stern waving hello. Suzanne was coming down the stairway to the platform, a few feet above the waterline.

"Koo Koo, get in the port corner and hold us off. Ray, take a position right behind the davit. We don't want to be bashing against the landing platform." Rod looked around to make sure there were no other boats or hazards, then brought *Jus' Restin'* slowly up to the platform and the waiting Suzanne. She looked marvelous as usual, wearing the khaki uniform of the ship's company. She was obviously on duty.

"Ahoy! I won't keep you long, but I hope this will bring a smile to you and the crew. There should be plenty." Rod tipped the bucket for Suzanne to get a peek at the contents. "Bluefin tuna fillets, with a nice ice wine. Bon appetit!" said Rod as he passed the bucket to Suzanne.

"Merci beaucoup!" She pushed the ice aside, exposing the deep reddish-purple tuna steaks. "This will be *delicious*! And, oh, I have good news for you: we have been marking the tuna you have been searching for on our side-scan sonar. Just a few so far, but they keep coming, most everyday. They are gone now, but I can let you know when they reappear, if you like." She smiled, knowing this was news the captain could use.

"That would make my day, for sure! Please do so. We lost a giant last week, just a few miles northwest of here, but recovered a little with these schoolies from the Cape. Any assistance would be greatly appreciated!"

"Then I shall call you – soon I hope," she said with a sly smile, turning and climbing up the stairway. She met Ahmed at the top of the stairs and they both waved as Mumbles and Koo Koo pushed away from the platform.

Koo Koo flew into the pilothouse, and pressed Rod for information about Suzanne. Rod would hear nothing of it and just started humming the words to an old Ricky Nelson song, one of his favorites as a kid, "Travelin' Man".

"Koo Koo, take her to the slip! Mumbles, hoist the tuna flag!"

It was the perfect ending to the weekend. Rod reached down through the ice, grabbed the last ice-cold beer and sat in a deck chair in the cockpit. He felt the wind in his hair and the warm air from land as they made their way across Ipswich Bay, heading for the serenity and security of Plum Island Sound. Rod felt all was right with the world, and it was.

Chapter Ten

Lobzilla

𝕴t was another typical Sunday afternoon at Harborside. The *Jus' Restin'* made her way under the old bridge and past the outskirts of Bourbon Street, spinning around on the current and backing into her slip. The Golden Cleaters were on active standby, but their assistance would not be required today. Mumbles and Koo Koo went over the side and made the lines fast as the engine was shut down.

Rod just stood at the helm feeling relieved. "You *always* bring me home – you're a good boat!" he whispered under his breath, tapping the stainless helm wheel with his fingertips.

People notice things at the marina, and having a tuna flag on the starboard outrigger was as good as ringing a dinner bell. People started showing up at the slip to see what had been harvested from the sea that day. After Mumbles put the tuna gear on the dock, Koo Koo started with the wash-down. With the cockpit void of extra gear, Rod pulled the bluefin out of the fish box and placed it on the top for all to see. Rod overheard someone say that it was just a baby, which took away a little of the moment. But the guy was right: it was a juvenile, but legal and would eat just as well.

Before cutting up the tuna, the threesome took a few moments to check out this speedster from the ocean. A marine engineer could not have designed a sleeker, faster predator. The pectoral fins are attached as if they're on hinges: they fold back into recesses along the body in order to minimize resistance. The dorsal fin folds down like a handheld Japanese fan into a slot, similar to the slots for car windows.

What really amazed these fishermen were the tuna's eyes. Their delicate clarity is such a contrast to the thick, tough, armor-like skin that covers a tuna's body. The eyes are right behind the hard flesh, independent and yet protected from injury during high-speed runs. This fish, when putting on a burst of speed, folds in all extremities and with rapid pulses of its tail, it zooms through the water like a torpedo. Even faster. It was readily apparent how this creature, at full size, attains speeds in excess of 50 mph.

Archie appeared through the small crowd of onlookers. He was a bearer of good news. "Hey Cap, don't forget. Labor Day's next weekend. The Middle Ground Open. Tee time is 09:00. Be there, and no excuses this year!"

"Well, you're right, I've missed it in the past – always too busy. But no way, not this year! I'll have the whole family there for the summer's grand finale. It should be a lot of fun." Rod reached into the fish box and took out four thick fillets. "Hey, here you go: a little something for your grill. This might make up for some of the chow you've been feeding me over the years." After seeing all the hungry faces around him, he went and got more. "And here's a few more for anybody who wants to join you on the grill!"

"I'll have Edith there, ah, whip these babies right up! Thanks Cappy!" Archie said. The crowd followed Archie back to Bourbon Street where the afternoon party was about to kick into high gear.

Rod spent the rest of the afternoon cleaning the boat, stowing the gear, and kicking back and reflecting on the weekend. With a long set of Mark Knopfler's music in the background, time went by nice and easy. Before long, Koo Koo and Mumbles were heading home; everyone else had also hit the road. Rod found himself alone with his thoughts, the weekend becoming just a memory.

He couldn't stop thinking about his whale encounters. He could understand the reason for the first one – it was simply his fault. What was he thinking, having bait running that deep with those huge creatures cruising and feeding? The span of their pectoral fins, which had to be close to 30 feet from tip to tip, made them likely victims of that style of fishing. Plus, it was bound to have happened with that many whales in the water.

But the second meeting, now that was different. Was it just a case of the law of physics taking over when two bodies try to occupy the same space at the same time? Or was the whale sending him a message? Did she have a calf with her, making her feel threatened? Rod chewed on the possibilities, but resigned himself to deciding that it was a chance meeting that fortunately didn't lead to disaster. With the 406 EPIRB and the survival gear inside the pilothouse, their hopes would have been pinned on the raft riding the overhead, or on another vessel if one had noticed their plight. It was a very, very close call.

Monday morning was overcast with a cool light drizzle. No fishing charter today, so there was time to relax and perform shore duties. After the two-wheeled cart was retrieved and the cooler was placed on its pedestal, Rod made some stops throughout the marina to repay outstanding debts and to gain some bonus points by sharing his good fortune.

First on his list was Chet, who was sitting on the front porch of the bathhouse. Chet had shared many secrets for fishing these waters, and Rod always made sure to take care of him. Next were the mechanical bays. He wanted to spread cheer to the crew that supported *Jus' Restin'* with quick turnaround times whenever problems arose. These guys were a great bunch, with a work ethic to match.

Lastly, a trip to the bait freezer. This would build a reserve supply for future events, such as the upcoming weekend. Charters had caused Rod to miss the Middle Ground Open in the past, but for some reason the books were clear this holiday weekend. If anybody called, he would tell them the truth: the boat had the weekend off for family time. Rod preferred telling the truth since down the road he wouldn't have to remember what he had said. It was a lesson his father taught him and he learned it well.

Ah, the Middle Ground Open. *This is going to be fun,* thought Rod as he headed down the road towards Newburyport and Captain Jack's Grille. The Middle Ground Open is the finale of summer activities for the boaters of Harborside Marina, a beach party on an island in the center of Plum Island Sound. It was great fun. The centerpiece was a miniature golf match that depended on the tide. Luckily it was going to cooperate this year.

High water would be around 08:00 on Saturday, so the course designer (who happened to be the captain of the *Happy Times*) would lay out the course as soon as the tide began to ebb. Authentic cups and flags, procured from golf courses over the years, would be set out with the eighteenth hole back at the center of the festivities. This course had hazards not normally seen on a golf course, and they changed every year. One infamous hole had ripples of sand that were six inches deep, a foot apart, and spread across 25 feet! It was like an old-time washboard. Natural water traps were everywhere, too, and the difficulty of the course always depended on the creativity of the designer – the guy with a Hawaiian shirt, straw hat, and a grounds crew with coolers in tow.

There were rules: one club and one ball. Other than that, the rules of miniature golf applied. The course ran clockwise around the grassy center of the island, culminating at the beach party. Here, family and friends would gather with grills smoking and music playing, kids fishing for anything that would bite, and teenagers digging steamers for the boiling pots. It promised to be memorable, and Rod was looking forward to some over-due family time with his three girls.

The rain had stopped by the time the truck pulled up to Captain Jack's Grille. It was still early: Cari, G, and the rest of the staff were just getting the tables ready for the lunchtime crowd.

"Hey G-man, do these look at all familiar?" Rod opened the cooler and pushed the ice aside, exposing the tuna fillets just as Jack came out from the kitchen. Everyone eyeballed the deep red fillets – they knew they were going to be a big hit on the evening menu. It was a good thing Rod had separated what he wanted to take home, because Jack immediately spirited the tuna off to the kitchen for safekeeping.

"Hey Dad, glad to see you got lucky," said a happy voice with a big hug attached.

"You have no idea how lucky!" he said with a sly smile. "Oh, before I forget." Rod reached in his rear pocket and pro-duced the folded flyer that announced the Middle Ground Open. "This Saturday is the big shindig at the marina. I'd like the whole family to go if that's possible. You can even invite G if you want." Rod winked at his daughter. G was a good guy and had received Rod's initial approval.

"We both have to work the evening shift, but we'll party until the last moment. You can bet on that!"

"And tell G to bring a golf club and ball, preferably a 7-iron. There will be a golf tournament and he's my partner." After a frosty Fisherman's Brew, strictly a quality check, Rod was on his way home.

The next two days were spent mowing the lawn and knocking multiple items off the honey-do list. Amy had just arrived from Wyoming, with all kinds of tales to tell about her life on the ranch. Rod missed having his Little Buddy around to fish and ride the motorcycle with him. Lilly was working the final strokes of a long stretch of evening shifts until Friday, when her vacation would begin. All appeared well on the home front.

On Thursday morning Rod and Kasey returned to the boat. They had a charter for three couples from the nuclear power plant in Vermont where Rod had worked over the years. It would turn out to be one of his best charters ever. They arrived right on time, six of the most outgoing, positive, fun-loving people to have come aboard. There were only a few requests for the captain: they just wanted to do a little bit of fishing, see some whales, then spend the rest of the time eating, drinking, and steaming around Cape Ann enjoying the sights.

No problem. This would be a dream charter without any pressure. Rod was asked to handle the food, so he went to a local market that had the finest marinated chicken & steak tips. He also bought Gulf of Maine shrimp accented with a Cajun dipping sauce that was going to make their foreheads sweat.

Rod figured his Lighthouse Tour – circumnavigate Cape Ann, with an afternoon picnic at Wingaersheek Beach on the Annisquam River – would fit the bill. The day went by flawlessly for captain and crew. The ocean was calm as they enjoyed the first lighthouse, a relatively small light on tiny Straitsmouth Island just outside Rockport Harbor. There was a slight sea swell on that morning, which made for breaking waves on the rocky shore. This gave the photographers onboard a chance to capture some classic New England seacoast scenery.

Next was a super fishing stop tucked into a cove directly under the watchful eye of Thacher Island's southern lighthouse. There are two identical lighthouses on this island called the "Eyes of Ann," which protect Cape Ann. Rod anchored and let *Jus' Restin'* drift back until her stern was a hundred feet from the rocks where the striped bass are known to hang out. Rod knew the cove well since it was one of his diving secrets. A few years before, he had taken a lobster there that he dubbed "Lobzilla." Even without its crusher claw it still weighed over nine pounds.

This site also held the record for the all-time funniest mishap aboard *Jus' Restin'*. It happened on the day Lobzilla was caught. Mumbles was on board that day and using the head while Rod prepped the boat for the imminent return of three submerged divers still trying their best to catch lobsters. Rod threw the life ring over the stern with the safety line attached, since there was a pretty good current pushing into the cove.

Bubbles were breaking in a tight group – it looked as if whales were about to feed – when the divers surfaced about 100 feet behind the boat.

At that moment Rod heard Mumbles pumping hard on the head pump handle. He was horrified...he realized he hadn't changed the tank valve position from the last offshore trip. Mumbles was pumping directly into the sea! A macerated plume of Mumbles and two-ply was now just below the surface, drifting directly towards the divers.

"Mumbles! Quick! Fill the five-gallon bucket from the starboard side!" Mumbles was never one to move very fast and always wanted to know why.

"Just do it!" Rod whisper yelled through his teeth.

Rod got the divers' attention by holding up Lobzilla. He didn't want any of them to put their masks in the water and peer down, only to discover the sewage that was attaching itself to their dive gear. As each diver climbed the ladder, Mumbles hit each of them with a bucket of clean seawater; Rod claimed he was rinsing off the "seaweed" that was clinging to them. It was hysterical, and they never did find out what had happened!

Rod was still reminiscing when his charter folks hooked up with some stripers. Before long, there were a couple of keepah's in the cooler. Everyone was satisfied that the fishing requirements had been completed, so it was time to get to the eating and drinking phase of the tour.

Eastern Point Light, a USCG station with a long rock jetty reaching out to mark and protect the entrance to Gloucester Harbor, was the next stop. Many people were spread out over the rocks fishing for flounder and stripers. Behind the jetty, sailboats hung lightly to their moorings and enjoyed the protection of the sea wall and calm winds. *Jus' Restin'* rounded the jetty point and steamed past Ten Pound Island Light and into the old seaport of Gloucester. Here they would cruise and "sight-sea" the waterfront. In view were the timeless fishing fleets, the fish processing facilities, and the harbor's many working docks. The tour finished with a very special monument: the Gloucester Fisherman's Memorial, an eight-foot bronze statue of a fisherman at the helm of his ship, braced for the wind and stormy weather. Inscribed are the names of fishermen who never returned to Gloucester, lost forever to the sea.

Rod picked up the radio and called the operator of the Blyman Bridge, a drawbridge that would lead them to their afternoon picnic on the Annisquam River. While they waited for the bridge to open, one of the guys noticed a strange pole near the beach. It looked like a horizontal utility pole, about fifteen feet above the water. Rod explained that it was a greased pole, part of the summer festival. Contestants were supposed to try to get to the end – walking, sliding, or however – without falling in. Very few succeeded.

After a twenty-minute ride through the picturesque Annisquam River, they arrived at the mouth at its northern entrance just in time for lunch. The ladies had stopped at the dollar store before leaving home to purchase pirate hats, scarves, and brightly-colored sunglasses. While the crew went exploring, Rod cooked and got everything ready. When the crew returned, the wine flowed, the music rolled on, and everyone thoroughly enjoyed themselves. It was a fun-filled day – those folks knew how to party.

After a short cruise back to Harborside, the day came to a close and the ladies broke out the crème de la crème: "Better than Sex" chocolate cake, which they all enjoyed on the porch of the boathouse as the sun set over the backwaters of the Parker River.

Two days later, after a lazy day off, it was time for Labor Day weekend. The family showed up at the marina at 08:00, loaded the food, drinks, and extra chairs on board. They then left the marina and sailed off to secure a good anchorage by the nineteenth hole. The greenhead flies were gone now, their carnage just a memory. A site next to the grassy center of the island was selected; blankets and chairs were put in place to mark party central for *Jus' Restin'*. The tuna flag was flown on the end of the harpoon, a signal for what would be shared with those who wanted to enjoy some bluefin.

The day was spent shaking hands and telling stories, eating and drinking the best the area had to offer, and celebrating the traditional end of summer in New England. But everyone knew the best weather of the year was still coming: Indian Summer, when New England becomes a Shangri-La.

In the early afternoon, with the temperature in the high eighties, a cell phone started ringing. Everyone instinctively went for their hip. Rod laughed, thinking they all would have made great gunfighters in the Wild West.

"Dad, it's for you. The ID says it's someone named Pierre. Should I take it?" asked Amy, holding out the cell phone in one hand and throwing a long blast of the Frisbee for Kasey with the other.

"No, no, that's OK, I'll get it. Toss it here." Rod could hear the submarine's dive claxtons going off in his head. DIVE! DIVE!

"Bonjour Rod, am I interrupting you?" asked the soft sexy voice from the other end of the airways.

"No, no. Not at all. It's great to hear from you. What can I do for you today?" he asked as he walked away from the crowd, his mind drifting off to thoughts meant only for deep water.

"First, on behalf of the crew and myself, I would like to thank you for the wonderful tuna and that lovely bottle of ice wine. They went very well together, although I have to admit – I didn't share the wine. I enjoyed that special gift from you all by myself." There was a moment of silence before she continued. "But I have news for you! We have completed our survey of this section of the chart, and are presently under way towards our final area, which is northeast of Eastern Point. But here is the real news..." The pitch of her voice began to rise. "I have been spotting bluefin tuna! Very, very large fish along a thermal gradient, just about eight miles off-shore. I have the coordinates if you would like them."

"You can bet I would!" he said, his heart and adrenalin pumping. This could be it! The break he'd been looking for! "Were there any other boats in the area when you saw the fish?"

"Negative. No boats in the area."

This was the answer Rod wanted to hear. He found paper and pencil, and Suzanne repeated the coordinates to make sure he'd gotten it right. He had.

"I can't thank you enough. We're going to go get 'em! As soon as I can put a crew together, we'll be out there. Thank you so much, you've made a great day even better!"

"Well, good luck Captain Rod. Catch a big one!"

With that, she was gone – again. Rod's mind was spinning. *Big tuna offshore and nobody knows they're there but me! Gotta get a crew together, fast! Gotta get bait! Check the weather, check the tides! Oh, baby, it's tuna time!*

Rod looked at his family. They were all having a great time. Behind them, *Jus' Restin'* swung on her anchor...twisting slightly against the wind...pacing and pulling on the anchor, as though she was calling to him. She'd overheard the conversation and was eager to head out and hunt tuna.

Chapter Eleven

Hump 109

"**G!**Come here – we have to talk!" said Rod, eager to put a plan together. He filled G in on the latest intelligence and asked if he could break away. G said he had to work that night, but that he'd get out to the boat as soon as he was off. That would work. Next, Rod called Bob Dude to see if he was available. Sarah answered the phone and once Bob was briefed on the details, he was ready; he wouldn't miss this for the life of him!

The only person who wasn't too thrilled with the plan was Lilly. She'd just started her vacation and now Rod was fishing with the boys. But she said one of the girls at work was looking for someone to swap a weekend shift with, so she would just start her vacation a couple of days later and make it up on the other end. She wasn't happy with the turn of events – her husband was putting the boat first again – but with finances the way they were it was a logical decision. She reluctantly OK'd the plan.

Rod called the bait dealer for an iced tote of mackerel to be left on the loading dock. The shop would be closing shortly, but Rod said he'd leave the cash in the coffee can in the freezer. Cari and G had to be at the Grille by 4 PM, so he shuttled them back to the marina, along with a few others who had to go home early. He and Amy picked up the bait, loaded it in the boat, and headed back to Middle Ground to enjoy the rest of the day's activities.

The Golden Cleaters were on full alert because many boats, including the *Jus' Restin'*, were backing into their slips at the same time. The boys were busy, intoxicated with their responsibility, and earning extra hazardous-duty pay.

Rod lay awake most of the night thinking about the next day. This time there would be no mistakes. Fog started rolling in around midnight. He was listening to the marine forecast calling for heavy fog, with a visibility of one mile or less. Cold fronts approaching from the west were due to arrive mid-day to late afternoon. With temps in the eighties, thunderstorms were predicted as the fronts moved through the area, bringing with them high pressure and fair weather. They would have to hit 'em early and get off the water in case it got rough.

He could hear the rumble of Big Bob's Harley coming down 1A as Gerald pulled into the parking lot. It was just after 04:30. No time pressure to leave, especially with this fog and darkness; besides, the sun wasn't rising until 06:10. They prepared the boat and brought on 60 pounds of ice. G headed out for coffee while they waited for daybreak.

Soon enough, Rod gave the command to cast off the lines and *Jus' Restin'* cleared the slip at 05:30. The faint glow of Chet's cigarette could be seen as they made their way past *Checkers*. Rod waved to Chet, who returned the gesture, his figure backlit by the dim cabin lights. He called up the newest waypoint, numbers given by Suzanne the day before: 70° 21' N by 42° 41' W. The GPS indicated eighteen miles from the #2 buoy coming out of Plum Island Sound. It was a straight shot across Ipswich Bay, off Halibut Point, and around the backside of the Salvages Islands. The fog was so thick, there might as well have been a blanket over the windshield; this indeed would be an instrument ride.

Rod pulled up the chart from the cuddy and plotted the numbers. To his surprise, the spot was just a tad southeast of the 180' line – only a little farther down the line! His hopes went to the limit. Tuna seemed to love this depth. The sounder showed some bluefish, and in a matter of minutes, four of them were caught and put in the livewell. Fishing live bluefish, with a chum slick of mackerel, was going to be the winning combination – they were sure of it.

Rod, G, and Bob Dude were in the pilothouse going over the game plan as they slowly approached the fishing spot. "Same responsibilities as last time," said Rod. "We need to be on the lookout for any change in water temp, maybe a debris slick on top, a rip line. The fish should be in this area. We've just got to find them."

Bob grabbed the paper towels and wiped the heavy moisture from the inside of the windshield as Rod continued.

"The fog is really heavy, but the radar isn't showing any boats in our vicinity. I'll keep it on the three-mile range and monitor it closely, and set our fog signal on auto if anyone comes within range. It's aggravating hearing that blast every two minutes, but it's necessary." Rod took a long look at his watch and did a few mental calculations. "It's 07:00 now. Slack tide is in two hours – primetime, just like before." He gave the crew two thumbs up. Bob and G were ready as Rod laid out the activities. "We'll get the bluefish rigged with nylon. G, I think you know how to do that. Then we'll try looking. If we don't find them we'll start chunking."

The boys nodded in agreement and the plan was set. Bob and G rigged the bluefish while Rod zeroed in on the coordinates. After the fish were rigged, they were put back into the livewell, ready to go.

"Hey, what was that sound?" asked Bob, cupping his hands to his ears while peering into the fog. "I heard a whistling sound, but I can't see a thing."

Rod shut down the engine and came out on the deck. He turned his head slowly from side to side trying to locate the sound, staring out over the stern. After a moment he just shook his head in disbelief as he headed back into the pilothouse muttering, "Whales...here we go again."

Everyone nervously went about their business, going over and over all the details, checking equipment, waiting for the action to start. It wouldn't be long.

"Bob, G! Quick! Look at the sounder! Red arches! Right under us, 90 feet down! Set out the bait, one for that depth and one on free swim. Starrrrrrrrrrrrrt chunking! Let's bring 'em in and keep 'em close!"

Big Bob and G hustled about their duties; they had both rods in the water in no time at all. Rod cleared the decks and prepared the harpoon, tail rope, and gaffe. A glance at the radar indicated the surface was still clear of boats. But a scan of the instruments told him something wasn't right. The engine temperature gauge was reading 195 degrees, which is 25 degrees above normal. Rod didn't have a chance to figure it out before pandemonium broke out.

"Fish on! Fish on!" cried out G, the 90-footer peeling line at a breakneck pace.

"G, stay on the reel. Bob, pull the other line in and put the bluefish back in the livewell." Rod looked around the deck and saw that everything was ready. "OK, OK, take your time now, steady as we go."

Rod was calling for caution, but everyone was excited. He needed to check out the engine while the fish was fresh and taking line. He shut down the motor and buzzed the props to the full up position. Leaning over the stern he saw that the water intake holes were clear, so he set the drive back into the sea. Next he went to the toolbox for a 9/16-combination wrench and lifted the engine cover. In less than fifteen seconds the top plate was removed from the heat exchanger.

It was not what he hoped to see: some of the rubber impeller vanes in the seawater pump were broken. Rod hoped the higher temps were being caused by the fact that these pieces were covering some of the cooling tubes, and that the impeller wasn't too badly damaged. He removed the pieces, reinstalled the cover, and restarted the engine. The water temp dropped to 185 degrees. He could live with this, but he didn't know how long his degraded water pump would last. But if it failed, he would call Chet and get towed in; he wasn't leaving these fish...not today, *no way*.

The tuna was kicking G's butt, taking more line than he was getting back. Big Bob took over and really put the pressure on the fish. He started to gain some line. In 45 minutes, with everyone taking turns, the fish was on the surface.

"When the sinker gets to the tip, just pull on it and the rubber band will break off in your hand. Keep bringing the fish closer." Rod had his eyes fixed on the big tuna. "I won't miss this time, I promise you!" He stood by with the harpoon in hand. The gaffe and tail rope were ready. "Just keep reeling. Steady. Keep 'em coming in."

The fish was less than ten feet away and coming closer. Rod raised the harpoon and drove it as hard as he could, directly into the tuna's head. With a tremendous splash, the fish surged down, taking line from the reel along with the harpoon line. There were now two lines into the fish. After a short burst the reel began to slow. Bob hauled back the quarter-inch nylon while G kept pressure on the fish.

"Work him to the port side. I'll have the tail rope ready. G, when he gets really close, leave the reel and get on the gaffe. You want to gaffe his tail. Hold it close to the gunnel. I'll rope him."

The fish was now alongside the boat, suffering the effects of the fight and the harpoon dart buried in its head. Bob pulled the fish ahead to mid-ship, while G pulled the gaffe into its tail. Rod was ready with the tail rope, making it fast with a snap of the stainless swivel.

"Tail rope on!" was the cry, as jubilation rolled over the crew.

"I'll rig the block and tackle right after I make the incision to bleed him," said Rod. He got his short stubby knife especially designed for this purpose; he measured the fish for the cut and pushed in the knife as G and Big Bob watched. Deep red blood gushed from the lateral artery of the beautiful giant.

It was a magnificent creature with brilliant blues, greens, and yellows – spectacular even in the fog. The fish would hang beside the boat until it bled out. Next, using the head hook attached to the block and tackle hanging from the davit, the fish would be hauled aboard. After ten minutes, the bleeding was complete. Rod got the tape measure; to sell this giant it would have to be a minimum of 73 inches. The fish was brought aboard the boat and lay on the deck. G-Man held one end of the tape and Bob, the other.

"86 inches! Woo! Hoo!" yelled Bob. Everyone was so excited that they failed to notice the three red arches on the sounder screen as the fish alarm went off. It was set for large targets only. "Look! There's more tuna under the boat. What do you want to do?"

"There's a two-fish limit – let's go for it!," Rod replied. "Get another blue in the water. Let him free swim. Drop another one right on their heads. One of these bad boys will come and get him. Bingo!" He was ecstatic. This was the culmination of everything he'd worked and planned for. It was all coming together.

Rod had never gutted a fish this big, but G was an old hand. His experience with the smaller yellow fin would now pay off. While G and Rod worked the fish, Bob rigged the rod with another bluefish and set it out on its leash with about 50 yards of mono.

"Get some chum in the water – ring that dinner bell!" yelled G.

Bob grabbed the chuminator and began setting out hors d'oeuvres for the tuna. G made quick work of the butchering, packed the fish cavity with ice, and slid the fish into a large, extra heavy-duty insulated zipper bag designed for these fish. Everyone took a best guess at the weight. Rod thought 500 pounds, while G and Bob were thinking closer to 575.

Rod gave Kasey, who had stayed holed up in the cuddy most of the trip, a bowl of water. Bob, meanwhile, was just getting the other rod down from the overhead when G went wild again. "Fish on! Fish on! Whoa! Whoa! Whoa! Look at this baby go! He's gotta be huge!"

The guys hadn't had much experience so far – one caught and one lost – but all indications were that this one was special. It wouldn't stop taking line! He'd only been on for three minutes, and half the line was off the spool. There was no sign he was letting up. Rod fired up the engine, which had been shut down while they were preparing the tuna on the deck. He knew he might have to chase this fish to try to get some line back; soon he was doing just that.

They gained and lost, gained and lost, for the next three hours before the fish finally started to tire. A calm routine had come over the boat when the radio broke the silence.

"Securite, Securite, Securite, hello all stations, this is the United States Coast Guard, Boston Group. The National Weather Service has issued a severe thunderstorm watch for coastal Massachusetts to include the Merrimac River south to Cape Cod, until six pm. These storms could bring torrential rains, possibly including large hail. All craft should be on watch for changing weather conditions and seek appropriate shelter. This is the United States Coast Guard, Boston Group, out."

Yogi Berra summed it up when he said, "It's déjà vu all over again." Rod switched the radar to the 24-mile range. There was nothing to see, so a slight feeling of relief swept over him. He checked his position, about two miles ENE of where they'd started, but still fifteen miles from Rockport and safe harbor. They would have to land this fish quickly.

The fog still hung thickly as they worked the tuna closer to the boat, 100 feet away now, his tail fin just breaking the surface. This fish was even bigger than the one they lost! He started taking line again, but that was short-lived. Bob took over the reel as G and Rod stood by, ready to put on the finishing touches.

The harpoon was merciful, so the end came swiftly. As the fish hung on the tail rope, the crew moved the first tuna to the starboard side of the deck to make room for the next one. The head hook was pulled through the tuna's mouth and the block and tackle was attached. The full weight of the fish hung on the line, causing *Jus' Restin'* to list heavily to port, so Rod told Big

Bob to pull from the starboard side. When the head hook hit the top of the davit pole, Bob tied the line to the starboard mid-ship cleat. Then G untied the tail rope from its cleat, and the three men pulled the tuna's tail into the port quarter. The rest of its body followed over the gunnel. Rod slowly released the line on the davit and the big fish lay down on the deck.

Rod grabbed the tape measure and handed it to Big Bob and G to do the honors, while he watched from the doorway of the pilothouse. They stretched the tape from the fork of the tail, along the hump of the body, to the tip of the nose.

"98 inches! That's over eight feet! Yeow! This one's gotta be over 700!" yelled G, as they all exchanged handshakes.

Rod was trembling was excitement, the adrenalin pumping. Two fish in the boat! He thought of his father and how proud he would have been. All of his preparation had finally paid off. He had proved that with patience, planning, and a little luck from the French, a payday had come together. Then, while looking around the boat and taking in the moment, it hit him right between the eyes: the whole upper quarter of the radar screen was BLACK!

*

Eric stood in the hangar doorway 100 miles away looking skyward, as the flight officers leaned into the wind, making their way across the tarmac.

"Looks like she's going to blow pretty hard. Are we ready to fly?" asked the aircraft commander.

"Yes Sir, we're ready for any call," snapped a saluting Eric, the powerful orange and white Jayhawk resting in standby behind him.

A Falcon jet was also there, along with a backup Jayhawk. The last member of the crew could be seen in the distance, running along the edge of the tarmac and heading for the hangar. He was a huge man in his early twenties, wearing shorts and a tee-shirt and looking like the Terminator. He was just finishing up the five-mile run from his home to the air station. He sprinted the last hundred yards, hitting Eric with a high five as he ran past. The rescue swimmer was now present and accounted for: the crew was complete. Eric pushed the pendant button and the 30-foot-high hangar door rumbled to a close.

*

"We gotta make a run for it! There's a storm coming – radar indicates ten miles away," said Rod.

The echo of his own words settled in his mind as he started doing the math. The storm was already six miles offshore, moving towards them. He would have to steam through at least a portion of the storm before reaching a safe haven. As Bob and G scrambled to get the second tuna into the bag, Rod fired the engine and set a course for shore. He chose Foley Cove, which would keep them clear of the rocky Salvages Islands right offshore from Rockport.

He kicked the engine into gear and took her steadily up to power. Just as the boat hit 3,800 RPMs, the fog started to thin and the visibility opened up for the first time that day. It was like coming around the tip of Foley Cove a few weeks back, but this time it was even worse. There was no sunshine, only a huge storm coming directly their way. He could feel the air getting cooler.

They'd traveled about two miles when the engine power suddenly dropped. Rod scanned the instruments. Oil, OK. Volts, OK. RPM, 2,800. Temperature, 210 degrees! He knew he was in deep now. The engine had a protective electrical circuit that initiated if the temperature exceeded 205 degrees F, or if the oil pressure dropped below 5 psi. The engine would only run up to 2,800 RPMs, maximum. This was designed to preserve the engine but still maintain limited power. It was clear that his luck had just run out. They were sliding fast down the curve of life's sine wave. He pulled the throttle back to 1,000 RPMs and continued on course, heading into the oncoming storm.

"Get inside, quick!" yelled Rod. He proceeded to break the news. "Make no mistake about it: we're in a lot of trouble. The engine isn't going to last very long. It's overheating and losing power. This storm is coming and there's no way we can make cover."

"Well, what are we going to do, Captain Dude?" asked Bob, ready for action.

"I'm thinking as we go – I'll be giving orders to prepare the boat." Rod pondered what to say. He wanted to tell them the right things to do, in the right order. "First, secure the tuna to the deck. We've got to keep the boat stable, so we can't have these fish sliding about the deck." Rod scanned the cockpit for whatever was available. "Use whatever you need, cut lines if you have to, but I want small holes punched in the top corners of each bag. Put a rope through the gills and out the hole, and tie the line to the mid-ship cleats. Do the same thing around the tails, out through the other hole in the bag, and tie that line off to the cleats in the stern corners. Make sure the zippers are closed tight. When that's done, come right back!"

They headed to the deck and got to work. More lightning and now heavy thunder rumbled in the distance. Rod grabbed his lifejacket from the back of his helm seat. "Kasey, come here, baby!"

Kasey was right at his side as he took the jacket and threw it down on the deck of the pilothouse. He took Kasey's front legs and put them through the openings he would normally place his arms through. He lifted the jacket and clicked the buckles on top of Kasey's back. He pulled them as tightly as possible but the jacket was still too loose. He got a roll of duct tape from the tool compartment and overlapped the jacket until it was snug, then wrapped the tape around her three times. The collar from the jacket was now under Kasey's chin: this would work if she had to swim for it.

"OK Kasey, you're as ready as you'll ever be. Good luck baby!"

He gave her a hug and a kiss on the head. She was starting to shiver – the storm was getting closer and she could probably smell the ozone from the distant lightning. Kasey's acute senses might not have been able to actually smell the storm, but Rod could certainly smell the engine coolant. He looked at the temp gauge: it was approaching 220 degrees. Just then, steam started coming from under the engine cover.

"Shutting down the engine before she blows!" yelled Rod, but it was too late.

The coolant blew and steam poured from the engine compartment. The storm was only six miles away now. Rod looked at the depth sounder: nearly 280 feet of water. There was no way they'd be able to use the anchor on the pulpit, it was just too small. Besides, it only had 300 feet of scope. It was useless. Rod came out on deck and saw that Bob and G were just finishing with the tuna. He checked the lines to make sure the fish were secure.

"Get the survival suits out of the cuddy! You guys take the ones in the big orange bags – mine is the reddish-orange Mustang bag – and bring them out here with you. Leave your shoes on: the suits are big, one size fits all. I need to rig a line to the bow. Go, go, hurry!"

Rod lifted the engine cover and grabbed a line that he stored in the engine compartment. It was a twenty-foot, ¾-inch nylon Y-bridal sling that Chet had made especially for emergency towing. In normal use, he'd attach the eye-loops to the cleats in the stern corners and tie the bitter end to a line from another boat, allowing him to tow it to safety. But now he planned to take this line and attach the loops to the two bow cleats, bringing the bitter end back around the outside of the bow rails and onto the deck. This loose end would be tied to the tuna anchor line. With 500 feet of line and a much larger anchor and chain, they would try to anchor *Jus' Restin'* and lay into the storm.

Rod knew that for the anchor to work properly, he needed much shallower water. He tapped the buttons on the GPS to get a bigger view of the area and to his surprise, waypoint Hump 109 appeared in the corner of the screen. This was a spot *Jus' Restin'* had fished many, many times. It was called Hump 109 simply because at low tide the top of the hump was only 109 feet below the surface; it was like an underwater mountain. Where they were right now was all sand and gravel, so the anchor would never hold against the velocity of wind that was coming their way.

He checked the distance to the 109: just over a mile. He would get there even if it meant sacrificing the engine. He fired the engine again and kept it at just above an idle; luckily the current was headed in the same direction. At this point he'd take any help he could get.

Suddenly it dawned on him. Help is what he *really* needed. He took the 406 EPIRB radio, which was secured next to the rear window, out of its holder and gave it a long look. It was time. He remembered Eric's words, *If you think you are going to need us, don't wait to call. Hey, it's what I live for!* Rod pushed the button to "Manual." The strobe light charged up and started to flash. He was confident the unit was sending a signal to the satellites overhead.

He grabbed the mike to the VHF, gained his composure, and began: "Mayday, Mayday, Mayday, this is the vessel *Jus' Restin'* on channel 16. We are approximately eight to ten miles east of Rockport. Engine is in distress, severe weather approaching, and we are abandoning ship for the life raft." Rod read their coordinates from the GPS and waited for a response.

Coast Guard Station Gloucester immediately responded, repeating the coordinates and notifying Rod that help would be dispatched right away.

Big Bob and G were on the deck with their survival suit bags. Rod grabbed the one G was holding, threw it at the deck, and jerked back on the strap. The suit flew out of the bag. Bob did the same with the other bag, but this time two mice that had taken up residence, and had enjoyed a nice summer at Uncle George's, scurried across the engine cover and over the transom, then fell into the water.

"Hey, even the rats are leaving the ship! Are we sinking?" laughed Bob, the gravity of the situation still not registering.

"Not yet! Get 'em on!" was all Rod could manage as he returned to the helm and checked the engine. Temp was nearly off scale. He knew the engine would either seize or catch fire, so he hastily filled the five-gallon bucket with water. As it turned out, he wouldn't need it because she stalled and the cylinders seized tight.

He checked the GPS. They weren't far from the hump, and if the current stayed true, he could drop the anchor about a quarter-mile in front of it. Even if the anchor did drag in the wind, it should eventually catch the hump and hold on. It was the plan and it was all they had. The leading edge of the storm was two miles away, its imminent arrival announced by a stiff breeze.

*

The EPIRB's emergency signal automatically relayed itself to Mission Control Center, whose personnel then relayed the information to the Search and Rescue SAR centers. The information came into USCG Air Station Cape Cod and USCG Station Gloucester simultaneously.

Both stations scrambled to answer the call. Station Gloucester was already preparing to launch their 47' MLB. This motor lifeboat was the latest edition to their fleet, a formidable boat that had its testing and training grounds at Cape Disappointment, Oregon, running "the bar" of the Columbia River. Today's weather would put the boat and its crew to the test. The storm was well under way at Gloucester Station when the crew left the dock. With the blue lights flashing and the sirens wailing, they headed out past Ten Pound Island for Eastern Point. The sea built from ten to fifteen feet as they rounded the end of the jetty and headed NE towards the approximate location of *Jus' Restin'*.

The alarm echoed loud in the hangar as the ground crew hustled to get the big orange and white helo out on the tarmac. The flight crew was already on board, preparing for takeoff. The rain was coming down hard, in sheets, as the turbines began to wind up to power. The crew went through the pre-flight checks and within ten minutes of the call, they were airborne, heading fifteen degrees magnetic for Cape Ann.

"Where are we headed, Sir," said a voice into the pilot's headset.

"Heading North-North-East for Gloucester. Got a 406 hit from a F/V, the *Jus' Restin'*, approximately eight to ten miles offshore. Don't know the nature of the distress as yet."

Eric's heart sank as the words rang in his ears. Uncle Rod!

*

The storm would be upon the crew of the *Jus' Restin'* in a couple of minutes, so it was time to play the only ace they had left.

"Bob, help me get the raft down from the overhead!" said Rod. The two of them climbed the sides, and Rod released the pelican hook that held the raft to the roof. They slid the raft over the port side into the water, the 25-foot painter line paying out of the hole from its hard fiberglass container.

"OK baby, do your thing," Rod sputtered as he pulled hard on the painter line. The raft's container responded by popping the cover and allowing the orange and black four-man Viking life raft to come to life. Her pressure cylinder brought her up to full size and shape and fully functional in less than twenty seconds. She was a four-sided raft, deep seated, with a bright orange spray canopy to keep out the wind and water.

"Our chariot awaits!" exclaimed G, looking like Gumby in his big survival suit. A wave of relief came over him at the sight of the raft.

"You two guys get Kasey and yourselves into the raft – now! Hurry, it's starting to blow!"

Rod pulled the painter line and the raft came up alongside, bouncing against *Jus' Restin'*. G was the first inside. Bob passed Kasey to G and then climbed in himself. Rod tossed in the EPIRB and the flare kit as the others took seats on the floor and waited for their captain.

"You're still tied to the boat. I'm going to wait until the last minute before I get in. I still have to set the anchor."

Rod looked at the GPS: they were almost to the hump. He stepped outside and tied the anchor line to the towline that was attached to the bow. The anchor was ready. It was starting to rain, and the wind continued to pick up velocity. The waves were right behind, pushing the boat sideways. He'd have to drop the anchor soon or *Jus' Restin'* would capsize, being adrift like this in the building sea.

He looked again at the GPS. The course of the boat was steady, straight towards the hump. He couldn't wait any longer...he grabbed the anchor and let it go! It was heavy going over the side, its 30 feet of chain rattling hard against the gunnel. Rod paid out all the line as fast as he could, making sure there were no knots. Down, down, down the anchor slipped, flying through the water, spiraling into the silence and darkness. It came to a hard rest on the dark gravel bottom. Its chain piled up behind the anchor as the 500 feet of crisp white nylon line headed lazily back to the surface.

Rod went back into the pilothouse and waited for the anchor to grab. It didn't take long for the nylon line to stretch and pick up the chain, pulling the flukes of the anchor through the gravel. With a fair bite right off, *Jus' Restin'*'s bow came about into the wind and began to ride the waves much better.

Next, he got a pencil and notepad from the plastic box on the dash. He scribbled down the exact coordinates of their location from the GPS, peeled off the paper, and placed it in the plastic waterproof key caddy in the ignition switch. Then he stepped outside, kicked off his boat shoes, and got out his Mustang suit. He'd practiced this routine at home on the living room rug countless times, but doing it on a rolling boat was different. After he got the suit on, he got his keys and cell phone from the pilothouse and put them in a zip-lock bag, then put the bag in the suit's inside pocket. Finishing up, he pulled the hood over his head and zipped it to the top.

The wind had really picked up, and *Jus' Restin'* was straining on the anchor as it rode up and over each wave. The boat suddenly lurched to port and began to drift sideways. The anchor had lost its hold! Rod looked at the raft pulling on its painter line, still tied to the overhead. It was time to cut the line, swim to the raft, and join the others. He went back into the pilothouse and grabbed his fishing knife. As he was coming out again, the anchor grabbed bottom, the bow came around hard to starboard, and he was thrown towards the port gunnel. He stumbled and fell, sending the edge of the knife along the line to the raft, cutting it free.

The raft started blowing away on the wind as Rod tried desperately to get to his feet. On his knees and looking out over the gunnel, he saw that the raft was now 100 feet away and rapidly gaining distance. His hopes sank. Bob held Kasey tightly as she barked frantically for Rod. There would be no returning to Kansas today: the balloon was gone!

"*Jus' Restin', Jus' Restin', Jus' Restin'*, this is Coast Guard Helo 6-0-0-4, Coast Guard Helo, 6-0-0-4 on channel 1-6, over."

Rod fought his way back into the pilothouse and grabbed the mike. "This is *Jus' Restin'*, go ahead Coast Guard."

"*Jus' Restin', Jus' Restin', Jus' Restin'*, this is Coast Guard Helo, 6-0-0-4, Coast Guard Helo, 6-0-0-4 on channel 1-6, over."

Rod repeated back to the helo. No response. Their signal sounded garbled, not like the normally clear audio. He looked outside to see the antenna mount broken and the antenna lying over the side, its tip in the water. At that moment the boat dropped into a trough and a wave crashed over the bow, pounding the windshield and flooding the stern with at least a foot of water. The tuna swayed awash on the deck, their lines staying taut.

She's going down, Rod thought, and there was nothing he could do to stop it. He would save himself, but how? His mind raced. He knew that breathing in the midst of the foam from the breaking waves would be the biggest problem. The solution to that was in the cuddy. He kept a spare dive mask and snorkel in one of the storage lockers for divers whose masks were leaking or their straps broken. He went into the cuddy as *Jus' Restin'*'s bow went under again. This time a wall of green engulfed the boat...she was now totally awash, her gunnels even with the sea.

While water poured through the pilothouse, Rod grabbed the mask and turned for the doorway. He was still adjusting the mask when the final blow hit the boat; he took a deep breath and pushed up and away as *Jus' Restin'* slowly sank beneath the waves. Looking down, he could see her white shape fading below him, heading for the bottom. In a moment, she was gone and he was alone and adrift. The waves had to be fifteen feet or more, their tops turning to foam and being blown away by the howling wind.

The Jayhawk continued on course, buffeted by the heavy winds and heading for the coordinates and the signal emanating from the EPIRB. Eric tried hailing the *Jus' Restin'* again, but still no answer. It had been nearly a half hour since they'd gotten the initial call and he knew they must be getting close. He continued to scan the waters from his shuddering perch 100 feet above the surface.

Bob and G had pulled the canopy flap down over the raft entrance, because the raft was being tossed about by the wind and crashing waves. With just a small window, it was a living hell inside – they didn't know what was going to happen next. They held the shivering Kasey between them and kept their fears and doubts for their captain to themselves.

Even though the wind was deafening, G swore he could hear a helicopter. He persuaded Bob to open the canopy, only to have water gush in. Sure enough, the helo was out there but had yet to spot them. Bob pulled open the flare kit and grabbed an orange smoke. He leaned out of the raft and ignited it, but the wind blew the sparks and smoke back inside. He threw it in the water.

"Here, fire one of these!" yelled G, passing the pistol launcher with a signal flare loaded in the chamber.

Bob pointed it skyward and pulled the trigger. BANG! It was off, exploding overhead. That did the trick! The next sound they heard was the reassuring high-speed whirring of the rotor blades from the Jayhawk as it approached into the wind.

"Prepare to deploy the swimmer!" was the command from the pilot as they hovered over the bright orange raft thrashing in the surf below.

"Scratch, you ready to go?" called Eric while directing the pilot to the raft.

When they were about fifteen feet above the highest crest, Eric gave his swimmer the signal to jump. He gave Eric a thumbs-up and timed his jump to hit the crest of the next wave as the raft rode up and over the top. One push and he was freefalling to the water below.

Eric lowered the basket to Scratch, who was already at the side of the Viking. "Hey guys!" he yelled, holding onto the grab lines on the side of the raft. "My name is Scratch and I'll be your rescue swimmer today. Is everyone OK?"

Bob and G signaled that they were all OK. Scratch took control of the rescue, issuing commands to get the crew safely out of the raft and into the basket. First, the G-Man scrambled out over the hard rubber raft. Scratch told Bob to let Kasey go up with the G-man, since Big Bob and Kasey together would be a tight fit. Big Bob climbed to the opening of the raft with Kasey under his right arm, as if he was a running back going for a touchdown at a Thanksgiving Day game. He passed the flailing and terrified Kasey to G's outstretched arms. The two of them sat down in the basket, and Scratch gave Eric the hoist signal.

Eric raised the winch line with the G-Man and Kasey swinging and spinning in the wind. When they reached the helo door, he stabilized the basket and pulled them safely inside. Eric pointed G to his seat and, with Kasey in G's lap, fastened the seatbelt. He slid the basket into its storage site and attached the "quick strop" sling to the cable. He sent the sling on its way to the rolling water below.

Scratch grabbed the sling and attached it to himself and to Big Bob, and cinched it tight. Using his diver's knife, he punctured the Viking several times, scuttling the raft in order to prevent a search if it was discovered by another vessel. He then gave the up signal, and they were hoisted back aboard the Jayhawk. Scratch and Big Bob came through the doorway; Eric was overjoyed that his uncle was safe until he came face to face with Big Bob.

"Who are you? Where's Rod?" he demanded, panic written on his face.

"He stayed with the boat," gasped Bob. "We lost him about ten-fifteen minutes ago."

"Sir, the captain is unaccounted for," Eric relayed to the aircraft commander, "his crew says he stayed with the vessel. They last saw him ten to fifteen minutes ago."

"Very well, we'll continue searching," the pilot said as they commenced an expanding square search pattern.

*

Rod drifted alone on the sea, the wind and waves thrashing him with their fury. The mask and snorkel were the best things he could have done for himself. He could see fairly well, and was able to keep the water out of his mouth and time his breathing to get the air he needed to stay alive.

His thoughts ran wild while he and the Lord had a heart-to-heart talk. How could he have gotten himself into this predicament? He'd pushed the envelope and was paying the price. He prayed that the raft would protect Bob and G, and he thought of Kasey who might die from sheer fright. And he thought of the tuna, lying there in their natural environment, 100 feet underwater. But now they were dead, tied fast to a boat that would not release them.

His thoughts drifted to *Jus' Restin'*. He offered up an apology to her, knowing she was where so many ships had gone before her. He was proud of that boat and the experiences they'd enjoyed together, and he vowed then and there to raise her again.

Finally, his thoughts went to home and the ladies in his life...the four of them had enjoyed so many wonderful times as a family. All he wanted was to get out of this alive, to be with them again. He would survive. That's all there was to it.

*

As the helo began its sweep, Bob told Eric that Rod had referred to the Hump 109. Eric relayed this information to the pilots, to aid in their search pattern. With the newly upgraded FLIR (Forward Looking Infrared Radar), Eric was sure they would find his uncle soon. After another ten minutes, the FLIR found its target: Rod's heat silhouette was showing on their screen.

"Prepare to deploy the swimmer," the commander ordered over the headsets. Eric dropped to one knee, and his palms flew out to both sides as if an umpire had just called Uncle Rod safe at home plate!

"Excellent job, Sirs!" Eric said through his mike to the pilots. "Scratch, what'll it be? Sling or basket?"

"The sling's the thing! I'm ready," barked Scratch, already moving towards the doorway and preparing to exit.

The Jayhawk took a hovering position over Captain Rod, who gave them a visual – a fist to the top of his head – to signal that he was OK.

"Swimmers away!" Eric said to the pilots. Scratch hit the water and began his swim towards the very tired captain. When he reached Rod he placed the sling over his outstretched arms and gave the lift signal to the hovering helo. The two of them headed skyward, leaving the hostile waters behind.

Eric reached out for the final time, pulling Scratch and his dear Uncle Rod to safety. He secured the hoist and closed the door. Bob released Kasey and in a flash she was shivering and whining at Rod's side, still in her duct-taped lifejacket. He held her close. Bob, G, and Eric all patted Rod on the back. The captain gave Scratch a long and grateful handshake: he had saved his life and he would be forever thankful.

"Look!" said Bob. "Captain Rod even saved the mother-in-law's cup!" They all laughed when they saw Rod holding the cup tightly in his left hand.

"*Jus' Restin'* sank. It was the only damn thing left...found it floating beside me!" he gasped, the full weight of the situation now engulfing him.

"Coast Guard Sector Boston, Coast Guard Sector Boston, Coast Guard Sector Boston, this is Coast Guard Helo, 6-0-0-4, Coast Guard Helo, 6-0-0-4 on channel 2-3, over."

"This is Coast Guard Sector Boston, go ahead Coast Guard Helo, 6-0-0-4 on channel 2-3, over."

"Coast Guard Sector Boston, this is Coast Guard Helo, 6-0-0-4, we have the entire crew of the F/V *Jus' Restin'* onboard at this time, and all are in good condition. We are returning the crew to their homeport at this time, over."

"Coast Guard Helo, 6-0-0-4, this is Coast Guard Sector Boston, understand, mission accomplished. Congratulations on a job well done. Coast Guard Sector Boston returning to channels 1-6 and 2-3."

"Coast Guard Helo, 6-0-0-4, returning 1-6 and 2-3, over."

As the crew of *Jus' Restin'* sat back in their seats, silently reflecting, Eric relayed the location of Harborside to the pilots. They made their course corrections, and the powerful Jayhawk headed across Ipswich Bay at 100 knots towards Plum Island Sound and the clearing blue skies of the western horizon.

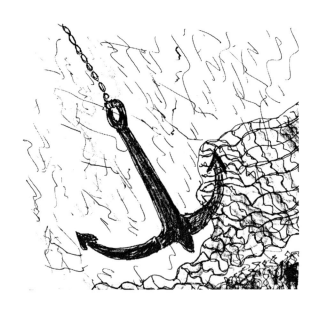

Chapter Twelve

End of the Line

Harborside was nearly deserted. Even though it was the Sunday of Labor Day weekend, the morning fog, coupled with a stormy forecast, was keeping all but the diehards away from the marina.

The aircraft commander of the Jayhawk made his final approach over the barrier island shore, followed the channel, came in over the old bridge, and hovered to the west of the large parking lot. He and his co-pilot concurred that there was sufficient room for a safe landing. He set the big white and orange bird down on the far side of the lot near the marsh.

The loud arrival of the helo attracted people who were already there, as well as those who happened to see it from Route 1A or had been listening to the rescue on their VHF radios. When the door slid open, Eric and his survivors jumped out to the cheers of the crowd. It was a grand scene as Kasey, still in her lifejacket, bounded out the door, followed by G and Big Bob, and then Captain Rod and Scratch. The Jayhawk's engines continued to wind down while the officers relaxed and completed the data for their report.

While reaching into his survival suit to get his cell phone and keys, Rod pulled aside Chet, who was at the front of the crowd, for a quick conference.

"Chet, I need to hire *Checkers* for the rest of the day. I've got two tuna on the deck of *Jus' Restin'*. She's in about 100-125 feet of water and I need to dive down and bring those fish up. There's gotta be $20,000 worth of bluefin down there if I can get them before the dogfish sharks do." He looked overhead and added, "The winds are gone and the skies are clearing, so I'd like to go as soon as possible."

"She's all yours, just tell me what you need," replied an eager Chet. He was an experienced diver himself, having built an underwater scuba sled in his younger days. He wouldn't be diving, but he and *Checkers* would be an invaluable asset on the surface.

Rod made the first of several calls in quick succession. "Uncle George, I need you to get all my dive gear from the shed and bring it to the marina, pronto! Take everything you can find. If you think it's in any way related to diving, bring it and please hurry. I'll explain later but please, hurry!"

P.J. was next on his list. "P.J., I need you at the marina right now! We're doing two dives at 100-125 feet and lifting two tuna to Chet's boat. *Jus' Restin'* sank with the fish onboard. We need to hurry. It's after two o'clock now, but this shouldn't take long if we can locate the boat quickly. I don't want to lose the fish!"

"I'll be there as fast as I can. Probably take half an hour. My gear is in my cruiser and I'm on the highway as we speak. I'll get someone to cover for me."

Lastly, Rod called Lilly. "Lilly, have you heard the news?"

"No, what's going on?" she asked, concerned that something was wrong.

"Well, there's good news and bad. A big squall sunk the boat offshore. Relax. Everyone is fine. G, Bob, Kasey – and hey, we even got rescued by our own Eric! But I've got to go find the boat. You won't believe it, but we finally hit the tuna! There are two giants lashed to the deck, and if we can get them up it should be a big payday!"

"Do you want me to come down to the marina to help out? I'll call in to work."

"No, no, I'll be fine and we'll be heading out before you could possibly get here. P.J. and I are going to dive down and bring them up. I'll call you later and keep you posted. Don't worry. This should be a routine dive."

"I'll call the girls and let them know what's going on. Keep me posted and be safe!" Lilly knew there'd be no stopping Rod, that he was determined to salvage the fish.

The storm had moved far offshore, so the weather was calm and clear when Rod went back to the Coast Guard crew to give them the data they'd need to complete their paperwork. Rod took a moment to convey his appreciation to Eric and Scratch.

"You guys, you're the best! You should be proud of yourselves – I know I sure am." He gave Eric a hug and Scratch a high ten. With the crew back aboard, Rod saluted the officers, and the Jayhawk rose above the marina yard, dipped its nose, turned south, and winged its way back towards Air Station Cape Cod.

Rod was now a man possessed, scrambling to get his dive tanks from the box at his slip. It felt strange to see the empty slip. His mind envisioned *Jus' Restin'* lying on the deep, dark, cold bottom of the Atlantic Ocean. The water temperature at that depth was a consistent 38 to 40 degrees; he was confident the fish would be fine, but he had to get to them soon.

As soon as Uncle George pulled into the yard, Bob and G grabbed the gear and loaded it on board *Checkers*. In the distance a siren was wailing – P.J. was really putting the pedal to the metal! In a flash, he was onboard with all of his gear. Rod turned Kasey over to Uncle George, and *Checkers* was now ready to head out on her salvage mission.

"Chet, don't spare the horses – let's go!" Chet responded with more throttle than he was used to giving because when he was towing, time on the hook was money in the bank. Rod took the key case from his pocket and pulled out the coordinates of *Jus' Restin'*'s last known position. He plugged them into Chet's GPS and saw that a 40-minute ride at their current speed was predicted. Rod and P.J. prepared their equipment, got their wet-suits on, and discussed the dive plan.

First, locate the boat, then anchor in such a way that they would drift back on the current and end up directly above *Jus' Restin'*. Next, they would descend to the boat and bring up the fish one at a time with *Checkers'* towline. They had two lift bags, but Rod and P.J. didn't think they would be needed. While tying the first fish, they'd grab *Jus' Restin'*'s block and tackle, which Chet would then hang on *Checkers'* davit to haul the fish on board with. This scenario would be repeated for the second fish.

Checkers was approaching the coordinates; the GPS indicated it was 500 feet away. Chet powered down as Rod stood on the roof, looking ahead for any telltale signs. The GPS was very accurate so they knew they were close.

Then Rod saw it. He couldn't believe his eyes. His luck was changing again, heading up that curve to the good side. Floating on the surface, swirling gently from side to side, was the life ring he used in case divers missed the boat! She was calling out to him, sending a signal just as a distressed submarine would do.

"Yo baby!" Rod yelled, pumping his fist for all to see. She was right under them, awaiting rescue. "Bob, G: help Chet set the anchor. P.J.: let's get it on!" The excitement of the moment was infectious. Chet was an exceptionally good captain and had *Checkers* on position in nothing flat. The plan was reviewed and everyone was in agreement. Big Bob gave Rod and P.J. a final equipment check before they went overboard to the bottom of the sea.

It was nearly 16:00, so light wasn't penetrating the depths as much as it would, had it been earlier in the day. But their eyes became accustomed as the gleaming white hull of *Jus' Restin'* came into view, lying upright, her bow at about a fifteen-degree angle towards the surface. Dogfish sharks were everywhere – at least 50 of them. There was a faint smell of blood in the water, but the sharks hadn't figured out the source as yet.

Rod reached the boat first and checked his pressure gauge and depth: he had plenty of air left at a 115 feet. Ten feet deeper and that buoy would have been under the surface, making the location much harder to find. He untied the smaller tuna from the cleats on the starboard side, and P.J. tied the line on the tuna's head to the towline. Rod got the block and tackle hanging from *Jus' Restin'*'s davit and attached this to the towline. P.J. gave four hard tugs on the line and Big Bob, G, and Chet hauled the tuna up.

It was a nice and slow assent to the surface. Rod and P.J. gave each other reassuring thumbs-up, knowing things were going their way. After a few minutes the tuna was hanging beside the boat. G-Man took the block and tackle from the line and rigged it to *Checkers'* davit, as the topside crew hauled the tuna onto the deck. Rod and P.J. came aboard and Big Bob changed out their tanks.

"One down, one to go," said Rod, looking at P.J. nervously. "Did you see what I saw?"

"You mean that big bluedog? Yeah, I saw him!" laughed P.J.

"I hope he keeps his distance – I'm not a big fan of sharks!"

In no time, P.J. and Rod were rolling over the gunnel again, going down the buoy line. The biggest tuna lay on the deck, awaiting their arrival. They untied the fish and retied it to the towline to get it ready for the trip to the surface. Rod banged his tank with his knife to get P.J.'s attention. Using hand signals, he told P.J. that he wanted him to take the fish up so he could stay down ten more minutes. P.J. nodded and gave the four-tug signal on the rope; the second fish, with P.J. hanging on for the ride, was lifted from the deck.

Rod was alone now, surveying *Jus' Restin'* for damage. She was upright, resting on a rock ledge, listing slightly to starboard. He swam with his flashlight along her hull and couldn't see any obvious signs of damage. She was in great shape and would be able to float on her own if he could raise her and pump her out.

I'll be back, he said, just like Arnold, to his boat lying there in the cold dark water. *I'll get you out of here.* Then he took hold of the buoy line, put a shot of air in his BC, and began his ascent to the surface. Topside, the boys were just getting the big fish onboard. P.J. and Rod took off and stowed their gear as Big Bob hauled the anchor. Chet fired the engine and *Checkers* headed home to port.

Rod pulled out his cell phone and made the call he'd been waiting a long time to make: to the fish dealer! He said he had two giants coming to Harborside Marina. The dealer replied he'd be there within 30 minutes and await their arrival.

"Hey Chet, got any navigation fluid on board? I think it's time for a toast!" Chet motioned Rod to take the helm, as he went to his special hiding spot and produced a very fine single malt scotch. "I'd like to propose a toast to *Jus' Restin'*, aargh, she's a fine boat and she'll sail again!" Rod said with a huge smile and a laugh. "And to the Big Guy above, who saved our souls today."

"Here, here!" was the raucous response as they pushed past the Dry Salvages and set a course for the #2. It was a triumphant trip through Plum Island Sound back to Harborside. A crowd was assembling for the second big event of the day as *Checkers* approached the service dock. The fish buyer's truck was backed up into position, its hoist lowered over the edge of the dock, ready for the fish.

Rod opened the smaller fish's bag and put the head hook from the hoist through the existing hole in the fish's lower jaw, which they'd made earlier in order to lift it aboard *Jus' Restin'*. The fish was brought up to the truck and transferred to the scale.

"560 pounds!" yelled G, leaning in for a closer look.

The dealer agreed and lowered the fish to the floor of the truck. He then pushed a needle-like device into the tuna's body and pulled out a sample of flesh. This he rolled on his fingers to check the fat content. Next, he cut a section at the tail, again checking for fat content. He tried to conceal his findings, but it was apparent he was pleased: this was a quality fish. The crew stood silently as the fish dealer and his assistant did their work. When they were ready for the second fish, Rod and Chet opened the bag and removed the giant's head and tail ropes. The fish was put on the hook and taken to the scale. The crowd leaned forward, straining to see the flickering yellow digital scale give up the numbers.

"827 pounds!" the dealer shouted. Everyone went wild. Rod couldn't believe his eyes. He'd done it – he had finally landed the big one! The dealer went through his routine again, plugging and cutting the tail of the fish. He appeared pleased with this fish as well.

After conferring with his assistant, the dealer punched numbers into his calculator and then summoned Rod. They went far inside the truck to discuss the price; Rod had never sold a tuna before and could easily have been at the mercy of a shady dealer. But he believed a man was as good as his reputation, and he'd always heard good things about this one.

The dealer handed Rod a slip of paper. Total weight of the fish: 1,387 pounds. Price per pound: $17. Bottom line: $23,579! Rod felt lightheaded. What a day's pay...but what a day's work! Rod always said that, like poker, you had to put it down to pick it up, but putting *Jus' Restin'* down on the bottom of the ocean was a little much. He accepted the offer, and the dealer cut him a check right on the spot. Rod tucked it into his shirt, exited the rear of the truck, and gave a double thumbs-up to the cheering crowd.

The sun was setting as the fish dealer closed the doors of his truck and waved goodbye. He was off to the processing plant where the fish would be prepared for the trip to Logan Airport, and then on to Japan.

"OK everybody, here's the deal: we're going to Captain Jack's and I'm buying!" promised Rod. It didn't take long for a procession of vehicles to start heading north on Route 1A towards downtown Newburyport, with Big Bob leading the way on his Harley.

It was a wild scene at Captain Jack's that Sunday evening for the private party in the corner room. A joyous time for all involved...surviving the storm, being rescued by a helicopter, and recovering the tuna one step ahead of the sharks. It was truly a remarkable day. A local newspaper reporter was there and got the whole scoop – it was going to make a great story for the Labor Day edition.

"Well, P.J., what do think?" Rod asked, pulling the corner of the check out of his pocket for P.J. to get a peek.

"Whoa, what a chunk o' change!" said P.J., shaking his head in astonishment.

Rod motioned to keep this information to himself. P.J. winked in acknowledgement. In the background G-Man popped a bottle of champagne and filled glasses for Big Bob, P.J., Jack, Cari, Amy, Chet, Archie, Budman, The Golden Cleaters, Dogfood Dave, and Uncle George, who had Kasey at his side on her leash. Lastly, he passed a glass to Captain Rod.

At that moment, Lilly popped through the door. "Don't forget me!" She rushed over and gave Rod a big hug and whispered that she'd sneaked out of work for a little bit, not wanting to miss the celebration.

"Congratulations Captain! And here's to the raising of *Jus' Restin'!*" said G.

"Hooray!" cheered Amy and Cari, joining their mom and dad in a family hug.

"I'd like to thank everyone for coming here tonight, and please continue to enjoy yourselves. Jack, put it all on my tab – I think I'm good for it!" Rod laughed, patting the check in his shirt pocket.

The party was well under way when Rod said goodbye to everyone, working the crowd as he left. Chet slipped a business card into Rod's hand, which made its way into his pocket. Uncle George and Kasey walked outside with him into the cool evening air. The weekend crowd was window-shopping at the stores along State Street.

"Well, chummy, the boys Down Home must be smiling on you tonight. You had a big day, with many more to come. Your father would be very proud of you. I'll take Kasey with me for a couple of days if that'll help you out."

Rod bent down and gave Kasey a long hug. Tears filled his eyes – he'd almost lost man's best friend today. "What do you say Kasey? Care for a little shore duty with Uncle George? Keep those paws on the ground for a while?" Rod mouthed the word "speak" and Kasey gave a little yelp. "There's your answer. She's all yours for now!"

They hugged and said goodbye, and Rod got in his truck and headed for home. He'd barely hit the shower when the phone started ringing. The calming waters of the shower were running over his tired body, helping him decompress from the events of the day. The shower was the place where Rod hatched many ideas and dreams. After he dried off, he went into the living room and saw the voicemail light flashing. He punched in his code, waited through the introduction, and heard Sarah's frantic voice.

"Captain Rod, Bob crashed his motorcycle! He's in an ambulance on his way to Memorial Hospital!" That was all there was.

Rod got dressed, raced to his truck, and headed for the hospital. He'd been in a few motorcycle crashes himself and they were never pretty. Saying a small prayer, he continued on and arrived around ten o'clock, just after the ambulance. Sarah was in the emergency room, crying. The details were sketchy, but after a few minutes a nurse appeared through the swinging doors and gave a prognosis.

"He has a broken leg, a serious one, but that appears to be the extent of his injuries. We'll know more soon. Please make yourselves comfortable in the waiting room."

Sarah and Rod took a seat; Big Bob's mom, dad, and sisters arrived shortly after. They were a tight-knit family and would stay by his side no matter what. Rod was nearing exhaustion and told Bob's family that he would wait in his truck for Lilly's shift at the hospital to end. If there was any news, they could call his cell phone and he'd be right back inside.

P.J. walked though the front door of the hospital and took the elevator to the nurse's station on the second floor. "Hey Lilly, how's Bob doing?"

"He's got some issues, but he should recover 100 percent." She looked down at the chart and then back to P.J. "Any action nearby tonight? I'm feeling lucky!"

P.J. knew exactly what she wanted. Being on the vice squad, he had his finger on the pulse of the gambling in the area.

It was his weakness, too – it was like the fox guarding the hen house.

"There's a hold 'em game I know of, a little steep though. But, hey, with the money Rod made today, you needn't worry about it."

"Really? How much to get in? And how much *did* Rod make today?"

P.J. knew he had spoken out of line, but it was too late. He figured Rod probably forgot to tell her and would bring her up to speed in the morning.

"The fish paid over $23,000. Getting into the poker game is chump change compared to that: two grand up front."

Lilly's mind was whirring. "If I can get out of here, can you get me in? I've got the cash in my locker."

"Sure. But you keep me out of this as far as Rod goes. He'd flip if he knew I set this up."

"No problem." Lilly completed her turnover and left through the back door of the hospital, heading through the parking lot to the waiting P.J.

Knowing his wife didn't like to be disturbed at work, Rod had parked in the rear parking lot, in the shadow of a large oak tree a few spaces from her car. Here he would wait for her or news about Bob; in a matter of minutes he fell into a deep sleep. He'd been out for the count about a half hour when the buzzing of the phone lying in his lap pleasantly woke him. He flipped the lid and saw Lilly's name.

"Hey there…" he answered, but was cut off mid-sentence.

"Hey Rod, it's really gotten crazy here tonight. I have to work a double shift, so I won't be home until after seven in the morning – I'll see you then." With that, she was gone.

Still groggy, Rod stared at the phone. *Well, OK then, looks like I'm going home. Sarah will call with updates, so there's no reason to stay here any longer.*

As he reached for his keys he heard a horn beep. He looked out his window and noticed a familiar figure walking between the cars on the other side of the lot. Lilly! She opened the passenger door handle of somebody's car and got inside. The headlights came on and the vehicle headed for the exit at the far side of the lot. Rod quickly started his truck and went in the same direction. *What's going on here? Who is she with and what is she doing?* He would find out. But since the shift was ending, other vehicles got between him and the mystery car. He soon lost them in traffic. A number of scenarios flooded his brain. Lilly hadn't seen him and, anyway, there was nothing he could do about it now. He'd go home to bed and let the charade play out in the morning.

Rod was up early and having coffee on the patio when Lilly arrived at 07:30. She smiled and commented that it had been a hectic weekend and that she was glad she could start her vacation now. Then she went into what seemed to Rod like a nervous monologue.

"Bob did fine in surgery, a compound fracture, but he'll be OK with therapy. I talked with Bob last night and he recounted your day on the water. That's unbelievable! And Eric and the helicopter – wow!"

"You can read the whole thing right here in the newspaper," Rod said as he pushed the morning edition over to her. The story of his rescue was on the front page. He watched her mannerisms closely, looking for anything out of the ordinary.

"I particularly liked the article about the storm – it answers a lot of questions," he said, pointing to the weather story on the back page. "It seems that radar tracked two storm fronts near Rowley. Storms in the northern hemisphere rotate counterclockwise, so when these two came together they spun off a smaller, more intense storm that rotated clockwise. It didn't last long, but it was powerful and managed to find us. Put us on the bottom! It was a good thing we had the safety gear, or we wouldn't be enjoying this coffee together." Rod and Lilly exchanged a glance, both realizing this had been a very close one.

"And over $23,000 for the fish: that'll take care of some college payments. Nice job!" Lilly said. She gave him a hug and a pat on the shoulder, then went into the kitchen.

Her words rang like a hammer banging a gong in his head. Nobody but the fish dealer and Rod knew how much the fish sold for...except P.J.! Rod was falling end over end down life's curve again, and he couldn't see bottom. He got up from his chair and walked into the back yard, alone with his thoughts. Was P.J. the driver of the mystery car? There had to be a logical explanation, but then again, anything was possible these days. He'd get to the bottom of this. But for now, it was time to dive, and dive deep. He would be safe in the depths of his own mental seclusion.

He went back in the house and got the business card Chet had given him the night before. New England Salvage, the dive-salvage operation Chet had talked about. There was a phone number written on the back.

"New England Salvage, this is Jim."

"Rod Gray, Captain of the *Jus' Restin'*. I need to speak with someone regarding raising my boat. It went down yesterday."

"Saw your plight on the news yesterday, Cap. You're a lucky guy. Sure, we can do it, no problem."

Rod and Jim went into the details of the salvage operation that would raise *Jus' Restin'* from the ocean floor. The plan would call for divers to attach four lift bags to the outside hull – two on the port side and two starboard side – just below the gunnels. Then, with *Jus' Restin's* anchor line still attached, a compressor hose on on the salvage vessel would inflate the bags and *Jus' Restin'* would rise to the surface, held in position by her anchor. Once on the surface, a suction hose would be dropped into her bilge to pump out the water. From there, *Checkers* would tow her back to Harborside for repairs.

"So, when do we go?" asked Rod.

"Forecast indicates calm seas on Wednesday. I can have the gear and two salvage divers onboard our boat early – meet you on site, say 07:00? The tide should be near slack and cooperating."

"Sounds like a deal. I'll call you tomorrow with coordinates to rendezvous."

Lilly would be going to bed soon. After all, she *had* worked all night. Rod decided to head to Harborside, nail down the arrangements with Chet for the salvage operation, get it approved by his insurance company, and then kick back. He sat on the porch of the bathhouse with a beer; it was a little early, but it was five o'clock somewhere. Rod had a tendency to utilize beer to help solve problems, and this was no exception. Suddenly, his phone went off. He lifted the lid and saw the caller's name: Pierre.

"Good morning, Suzanne."

"Good morning Rod, I'm so glad to hear your voice! Are you OK? We were all listening to the radio chatter onboard our ship, hearing the Coast Guard calling you and no answer. I was so worried."

"Well, we're all fine, but like you said before, this job does have a few surprises!"

"You lost your boat! *Jus' Restin'* is gone! What are you going to do now?"

"There's a plan in place to raise her. You won't believe it, but we hit the tuna right where you said they were. Landed two beauties for a nice payday. We had to dive down to the boat to retrieve them, but it was worth the effort. I owe you for that! Hopefully, by the end of the day on Wednesday, she'll be back at Harborside ready for repairs."

"Well that is just wonderful. You are not wasting any time!"

"I've had that problem in the past but that's going to change." He paused, pondering his last statement. "How's your operation progressing over by Eastern Point?"

"Sad to say, we're almost done. No luck. The financial backers want the ship in Halifax, Nova Scotia, as soon as possible. It looks like the *Atlantic Zephyr* will leave this weekend for the Maritime Provinces."

"Well, that is sad news. I was hoping we could have a glass of wine before you left on your next adventure."

"I would really like that! Maybe we could meet somewhere? Somewhere *special*."

"I'll make it happen. We'll talk soon."

"Goodbye, Captain Rod," she said softly in her sultry French accent.

Rod melted back into his chair, his mind overloaded with new ideas and problems. Some good, some not so good. The trouble would be to figure out which were which, and how to deal with them. But he would try not to worry. As his father said, "Worry is interest paid on something before it's due." Again, it was time to run silent, run deep.

Rod decided he'd invite P.J. to the salvage dive if he was available. After a short conversation, P.J. was onboard with the plan. Rod was following the words of the great Chinese general, Sun-Tzu: "Keeps your friends close and your enemies closer."

Wednesday was just as Jim had forecast: clear skies, calm waters, and winds light and variable. Perfect sea conditions for the work that lay ahead. Rod, P.J., and Chet were already on the scene when the salvage boat called them on the VHF. Their vessel was quickly alongside, rafting together with *Checkers*. The salvage divers were busy preparing for their descent. Rod and P.J. were already suited up; it would be slack water in an hour, and they wanted to take advantage of the tide.

The captain and mate of the salvage boat inspected the lift bags and lines that would be attached to *Jus' Restin'*, and then started the compressor that would provide the lift to raise Rod's pride and joy. When all was ready, the divers and crew met at the gunnels of their respective boats and conducted a pre-dive brief. Rod, P.J., and the salvage divers were all equipped with 120-cubic-foot tanks. At a depth of a 125 feet, they calculated about a half hour of air was needed to attach the lift bags. They planned to try to raise her on the first dive, air supply permitting. Otherwise they would surface, decompress, and go back down with a second tank of air and finish the job.

Nobody was to swim under *Jus' Restin'* as she was rising, and the support crew was to monitor the bubbles closely so that they could maneuver the topside boats away from the rising vessel. Both concerns were paramount to everyone's safety. All agreed the plan was do-able, and after a round of handshakes, the divers were over the side and following the life ring line to the deck of *Jus' Restin'*.

She slowly came into focus, her outriggers rising high above her bright white hull, which reflected whatever sunlight could reach through the ocean depths. Codfish and haddock swam lazily about their new neighbor, who was soon to take her leave. The salvage divers went immediately to the task of attaching the lift bags. First, on both sides directly under the pilothouse windows, they utilized the mid-ship cleats and passed the lines under the hull, securing them tightly to the opposite sides. Next, they attached the last two bags to the hull at the port and starboard quarters. They secured them to more cleats and D-rings on the stern. Lastly, they secured them all together, front bags to rear, ensuring that there would be no shifting of position once she started to move.

It took nearly all the allotted time to install the lifting equipment, so they decided to surface and take a one-hour rest. Back on deck, Rod changed tanks and waited anxiously. He wanted to see his boat riding on the surface, which made the hour drag. He thought about how a couple of days ago he was fighting for his life on this now-tranquil piece of ocean.

"Captain Rod, ready to go?" boomed Jim from the salvage boat, snapping Rod back to reality.

He motioned he was, and without further delays the divers were back over the sides. Rod took up a position about fifteen feet from the bow. P.J. was at the stern, watching as the divers inflated the bags. These guys were good. They knew that a combination of patience and buoyancy would raise *Jus' Restin'* without incident. The bags slowly grew, responding to the air pressure being forced into them from above. After just a few minutes, she started to move! Rod watched with great excitement. *Jus' Restin'* came up nice and level – hanging there, levitating a few feet off the rocky bottom. The current began to move her to the south as she swung on her anchor line.

The divers signaled each other in their own code and more air was added to individual bags. She continued to rise, nice and slow, perfectly level. Rod was impressed! These salvage boys really knew their stuff. They carefully monitored the bags: if she was too positive, they would let out a touch to maintain a good ascent rate. On the surface, the two captains maneuvered on Chet's anchor, keeping their boats about 75 feet from the churning water created by the divers' rising bubbles.

Rod checked his gauges: 55 feet below the surface now, everything going smoothly. He thought of the *USS Squalus*, and the heroic efforts of the Navy divers who rescued all those sailors from a stricken submarine just a few miles ENE of their position. Thinking about being trapped at that depth, with air running out, made chills run up his spine.

The sun shimmered overhead, reflecting off *Jus' Restin'*. Only 25 feet to go. Rod's ears were popping, since the pressure was decreasing rapidly now. Fifteen more feet...steady and level. Her outriggers would be breaking the surface right about now, looking like periscopes.

"Here she comes!" shouted Chet, excited to see *Jus' Restin'* coming to the surface where she belonged. She broke the surface and floated just above the waterline, her gunnels awash. Chet maneuvered the rafted boats over to *Jus' Restin'* and the divers.

The mate from the salvage boat passed the suction hose over the gunnel into *Jus' Restin'*. Jim fired the pump's engine, and soon water was gushing out the salvage boat's stern. Once the water was down to the deck of the *Jus' Restin'*, the mate climbed aboard and placed the pump hose into the bilge. It was a powerful pump and made short work of enabling *Jus' Restin'* to float on her own once again.

The only job left was to retrieve the anchor that held *Jus' Restin'* to the bottom. Rod checked his console gauges: he had just over 2,000 pounds of pressure in his scuba tank. The plan was for the divers to remove the lift bags and return the equipment to the salvage boat while Rod made a final bounce dive to release the anchor. P.J. objected to the idea of Rod going down alone, but reluctantly agreed to stay topside and oversee the show. Dive training stressed not diving alone, but in the real world it happened all the time. Rod went back down the anchor line, his hand riding the 500 feet of line that sloped its way to the anchor.

He felt the pressure building again as he descended into the cold and dark water. The thermocline loomed ahead, its wavy appearance easy to see. Rod continued down, his right hand lightly grasping the line. Occasionally fair-weather clouds blocked the sunlight, so Rod turned on the flashlight that was attached to a strap on his mask. He noticed the different color markings at 100-foot increments along the line; soon he passed the mark that told him there was 100 feet to go.

The rocks began to take shape as he went over the top of Hump 109. The anchor line traveled over a huge mass of fishing gear, trawl lines, and nets that had been snagged on the hump during the hundred or so years of commercial dragger fishing. He finally came upon his shackle – 30 more feet of chain and he'd be at the anchor.

What came into view was more than he expected. Under the snarl of fishing gear was an old ship, her masts broken and rotted and lying across her decks in a mass of tangled lines and debris. Her hull was tucked under an overhang on Hump 109. Rod followed the chain and found that his anchor had ripped into the bow of this old vessel, tearing open the port hull and exposing the forward storage compartment. The storm had made the anchor pull with such force that the opening was big enough to swim into.

His light illuminating the way, he saw an assortment of trunks and boxes inside the ship. The artifacts were strewn about the bottom of the hull, covered with silt and marine growth. He found what appeared to be a small saucer – something from a dinner table setting – and rubbed its front and back. Dishes were always the artifacts that salvage divers looked for. He wasn't sure what it was worth, but it would make a great souvenir. He tucked the saucer into the pocket of his BC.

Rod backed out of the hull, knowing better than to dive into a wreck alone; he had a new appreciation for his own safety. He swam down the length of the vessel, running his glove along the lapstreak sides of her hull. He reached the stern and scanned the rounded, flared craftsmanship of this fine old craft. He tried to read the name on the escutcheon. Sea anemones were growing all over it, so he got out his knife and, starting from the right, scrapped away some of the growth. He made out a Y and then an N, which made him think the vessel was probably out of New York. He continued scraping until he exposed the last letters. It hit him like a ton of bricks...it was the *EBONY!* The quarry of Suzanne and the *Atlantic Zephyr!*

His heart pounded and his mind raced. This was a Pandora's Box if there ever was one! Discovering a ship filled with silver and gold could bring him fame and fortune. But at the same time, he might unleash untold secrets upon mankind. He hovered in the murky waters of the ocean floor, staring at the stern of the old ship and pondering the situation. He was struggling to catch his breath, at first he thought it was all the excitement of the moment. A quick look at his console revealed a new problem, one a diver fears most: he was out of air!

He hadn't paid attention to his air supply – he'd let the excitement of his find override his training, and now he was in trouble. Again! The pressure gauge read empty, but strapped onto his primary tank was his back-up pony bottle, the yellow thirteen-cubic-foot tank that he'd used to free the line from the shaft of the lobster boat in Foley Cove. He swapped regulators and got a breath of air. This, he knew, wouldn't last long because it hadn't been topped off since that last dive, and it would expire quickly at this depth.

He swam for the anchor line and up to the shackle that secured the chain to the nylon line. With his knife still in hand, he cut the nylon free, causing it drift up and away on the current. *Jus' Restin'* was freed from the wreckage.

Now he needed to focus...focus...focus. Slow his breathing down as much as possible, while pulling himself up hand over hand. He had to be smart, or he would never make it to the surface. He dropped his weight belt and continued upwards with steady kicks, exhaling slowly, his lungs expanding as he rose. He held his depth gauge in front of him: steady, kick, focus, focus, exhale, inhale. He was passing the 90-foot depth when the pony bottle expired. It was only 90 feet to the surface: the same length as his driveway at home, a walk he did everyday to get the mail. He took the inflator hose from his BC and put it in his mouth. The expanding air in the BC provided him with a needed breath of air. He continued, blowing out very slowly until the BC provided another life-saving breath.

He looked up towards the light and saw a silhouette. It appeared angelic, as if this was the end of this life and he was being prepared for the next one. He kept looking at the figure against the sunlight, his lungs burning for air. The BC was now empty. The silhouette came closer and closer. Rod felt warm and his vision went blurry. At the moment Rod was sure the end was upon him, a hand from the "angel" pushed a regulator into his mouth. It was P.J., coming to the rescue!

Oh, the feeling of air filling his lungs! He took several deep breaths, then he and P.J. broke the surface a good 300 feet from *Checkers*. They floated on the water for several moments so that Rod could regain his composure. Finally, Rod mustered a thumbs-up. No words were needed – no words could express the feeling of gratitude Rod held for P.J.'s vigilance. But his emotions were decidedly mixed.

Rod and P.J. surface swam on their snorkels to the boat. *Jus' Restin'* was afloat, tied to the starboard side of *Checkers,* with a ladder at the stern set out by Chet. Back on board, the divers now wanted to know why the anchor line had gone slack. What was with that?

"The anchor was jammed, mashed into the rocks as a result of the storm. I cut it free and left it there to rust."

"Very well then. It looks like our work here is done. I'll send you the bill, Cap! Good luck!" laughed Jim.

Rod went to the gunnel and thanked everyone for a job well done. "There will be a nice tip for all of you – you've earned it!"

He pulled in the slack from the anchor line and piled it on the deck in a heap. The boats drifted apart as Chet fired up *Checkers* and eased out the towline that was attached to *Jus' Restin'*. Rod made the return trip sitting on the engine cover of his boat. P.J. took the helm as Chet adjusted the catenary until she was riding smoothly at the right distance off *Checkers'* stern.

Chet was all business navigating *Checkers* back to Plum Island Sound. He was happiest when he had a boat in tow, and was proud to bring *Jus' Restin'* home to Harborside. With any luck, he might get his picture in the next day's paper, so he "tipped" the newspaper with his cell phone, just to be sure.

Rod's emotions were all over the ocean. He was envisioning the *Ebony* lying on the bottom, holding all kinds of possibilities in her hull. And nobody – but nobody – except him knew she was there! He suddenly felt a huge burden on his shoulders. There would have to be some serious thought and planning before he could make any kind of move. It was time to run as silently and as deeply as he ever had in his life...this twist could take him to near crush depth!

Back at Harborside, the mechanics were waiting with a forklift to bring *Jus' Restin'* into the workshop. Essentially, seawater had ruined everything. They would have to completely gut her: new equipment, engine, wiring...the works.

"I think we'll put some real horses in her this time. The only thing she won't be able to pass will be a gas dock!" laughed Rod as he walked with the onlookers alongside *Jus' Restin'* on her way to the repair bay. He ran his hand along her hull and under his breath he muttered, "I always said you'd catch the big one, but you outdid yourself this time."

He envisioned *Jus' Restin'* during the storm, her anchor trolling through the water as if she was the one doing the fishing, then hooking the *Ebony* and refusing to let go. She would go to the bottom before she would give up her greatest catch ever!

"G.W., have your way with her, pal! Make her better than before, whatever she needs. I'm serious: I want real horses installed," Rod told his mechanic.

"You got it Cap! I'll turn it around as quickly as I can, just in time for the next bite."

Rod stopped in his tracks and looked at the people who were standing around, watching and listening to what was happening. "Have it your way," he said with a chuckle, causing everyone to burst into laughter. "Make it so!"

Back home, Rod spread his dive gear out on the driveway to wash out the salt. Then he remembered the dish – he'd forgotten all about it! He opened the pocket of his BC, and there it was, the bottom half of a cup and saucer. He ran the hose over it to see if there were any identifying marks. There were some letters on the back, a symbol similar to a crest, but most of it had faded or was stained from the sea life that had attached itself and made it home for the last 60 years.

He went inside to his computer, and sat and stared at the screen. Suzanne had called this "Ivy" or "Old Ivy"...he couldn't remember exactly. He typed in Old Ivy, and scanned ten pages of sites, but to no avail. Then he remembered that when she said it, he laughed a little and thought about elephant tusks. Ivory? He typed in Old Ivory and bingo! Two pages for Old Ivory porcelain china appeared. He typed in Old Ivory antique dealers, and got a hit for a dealer in York, Maine, called Red Fox Antiques. Not more than twenty miles from his home. He put the dish in the trunk of his motorcycle, got on the bike, and headed for Maine.

He found the antique shop along Route 1 and pulled into the parking lot. An elderly woman, very pleasant, introduced herself as Pearl and asked how she might be of help. Rod reached into his leather jacket and produced the little saucer for her to inspect.

"Oh my, this is a rare one, where did you get it?" she asked, never taking her eyes off the dish. She looked it over very closely, admiring the fine craftsmanship.

"Picked it up at a yard sale. Thought it might be of value. A friend sent me to you." Rod played Mickey the Dunce as best he could, hoping she would be able to identify the piece and validate his beliefs. "Could you tell me what it is and if it's worth anything?"

"What you have here, Sir, is a very, very rare piece of Old Ivory." She continued to inspect the dish carefully. She took it over to a small sink, washed it, and dried it with a soft towel. "This particular hand-painted pattern hasn't been seen in years, since before the war." She looked at the calendar behind her. "We have an exclusive auction here each year for items like this. You might want to sell it; it's very valuable. I'd be interested in purchasing this piece right now."

"How valuable?" Rod queried, pretending to be surprised.

She thought for a moment, then replied, "Maybe $1,000 or more."

"Whoooa, isn't that a pleasant surprise!"

"Are there more pieces where this came from?" she asked, realizing this was a true gem.

"No, this was the only piece. Guess I just got lucky!" He felt like he was holding pocket aces against Doyle Brunson, playing Texas Hold 'em with a huge pot on the table.

"Well, if you find any more and decide to sell, please bring them in. I would love to buy them."

He thanked the woman for her time and left. The pieces of the puzzle were coming together. But he needed more information – he had to go to the source. What he didn't see was Pearl peering through the shades and jotting down his license plate number on a business card she kept in a small lock box under her counter.

On the way home, Rod stopped at the hospital to visit Big Bob. He was awake, with his right leg elevated and encased in a huge cast from his toes to his upper thigh.

"Captain Dude! Glad you could come." Bob was upbeat as usual; he wasn't going to let this keep him down for long. "Let this be a lesson to you. Alcohol and hot top don't mix. The woman who hit me was drunk, and I hit the street. They're cutting back on the pain medication and it's starting to hurt. Afraid I'm going to be in rehab for a while."

"Well, if you need anything, just let me know. The tuna will help pay your expenses. What a day!" Rod gave Big Bob a wink: his share of the catch was going to take some of the pressure off the expenses that were sure to mount. It was an enjoyable visit. He recapped the story of raising the boat, but didn't mention a word about the *Ebony*. They said their goodbyes and Rod headed for home.

Back at the house, all appeared normal. The girls wanted to spend some quality time with their mom, so Rod decided he was going to get away for a while – on terra firma this time. With more than a week of comp and vacation time left, he could finally be alone with his thoughts. He would take the motorcycle and do something he hadn't done in a few years: a Road Trip.

The next morning he said goodbye to Lilly and the girls, loaded the truck, and went to Uncle George's. Both Uncle George and Kasey were as glad to see Rod as he was to see them. Rod was in his comfort zone.

"So Captain, tell me, where are you headed?" asked Uncle George, who had always wanted to go on a real road trip himself.

Rod smiled and continued to load the bike. "I think I'm going to take a ride north, up to Canada. Along the Saint Lawrence River, around the Gaspé Peninsula, and then check out the Maritime Provinces." He reached into his jacket and got out a small envelope. "If anything happens to me, please give this to Lilly. But you *must* hide it where only I would think to look. OK?"

"Sure enough, but you'll be back before you know it. Good times always go by too fast."

"Maybe. The first stop on the tour is going to be Montreal."

"But Rod, they only speak French there – how are you going to deal with that?"

At that moment a Harley downshifted and pulled into the driveway.

"With my interpreter of course!"

Coming to a rumbling stop at their feet was D.C., Uncle George's son. He hit the kill switch and sat there, his hands draped over the handle-bars. He posed quite a sight: 6'3" like his father, full salt and pepper ZZ-Top beard, and a short ponytail sneaking out from under his orange and black Harley-Davidson dew rag. He rounded out his image with a genuine Cuban cigar smoldering in the corner of his mouth. D.C. was a computer expert, had retired from the Coast Guard, still traveled extensively, and spoke several languages. He didn't know it yet, but he was about to embark on a new adventure as Rod's ace in the hole.

"Hey Pop, you coming with us?" D.C. laughed, pointing to the back seat of his Electra-Glide.

"Next time!" George shot back. But he really did want to go along.

"Rod, just had the engine retooled – lots of horses now! Check this out." He hit the starter and the Harley roared to life, causing the big v-twin to shake with power.

"Well, you're going to need them all to keep up with me!" laughed Rod.

D.C. and Rod always traded barbs over the Harley-Davidson vs. Metric rivalry, making for lively conversation. In short order they were on their bikes, as Uncle George held Kasey tightly on her leash.

"We'll send you a postcard from St. Catherine Street. Remember: loose lips sink ships. Take care of my dog and she'll take care of you."

"Understand. Carry on," Uncle George replied with an envious smirk.

The motorcycles came to a stop at the end of the driveway. First things first – time for some tunes, an appropriate riding song. Nothing was better than the Traveling Wilburys' "End of the Line." Rod found it in his iPod and let it rip nice and loud. He kicked the bike into gear and rolled the throttle on, the Wing flying up old Route 1A north to Canada, the music playing in his ears, D.C. and the Harley right on his tail. They were headed up the curve of life again and the sky was the limit!

Chapter Thirteen

Maritime Surprise

The traffic was getting lighter and lighter the farther north they traveled. D.C. and Rod now rode side by side in each lane of the super smooth two-lane highway, cruise control locked right on 80 mph. It was a spectacular autumn ride. They cruised the Interstate through New Hampshire and crossed the Connecticut River into Vermont, where the splendor of fall foliage peaking could be seen at the foothills of the Green Mountains. The weather was cool, crisp, and clear. The air even smelled of autumn: an occasional whiff of ripe wild Concord grapes and woodstoves permeated the rush of wind around the windscreens of the motorcycles.

A road sign indicated that the last exit before the Canadian border was ten miles ahead. D.C. motioned to Rod to take the exit – time for bladders and fuel. Just off the exit was a service station and a greasy spoon. After fueling the bikes, they went into the restaurant, where the smell of burgers and a deep fat fryer filled the air.

"Canadian customs isn't far away. Are you holding?" asked D.C. nonchalantly.

"Are you out of your mind? Between nuclear power plants and charter boats, I'd have to be crazy!"

"I wasn't talking about drugs, numb nuts. Do you have any weapons? Guns?"

"Negative on that, too! Do you?"

"As a matter of fact," replied D.C., glancing around the diner, "I do."

"Since when do you carry weapons? And what are *you* packing?" laughed Rod, only half-heartedly joking about D.C.'s surprise disclosure.

"Always." D.C. pulled open his leather jacket, exposing a shoulder holster with a pistol grip visible. "This trip, a Sig-Sauer 229 Elite Stainless: a personal favorite."

"And you need that for what reason?"

"You never know...until you need it. Helps level many a playing field." D.C. chuckled and zipped up his jacket. At that moment the waitress arrived with their Vermont Long Trail Ales.

"Always like to drink the local water!" laughed D.C. He picked up his ale, clanked the top of Rod's bottle, and smiled at the waitress. "We're going to need a couple more, I'm sure." She smiled and went to the kitchen to check their order and round up two more ales.

The conversation moved to the road trip. D.C. had agreed to go with little to no information because he would take any excuse for a road trip. Besides, Canada was his favorite terrain. They'd ridden together in the oppressive heat of the West, but they preferred the cool climate of the North. Their motto was, "Whenever possible, *never* travel the same road twice." With lunch behind them, they went outside to the bikes.

"OK D.C., here's the basic plan." Rod opened the accordion-like map on the trunk of the Goldwing and traced the route he had envisioned. They would cross the border into

Canada at Philipsburg and go straight to Montreal where they'd raise a little hell in the red light district of St. Catherine Street until their one-dollar bills ran out. Then they'd continue on to Quebec City and cross back over the St. Lawrence River, continuing along the scenic highway that encompasses the entire Gaspé Peninsula. Finally, they would cross into New Brunswick at Campbellton.

"Hey, looks like we're going through Moncton, home of the "Moncton Mauler," laughed D.C.

The "Moncton Mauler" was the nickname the two Georges had given their colorful brother-in-law from Moncton in the fifties. He was a huge fan of Big Time Wrestling. Just mentioning their uncle, a cantankerous guy who was always pulling pranks and keeping everyone entertained, made them laugh.

"After Moncton, maybe another 100 plus miles, we'll cross into Nova Scotia and be in Halifax before you know it." Rod held the map open for D.C., who nodded his approval.

"How come we're going to Halifax?" D.C. asked, not appearing to care one way or another.

"Always wanted to check it out."

"Fine with me. Let's roll!" D.C. hit the starter of the Harley and she roared back to life. He thundered out of the parking lot, while Rod's Goldwing followed silently close behind. After a short run they approached the border. The officials waved them to separate inspection stations.

Rod answered all questions courteously, but it soon became apparent that his motorcycle was going to have to submit to a strip search. 9/11 had changed everything. While Rod was opening the luggage compartments, he noticed that D.C. was sitting on his bike, laughing and joking with his customs agent. As soon as D.C. saw Rod's predicament, he stopped joking and spoke in earnest to his agent, who quickly motioned to let Rod come on through. He was given back his ID and granted passage. D.C. shook hands with his agent and then pulled up alongside Rod.

"Do you know that guy?" asked Rod, impressed by the influence D.C. wielded.

"Let's just say it helps to speak the lingo." D.C. dropped his sunglasses, giving a wink as he gunned the Harley and sped ahead.

Next stop, Montreal. The sun was setting as they backed the bikes up against the curb of the infamous St. Catherine Street, right in front of the Beer Gardens. "As good a place as any to get started – let's go in."

It was all Rod needed to hear. Montreal is "Green Bottle Beer Country": Moosehead, Molson Golden Ale, Labatt. Add the bright neon lights, loud music, the sound of foreign accents, and the smell of French perfume...a little bit of heaven on a Saturday night, and just the trick they needed.

The cousins worked both sides of the street, enjoying the food, drink, and all varieties of entertainment for which the area was famous. After a few hours of frivolity, the effects of partying began to take hold. They decided to find a place to sack out for the night and head for Old Quebec City in the morning.

*

Captain Dodge heard the foghorn from the Eastern Point Lighthouse moaning out its low throaty signal and reverberating through the fog. He leaned against the rail outside the bridge of the *Atlantic Zephyr*, tied fast to the pier in Gloucester Harbor, and enjoyed his old faithful pipe. He'd spent the last three months in a futile search for the *Ebony*, utilizing the finest sonar equipment and GPS navigation to survey and map the bottom terrain off Cape Ann. The wrecks that were located were photographed and, in some cases, explored by Ahmed's six recovery specialists. Not a trace of the *Ebony*.

Having come up empty off Gloucester, Dr. Ahmed Jafari and his backers from King Saud University decided to pursue another lead, an area of promise just north of Halifax, Nova Scotia. With winter a couple of months away, they wanted to leave as soon as possible. It was nearly midnight when Ahmed joined the captain on the rail.

"Any sign of my crew, Captain?" asked Ahmed, checking his watch under the deck light. "I told them to be back on ship by midnight."

"They still have some time. I hope they manage to keep out of trouble, unlike the last time you gave them shore leave. The Portuguese fisherman here in town might not take too kindly to drunken antics on a Saturday night."

"Do not worry Captain, my men can handle *any* situation they might encounter, believe me."

"Well, I hope they don't need to. I'd like to leave this dock early, with no issues. We don't need to draw unwanted attention to this boat."

Captain Dodge and his crew, which included Suzanne, had taken Ahmed, his personnel, and their gear (stored in sealed containers) aboard in Jeddah, Saudi Arabia, the previous June. The two crews only mixed for official work activities. The captain preferred his seclusion; he directed Suzanne to coordinate the search activities with Ahmed.

Having just put the finishing touch on a bottle of Pinot Noir, Suzanne lay in her bunk contemplating her next move. She had strong feelings for Rod, but knew nothing of him outside their brief encounters. Did he harbor the same emotions for her? He'd said they would meet again – "someplace special" – but the boat was leaving early in the morning and there was still no word from him. She decided to let him make the next move, whatever and whenever that might be. She turned out her light and fell asleep to the sound of the lonely foghorn.

A light breeze had lifted the fog, and the sun shone brightly as Captain Dodge gave his initial orders. The *Atlantic Zephyr*'s bow thruster eased her prow into North Channel, and her port stern spring line held her close as she pivoted on the pier. The captain skillfully maneuvered his ship; she was soon headed 180 degrees about and easing through Entrance Channel towards the Eastern Point jetty. The *Atlantic Zephyr* was a sleek, shell-white vessel, just over 140 feet in length. She would cruise to Halifax at a steady steam of ten knots, gracefully covering the estimated 350 nautical miles and arriving late Monday afternoon or early evening.

*

D.C. was up and thrashing around the motel room – his way of letting Rod know it was time to get moving. Once breakfast was behind them and the bikes were loaded, they were off to Quebec City. It was a short ride through the city, across the Saint Lawrence River, then northeast along the eastern shoreline.

The weather report had predicted a low-pressure front coming in from behind, and the forecast was proving to be correct. After barely 100 miles it began to rain. Both of them had logged many miles in rain, hail, and even slush, but if foul weather could be avoided, why not adjust? By 11:00, it was time to reconsider the route. They stopped at a local pub to compare the weather map to the road map.

"We'll have this figured out in a couple of minutes," said D.C. confidently, booting up his laptop.

Rod asked the waitress if she'd mind changing the TV over the bar to the weather channel. Between the computer, map, and weather channel, the boys decided it was time to take a detour to the southeast where the weather looked more promising. They'd skip the long route around Gaspé, and instead take a road out of Quebec, into New Brunswick, around the tip of Maine, along the St. John River, and eventually into Fredericton, New Brunswick. It turned out to be the right decision.

The weather steadily improved until the sun began to streak through the clouds. By late afternoon it was blue skies and warm air as they entered the outskirts of Fredericton and decided to find a motel and a place to eat. D.C. discovered a fine upscale restaurant on the waterfront, with window seats overlooking the docks. They scanned the menu and ordered their drinks and dinner. It was pretty much big boy's talk of fishing and riding until D.C.'s third scotch arrived.

"OK Rod, what's the deal – why are we going to Halifax? I've got a feeling this is more than a scenic tour." He sipped his scotch and waited patiently for Rod's answer.

Up to that point Rod had kept everything to himself: not a word of his secret to anyone. He'd thought long and hard about bringing D.C. into his confidence. If he was going to open the door, now was the time. He decided the moment was right but he wouldn't divulge everything at once.

"We've talked about the events of the past couple weeks – the *Jus' Restin'* sinking and all," Rod began, choosing his words carefully.

"Pretty lucky if you ask me! Glad you made it, cuz." D.C. lifted his glass to salute.

"Well, there's more luck involved than meets the eye. The anchor wasn't snagged on the bottom: it was hooked into the bow of a shipwreck. I know this because I dove down to release the hook." Rod picked up his drink and winked.

"Now *I'm* hooked! What kind of shipwreck? Maybe some other goodies inside? Jesus, some guys have all the luck! But what does this have to do with Halifax?" fired off D.C..

"Easy cousin...there's a woman involved."

"There's always a woman involved!" laughed D.C., drawing attention from the other diners. His scotch balls were making themselves known.

Rod turned his head away and gazed out the window at the fishermen on the dock below. Quietly he said, "We'll continue this conversation in the motel room."

They paid the check and headed out to the bikes, which were parked next to the awning over the entrance. D.C. was about to get on his Harley when he saw a twenty dollar bill lying on the ground under the motor.

"Hey, looks like my luck's about to change, too!" He bent down to pick up his newfound fortune, but when his fingers were within an inch of the bill, it moved as though an undetectable breeze had it in its control. He reached again and the bill again jumped beyond his grasp. He grabbed for it a third time, but the effects of the scotch had taken their toll: he stumbled and nearly fell over.

Out of the corner of his eye, Rod noticed that the bushes about 30 feet away were rustling with the sound of snickering kids. It seems they had taken a real twenty, glued it to a weight and some fishing line, and were having their fun with tourists leaving the restaurant. Other patrons who'd been duped were watching the pranksters pull in the line and run away across the parking lot, laughing at their latest victim. D.C. watched the twenty-dollar bill bounce across the parking lot as the onlookers laughed at him with glee. He looked at Rod, reached into his jacket, and put his hand on the Sig.

"You laugh and you're first!" he joked, knowing he'd been had. "I feel like I've been done in by the Bushman of San Francisco."

"I hope you're not always this easy. Come on, let's go," laughed Rod.

After a short ride in the cool evening salt air, they returned to the motel. D.C. went right back to interrogation mode – he especially wanted to know more about The Woman. Rod explained how he'd met Suzanne and Ahmed in the first storm, her surprise return for a sunset cruise, and how she'd supplied him with the tuna coordinates.

"That still doesn't tell me how she's involved with Halifax. What's the connection?" he pressed.

"The day of the sunset cruise, Suzanne brought a lot of wine – which we happily consumed. Conversation turned to what brought her to this area, as she's clearly not a local. During the course of the evening, Suzanne said she was on a research ship, the *Atlantic Zephyr*, searching for *this* particular wreck, and that the ship's manifest declared it was carrying a unique type of antique dinnerware. Called it Old Ivory." Rod took a sip of his Diet Coke and continued. "I found a dish in that hull – it's the real deal all right. I had it checked: an antique dealer offered me a grand for it, validating what Suzanne said about its origin."

"Not bad: a kilo-buck for one dish? There must be more than just dishes though. Anything else?" D.C. was digging. Rod decided he could handle more.

"Suzanne said that the *Ebony*, although this wasn't listed on the manifest, was transporting jewels and gold liberated from the Germans, who had stolen it during WWII."

"Oh, baby! The plot thickens! Ya-ya-ya! See any of the shiny stuff?" D.C. was on the edge of his chair now, hanging on Rod's every word.

"Not yet, but I'm sure it's there. Only made the one dive, and that was short-lived. Barely made it back to the surface!"

Rod rubbed his chest, remembering the burning in his oxygen-starved lungs.

"Well, that's all fine, but what do you need the chick for? *You* found it, not her! It's all yours!" D.C. leaned back, pulled out his lighter, and proceeded to spark up a big Cuban cigar.

"That may very well be true, but there's more." Rod knew that from here on in, he would have to choose his words wisely and sparingly.

"More?" replied D.C., resuming his perch on the edge of the chair and blowing the stogie smoke out the side of his mouth. "What 'more' could there possibly be?"

"Well..." Rod hesitated for a long moment. "For now, let's just say an item of 'scientific interest.' I'm hoping Suzanne can shed some light on it."

"Scientific interest? I'm all ears."

"Hey, I've already told you more than I know." laughed Rod, realizing that what he'd just said was pretty close to the truth. "The *Atlantic Zephyr* is due in Halifax Harbor any time. We'll look for her tomorrow. When we find her, we'll find Suzanne – and hopefully get the information we need." Rod looked at his watch and abruptly stood up. It was almost 11:30. "Well, that's it for tonight. I'm going to sleep."

Rod closed his eyes. He knew that once the word got out that the *Ebony* had been discovered, it would be difficult, if not impossible, to keep others from trying to locate her and plunder the cargo. His primary mission would be to determine what the items of scientific interest looked like, so that he could dive back down and retrieve them prior to claiming the remainder of the booty. He would need to convince Suzanne to willingly give up whatever information she had without revealing his scheme. Deception was never a strong suit for Rod, and he knew his task was not going to be easy – especially with the gravity of the situation and possible consequences of failure.

D.C. took the lead the next morning and never gave it up. He was on a mission to get to Halifax and Rod had better keep up. "Sparks were flying" was not just an expression when he was on the move because he would lay that bike over in the corners, and grind the pegs on many a tight turn. He literally enjoyed life on the edge.

It was mid-afternoon when they rolled into the seaport town of Halifax. An Indian summer day and the weather could not have been more accommodating. The road they ventured on led to the wharf, where many large ships – mainly cruise ships – were tied up. They parked the bikes and walked the touristy shops and restaurants, stopping here and there for samplings of the local food.

"Well, is your boat here?" asked D.C., looking about. "I don't see it anywhere."

"I don't think so, but we need a better view." Rod leaned over to the tourists sitting beside them. "Do you know where there's a good spot overlooking the city?"

"Sure," replied one of the ladies. "Go right up that street over there – it'll take you to the top of Citadel Hill. You'll be able to see the complete harbor, everything. Best view around."

"Thanks." Rod turned back to D.C., "Indians always take the high ground. Let's check it out."

When they arrived at the top they found a huge fortress: Fort George, built by the British in the 1700s. Approximately 250 feet above sea level, it offers a commanding view of the harbor and its approaches. They were just completing a self-guided tour of the grounds when Rod reached into his blue jeans, fumbled through his change, and got out a quarter. He walked over to one of the tourism binoculars and inserted the coin. He panned the viewfinder to the right, looked up over the top, and then returned to the eyepiece. He stepped back and motioned for D.C. to come forward.

"Here she comes, right on time. Take a look."

"Beautiful boat," remarked D.C., admiring the vessel. Turning to Rod he asked, "Now what do we do?"

"First we need to find a place to stay and then figure out a way to meet Suzanne."

It didn't take long to find a motel close to the wharf. Rod asked for a room with two double beds, but D.C. cut him off.

"I got a feeling I'm going to get lucky in this town! Give us two rooms, and keep us as far away from each other as possible," he laughed. The clerk handed them each a registration card and asked if they wanted Jacuzzi tubs. He'd barely gotten the words out of his mouth when D.C. answered, "Absolutely! We've been riding hard, cuz – we need to relax a little!"

"After you unload your motorcycles, there's a garage next to the motel where you can keep your bikes out of the weather," said the clerk. "I'll give you the code. They'll be secure there."

Rod opened the door to the room and looked at his surroundings. Nice. This would make a fine place to hatch his plan. Looking out the window to the far end of the motel, he could see D.C. unloading his bike at his room near the office. Rod sat on the edge of the bed and began to put the pieces of his plan in order. First, he had to make a couple of cell calls.

"G.W., how you doin'? Any progress on retrofitting *Jus' Restin'*?"

"You're gonna love this, Cap. Got a deal on a new 502 cubic inch with over 500 hp. This baby is hot! Huge carburetor, racing cams, new outdrive – the works. Came in on the truck yesterday morning. Jason's handling all the electronics and wiring. She'll be a sleeper on the water until you whack the throttle. That new carburetor pours in gas like a toilet flushing water. You're gonna need that 173-gallon fuel tank now! Also ordered you a new Viking for the overhead. Hoping to have her back in the water, E.O.D. tomorrow."

"Whoa, you da man, G.W.! I appreciate what you're doing here. I'll make it right with you – keep up the good work, pal. You're awesome!"

Next, a quick call to Uncle George, requesting him to take the dive tanks from the shed to the dive shop and have them filled. He would need them as soon as he got home. They chatted a moment about the trip and Rod asked how he and Kasey were getting along. As usual, there were no problems. Rod said all was well with him and D.C., that they were having a great time together and would be home in a few days.

Rod was getting dressed after a soak in the Jacuzzi when D.C. knocked on the half-open door, carrying a bottle of single malt scotch. "What do you say – a little happy hour to help us nail down our plan?"

"Sure," replied Rod. "Sit down. Here's what I've been thinking..." He pointed his index finger towards the wharf. "We'll head back down to the docks and restaurants. I'll make contact with Suzanne and try to arrange a meeting, maybe at that bar we saw. It looked like a good place. Then I'll share a little wine and talk with Suzanne and try to figure out what I'm looking for on the bottom of the ocean."

"Sounds fine to me, but I ain't playing your illegitimate brother when she shows. I don't want you to even acknowledge my existence. I'll have your back. You need to play this charade on your own. Remember, I'll *never* be far away."

"Probably best. She may open up more without a stranger around."

"Now you're thinking, cuz" agreed D.C., passing a glass to Rod.

The bar was a short walk from the motel and soon they had seats overlooking the waterfront. To the far right, over the top of the next building, D.C. pointed out what appeared to be the bridge of the *Atlantic Zephyr* tied to the pier. While Rod ordered the drinks, D.C. stepped out to reconnoiter the ship. It was the *Atlantic Zephyr* all right. Rod checked his watch: it was almost 19:00 when D.C. stepped back through the door into the bar.

"OK, pal, time to put Operation Scientific Interest in motion," chuckled D.C.

Rod pulled out his cell phone and selected "Contacts, Pierre." He pressed SEND and the phone began to ring.

"Bonjour, this is Suzanne," said a soft voice on the other end.

"Hello Suzanne, it's Rod. How are you?"

"I'm very well, thank you! I was so sad I missed you before we left Gloucester. I was thinking I would never hear from you or see you again."

"Well, I think you're in luck. If you're on your boat, which I'm hoping you are, I'm barely a couple of hundred yards away as we speak."

"You are here? In Halifax? What a terrific surprise!"

Suzanne was excited to hear his voice and the prospect of seeing him again, and this was evident in her response.

"I was hoping we could share that wine I promised you."

There was a short silence. Suzanne was already planning her exit from the ship.

"The crew is about to head into town for liberty. Ahmed and I were going to have dinner together, but he can just say hello and then rejoin his crew. I can't wait! This is wonderful! Where can I find you?"

"That's easy. Sitting right here in Rudy's Tavern, along Cornwallis Street as you leave the pier. Can't miss it. I'll be inside standing by." Rod hung up. He turned to give D.C. a thumbs-up, but he was nowhere to be found.

It wasn't long before Suzanne, followed by a smiling Ahmed and his swaggering crew, entered the pub. Her eyes met Rod's as he turned from the bar, having seen her reflection in the mirror when she entered.

"Captain Rod!" she exclaimed, giving him the hug and kiss he'd been dreaming about. "This is too good to be true. How did you know I would be here?"

"You told me your destination, and I figured you would port before starting your next survey. Took a chance and it paid off." Rod smiled. He, obviously, was glad he'd made the effort to meet her again.

D.C.'s digital camera was clicking away from a cyber café across the street: he was shooting pictures of the entire entourage as they entered Rudy's front door. He reached into his pocket and produced a thin cable, with which he hooked his camera to a computer. First he furiously typed in some words, then a series of numbers, then slowly tapped a few more keys. He glanced across the street while the computer did its thing. He nonchalantly scanned his surroundings.

"Captain, it is so good to see you again! I have told my crew all about you!" said Ahmed. He turned to his men, who acknowledged Rod. "What brings you all the way to Halifax?"

"Figured I needed a little time on firm ground after my adventures, so I decided to take the motorcycle on a road trip. A few days to get away, that's all."

"We monitored your radio traffic during the storm. We were worried about your safety, but here you are safe and sound. You are a fortunate man!" said Ahmed. He then spoke to his crew in a foreign language; they headed for the door, and Ahmed turned back to Rod and Suzanne. "Again, it's good to see you Captain Rod. Enjoy your trip. Suzanne, remember we leave at 06:00. Have a good evening." He left the tavern to join his group waiting outside, and they all wandered up Cornwallis Street in search of their own adventures.

"I had a chance to peruse the wine list, and selected an August Briggs Pinot Noir," Rod said to Suzanne. "I have to admit: it was the waitress's recommendation." He motioned to the waitress, and she brought the wine as planned.

They drank the wine and talked about the sinking and subsequent raising of the *Jus' Restin'*, and about the tuna Rod caught. Suzanne ordered another glass of wine, staying with the same choice, since it was a refreshing surprise.

"So, now you are here in Halifax. Again searching for that same boat?" Rod asked, knowing where he wanted to navigate the conversation.

"Yes. I thought our best chances were in Cape Ann, but they pulled the plug on us. Gave us new coordinates...we'll try them and see what happens." She didn't sound very confident of her chances of success.

"You said you thought there might be something 'special' on board, based on a rumor you overheard. How would you know what to look for?"

Rod was reaching, trying to get a basic description, but what he was about to get was more than he'd envisioned. Suzanne thought for moment about how fruitless the search had been, and the dim prospects of success in this remote location. It seemed to her that the project was turning into a worthless endeavor.

"It's all right here," she said, pulling a memory stick out of her shoulder bag. She motioned the waitress to their table. "Is there computer access here?"

"No, but right across the street," she said, pointing out the bay window, "is an Internet café. And the best part is they serve wine, too!"

Rod paid the check and left the waitress a substantial tip. The two of them crossed the street to the café. Once inside, Rod spotted D.C. but was careful not to acknowledge him. They sat at a computer and ordered two small glasses of wine. Suzanne removed the memory stick from her pocket and placed her jacket on the back of her chair. Rod couldn't help but notice how stunning she looked in the soft lights of the café – every time he laid eyes on her she looked more beautiful.

"Do you like Paul McCartney and Stevie Wonder?" Suzanne asked. "I filed this under Ebony and Old Ivory. Cute, huh?" She smiled as she scanned and called up the picture file. Rod moved in close behind her in order to view the screen from a better angle. Again, that perfume! She opened a series of photographs taken years before: black and whites, but good quality film.

"Looks like people loading a ship," said Rod, talking directly behind Suzanne's ear. She turned and gave him a little peck on the cheek.

"As you can see, it is the *Ebony* being loaded at the dock in Bordeaux prior to her departure. She was carrying a substantial amount of cargo."

While Suzanne continued to scan the pictures, Rod glanced at D.C., who appeared not to be paying attention to them. When Rod turned back to the computer screen, D.C. looked back up, indeed monitoring them closely.

"You talked about how you overheard something of the scientist's work." Rod was pushing his luck but he had to find out if she did, in fact, know more.

"Yes," she continued, "I believe they are looking for this."

She magnified a picture of a nondescript item. Rod rolled the mouse wheel to further enlarge the picture, and leaned in for a closer look. It appeared to be a cylinder, possibly a section of pipe, about three inches in diameter. It was dull and most likely made of lead. There were no visible threads at the end caps, so he figured they must have been soldered. If he was right, this item of scientific interest would be watertight and corrosion-resistant, its contents undamaged even after all these years lying on the bottom of the ocean.

*

It was a busy day in Pearl's shop in York, Maine. Pearl stayed open a little later than usual, because she was enjoying the brisk business and companionship of several longtime friends and customers. Just as she was about to leave, something caught the corner of her eye: a business card. She picked it up from under the counter and dialed the telephone number into her antique rotary phone.

"Hello, Mr. Jafari, is that you?" she asked in her frail voice.

"Yes it is. To whom am I speaking?" Ahmed asked.

"This is Miss Pearl, from Red Fox Antiques. You stopped into my shop a couple of months ago. You were looking for Old Ivory."

"Yes, Miss Pearl, I did. How may I help you?" he answered, having a hard time hearing over the noise from the bar.

"It is I who can help you, Mr. Jafari," replied Pearl. "I apologize for getting back to you as late as I have, but I misplaced your business card."

"That is no problem, Miss Pearl. What information do you have for me?" Ahmed's interest was peaking. He walked outside into the quiet night air, hanging on Pearl's every word.

"Last week a gentleman with Old Ivory came into my shop," she began. "It was the exact pattern of which you inquired. It was stained and smelled a little strange, as if it had been, maybe, underwater for a period of time."

"Did the man leave an address or phone number where he could be reached?"

"No, he did not."

"Well, could you do your best to describe him to me?"

"Oh, certainly. He was a tall man, over six feet at least. He had snow-white hair and a scruffy goatee. Maybe it just needed to be trimmed."

"This is very helpful, Miss Pearl. Do you remember anything else?" Ahmed pressed for any clue that might help him identify the mystery man.

"Oh, yes – I almost forgot. He was riding a big black motorcycle. I couldn't see the license plate number, but I think it was from New Hampshire."

"Why, Miss Pearl, you have been a tremendous help! I will send a little something your way. Thank you very much." Ahmed stared at his phone. It didn't take a genius to do the math here. He was sure Rod was the mystery man, and he was right here in Halifax!

While sipping wine at the Internet café, Suzanne and Rod chose a restaurant from the city's webpage. Suzanne excused herself and headed for the ladies' room. She wasn't two feet inside the door when D.C. was at Rod's side.

"We have to leave – NOW! This is bigger than you know!"

"But why? What's the problem?"

Rod wasn't in the mood to go anywhere with D.C., not with Suzanne and dinner a few moments away. Right then Suzanne's cell phone, which was lying on the table, beeped one time. D.C. looked towards the ladies' room, then picked up the phone and flipped the lid. TEXT MESSAGE. He read the text and then turned the little screen for Rod to see: "Captain Rod has found the Ebony. Do not leave him. We are coming. Where are you?"

D.C. tossed Suzanne's phone in her bag and grabbed Rod by the arm. They flew out the front door and down a side alley.

"What's going on? Tell me now!" demanded Rod.

"No time. We must stay clear of Ahmed and his men. They're not who they say they are. We need to get our bikes and get out of here!" D.C. was adamant and meant business. The Sig-Sauer was now out of its holster, held low along its master's side. The two men sneaked back to their motel.

"What about Suzanne?" whispered Rod, concerned for her safety. "Are we just going to leave her?"

"There's nothing we can do about her right now. We have to get out of here! Get into your room, pack your stuff, and when I call your cell, come to the garage. But NOT until I call. Move!"

Suzanne returned to the table and sat patiently sipping the last of the wine and waiting for Rod, whom she assumed had also gone to the restroom. She looked out the window and saw Ahmed walking hastily up the street, looking in the windows of every restaurant. One of his henchmen was working the other side of the street. She glanced at the men's room, expecting to see Rod appear at any moment, but the door stayed closed. She turned back and saw Ahmed peer through the window, and then silently enter the café.

"Where is Captain Rod?" he demanded in a low voice. This was a side of Ahmed Suzanne had never seen. "I said, where is Captain Rod?" He glared at Suzanne and she pointed timidly at the restroom.

One of the henchmen entered the café; Ahmed motioned for him to stay where he was. Ahmed approached the restroom door and slowly opened it. He pulled a handgun from his jacket pocket and entered, scanning side to side. It was empty: Rod was gone. He turned back to Suzanne. "I sent you a message to keep Rod with you. Where did he go? Why did you let him leave?"

"I never received any message, Ahmed. Why, what is wrong? Why are you looking for Rod? Why are you so upset?"

Ahmed fumbled through Suzanne's bag and grabbed her phone. He flipped the lid and showed Suzanne the message. She read it and nearly fainted.

"What did you tell him? What does he know?" Ahmed demanded, shaking Suzanne.

Suzanne was in shock over the news, but was more distressed at the way she was being manhandled by Ahmed. She was afraid for her safety. She quickly surmised that it was in her best interest not to divulge any of her and Rod's conversation about the *Ebony*.

"I told him nothing about the *Ebony*. We only talked about how he caught the tuna and lost his boat in the storm. We were just getting ready to go to dinner when you came in."

"He must have seen the message, because he's gone." Ahmed told his men to continue searching the port for Rod. "Suzanne, return to the ship and tell Captain Dodge to prepare to get under way. The *Atlantic Zephyr* is going back to Gloucester."

D.C. and Rod were ready to depart in a matter of minutes. D.C. reached into the top pocket of his saddlebag, got out a short stainless steel cylinder, and screwed it onto the barrel of the Sig. He squinted through the curtain: all clear. He exited the room and walked to the garage while Rod watched from the window. D.C. rolled up the garage door and loaded the Harley; when he finished he scanned the lot again – still clear – so he called Rod, who immediately joined him.

"You know the way out of here. I'll follow you. Don't stop for anyone." D.C. said.

The bikes came to life; the thunder from the Harley echoing in the garage could be heard two blocks away. Rod took the lead, turned the corner and then stopped for a red light. One of Ahmed's men appeared from out of nowhere, blocking his path. D.C. followed from behind, his headlight shining brightly on the man as he lunged for Rod's arm. It was the last move he'd ever make. Phut, phut went the Sig and down the man fell, in a lifeless heap. D.C. got off the Harley, grabbed him by his feet, and dragged him into the nearby bushes. He climbed back on his bike and caught up to a stunned Rod.

"I told you not to stop!" D.C. shouted. He scanned the area: it was clear in all directions. "Now, let's go, *and keep going this time!*"

Chapter Fourteen

The Coast is Clear

Nearly an hour and a half later D.C. signaled for them to turn into the back parking lot of an all-night diner on the outskirts of Moncton. Rod got off his bike and proceeded to get right into D.C.'s face. D.C. held him off.

"Go inside, get us some coffee, and when you return I'll answer all your questions." D.C. was calm; after all, he had the helm now. "Just go, please."

While Rod was in the diner, D.C. removed his laptop from his saddlebag and booted it up on the seat of the Harley. He went through the same series of keystrokes that he used in the café. When Rod returned he minimized the screen.

"I'm all ears, D.C. What the hell is going on here?"

"When you first told me about the *Ebony*, I thought it was just a story of good fortune and I took it for face value. But you piqued my curiosity when you enlightened me on the item of scientific interest. I did some research and decided to take a low profile once we got to Halifax. While you were in Rudy's, I shot and uploaded pictures of Suzanne, Ahmed, and all of Ahmed's people."

"Uploaded to where? I don't understand. Plus, you shot a guy! For all we know, you might have killed him! And now I could be an accomplice to murder!" Rod was whispering at the top of his lungs. D.C. continued to explain.

"It'll be clear in a minute." He maximized the screen and a full view picture of Ahmed appeared before his eyes. "I'd like you to meet an Iranian named Vali Davood Pahlavi." D.C. paused as Rod took in the scene of a man in military clothing in an unknown desert location. "And here are two of his comrades," he added, scrolling to the next screen. Rod had seen them both earlier that evening at Rudy's.

"I still don't get it. How do you know this? What's your angle?"

D.C. reached into his pocket and pulled an ID from his wallet. He handed it to Rod and maximized another page, throwing the knockout punch. Rod looked at the screen in amazement. United States Department of Homeland Security! Next, he looked at D.C.'s ID, which indicated Top Secret clearance and pictured a clean-shaven Chief Warrant Officer 04 in uniform. Rod was bewildered.

"After 9/11 I voluntarily activated myself back into the Coast Guard. With my military and computer backgrounds, I got spun off to counter-terrorism. Since then, I've been working on a number of operations you'll never hear about. You and I, quite simply, stumbled into this one. But I need to know one thing. Did you find out from Suzanne what we're looking for?"

Rod thought long and hard, then decided he would give up the information about the item of scientific interest. But he wouldn't yield the *Ebony's* coordinates – not just yet. Under the amber lights of the road stop, Rod brought D.C. up to speed.

"Well, that explains the Iranian interest. They've always wanted The Bomb, but whenever they get anywhere close, the Israelis target their facilities and kick the crap out of them, negating their progress and sending them hurtling backwards. This information could give them the edge they've been seeking...and with all that oil money, they'd look forever."

"Ahmed – or whatever his name is – now knows that I know where the *Ebony* is located. He's going to try to find me, so we need to get to the *Ebony* before he does. Let's put our heads together here, cuz."

"One thing is in our favor," said D.C. "Although we know that he knows that we know where the *Ebony* is located, he doesn't know that we know who he is and what he's up to. He thinks he has the upper hand, and we'll use that fact to our advantage."

"I've got a couple more questions. I'm concerned about Suzanne, and how about the guy you shot?"

"Negative on Suzanne: no information yet on whether she or the crew members of the *Atlantic Zephyr* are in collusion. Regarding the man who was about to drag you away: I'll relay all pertinent information and that problem will disappear. If he'd gotten ahold of you, cuz, life for you would be a lot different now."

"One last thing. Ahmed – what's his story?"

"Ahmed and his men are terrorists. Plain and simple. We lost track of him several months ago. They do, however, possess some unique skills, which typically are nonexistent for this type of terrorist. Namely, underwater tactics. We need to be ready for them – and trust me, we will." D.C. closed down the laptop and motioned Rod towards the gas station across the street. "Let's fill 'em up and ride."

*

Captain Dodge was sipping his coffee when he noticed Suzanne sprinting up the gangway. She came directly to the bridge and stood before him. "I just left Ahmed. He wants you to prepare to leave for Gloucester. Right away."

"Well, I'm afraid that's not going to happen, not for at least twelve hours," the captain replied calmly. "The starboard turbine is down for maintenance. We've got a fuel issue. Why, at this time of night, is he in such a hurry to go back to Gloucester?"

"For some reason he believes that Captain Rod has found the *Ebony*."

"Well, has he?" Captain Dodge snapped backed, looking Suzanne directly in the eyes.

"I don't know. He and I were getting ready to have dinner and he disappeared. Then Ahmed came looking for him; his men are still looking."

"Sounds to me like he does know. And if Ahmed's men are looking for him, Ahmed must have information that he does." He stirred his coffee slowly, took another sip, then picked up the ship's phone and called his chief. "Smitty, get the crew up and complete the turbine repair. We need to get under way ASAP."

About an hour later Ahmed returned to the ship with his men. One of them appeared to Captain Dodge to have passed out – he guessed because of too much drink – and the others were carrying him. The captain intercepted Ahmed on the bridge.

"Looks like one of your men had a little too much party," he observed as the other men went below decks with the "drunk" draped on their shoulders.

"It's a good thing we found him – he was passed out in the bushes. No substitute for technology," said Ahmed, holding a small GPS personnel locator in his hand. "All my men carry them." He abruptly changed the topic to departure time.

Captain Dodge informed him of the ongoing maintenance activity. Although they were making progress, it would be at least noon before they could functionally test the turbine. Upset at the delay, Ahmed stormed off to his cabin; he needed to go to Gloucester and get Rod under surveillance. He knew Rod would be heading for the *Ebony* now that his secret was out. Ahmed found a morning flight to Boston and booked it for one.

*

It was just past sunrise when the motorcycles rolled into Rockland, having crossed the border at Calais. They'd traveled Route 1 south throughout the night. Rod couldn't help but think back to his childhood days as he approached the "Lobster Capital of the World." Life had certainly changed from those carefree times.

"It'll take at least two to three hours to return to Portsmouth, and then we need to prepare to go offshore to the *Ebony*," Rod said to D.C. "I'll call G.W. and see when *Jus' Restin'* can get back into the water." D.C. nodded and entered the diner for breakfast.

Rod placed the call. "G.W., what's the latest? How's the boat? I'll need her as soon as you give me the green light."

There was a short silence, but there usually was when G.W. had something to say. He always thought before he spoke – something Rod wished he'd learned years ago. "Hey Cap. We're looking really good. I've had her running in the shop. Whoa, baby! She's got some kind of power. The last of the electronics go in this morning with a sea trial this afternoon. Will you be there for the ride?"

"Not really sure but don't wait for me. Get her ready. Shake her down good and top her off. We'll talk later. Thanks, G.W." Rod was pleased. The shop had come through again.

"Rod, I've been thinking," said D.C., "you should stay clear of your house. Give Lilly a call and make sure she leaves and stays somewhere else for a while. Your house could become a target. Nowadays, anyone can find out where you live."

To D.C.'s surprise, Rod disagreed. "I've got to go by my house and get a piece of gear. Imperative. I'll be in and out in a flash. We can meet at your father's house later. We'll leave from there in the morning, get the boat, and sneak out to the *Ebony* before anyone else can." He thought for a moment and continued. "Nobody but me knows where the *Ebony* is. If people are watching, they're going to have to follow me to find it. We'll have to keep a sharp eye for anyone or anything out of the ordinary. Anyone suspicious." D.C. agreed to the plan.

The final leg to Portsmouth went by quickly. D.C. waved goodbye as he leaned into the exit that led to his home in York. Meanwhile, Rod continued over the Piscataqua Bridge towards his own home ten miles away. He hit the garage door opener and the Goldwing slipped inside; the door immediately closed behind him.

Neither Lilly nor the girls were home. The girls had gone back to college, but Lilly should have been there. Rod went into the kitchen and scanned the scene. The only thing unusual was an envelope with his name on it at his place on the table; Rod picked up the envelope and took out a folded piece of paper. It was from Lilly, dated the day he left for the road trip. He read the letter, shook his head slowly, and read it again...some pieces of life's puzzle began to fit into place.

Lilly explained how she felt that life was passing her by, that she was always in the background while her husband chased his dreams, trying for his "big score." She went on to say that although Rod thought she'd kicked her desire to gamble, she had actually been pursuing it with renewed vigor, buoyed by a game where she made her own big score. Meanwhile, Rod had thought she was working. She regretted lying, but she was determined to chase her dream of becoming a professional gambler. She was on her way to Las Vegas! Rod put the letter back in the envelope and set it on the table where he found it. Still didn't explain how P.J. fit into the equation, but there was nothing he could do about it now. He knew she would be safer away from here, and he had bigger fish to fry.

*

Ahmed assembled his men at 07:30 in his stateroom below decks. He discussed the events of the night before and the progress towards setting sail for Gloucester – the captain had indicated an earlier 10:00 departure time. He directed Rasheed, his second in command, to dispose of their fallen comrade's body at sea under the cover of darkness. He further explained that he would be boarding a flight to Boston, and would keep Captain Rod under surveillance until the rest of the men arrived in Gloucester on the *Atlantic Zephyr*. He got his satellite phone and glanced towards the locked case of weapons in the corner of the room. The only weapon he would have, until he arrived in Boston, would be his wits. Once there, he would rendezvous with a contact and the weapon problem would be solved. He wished his men well, ensured them that they would succeed and departed for the plane.

Captain Dodge was in the engine room leaning over the rail, overseeing the early completion of the corrective maintenance to the starboard turbine. His engineer reported that they were nearly done and would test the engine shortly; the captain acknowledged the effort of his engineer and crew. His mind drifted back over the story of Captain Rod. How did he find the *Ebony* while he, with all his sophisticated gear, had been unsuccessful? He suddenly stood up and left the engine room.

He entered his stateroom and went directly to his half-open safe, then got out the ship's log and flipped backwards through the pages. He found a piece of paper and jotted down some notes, returned the log to the safe, and this time, closed the door and spun the tumblers. Then he went downstairs one level and knocked on a door.

"Good morning Captain," said Suzanne, smiling.

"Good morning, Suzanne. I want you to call up these coordinates from your sonar files." He handed her the note and stood by as she sat at her keyboard and entered the numbers. Within a moment the screen showed a picture of the ocean floor, complete with multi-colored contour lines and a large hump rising up from the center. "Show me a complete scan of that rise, from all angles."

Suzanne worked the keyboard, and the screen began to revolve around the point in question. When the scan was completed, the two of them looked at each other.

"There must be an acoustic shadow hiding it."

"I don't understand, Captain. Hiding what? What do you expect to see?" asked a bewildered Suzanne, pointing to the screen.

"The *Ebony*, of course! These are the coordinates I wrote down when Captain Rod broadcast his mayday. This is where his boat sank! I believe that he found the *Ebony* while recovering his own boat. How else would he ever find it? Especially ten miles offshore."

Suzanne continued rotating the screen and pondering Captain Dodge's conclusion. She looked for something that might corroborate his assessment of the clues. It certainly wasn't out of the question – as a matter of fact, the probability was quite high. *And I thought he had come to see me,* she sighed.

*

It was late afternoon when Rod and D.C. rendezvoused at Uncle George's Essex home. They brought the dive gear from the shed into the living room and began an intense check of the equipment. Both 120-tanks were verified at 3500 psi, and the pony bottle was all set at 3000 psi. Rod personally checked each piece of gear and loaded them individually into his dive bag. Then he put a case on the coffee table and opened its contents.

"D.C., check this out." Rod held up a mask with an underwater receiver and push-to-talk button. He passed the control panel over to D.C. "With this outfit, we'll be able to communicate: you in the boat, me in the water."

"Cool, I'm digging it, Captain. And I like this item, too." D.C. held up a bright yellow underwater halogen light. "It'll probably be pretty dark when we arrive. Good idea."

Uncle George had finished preparing dinner, and the three of them took their seats around the table.

"Uncle George, do you have that envelope I left with you?"

"Sure do." George got up and walked over to a Frisbee hanging on a nail on the wall. He brought it back to the table and handed it to Rod, who looked inquisitively at his uncle. "Turn it over," he said, smiling.

Kasey was getting excited in the background, thinking it was her time to play. Taped to the underside was Rod's envelope. He peeled it off and gave Kasey the Frisbee; she sat down, Frisbee in mouth, and waited patiently to go outside.

Rod opened the envelope. "Gentlemen," he whispered in a low voice, "what we have here are the coordinates to the *Ebony*. Tomorrow morning we will dive that wreck and retrieve the item that many people are seeking."

Kasey got up and anxiously headed for the door and barked. "You guys sit tight – I'll take her out," said Uncle George. "It's getting to be our routine. We'll be right back." He grabbed the leash and the two went out the screen door.

Rod and D.C. were discussing the logistics of the next day when Kasey began barking violently behind the house. "That isn't normal," said Rod, his eyes meeting D.C.'s. They bolted for the door. D.C. cleared the stairs in the near darkness and tripped over someone lying on the ground. His father! Kasey was now barking in the front of the house. Rod ran towards the street in time to see a man jump in a car and speed away, nearly hitting Kasey.

D.C. carried George up the steps and into the kitchen. He sat him at his place at the table, blood flowing profusely from his nose and above his right eye. "Dad, are you OK? Talk to me!" He examined his father's bruised and beat-up face.

Uncle George was seriously hurt, but managed to speak. "When we went outside, we surprised a guy skulking under the kitchen window, listening to you both. When he saw Kasey and me, he charged and started punching me. Kasey went after him and he bolted."

Rod came over with a wet towel and wiped the blood from his uncle's face. "She's a good girl, my Kasey-Girl." Rod patted his dog, who stayed right there by George's side.

Rod and D.C. looked at each other. Ahmed! He was the only logical culprit. "He'll get his. Mark my words," D.C. said. He meant what he said. "If he heard us talking, then he knows our plan. But he still doesn't know where we're going – he's going to have to figure that out. *We'll be ready.*"

Even though it was clear his father would be all right, D.C. insisted that his sister Bertie come by and take him to her house. While D.C. prepped him for the ride, Rod excused himself to make a couple of phone calls.

First, he placed a call to P.J., but his phone went right to message answering. He would try again in a few minutes. Next, he called a friend to ask for a favor. They talked for about ten minutes, then Rod ended with, "and it must be done first thing – no excuses." The person on the other end agreed, and Rod hung up. He speed-dialed P.J. again. Same result, so this time he left a message to be at the boat by 06:30. P.J. must let him know one way or the other if he could make it – very important that he respond ASAP.

*

Captain Dodge was in his stateroom updating the ship's log when he was summoned to the bridge. The *Atlantic Zephyr* had been running smoothly at full power for several hours, back to the waters of Cape Ann.

"Sir, satellite phone for you." The first officer handed him the phone.

"Captain Dodge speaking."

"Captain Dodge, this is Ahmed. I want you to bring the ship to approximately ten miles east from Thacher Island. Maintain the ship under way, but stand by until I send further instructions."

"Understand: ten miles off Thacher, ready state. Is that all?"

"That is all for now. I hope to have more information for you in the morning."

The phone went silent. The captain scanned the radar and stared out over the bow: the ship's lights cast an eerie glow over the decks. He didn't hear the splash from the stern.

*

It was 05:00 when D.C. started banging around the kitchen, preparing bacon and eggs and waking Rod from a sound sleep. When breakfast was over they loaded Rod's Ramcharger with all the gear from the living room. Rod noticed a new bag, one he hadn't seen before, in the back of the truck alongside his dive equipment.

"What's that?"

"That's my stuff," replied D.C., as he closed the rear deck lid. "That's all you need to know."

Rod backed the truck to the top of the ramp, then D.C. opened the tailgate and unloaded the gear. Rod looked down at the service dock...there she was, *Jus' Restin'*, moving ever so slightly against her dock lines, as though she was swaying to the music of an unheard song. He couldn't take his eyes off her. She looked as good as the day he first put her in the water.

He grabbed some gear and went down the ramp to the dock. Stepping over the gunnel, he saw the anchor line that had connected the *Jus Restin'* to the *Ebony* coiled in a tote box. He opened the pilothouse door and, although familiar, it was completely new: the instrument panel, the integrated radar, the GPS, the sounder. The helm wheel and compass were all that remained of the original. There was a note from G.W. attached to the wheel, simple and to the point: "All systems 100 percent GO. Good luck Cap."

D.C. was stowing the last of the gear as Rod reached for the ignition key. He turned it one position and the instrument gauges came to life. He checked the fuel: full. After hesitating for a moment, he turned the key one more position and woke up the beast under the engine cover. The boat rocked from the torque of starting. He opened the engine cover, and he and D.C. eyeballed the new motor – Rod laughed and muttered "whoa!"

"You boys are up early. Can't wait to try her out, huh?" asked Chet, standing on the stern of *Checkers* two slips away and taking a drag on his cigarette. He was about to head up for his morning shower. "By the way, some guy was here yesterday looking for you. Said he wanted to book a charter." Chet took another long drag on his cigarette. "Looked like that same guy you saved the day of the storm. Anyway, I told him he might find you at your uncle's place. Did he ever show his face?"

"Not exactly, but, we made contact," replied Rod, looking at D.C.

"As a matter of fact, we're going to take him out – today," said D.C., smiling as he picked up his bag from the deck and carried it into the pilothouse.

While the engine warmed, Rod turned on his new electronics. Everything was essentially the same. No problems here. He took the paper from his pocket and punched the coordinates for the *Ebony* into the GPS, noting the time of entry: 06:35. Still no word from P.J., so he told D.C. that he was ready to shove off. D.C. cast off the lines and *Jus' Restin'* drifted away from the dock, riding the outgoing tide. As they passed under the bridge, Rod's eyes scanned side to side. Something caught his attention at the town dock and landing: P.J. was sitting on top of a pile of neatly-stacked dive gear. Easing the helm to port, Rod brought *Jus' Restin'* alongside the dock. P.J. stood up and grabbed the bow rail to hold her position.

"I understand you could use a little help?" he asked in a low-key voice.

"That's right. Pass your stuff to D.C."

Once P.J.'s gear was on board and the introductions were over, *Jus' Restin'* continued out the channel past Willy the Clammer's house. Willy's skiff was gently swaying on a line tied to the dock. D.C. was busy talking on his cell phone in the cockpit when P.J. entered the pilothouse, closing the door behind him.

"Before I fill you in on what's going on, I have a couple of questions…" Rod began. But P.J. didn't let him finish.

"I'm sorry Rod, but a lot of this is my fault. I never should have taken Lilly to that poker game. I enabled her. She hit it big and it just fanned the flames of her gambling. She called and told me what she was doing and where she was headed. I tried to talk her out of it, but she's convinced she's got what it takes. I'm so sorry Rod." P.J. just stood there, disappointed in the turn of events and how he'd been the catalyst.

"How long has this been going on? And what's your relationship with her?"

"Probably a year or so, maybe a little longer. I set her up with a few small action games and she got hooked. She kept asking for bigger action. I got caught in the middle of you two. But there's nothing between us if that's what you're asking."

Rod looked into P.J.'s eyes and chewed on his remarks for a moment, then turned and shook his hand. "Thanks for the honesty. I wasn't sure what was going on, but the picture is a lot clearer now. I'll deal with it – it's my problem."

Rod decided to bring P.J. up to speed on the day's mission. P.J. was floored. "You can't be serious!"

"Never been more serious," said Rod as they passed the #36 buoy. "Now take your seat."

Rod banged on the rear window to get D.C.'s attention, then stuck his index finger in the air and spun it around to signal throttle up. Sitting on the engine cover, D.C. signaled back to let her go. Rod pushed the throttle forward and *Jus' Restin'* was out of the water, skimming along through the channel at a little over half-throttle. The GPS said they were nearly at top speed with the old engine, so he decided to take it easy until she had a few running hours and he was used to the power and new handling. He kept an eye out for anything out of the ordinary; the only other boat on the water was a big Carolina Classic, which was striper fishing off Emerson Rocks at the end of Plum Island.

When *Jus' Restin'* past the #2 buoy, Rod called up the GPS and selected "Ebony," his only waypoint in the memory, and the course was plotted. He came about onto the heading and steered for their destination. They were about four miles beyond the #2 when Rod called D.C. into the pilothouse. He motioned towards the radar, which was set for a 1.5-mile range, and pointed to the target a little over a mile behind them.

"Picked up a bogey – I think it's the boat from Emerson Rocks. He's been shadowing us a little over a mile behind. We'll see if he stays with us in the fog up ahead."

They traveled another mile, deep into the fog. D.C. continued watching the radar screen intently. As they slowed down, the gap closed and then remained constant. When they sped up, the gap opened back up – then again stayed the same.

"That's our boy!" D.C. proclaimed. He was ecstatic. He knew that Ahmed was directly off the stern.

D.C. took the helm while the other two prepared for the dive of a lifetime. Rod told P.J. to take one of his larger 120's so that they would have an equal and adequate amount of air. P.J. got a spare regulator from his bag and attached it to one of his 80s. "We'll take this as a backup – plus your pony bottle."

Rod remembered the last time he was here and didn't want a repeat performance. He gave P.J.'s idea a thumbs-up and a wink.

"I have an idea," said Rod. "We don't want to anchor and give away our spot. With this fog, and if that's Ahmed behind us, he'll follow *Jus' Restin'* until he thinks he can pounce. When we're suited up and ready, D.C. will slow the boat to headway only, and you and I will slip over the side. We'll have 100 feet of the big anchor line dragging behind with a couple of hand loops in it. Then D.C. will steer for the *Ebony*."

He looked at the high flyer to port, leaning against the tide. "Considering the current, when the GPS says 150 feet to go, you signal us, D.C. We'll release our towline, drop down, and ride the current right onto the wreck." P.J. nodded in agreement. "D.C. keeps going at the same speed, cruising around like he's using sonar to look for the *Ebony*, and then returns in no more than 45 minutes. Picks us up and off we go."

"I like that," said D.C. "I may add a twist or two while you're down, but that shouldn't affect you guys."

"Whatever you do, don't be late! We don't want to be bobbing defenselessly on the surface." Rod pointed to the underwater communications console. "You can talk to me by lowering that cable into the water. Put a weight on it to keep it under, otherwise we won't be able to communicate."

"Got it," said D.C. "Let's go – time's a wastin'."

D.C. pulled the anchor line from the tote box and played out the 100 feet as planned. P.J. and Rod positioned themselves on each of the gunnels, ready to roll out. D.C altered course a touch as the GPS zeroed in on its target; at 500 feet away, the divers rolled out and grabbed the line as it came by. When *Jus' Restin'* was 300 feet away, D.C. held up three fingers, then two, then a thumbs-down at 150 feet to target. Rod and P.J. disappeared under the surface and drifted silently down to the *Ebony*.

Fifteen minutes later Ahmed continued to keep his distance, interpreting – luckily – *Jus' Restin's* maneuvers as a search for the *Ebony*. He was convinced they were very close. He called Rasheed via his satellite phone, and ordered him to assemble the men and prepare their incursion.

Next, he called Captain Dodge, who was on the bridge at the appointed position. The captain jotted down the coordinates where he was to take the *Atlantic Zephyr* and await further orders. He compared the new coordinates to the ones from the ship's log...he was correct about the *Ebony*'s location! He then walked to the rear of the bridge and looked down at the activity on the stern: Ahmed's men were busy preparing the Zodiac to go over the side. Two of them were suiting up to dive. The one piece of the puzzle Captain Dodge hadn't anticipated was that Rasheed was carrying a weapon.

＊

D.C. looked at the GPS: *Jus' Restin'* was passing right over the *Ebony*. He reached to the control console and pushed the yellow button.

"Rod, do you copy?"

"Loud and clear," said Rod from 125 feet below. "Found plenty of what we expected but not our primary. Still looking."

"Very well, I'll contact you again in ten minutes."

D.C. moved to the radar and switched scales to the six-mile range. Nothing. Then he flipped to the twelve-mile range. Bingo! Less than eight miles away was a very large vessel. He watched its movement, and after a couple of minutes, it was obvious that it was slowly closing in on their position. It was time to play his ace; he took his satellite phone out of his bag and called in the data.

Ahmed continued to maintain his distance from *Jus' Restin'*. He was waiting patiently for the *Atlantic Zephyr* to get into position so that his men could move in and claim their prize. He was determined to thwart Rod's attempts at recovery – his country was depending on him!

Down below, the search continued. The *Ebony* was suffering the effects of being submerged for so many years, making for a dangerous diving situation. Twice, large sections of timber collapsed as P.J. and Rod rooted around in the cargo hold. They were nearly ready to move to the last hold when P.J.'s light illuminated what looked like a safe. He tried the handle but it wouldn't budge, due to the corrosion that had solidified the mechanism. Then he saw what appeared to be their quarry: a pipe, covered with silt and sea anemones, jammed between a piece of timber and a rib of the hull.

Rod looked back from outside the hull and saw P.J. struggling to free the pipe. With all the strength he could muster, he finally wrestled it free, pulling the timber with it. A huge cloud of debris billowed out of the hull opening. When the current cleared the water, Rod swam to the hull opening and saw that P.J.'s legs were trapped under the timber!

P.J. passed the pipe to Rod. Taking his knife from its sheath, Rod vigorously scraped away at the sea life...this was it! Pandora's pipe. His attention quickly returned to P.J.

"Rod, do you copy?" D.C. suddenly said, startling Rod, who was assessing their new dilemma.

"Roger, D.C. Good news and trouble! Mission accomplished but we can't come up."

"Understand you have our objective. What's the problem?"

"P.J.'s trapped in the hull. We've got to figure out how to get him outta here quick. The air won't last long with us buddy-breathing."

"How can I help?"

Rod's mind raced. He could see by the look in P.J.'s eyes that he wasn't fooling around this time. There had to be a solution – he just needed to figure it out. He checked his air supply and then P.J.'s. He was down to 1,100 psi and P.J. had 1,700 psi. At this depth, Rod figured ten minutes for himself and fifteen for P.J. One thing was in their favor: they still had the aluminum 80 for backup, plus the pony.

"I got it!" Rod blared into D.C.'s headset. "Under the port side seat are two spare propellers. Take the 500-foot anchor line, and tie the props to one end of the line. Tie the other end to a stern cleat, then bring the boat right over our breaking bubbles and drop the props. I'll tie the line onto the piece of timber that's holding P.J., and *Jus' Restin'* can pull it away!"

"Gotcha Rod. They'll be coming down ASAP."

D.C. opened the compartment under the seat and retrieved the heavy stainless steel props. *These'll sink like rocks,* he thought as he tied them with a bowline knot. He returned to the helm and guided *Jus' Restin'* over the bursting bubbles.

"Coming down – watch your head!"

"Understand. Props away."

Rod kicked his fins and backed away from the hull. He saw a flash as one of the blades reflected the sunlight from far above, and then down they came, landing in the mud about fifteen feet from the hull.

"Got 'em. Give me some slack and stand by."

"Slack and standing by," replied D.C. from 125 feet above.

Rod untied the props, swam to the hull opening, and showed P.J. the line. His eyes opened wide – he could read Rod's mind. P.J. took his regulator from his mouth and blew Rod a kiss. This was one "bitter end" he was glad to see.

Rod was down to 500 psi as he surveyed the mass of timbers. He picked the piece just above the one that was holding P.J. captive – it appeared in the best shape, and Rod figured he could pull P.J. out if this major weight was removed. He tied the line with a clove hitch and a couple of half-hitches for safety. He needed *Jus' Restin'* to pull on a heading that would lift the timber up, back, and away; he looked at his compass and decided that 90 degrees due east would do the trick.

"D.C."

"Here, Rod. What do you want me to do?"

"I need you to steer a course due east of the bubbles. Nice and slow until the slack becomes taut."

"Roger that." D.C. idled the boat slowly to the east, playing out all the slack until the line tightened up. "She's tight!"

"OK. Gimme 1,000 RPMs," Rod ordered from below.

D.C. pushed the throttle ahead. The stretch came out of the line, but the timber wouldn't budge.

"Gimme 500 more." *Jus' Restin'* was pulling hard, but still nothing. "Gimme 2,000!"

Suddenly, P.J. waved, signaling that it was starting to move! Rod reached through the hole and grabbed P.J.'s arm. P.J. shook his head no, not yet – he was still pinned. Rod signaled to P.J. that he was going to ask for more and to get ready.

"Gimme 2,500!"

D.C. inched the throttle forward and *Jus' Restin'* pulled even harder. Finally, the timber started to lift. Rod pulled for all he was worth and P.J. slid forward through the hull.

"Neutral!" yelled Rod. D.C. heard the command and brought the throttle back to neutral. "He's out. We're coming up the line. Get ready to pull us in."

Rod grabbed the spare 80 air and handed it to P.J. Next, he grabbed the pipe and handed that to P.J. as well. He cut the rope just outside the hull and pulled the line back to his buddy, who had the spare air ready. Just in time! Rod's tank was bone dry.

After a fifteen-minute decompression stop at twenty feet, P.J., holding tightly onto the mystery cylinder, was first to break the surface. Rod popped up right behind, breathing on the spare air. The divers climbed aboard, and the three men stood in the cockpit of *Jus' Restin'* examining their find. Rod looked it over and nodded that this was what he'd seen in Suzanne's photo.

"Shush. Listen!" whispered D.C. The sound of distant gunfire could be heard through the fog.

*

It wasn't but a few moments after the call came in that the MH60J Jayhawk helicopter lifted off from its pad at the Portsmouth Navy Yard. It had been on "hot standby" ever since D.C.'s initial intelligence report. The chopper closed the 30-mile gap to the *Atlantic Zephyr* in just under twenty minutes, at over 170 knots. When it was three miles to target, it descended into the fog and slowed its high-speed approach. The MSST 91110, the Coast Guard's anti-terrorism team based in Boston, prepared to fast rope from the open doors onto the deck of the *Atlantic Zephyr.*

Rasheed saw the helo appear out of the fog, and realized this wasn't the friendly Coast Guard that had been flying over them the past few months. Aiming his AK-47 at the aircraft was to be his final, fatal move. The helo's twin M240H machine guns roared to life, spraying bullets at 750 RPMs over the stern and hitting Rasheed and two of his men. They crumpled to the deck. Several bullets hit exposed dive tanks, sending them rocketing into the air and splashing into the water.

Rasheed's other men elected for a trip to Gitmo, their bravado quickly evaporating as they threw their arms into the air in surrender. With the machine gunners providing cover, four DOGs (USCG Deployable Operations Group) slid down their fast ropes to the deck below. It was all over in less than a minute: the United States Coast Guard had taken control of the *Atlantic Zephyr.*

*

D.C. continued his cruising charade while Rod and P.J. stowed the gear and made ready for the run back to Harborside. Rod took the helm, and D.C. got his bag from the cuddy.

"Let's do a fly-by," said P.J., "and see if that was really Ahmed."

"That's not such a good idea," replied D.C. "First let's see who follows. There've been a couple of other boats fishing here. In this fog, I'm not positive which boat is which anymore. Let's let Ahmed show himself again – then we'll deal with him."

Rod and P.J. agreed. Rod called up the chart plotter and set a course for the #2 buoy back into Plum Island Sound. He pushed the throttle ahead and *Jus' Restin'* came to power, running west at 25 knots.

"Here he comes! This time he's closing the gap. Hit it Rod!" yelled D.C.

Rod pushed the throttle ahead, and *Jus' Restin'* responded with speed she'd never seen before. But the gap didn't widen: Ahmed was still closing in.

"D.C., take the helm. We have more power and I know we can outrun him, but we want to *catch* him. Let me know when he's an eighth of a mile behind. P.J., come with me." Rod dragged the tote box with the 500 feet of anchor line to the front of the engine cover. "He's following our wake. We'll use this line to foul his props – he'll be a sitting duck!"

They worked to spread the heap of line as far apart as possible, so that when they cast it over the stern it would cover a large area. D.C. watched the radar and sure enough, Ahmed was coming in quickly. When he crossed the 1/8-mile gradient on the radar screen, he signaled that it was time to launch the net. Rod and P.J. walked the rope to the stern, along both gunnels, and let the mess of anchor line fly.

Before Ahmed had a chance to register what had gone under the bow, everything came to a halt. The twin props from his boat choked on the line and both engines stalled. Ahmed crashed into the windshield, then fell backwards onto his knees – his boat was dead in the water. Scrambling low across the deck, he got out an MP5 from the camouflaged bag under his helm seat...it was him or the 72 virgins. Either way, he was ready for action!

"Look, he's dropped way off," shouted P.J. "Three-quarters of a mile back – we got him – perfect! Now it's our turn."

D.C. picked up the satellite phone and relayed their coordinates. Then he instructed Rod to circle back towards Ahmed at headway speed only. D.C. got his equalizer, an AR-15 with a laser-sighted M320 grenade launcher attached, out of his bag. Then he climbed to the overhead and sat down on the Viking life raft canister. After the beating Ahmed had given his father the night before, he made a decision: he would take no prisoners. The boat was now less than a quarter-mile away.

"Steady as she goes," D.C. said. "I want him dead straight ahead, directly off the bow. Let me know when we're 500 feet away."

Rod held *Jus' Restin'* on course, narrowing the gap in the dense fog. "She should be visible any moment – D.C., be ready!" whispered Rod.

Raising his weapon to eye level, D.C. switched off both safeties and continued looking through the scope.

Ahmed stood in the cockpit of his boat, his weapon also ready, watching his radar. *Jus' Restin'* was getting close, very close: he could hear the waves slapping on her hull. He raised his weapon and prepared to fire.

"500 feet," P.J. whispered.

The sun shone brightly overhead, and a reflective glow from Ahmed's boat appeared through the fog. D.C took aim and pulled the trigger. Five rounds burst from the muzzle of the AR-15, then another set of five.

Ahmed saw the laser beam's image on the overhead while he fired in what he believed was the right direction. It was too late. The laser beam had found its spot amid ship, the most vulnerable spot because it housed the fuel tanks. The grenade was on its way...with a tremendous blast, the boat exploded and disintegrated into flotsam. D.C. sat silently on top of the Viking, scanning the scene and insuring that nothing remained. When the last of the debris fell out of the sky and back into the water, he climbed down and stowed his weapon.

In a moment the sound of a helicopter could be heard. It approached, circled once, and then assumed a hovering position over the *Jus' Restin'*. A DOG officer stood ready in the doorway, and then rode down on the winch line. He stepped onto the deck and removed the harness. The helicopter backed away and took up a standby position.

"What was that ordinance we observed?" asked the officer, looking directly at D.C.

"Combatant. Refused to be taken alive. Blew himself to hell," said D.C. stoically. The officer was content with the explanation.

He turned his attention to Rod. "I believe you have something for me, Captain." It was a demand, thinly veiled as a request. Any plans Rod might have had for the information in the cylinder vanished into thin air.

"Yes Sir, I believe I do." Rod went behind the helm seat and retrieved the cylinder. He presented it to the DOG, who inspected it closely. He signaled to the helo.

"Thank you, Captain." He turned to D.C. "I believe that you, Sir, are coming with me."

"Yes, Sir."

D.C. was all business as he shook Rod's and P.J.'s hands. The helicopter moved in and hovered directly overhead. The rotor-wash blasted *Jus' Restin'* , causing her outriggers to chatter in the wind, as the winch operator lowered two strop slings. D.C. and the DOG officer slipped their arms, head, and shoulders through the lifting device. After a salute from the DOG, they lifted off to the waiting chopper.

Once inside, D.C. took a seat by the door. Looking down, he put his finger to his nose just like Santa, while the chopper turned, dipped its nose, and headed north to Portsmouth.

Rod and P.J. stood in silence as the aircraft flew away. Because their attention had been fixed on the thundering helicopter overhead, they failed to notice the pool of blood on the deck where D.C. had been standing.

Chapter Fifteen

Rock and Roll

The sun was setting on the Piscataqua River as Rod's motor-cycle weaved its way around the potholes towards the water's edge at Pierce Island. Across the river in the distance, the mercury lights from the Portsmouth Navy Yard were just beginning to come on, casting an eerie backdrop to the *Atlantic Zephyr*. She had arrived late that afternoon, and was tied to a pier that normally welcomed submarines returning from sea duty.

Rod shut off the engine and calmly surveyed the scene. It was a quiet evening, and the sound of cars driving over the hummin' Memorial Bridge could be easily heard in the distance. Every few minutes another boat returned from tuna fishing off-shore. He scanned the boats but didn't see fish on any decks, nor tuna flags proclaiming victory. That was just the way it went with tuna: you can't pick it up unless you put it down, so you have to try again and again.

He took out his phone from the rear compartment, flipped the lid, and saw that he had two missed calls and one message waiting. Lilly had called but didn't leave a message. The other call was from his financial guru, Paul Scott, who simply said to call back. Paul had been his advisor on all things financial since forever. He was well connected: if he didn't have the answer, he always knew someone who knew someone who did. And they were always top shelf. He pushed redial and in a moment Paul was at the other end.

"Hey Paul, give me some good news."

"I did what you requested – I set you up with a top flight admiralty lawyer. I relayed all the information about the boat's history, and he filed your claim in court first thing this morning. Naturally, the coordinates are sealed." Paul paused as he scanned his notes. "The attorney is doing his research, so your right to salvage is still up in the air. He didn't want to indicate one way or the other because it's apparently a complex process."

"Well, I guess the important part is that the discovery has been claimed and we're first. I've hired a couple of friends, non-divers, to guard the site until we get the green light to bring *Ebony's* cargo to the surface. We'll need a secure place to store everything."

"I already figured that one out. We can lease my home-town's abandoned police station – we'll use the jail cells and hire security guards. It's close and I know the town manager. It's a no-brainer."

"Good job Paul, let me know as soon as you hear anything."

Rod closed the phone and focused his attention across the river on the *Atlantic Zephyr* – he had no idea what had transpired because D.C. hadn't said a word. Where was the crew and what was happening to them? If he hadn't seen the story on the evening news about a research ship in for emergency repairs, he never would have known of her presence in Portsmouth. He'd watched the entire New England news channel broadcast, twice. There wasn't one word about anything that happened offshore that day, other than a missing boat rental that was feared lost. The news anchorman reported that the Coast Guard determined that the boat had caught fire and exploded, and that the ship's captain was still missing.

Rod opened the phone again and called D.C.; he needed some answers. Not there. He thought of how his cousin had been living a totally covert life, and how important it was that this remained a secret from his friends and family. The way he dispatched the two terrorists – he was cool under fire. But what bothered Rod was D.C.'s blood on the deck. How badly was he hurt?

He scanned the contacts and dialed Pierre. No answer, and no surprise. He figured she'd never to talk to him again after his last maneuver. He didn't like deceiving her, then leaving her in harm's way. On the other hand, was she involved in this scenario?

Rod started his bike. It was time to take a trip to Jack's and relax. He passed the exit to his home and kept right on going; he knew nobody was home. *Keep heading for Jack's,* he thought. It was just a short ride to Newburyport, but that night, with so many unanswered questions on his mind, it seemed to take forever. Only a few friends knew Rod's secret, and until he heard from the attorney, things would stay that way. Rod had determined a long time before that whenever he discussed a potential winner that wasn't already etched in stone, it would fall through.

"Ahoy, Captain Rod, come on in! Can we pour you a Fisherman's Brew?" asked Jack, standing next to a new man working the bar.

"Sounds like a winner. Who's the new guy?"

"I'd like you to meet Sam Alexander. He owns the breakfast place next door. We're going to knock down the wall, pull it together, and be partners."

"Just as long as our arrangement stays as it is, I couldn't be happier. You know, I could use a good breakfast spot. Good luck to the both of you!" Rod shook Sam's hand and congratulated them.

It was time for another phone call – this time to his cousin Bertie. She told Rod that her father, Uncle George, was recovering from his attack, although he was having trouble seeing with his right eye. She had brought him and Kasey back home earlier that evening.

After his two-beer limit, Rod pointed the bike down 1A towards Uncle George's. There was no traffic at the old wooden bridge at Harborside, so he stopped and shut off the engine. He looked over the edge and saw the boats in the marina, dimly lit from the lights in the parking lot above. All was quiet in the slips. Rod could see the faint glow of Chet's cigarette as he leaned out *Checkers'* starboard window, keeping a vigilant eye on the docks. Rod looked up and there was *Jus' Restin'* nestled back in her slip. A feeling of calm came over him; the two of them had been through some adventures over the past month. He planned to return to her in the morning.

He arrived at Uncle George's and put his bike away in the garage. Looking over his shoulder at the kitchen window, he imagined Ahmed standing there, trying to figure out a way to get to the cylinder first. Rod assumed he was wondering how to turn this situation around and become a hero for his country.

He thought about Kasey. He believed she'd never attack a human, but then he laughed – she'd probably thought Ahmed was trying to steal her Frisbee. He would have, had he known the coordinates were hidden there!

Kasey and a pitifully bruised Uncle George met Rod at the door. Kasey whined with joy at the sight of her master. They retired to the living room, where Rod enlightened his uncle about finding the *Ebony* and the infamous treasures. He neglected to relate anything else, since that was information only D.C. could share if he felt so inclined.

The next morning pancake mix, as usual, was waiting on the counter. Rod took the hint! After breakfast, he brought his uncle up to speed regarding Lilly's new adventure.

"Hey, we've all wanted to chase our dreams. You Rod, of all people, should know that. Just give her some space and see where it goes." Uncle George had a point. He'd take his advice – for now.

Rod's Ramcharger pulled into the parking lot at Harborside, just as a morning coffee break was under way. Rod and Kasey joined the group for a few laughs about the new and improved performance of *Jus' Restin'*. "She's amazing...The Bionic Boat! You made her even better than before!" Rod said, pointing at G.W.

"Everything comes with a price," laughed Skip, the marina manager, handing the bill to Rod. Looking over the invoice, Rod grabbed his heart, prompting Chet to offer some of his nitroglycerin. Everyone had a good chuckle. Rod personally thanked everyone for their support. Someday soon, he would reward them for being there when he needed them most.

Kasey proudly led Rod down the ramp to *Jus' Restin'*. They ran into Archie along the way. "Hey Cap! What's going on today? Heading out for tuna?" he laughed. Rod just shook his head and smiled. "By the way, you have a guest on the boat."

Rod didn't ask who, and continued following Kasey to the boat. Kasey eagerly jumped the gunnel when she saw Lilly sitting on the engine cover. Lilly patted her with one hand and held a folded white envelope in the other.

"I've been waiting for you. Seems like the story of my life." She turned her back on Rod and looked over the stern. "I've made a decision. I'm following my own dreams for once. I can't live my life playing second fiddle to this boat and that ocean." She turned to face Rod. "It's all in here. It's too painful to repeat and I don't want to argue – you can read it after I'm gone." Lilly handed Rod the envelope, kissed him on the cheek, and bent down to pat Kasey. "Take care of your captain and be a good girl." She glanced at her husband, then stepped over the gunnel and walked away without looking back.

Rod hadn't spoken a word. He didn't know what to say. He'd lived through desertion as a child so this was not unfamiliar territory. He sat for a few moments, gazing at the Parker River and pondering his new fate. He would persevere.

Kasey was waiting patiently for her master to open the pilothouse door. "On your spot, baby!" he said. Kasey bounded into the cuddy and the comfort of her pillow, only to find it wasn't there. "Hey, we're going to have to get you a new pillow!"

"Well, that shouldn't be a problem. You've got all the 'cushion' you're ever going to need." Rod recognized the voice right away...Paul Scott was on the dock with a smile on his face as big as the Cheshire Cat's. He was holding a large manila envelope.

"Lay it on me, brother. What's the good word?"

"This is from your lawyers in Boston. They still have a couple of questions about your instructions, but that can wait. Essentially, after meeting with the court magistrate, this appears to be how it's going to work." Paul took a deep breath. "If the *Ebony* had been lying within three miles of shore, Massachusetts would legally claim jurisdiction. The Feds *may* want to get their fingers in it, but the lawyers figure it this way..." Paul was fidgeting with excitement. "Your discovery falls into what's called the 'law of finds': the *Ebony* was not an official vessel of another sovereign country, so it's what the kids call 'finders keepers, losers weepers!' It's all yours!"

"Woo! Hoo!" shouted Rod. Kasey bounded out of the cuddy when she heard the elation in Rod's voice. "We're rich, Kasey!" He gave Paul a huge bear hug and yelped for joy. They excitedly discussed the logistics of salvaging the treasures offshore. The conversation would've gone on for hours if the phone hadn't interrupted them. It was D.C. Rod signaled Paul that he needed to take the call, and that it was private. Paul graciously excused himself and headed down the docks, vowing to call later.

"What's buzzin' cousin?" said the voice on the phone.

"I was wondering when I was going to hear from you! Did you get hit? There was blood on the deck. Come on, give me *all* of it – no secrets."

"All right, here's all the news that's not fit to print." D.C. began by recounting the capture of the *Atlantic Zephyr*, along with the surrender of the survivors of Ahmed's crew. He went on to describe how the investigation revealed that Ahmed was telling an elaborate cover story. "He had a convincing story, airtight credentials, and *big money.* The ship's owners never questioned his credibility or motives."

"And what about the blood?" asked Rod.

"Took a hit from Ahmed to my right thigh. Nothing too serious. Glad the Harley has electric start, though!"

"OK, so you're telling me Suzanne had nothing to do with Ahmed and his plans?"

"That's a roger. All unwitting participants. Actually, the *Atlantic Zephyr* steamed for Italy this morning, cleared of any wrongdoing. We'll deny any involvement with the boat, if it ever comes to light. I spoke with the captain, and all things considered, I don't think that's ever going to be an issue."

"Did you speak with Suzanne? Did you explain to her what I was up against, what we were trying to accomplish? National security and all that? What did she say?"

"She said she didn't trust me, that she wanted to talk with you. She quit the *Atlantic Zephyr* this morning. So cuz, it's all up to you now. Gotta go."

"Whoa, whoa, whoa – wait a minute." But it was too late; D.C. had hung up. What did the pipe reveal? Was the information intact? Would he *ever* find out? His unanswered questions were still hovering in the air when a Harley came to life in the parking lot; Rod looked up as D.C. waved and then threw in a couple of extra revs for effect.

Just then, Rod noticed Kasey's tail wagging...Suzanne was walking towards him past the *Happy Times.*

"Bonjour, Captain. Is this vessel hiring? I could use a job."

"You're in luck – we have an opening. Please, Suzanne, come aboard." He held out his hand and Suzanne took it and stepped over the gunnel onto the deck. Rod wasn't sure if she would slap him or kiss him. She opted for the later, and he was happy. Very happy.

"I need to let you in on a little secret." He smiled and pointed to the engine cover, motioning for her to take a seat. He went into the pilothouse and got the manila envelope, which was lying on top of the folded white envelope.

"I don't think I can handle any more secrets!" she laughed while making herself comfortable.

"Well, it's pretty simple. I needed to clarify some details, but I can at least implement the clause the attorneys were confused about."

"I don't understand. What attorneys? What are you referring to?"

"As I'm sure you can understand, the last month of my life has been – shall we say...exciting? None of it, *and I mean none of it,* would have been possible if our paths hadn't crossed. Call it destiny." Rod paused and envisioned a fine wine hiding inside Suzanne's travel bag. "I'm a Libra, so everything has to be in balance. To that end, I instructed my lawyers, upon you being cleared of any charges, to name you an equal partner in the salvage of the *Ebony*. Everything, right down the middle."

Suzanne was flabbergasted.

"May I take your response as a yes?" Rod laughed, stroking Kasey's neck. "I have friends anchored in a 54' Viking Sport Fisherman near the coordinates, faking tuna wishing while guarding the *Ebony*. Nothing short of a hurricane would make them leave! What do you say the brand-new partners fire up the *Jus' Restin'* and cruise out to share the good news?"

Suzanne gazed over at the stern of the *Happy Times*, thought for a moment, then turned back to Rod. "Very well, Captain." She smiled and began to cast off the stern lines. "Let's make it so."

Rod went back into the pilothouse and stood at the helm; the key turned and *Jus' Restin'* and her captain came back to life. Rod could feel himself heading up the curve again. He leaned down and patted Kasey, who was standing right by his side.

"Kasey, it's like they say on rock and roll radio: "The hits just keep on coming!"

Breinigsville, PA USA
03 June 2010
239154BV00001B/2/P

9 781608 4444